D0989533

WITHDRAWN
MAINE STATE LIBRARY
64 STATE HOUSE STATION
AUGUSTA, MAINE 04333-0064

Le Morte d'Avalon

By J. Robert King

Mad Merlin
Lancelot du Lethe
Le Morte d'Avalon

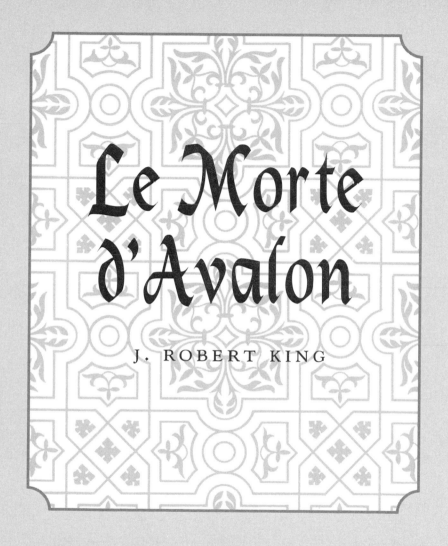

Le Morte d'Avalon

J. ROBERT KING

TOR®

A Tom Doherty Associates Book
New York

JAN 2 0 2004

This is a work of fiction. All the characters and events portrayed in this novel are either fictitious or are used fictitiously.

LE MORTE D'AVALON

Copyright © 2003 by J. Robert King

All rights reserved, including the right to reproduce this book or portions thereof, in any form.

This book is printed on acid-free paper.

A Tor Book
Published by Tom Doherty Associates, LLC
175 Fifth Avenue
New York, NY 10010

www.tor.com

Tor® is a registered trademark of Tom Doherty Associates, LLC.

ISBN 0-765-30594-1

First edition: September 2003

Printed in the United States of America

0 9 8 7 6 5 4 3 2 1

To Jennie:
The first one was for you, and the best one, too.

Acknowledgments

Thanks go once more to my editor, Brian Thomsen, for this book and the whole trilogy. Thanks go also to Natasha Panza for her guidance through production, and to Tom Doherty for the means of production. And thank you, family, for bearing with me.

Le Morte
d'Avalon

The Curse of Eve

Father smiled. He had a wide mustache and strong, fine hands. He cupped Morgan's jaw and knelt before her as if she were not just a duchess, but queen. "You understand, don't you?"

Morgan solemnly shook her head. At five, she was determined to understand. "Why not stay? The king'll come, won't he?"

"I don't want him here." Something moved in Father's eyes, like rabbits frightened down their burrows. Above his head, a black wind moaned in the wooden vault. "The king and I have matters to discuss, matters better spoken of in Castle Terrabil."

Morgan slid her hand into his and twined their fingers together. "Take me, then. I'm good at discussing things."

Father's mustache spread in a wider smile, but he seemed only sad. "You're my girl, Morgan." He stroked her hair, black to his blond. "You stay here and take care of your mother. When all this mess is done, I'll come back and catch you up in my arms and hold you."

"Hold me now." She wrapped him in a fierce embrace and felt—through her samite dress and his green-and-red tabard and plate and chain and chemise—his heart. Courage meant having heart, and hearts were full of blood. When you lost your blood, your courage was gone. "Don't go. King Uther is a butcher."

"All kings are butchers," Father said quietly, "but I am not a lamb."

She saw him laid open like a lamb, his blond hair soaking up his courage. "He'll kill you!"

"Oh, Morgan, don't say such things—"

"Stay, Father! What'll happen to us if you go?"

"What will happen to you if I—" he broke off. It was as if an invisible hand gripped his throat. "Take care of your mother, Morgan. I'm counting on you."

She blinked back her tears. "I will."

A soldier came to the door. Father moved in flocks of soldiers, clothed in metal and scars, and the man's eyes spoke dread. Father pulled back from her.

You will never touch him again, Morgan, not even through all that samite and steel. The voices never lied.

"He'll kill you!"

Father drifted back and away, as if a river pulled them apart. "I have to go." He grew smaller in her peaty eyes, turned, and murmured things to the man at the door. Together, they vanished down the corridor, heading for the black courtyard where more of their kind waited on huge, stomping steeds.

"Come, Morgan," said Mother, laying hands on her shoulders.

Morgan startled. She'd forgotten Mother. Her hands were smooth and strong from all their needlepoint, each stitch a little thread of worry. "Sit with me by the fire." She tugged her daughter off the stony floor and onto a thick woolen carpet.

Numbly, Morgan walked. She passed embroidered chairs like bushes in a garden and reached Mother's seat, there by the hearth. At the foot of it, Morgan knelt. The woolen carpet scratched her knees, and the fire made her face hot, but her shoulders were cold. "Why, Mother?"

Duchess Igraine settled into the chair and gave a long sigh. "Why what, Morgan?"

"Why does Father have to go?"

The roof creaked with wind or bogey feet. "He goes to protect us."

"How can he protect us if he leaves?" Morgan looked down at her hands. Gooseflesh prickled her whole body. "If he loved us, he wouldn't leave."

"No," Mother said. She reached down and took Morgan's hand. "He loves us very much. He'll battle King Uther for us. For me . . ."

Morgan looked at her mother. She was pretty. Her hair piled in curling mounds above her heart-shaped face. She had blue eyes and lips that curved like rose petals, and she wore lace and ribbon, lovely and strange. Mother had her flocks too, women who were doves.

Morgan was a raven.

"Your father defends my honor. King Uther would steal me away, but your father will stop him."

"Steal you away?" Morgan said, standing. "Is he a Saracen?"

"He is king, and he desires me. . . ."

"Do you desire him?"

Mother blushed. "Of course not."

"Have you told him you don't want him?"

"The wants of a woman matter little to any man, and nothing to a king."

"Let's go fight him, Mother. I could kill Uther."

"Morgan! You're only a little girl."

"Then you kill him."

Igraine's face grew redder still. "It's not women's work. Your father wants us to stay here, and stay we will."

"What Father wants . . . what Uther wants . . . why doesn't it matter what we want?"

"We are subject to them," Mother said, drawing Morgan down to kneel again. "God made us from their ribs, so we're really only parts of their bodies—the parts closest to their hearts. Should a man be ruled by a part of his body, or should he rule all the parts?"

"I have my own body," Morgan said.

Mother shook her head and took a deep breath. "You see, sweet child, God made Eve, and she brought sin into the world. Because of it, God cursed her saying she would have pain in childbearing but her desire would be for her husband and he would rule over her."

Morgan knew these stories in Cornish and Latin, and in both languages she resented Eve. "She should've killed that serpent. That's what I would've done. Then we would've been like the men, and no one would rule us."

"But men are ruled by God. God cursed Adam too, saying men must work by the sweat of their brows, their labors producing thorns and thistles, and at the end of their days they will return to dust."

Morgan was silent a long while, staring into the fire. She watched the logs, broad and strong, giving themselves up to ash. "Father's at the end of his days. God is turning him to dust."

Mother slid from her seat and knelt, trembling. Tears made her eyes shine like marble. "No, Morgan. Don't say such things."

"I didn't say it. You said it. God said it."

Mother stroked her dark locks. "Oh, now. It's all right. Men don't die forever. There was a Second Adam who lifted the curse of the First Adam. Christ undid the curse of works and death so that even in death we will live."

"Who was the Second Eve?"

Now the tears were streaming. "What?"

"Who lifted the curse of Eve?"

Mother shook her head. "There has not been a Second Eve."

Morgan turned away from the fire, and she stared into the dark arch where Father had vanished.

Say it, Morgan. You know it is true.

"Then I'll be the Second Eve."

1

Seeing as No Other

Morgan ambled down a crag above the tossing sea. Behind her rose Tintagel, its walls blazing with the last light of day. The stone battlements looked like teeth against the sky, and in the keep, a candle burned in Morgan's window.

She was supposed to be there, reading her lessons, but a voice had interrupted them: *A great evil is coming, Morgan. Flee to the caves. Follow the veins of the earth and save yourself.* Morgan had not hesitated, going to the window where a convenient trellis descended to the garden. She waited until the guards met in the corner bartizan and shimmied down. Beneath the rose bowers ran a pathway that Morgan herself had cleared—a thorny tunnel to the postern gate. It led beyond the wall to a switchback footpath amid a grove of alder, and it in turn to caves beneath the peninsula. One of them emerged in woods on the mainland, and freedom.

Morgan paused, pulling the candle and tinder box from her nightgown. The cave below her was black and ragged, and it roared with the sea. She was afraid of that dark beast, but even more so of King Uther.

He was the evil who was coming.

Uther had laid siege to Castle Terrabil, and for nine months, Father had been trapped. Scouts said that the siege was turning against him. Uther's forces were already advancing past Castle Terrabil, and if Father did not sally forth to take the offensive, King Uther would capture Tintagel as well.

Morgan tucked up her nightgown and stepped down into the toothy cave. Her hand trembled as she lit the candle and lifted it high. A cold wind breathed up from the darkness. Squinting, Morgan made out a stomach of stone and three separate passages that diverged from it. Only one would lead to escape.

Flee to the caves, the voice had said.

But Father had said, *Take care of your mother.*

Morgan hesitated.

High above, a signal horn sounded. The waves argued to drown out the sound, but the melody was clear. "Father?" The candle fell from Morgan's hand and guttered among black stones. She climbed away.

If Father had returned, everything would be all right. He would defend them and save them. He would know which cave led to freedom. Scampering along the rocks, Morgan edged around the coastline. She reached the ragged cleft between Tintagel and the mainland and stared up breathlessly.

The drawbridge was rattling down across that gap, and the trumpet sounded its call again.

Grinning, Morgan climbed. It had been hard to run the castle without him, even for a six-year-old. For the first time in nine months, the terrible burdens of war lifted from her.

Rocks bit into her feet, but she didn't care. She would

wash off the blood and put on slippers so he wouldn't see. A quick robe, fingers through her hair, a splash of water across her face, and she would run to him. He would see her and catch her up in his arms and hold her. . . .

Horseshoes pounded the drawbridge, sharp and savage like Saxon drums, and three men rode by overhead. One bore Father's standard, holly and berry, and it flashed in the failing sunset. All three galloped through the main gate.

Hands and feet scrabbled the stone, lifting her higher. Morgan would have to wash her hands too, and her eyes, but soon she would be with Father and would once again be a little girl.

The ragged animal that had clung above the sea was gone now. Morgan had washed in the bird fountain, plaited lily of the valley into her hair, and plastered her wounds with kitchen ash. She had hoped for a robe to wear, but it would be sweeter to be in her nightshirt when she felt his strong arms around her. . . .

Morgan ran. Her feet slapped the flagstones as she entered the courtyard, and nearby horses startled. They reared beneath the sickle moon and whickered as stable hands dragged them back down.

Ahead, Chamberlain Jordanus walked toward the tower stairs.

"Chamberlain! Is it true? Is Father home?"

The chamberlain slipped at the base of the stair and crashed to the ground. He must have been exhausted from his ride. Coppery hair and beard twisted around his leathery face, and he struggled against his armor. He looked drunk. That meant very good news, or very bad.

Morgan ran up to him. She reached out to help him up, but he didn't take her hand. "Where is he? Where's Father?"

Jordanus smiled vapidly. He patted her shoulder, and his hand felt heavy and limp. "Morgause, you good girl."

"Morgause?" He was drunk. "Morgause is still in Lothian. I'm Morgan."

"Of course you are."

"Where's Father?"

Jordanus shifted, and there came a small crackling. "It's bedtime for little girls."

"He's here—"

There was a thin space between the chamberlain and the first stair, and Morgan sprang through. One elbow made the space wide enough. She climbed. The stairs spiraled upward into darkness, toward her mother's chambers. That's where Father would be. Occasional lamps lit the wall and shot arrows of soot up to the ceiling. Behind Morgan, Jordanus rumbled like a bear and clattered after her. She laughed. He couldn't had caught her when sober, and certainly not with Father waiting above.

Morgan reached the head of the stair, latched onto the knob, and flung back her mother's door. It spilled light and perfume into that dark, dank place. "Father! Are you here?"

They were, Mother and Father both. Their faces rose from among mounded blankets and the footboard of her bed. Their eyes gleamed with mischief, and their cheeks were pink and bright. Both were bare—adults are not supposed to be bare—but the way mother's hair was piled on her head, it was as if she'd meant to receive him this way.

"What's happening?"

Before they could respond, the chamberlain staggered up

behind Morgan. "Forgive me, Duke, Duchess! I didn't want her to see this—"

"Get her out of here," Father said. The voice was his, but the words weren't. Father was disjointed like the chamberlain, but not drunk. It was as if someone else had crawled into his skin.

I will come back and catch you up in my arms and hold you, Father had said.

A great evil is coming, the voice had said.

Spiders of fear ambled down Morgan's spine. "What've you done with my father?"

"Shut up, girl, and get to bed," he growled.

Those words shattered the enchantment: He was another man, his hairy arms wrapped around Mother. He had a body like a bear and a peppery beard and eyes as black as coal. "You're not Father. You're a devil!"

"Get her out! Out!" the man shouted.

Jordanus grabbed Morgan's shoulder. His hands were puffy, as if he were wearing gloves.

"Mother! They're devils! You have to get away!"

"*You* have to get away," slurred the man who was not Jordanus, and he shoved her out of the room and back down the stairs.

Morgan slipped. The ash had failed in the cuts on her feet, and her soles were slick. She slid and tumbled down the black spiral. Edges of stone pounded her arms and back, but she didn't cry out. She could only think of the monsters that had come to Tintagel. The voices were always right.

Below the first curve, Morgan caught herself. Her fingers clung to the cold stone, and she sat on one tread and rocked in pain. She wouldn't cry. Her chance to be a little girl in her father's arms was gone, perhaps forever. She had to be grown up now. No one else could hear the voices or see the visions, so only she knew what was really happening. Only Morgan could defend the castle.

"I'll kill him," she told herself.

The man in the bed had no armor or weapons, and she could simply stab him until he was dead. It wouldn't take much of a blade, just one long enough to reach a man's heart.

At the head of the stair, the two devils were shouting at each other. A crash followed, and a clamor of steel on stone as Jordanus tumbled down the stairs.

Morgan stood and hurried downward. She didn't want to have Jordanus roll over her, and with luck, he'd be knocked unconscious. Then the way would be open to the other one. Morgan reached the bottom of the stair and charged out into the nighttime courtyard.

Overhead, the sky reeled with stars, and the Milky Way made a ragged road. Cold air wrapped Morgan. She felt lost in an enormous world.

Devil or man, the thing in Mother's bed was not Father, and he must die.

Morgan ran across the courtyard, leaving wan footprints in the starlight. No one remained. The three horses had been led from the bailey to the long, low stable at one end. From its doorway, golden lantern light spilled across new straw. Tails of hair lashed in the darkness, and a young man brushed the side of a horse. He wore a knife at his belt.

Morgan headed for that knife. She didn't know the young man, but he would know her, and he would obey. Morgan ran until straw poked the soles of her feet. She slowed, entered the doorway, and approached the mare. She was breathing hard, and the young man looked to her.

Surprise lit his face. "Mistress Morgan, you're bleeding."

"Give me your knife."

He set down the brush, and his hand slipped to his belt, but he didn't draw the blade. "What for?"

"Give it!" she demanded.

Though he was twice her age, he slipped the strap from the sheath, drew the knife, and flipped it in his hand. He caught the tip and held the handle toward Morgan. "It ain't my place to ask, but what do you want it for?"

Morgan took the blade. "There's a war on." She began to turn, but he caught her shoulder.

"You're not supposed to fight," the young man said. His eyes were concerned beneath sticky brown hair. "Let me fight for you."

She blinked. He was strong enough, but he wouldn't see through the disguise. "You can't fight this fight, and I can. Thanks for the knife." Her hand tightened on the hilt of the dagger, and she stalked away.

He stared at her as if she were mad, and maybe she was. The knife handle slipped in her sweating hand. Could she kill a man, especially one who looked like Father? If she didn't kill him, what would happen to Mother?

Setting her jaw, Morgan approached the tower stairs. The man who had pretended to be Jordanus was gone, and none of the Tintagel guards were nearby. Morgan started up the stairway, her feet silent on the stone. It would be all too easy. Morgan switched the knife to her other hand, wiped the sweat from her palm, and switched it back.

She had seen a cook cut the head from a chicken, and the thing's body flailed in terror. Would it be like that? She had watched archers shoot down a rabid dog, and it had had six shafts in it before it stopped running. Would she have to stab him six times? Or seven? Or ten? Once an escaped prisoner had jumped from the wall and fallen to the rocks, and his bones had cracked like green wood.

It would be horrible, but it had to be done.

At the top of the stairs, Morgan paused. She set her hand on the doorknob and gently turned it. Metal grated quietly, the latch cleared its well, and the door eased slowly open. Light and sound spilled through the narrow gap, and Morgan peered through.

Mother lay on the bed on her back, her hands gripping the headboard, and her knees pointing toward the ceiling. Between them was the man, and he was not Father. His back was meaty, mantled in black hair. He leaned above her, fists ramming into the linens on either side of Mother. He lunged repeatedly at her, but she didn't seem fearful or even sad. A trembling smile filled her face, and she made sounds of pleasure.

Morgan set the tip of the dagger in the doorpost and carved a small sliver from it. This man wasn't Father, and he was doing something to Mother, something that Father never would have done. She opened the door wider. . . .

The man looked different, slender and strong, with blond hair. He looked just like Father, but still he did this thing. Mother rolled him over, straddling his waist. She bent down to kiss his face and his neck.

What if it was him? What if Morgan killed her own father?

She backed away, watching the man and woman wrestle. Between door and post, the gap narrowed. The metal latch slid into its wood groove, leaving Morgan in darkness.

Numbly, she turned, descended the first few steps, and

sat down. The knife was hot in her sweating hands, and the blade dangled between her knees. She couldn't breathe.

Once a wild bitch showed up outside the castle walls, and the bailey dogs went crazy trying to get her. When a servant took rubbish to the midden, the dogs escaped. They ran down the bitch and climbed on her back and fought over her until at last they tore her apart. She and three other dogs died that day, and the men shot two more. That had been Morgan's worst memory, until now.

She stood up and walked listlessly down the stairs. It didn't matter if she got caught. Nothing mattered now. The world had changed around her, too big and strange to understand. Morgan could only float through the bewildering air.

Whatever that unspeakable thing was that they did, it somehow explained all of this: Father, Mother, Uther, Morgan. . . . She was staring at the key but was too fearful to turn it and open the door.

Morgan stumbled out of the archway. The stars scolded her. They saw everything—the imposters, the adult flesh, the wrestling, the dagger—and they disapproved of Morgan. She could hardly bear to walk beneath that piercing host.

They outlined the shadow of a young man, standing in the courtyard. The stable hand had followed her. "Is your battle done?"

Morgan shook her head darkly. She turned the knife in her hand and offered it, handle first, to him. "No, it's just beginning."

Morgan woke up vomiting. She knelt on her bed, the acid remnants of dinner falling from her lips.

She'd had a nightmare. In it, she was Mother, and a man climbed all over her and wrestled her until she couldn't move. She didn't know who this man was, a shadow that was Noman and Everyman. He was inescapable, and he did whatever he wished. Morgan couldn't escape or fight, but she could vomit, rejecting it all and breaking the spell of sleep.

On her knees, she awoke. Her fists were braced on the linens. It was done. The world spun nauseously around her, but she was still.

Father had knelt this way when he had died. The soldiers of Uther had put their swords in his back, and he had fallen on his face and lain in the mud, unable to move. This was no nightmare, but a vision, and now Morgan wished she had never awakened.

Say it, Morgan. You know it is true.

"Father is dead."

2

Messengers

Morgan sat at her bedroom window. The sill was cold with night, and the stars shone down on a black land. Three horses galloped away on the road and bore three imposters. They had come to a fortress above the sea, conquered it from within, and now returned to the darkness that had spawned them.

Morgan didn't even curse them, though she could have. She'd learned from warriors how to swear in complete sentences, but her fury was gone. Only grief remained.

This was her vigil for Father.

The thunder of hooves diminished and ceased among distant oaks. Then all was silent but for the chanting sea. It worried its coastline, and wind moaned among the castle stones. Tintagel was mourning its ruler.

But not the heavens. They didn't care. The stars sang in their merry watches, high and glad. Brightest and jolliest of all was Jupiter. One night, Father had shown her the great round orb, and on succeeding nights had tracked his motion forward and then backward and then forward again.

Old Jove has a wandering eye, Father had said, *and he takes many forms to woo women. Once, he even became a great white bull and enticed a princess on his back and swam away with her to Minos. There she bore him the minotaur.*

Memory gave way to vision, and Morgan saw a different beast-man: The boy had antlers, and his face was the fairest she had ever seen. He carried a great sword in his hand, and with it he slew the people of Dumnonia, and of Britannia, and of Caledonia. He would make all the isles bleed, and then the continent, and then the world. He was the Son of War and would baptize them in blood. The antlered boy would be born out of Mother, and his birth would tear her to pieces.

Morgan shuddered, trying to dispel the vision, but when she shut her eyes, it stared back at her. She was covered in cold sweat. Over and over, she whispered "it isn't true . . . it isn't true . . . it isn't true . . ." but each time a voice added the word *yet*.

Mother lay below, unknowing of the antlered boy who would tear his way out of her. She was softly sleeping and dreaming of a husband who no longer was. Let her sleep and dream and be with him one last time.

Morgan stared, unwilling to close her eyes. She sat motionless as stealthy hours crept over her. The black east turned gray, and light drew its colorless shroud across the sky.

Dawn is coming, dear child, said the kindest of the voices, an old and wise woman. *It will break your vigil.*

Exhaling raggedly, Morgan bowed her head and nodded. The voices had been with her always, a ghost village that spoke to her. They were her only true confidantes. Some were wise, others foolish, some angry and others glad, but all of them were women, and they all told the truth.

Dawn brings the terrible news that you already know. Soon, everyone will hear what you have heard and see what you have seen.

At the edge of the oak forest, a horseman appeared and rode at full gallop across the rumpled hills. He traced backward the trail of the three demons, as if to revoke their terrible deed. The messenger charged toward the arched gate and reined in. His despairing cry woke the guards, and they too shouted. The great bridge came sweeping down, and the portcullises went sweeping up, and the horseman charged across the wood. Hooves drummed the chasm, and the man rushed beneath the castle gates.

"Wake the castle! Wake the family!"

Morgan stood beside the window and stared down into the half-light. She had waited all night for this messenger, and mouthed the words:

"The army is routed. The duke is dead. King Uther is coming!"

Feet scrabbled to windows and fingers clung to sills. Sleepy folk cried out into the darkness. "What is it? What alarm?"

Like a bell tolling, the messenger rang out the news: "The army is routed. The duke is dead. King Uther is coming."

"To arms!" shouted a guardsman on the wall.

Another cried, "To the caves!"

"Gather the duchess and her daughter."

"We must surrender!"

"No time!" cried the messenger. "Uther is coming!"

From the windows, voices shouted, and from the doors, men poured into the courtyard. Without Father, no one knew whom to follow. The men boiled like fish in a kettle, and the women stood and stared.

Morgan peered down toward Mother's balcony. She sat

there, her nightgown in disarray and her legs in a V. She knew. Father was gone, and his killer was coming. The men heard only the threat, but the women felt the loss. Mother lay down and wept.

Morgan cried too. Her tears for Father had been spent, but these were tears for Mother. She was watching the woman die, just as Morgan herself had died. She couldn't bear to see anymore and turned watery eyes to the rising sun. Beneath it, the oaks seemed to be swimming.

Those weren't oaks, but heads and shoulders and swords advancing in a mob across the ground. There would be no resistance and no escape. Uther would take Tintagel, and all of them, on his own terms.

The peninsula gradually filled with armsmen, funneled by the land until they stood shoulder to shoulder from the channel to the Eire Sea. They did not storm the gates, but formed into precise lines on either side of the road, waiting for military review. As they gathered beyond Tintagel, the folk within the castle ceased their clamor. They knew they were in the hands of Uther.

Morgan withdrew from her window. She had wanted to allow Mother time to weep, but Morgan's heart was breaking now. She needed her mother, and perhaps Mother needed her as well.

After hours of stillness, she rushed past the canopy bed, threw back the bolt, and ran down the stairs. She reached her mother's door and saw the place where she had carved a sliver from the post. If she had entered it last night—somehow all this was apiece—and killed the imposter, then maybe Father would still be alive. Morgan threw back the door.

"Mother," she sobbed, and bolted past the bed where the nightmare had been and to the balcony.

Hearing her child's approach, Mother sat up and held her arms out.

Morgan fell into them and wept. Since sunset, the world had been wrong and dangerous. Beyond these arms, it still was, but within them, all was right again. "Don't let go of me. Even when he comes. I want to be with you."

"When who comes?" Mother asked blearily.

"The king, of course. He's on his way."

Mother shook her head in despair. "Didn't your hear, Child? Your father is dead."

"I know," Morgan replied, burying her face in her mother's bosom. "I've known all night."

"What are you talking about?"

"I saw it, in a vision, after that man came to you—"

"That man? That man *was* your Father, Morgan. That was the last time we will see him."

Morgan shook her head, flinging the tears from her eyes. "No, Mother. That wasn't him. Didn't you hear what he said to me? That wasn't Father."

"It was." Mother stiffened, pushing the girl from her breast. "I'm sorry for what he said to you, but he was your father. People don't just change into each other."

Morgan stared into her face, bleak and blonde like Father's, and she wondered again where her own raven hair had come from. "They do change. Like Jupiter—Father told me once—how Jupiter became a bull and took a princess and made the minotaur."

Mother's face had grown rigid, and she shook as if she were near to shattering. "Please stop it, Morgan. Please stop!" Tears made tracks down her white cheeks.

"I'm sorry," Morgan blurted. It was a lie, the first of what would be many between them. "I . . . I had a bad dream."

The lie was magic. Arms that had turned to stone melted around her, and Mother was Mother again. She held her daughter and spoke her own transparent lies: "Everything will be all right. King Uther doesn't want to hurt us. I won't let him hurt you."

The trumpet of Tintagel began a fanfare, and King Uther's trumpets joined the song. Torment turned to triumph.

"He's coming." Mother struggled to stand, unwilling to let go of Morgan. She craned her neck to see over the balcony rail, and Morgan looked too.

Across the chasm, Uther had captured the gate. Most of the guards knelt before it, their heads bowed and their weapons piled nearby. The oldest and staunchest guard lay in the road, blood spreading in a red carpet from his neck. Upon that carpet, men trod—a funeral procession of six warriors in chains. These were Father's men, among the few survivors. They wore his emerald and crimson proudly despite the mud and blood that stained them. On their shoulders their carried a bier.

"Father!" Morgan gasped. He was half a mile away, and yet she could see every feature. His golden hair was dulled with blood, his long and lovely face as pale as ivory. His tabard was neither green nor red, but now the color of rust. His body seemed almost chewed by blades. They had killed him, and well.

Mother tightly clutched Morgan and sobbed. "At least we had one more night."

"At least," Morgan said. She couldn't take her eyes from that body and watched until the procession passed behind the archway. Her gaze shifted toward the man who marched behind the bier. She knew him immediately.

King Uther lumbered like a bear, his black hair and beard

grisled in gray. Fine samite displayed his Pendragon emblem, and the chain mail hauberk beneath draped a barrel-shaped body. He marched solemnly behind his slain foe, but his eyes were turned up toward the balcony of Igraine, as if he had been there before.

"That's the man," Morgan said quietly.

"Yes. That is King Uther."

"No, the man from last night, from . . ." her mother's eyes flashed, ". . . from my dream."

Mother's teeth became a portcullis across her mouth. "He's blackmailing us. If we want . . . your father . . . we have to lower the bridge. If we lower the bridge, he comes in."

"We can't stop him," murmured Morgan.

Her mother drew a long, slow breath. "You're right. We'll have to lower the bridge and let him enter. I'll have to confront him. You must go back to your room and wait for me there."

"No, Mother! Not alone!"

"Hush, now," Mother said, placing her fingers gently on Morgan's lips. "I'll send someone to be with you."

Morgan nodded, miserable.

"Go," Mother said firmly. She was gathering herself, becoming the duchess of Tintagel. "Throw the bolt and wait for the servant. She'll help you barricade the door. I'll send her with swords, one for each of you." She paused, taking a last look at Morgan, and then dashed a tear from her eye. "Go. I have to get dressed. I can't receive the king this way." She gave a weepy smile.

She already has.

Morgan only turned away, ducking her head and heading for the door. She ran as if Uther and his men were already within. Through the corridor, up the stairs, and to her room—she flung back the door and leapt within. Turning, she slammed and bolted it and slumped down to weep.

In time, chains clinked as the drawbridge paid out. Mother would be half dressed by now. The timbers boomed into place. Father's body would be jolting along beneath the portcullises. The trumpets began a royal fanfare to hail King Uther as he crossed the bridge.

Morgan remembered the black hair all down his back, the lunging motion, the way mother lay there as if gladly slain.

"Morgan!" came a growl through the door. It bounced in its frame. "It's me, Meg, the midwife."

Morgan jumped to her feet. She shot back the bolt and leapt aside as the door hurled open.

There stood a woman who was Uther's equal—brawny and brutish, with powerful shoulders and massive hips and a face like a lion's. Brown hair jutted in a wide mane around her head, completing the effect. In one hand, she clutched a pair of sheathed swords. In the other, she grasped Morgan, snatching her up. Morgan was lost in that massive embrace, as she had been countless times since birth.

"Meg!" she said, though her voice was muted.

"Oh, sweet Morgan. Meg's here. Nothing's going to happen now." As if reminded of the door that hung open behind her, Meg spun around, slammed it, and locked it. "Let's pile this door closed."

Only then did she release Morgan, who stood tingling after that all-powerful embrace.

Meg stomped into the chamber, stooped at the foot of the bed, set her hands beneath the boards, and hoisted. The muscles in her neck flexed tightly, and she sidestepped to pivot the thing. Wooden feet shrieked on the stones. With a mighty heave, she flung the bed before the door. "Always start with the bed," she said.

Morgan still stood and gaped in amazement, glad she hadn't been standing in the way. "You've barricaded doors before?"

Meg shrugged as she dragged the wardrobe beside the bed. She tilted the case onto its side. "Midwives learn ways to keep out the men. A good barricade can stop the whole thing before it's begun."

"Before what's begun?" Morgan asked.

Pausing with a chair in either hand, Meg said, "You've seen the horses foal. You've seen them going at it in the fields."

Morgan nodded gravely.

"That's what I'm talking about. Keep the stallion out of the paddock, and you keep the foal out of the mare." She tossed the chairs atop the pile.

His back had been like an animal's, rippling and lunging. "People are the same as animals," Morgan muttered.

Meg brushed off her hands and walked over to the window. "Some days more than others." She stared out at the drawbridge, and her eyes narrowed

Morgan walked softly to the midwife's side. She stared out past the rail. Already, Father lay in the courtyard below. He had been brutalized, and seemed impossibly thin on the pallet. His men stood around him, their shoulders high but their heads bowed. The Pendragon's men filed in around them. Many marched into the castle proper, ready for a fight that wouldn't come. The rest formed ranks around the dead man.

King Uther was there, too, his shoulders held back as if he waited for someone.

"She's going to have another baby."

Meg turned her leonine face toward Morgan. "How do you know that?"

"I saw what he did last night," said Morgan flatly.

Flaring her nostrils, Meg said, "It doesn't always bring a baby. This time, though, it will. I felt it in her touch. She has the fever, and she smells right. There's a baby in her."

"It's not from Father."

Meg's face grew very pale. "You've been having more visions, girl?"

"King Uther was here. He looked like Father. He put a baby in her."

Clucking, Meg shook her head. "What they won't do. They got everything in the world right in their hands—all the power, all the land, all the gold—and still by hook or crook they take the one thing we got. They stake their claim and plant their seed and trade it between them like it was just ground."

Yesterday, Morgan would not have understood, but today she did.

In the courtyard below, the great hall doors regally swung open, and out of them walked Mother, except that she was Duchess Igraine now. Instead of disheveled bedclothes, she wore regal samite in the green and red of Tintagel. Her hair rode atop her head in a tight coif, and veils draped around her face. Within the veils, her face was serene. She looked as if she hadn't shed a tear. She strode solemnly forward, and the muttering of the crowd fell to silence. Ten paces brought her before King Uther, who beamed gladly at her. Igraine bowed her head and bent her knee. She continued on, lying down before the man who had slain her husband.

Your desire will be for your husband, and he will rule over you, said the wise woman within her—echoing the words of Mother . . . who echoed the words of God.

Morgan wept again. "If they can put babies in us," she said through her tears, "we should be able to take them out. I don't mean as babies; I mean take them out so that they never are anything at all."

"Child," Meg said, one hand on Morgan's shoulder and the other on the rail. "You grew ten years last night. I'd take it back if I could."

"Take it back, then, Meg," Morgan said sternly, seeing again the antlered boy and the blood of nations. "Take that baby out of Mother. He will be a horrible child, and a worse man. He'll kill the world."

At first, she could hear no response except the woman's breath—her panting, as if the higher part of her had given place to a lower animal. "I could never do such a thing . . . unless your mother asked me to."

"If she did, could you do it?" Morgan asked. "The child will be a bloody monster like the minotaur, the Son of War."

"It is a very great sin to do what you ask, Morgan."

"Is it worse than what they did? Or what the beast-man will do?"

"Women have been killed for doing it."

The little girl swallowed, and her eyes seemed old. "We'll be killed if we don't. Women get killed no matter what they do."

Meg stared down at her hands, big, with curved fingers and thick calluses. "There are ways, yes. Old ways. I can make a powder. If your mother agrees to take it, she will be sick for three days, and the child will vanish on a tide of blood."

Morgan looked down into the courtyard, where mother still lay prostrate before the king. He bent down above her, not kneeling but stooping, and held out his knuckles that she might kiss his ring. Even as she lay there on her belly, she lifted her lips to kiss the killing hand

"Yes, Meg. Make the powder, and I will convince Mother."

3

Burying Them

Morgan wore a dress that stank. The cooks had dyed it in a great rush, mixing ink and ochre to make it look black. The cloth turned out a sickly gray, and it was still damp, and it stank. When the sun hit her shoulders, little white ribbons of steam rose and curled around Morgan's face and made her gag.

"Hold still, Morgan," said Mother, tugging on her hand. Mother wore a real black dress with a black veil for her head. She was old enough to have gone to funerals before. In this dress, she almost looked beautiful, and that also made Morgan gag.

King Uther looked at her as if she wore nothing at all. He stood on the other side of the bier, and he fairly smiled across the dead man. The king wore red brocade trimmed in ermine, with a silk cape clasped at the neck by a gold chain. He was not mourning. This was not his father. Morgan couldn't imagine that this bastard had any father.

Bastard was a word that Meg had taught her, a midwifing term. Meg held Morgan's other hand, but softly, to comfort instead of correct. Meg wore a robe of true black, ritual wear for castings, though she had taken the talismans off. She had said there was no need to provoke the bastard.

Morgan sneezed.

At the head of the grave, the priest ceased his kyries. He stared pointedly at her, sniffed, and began again.

Morgan felt like a vagrant in her dank dress. She and Father were a pair.

He lay there in his riven tabard, his suit of plate and chain, and the tattered chemise that jutted from each wound like torn flesh. Uther had refused to let him be changed into his stately robes or have his wounds packed or even his body cleaned. Duke Gorlois would lie eternally in the clothes and filth in which he had died. And he stank. Even now, workers cast shovels of lime onto his body to kill the smell, but it was too little too late. His flesh receded beneath the white powder, losing its color and then its lines. He was becoming a ghost, but this ghost would not fly up into the sky. He would be buried beneath a ton of garden soil and stone.

The priest was done. His droning words fell to silence, and the air solidified like mortar. For a while, no one could move or speak. They all stared down at the bier and the long white mound that had the general shape of Father. Then the workers positioned themselves at the head and foot of the dead man, lifted the ropes tied to his pallet, and began to lower him into the ground.

Sunlight shone dazzlingly on the body. Father hung on four cords above Tophet gloom. This was his last moment of sunlight. Morgan's breath caught in a sob. The pallet shuddered lower, lime raining from its edges. The shadow of the grave crept slowly over Father until he was submerged in it. The bier sank and at last lay on the bottom. The workers flipped the cords down across Father, and they looked like snakes.

King Uther moved. He pretended to grimace, but it was really a grin as he strode to the dirt pile and yanked up a shovel. The spade seemed a sword in his hand. He walked up to Mother and thrust the shovel out to her.

She stared at the spade, its edge shiny. Crumbs of earth clung within its hollow. She grasped the handle, her fist looking small and white beneath his bear's-claw. She took the shovel from him, stepped to the mound of dirt, and dug the blade into it. It came up, streaming darkness down into the hole. Mother turned the shovel, and earth fell, brown atop the lime-shrouded face.

And at the end of your days, you will return to dust, for dust you are.

King Uther reached a meaty hand out to pat Mother's back—the bare flesh between her shoulders where the lacy collar drooped. She looked up at him as she once had looked at Father, and her eyes gave thanks.

But your desire will be for your husband, and he will rule over you.

Uther took the shovel and chucked more clods down atop his rival. Then he surrendered the tool to the workmen, who stooped to fling shovel after shovel into the hole. Dirt, sand, gravel, and stone, they pounded him and buried him.

"Good-bye, Father," whispered Morgan. She turned toward Mother, but she was already in the king's arms, weeping.

Another woman drew Morgan into her great embrace: Meg. Morgan clung to her tightly and cried.

———

It had been a bleak month since Father's funeral. The king and his retinue remained at Tintagel, exploring the castle and cataloging its stocks. The local troops were imprisoned in the dungeons they had once guarded, and even the staff were interrogated and sorted according to their loyalties. Two men were killed outright, and a dog was shot when it growled at the guard captain. While the king's men worked over the castle, Uther worked over Igraine. He was always with her except when she slept, and Morgan wondered even then. Mother hadn't a moment to spare for her grieving daughter.

At last, this bright morning, Uther and most of his men marched out. Morgan sat at her window and stared with grim joy. She had never heard a sweeter sound than those hundred hooves on the drawbridge. The chasm growled like a defeated beast as they marched away. Yes, Uther left a large garrison, but he himself—the black-haired monster that had killed her father and raped her mother (rape was another word Meg had taught her)—was gone. Now, Morgan would go to Meg and learn how the Son of War might himself be gone.

Sliding on her summer sandals, Morgan ran for the door and down the stairs. She silently passed Mother's room, descended more stairs, and rushed out into the windy courtyard. Morgan almost skipped, almost laughed. Today was the beginning of freedom.

She ran into the garden, and her joy was done. There amid the final flowers of summer lay the grave. It was marked with a simple cross, tacked together as hurriedly as Christ's own. The ground before it wasn't even a mound, but a depression, sunken and sad. Morgan stopped beside the spot. It was Father's tomb and hers. Her childhood lay buried with him. Even between the two of them, they did not fill out the ground.

But all graves lead to resurrection, said the wise old voice in her mind.

The ground suddenly filled itself out. There was no longer a grave, nor a shabby cross, but a garden world. Tender shoots rose to her waist, with wildflowers in purple, orange, yellow, and white. Atop the sea of grass, a breeze meandered like the idling hand of a god. A great tree stood nearby, and beneath its spreading boughs thrived a young forest. Other sylvan islands rose amid the billowing hills, but most of the world was grass. Creatures moved among the stalks, and birds twined their ribbon trails through the air. Continents of cloud sailed across the sky or piled toward the sun or struck down with storms.

Have you ever seen so beautiful a place, my daughter? Morgan fell to her face and buried her eyes in the fecund world, but still her ears could hear. *It is the world as it should be, the Garden of Delights. Have you seen so beautiful a tree? It is Yggdrasil, the Tree of Knowledge and of Eternal Life. From it everyone should eat, and know, and live forever.* These were the words of the serpent, and yet the voice of the wise woman. *You can bring them to the tree, Morgan. You can throw back the garden gates so all the world may live in beauty.*

"I want to. Show me how."

The antlered boy will be your foe. While he lives, the world will die. He will bathe Britannia in blood. Oppose him.

"I will," she vowed quietly. "I will."

The garden and the great tree were suddenly gone. Only that long trough remained, and her moldering Father beneath it.

Morgan trembled. "Oppose him. . . ." She knelt and let the tepid sun warm her shivering back. In time, she rose again and staggered away from the grave.

Morgan crossed on through the garden to its far side.

There, a cellar door stood open. Rough-hewn steps descended into a cool, wet, fresh place. Morgan walked down the stairs. Once, she had been afraid of the haunted hole, as the castle children had dubbed it, but now she knew the woman who lived below. Morgan walked along a wide stone trough where a spring bubbled. Jars filled the slough, storage for the cold wares of the kitchens. Morgan went through a ragged door. More steps spiraled into darkness. She would have been terrified of that darkness, but Meg had shown her the way.

Through three turns and down three fathoms she went, all of it in darkness. Then the way opened again. The grotto was cool and wet, but living scents filled the air. Morgan smelled Meg before she saw her—a scent that was clean, rigorous, and natural. One more step brought her out of darkness and into the yellow glow of Meg's chambers.

They were utterly different from Mother's. Mother lived high in a tower, with white marble and gold leaf. Meg lived in a dark, low place, a natural grotto she had discovered beneath the spring cellar. Waters ran there, as they had since the world began, and with liquid hands they had sculpted the limestone into smooth curves, round rooms, and burls that might have been hobgoblin stools. It was the sort of place that priests would try to exorcise, but they would have misunderstood its spirits—not evil, but good.

Meg stood in the midst of the chamber, a tunic of thick homespun draping from shoulders to knees. A rope belt cinched the clothes at her waist, and hemp sandals like Morgan's own covered her feet. These were her work clothes, and all around her were the accoutrements of her craft: dried herbs, compound vials, pestle and mortar, pots and braziers, knives and needles, cauldrons and altar stones. On a peg in the wall hung a tin whistle with a leather thong, and beside it a little drum.

Even now, Meg hummed an ancient lay, the sacred texts of her mystic faith.

"I heard the horses," she said, one hand fondly cupping a knob on the wall. "I knew they were going and you'd be coming."

Morgan only smiled in greeting and moved to a low ledge, where she preferred to sit when Meg did her work. "It's time. The bastard king is gone."

Meg lifted an eyebrow. "Words like that sound bad from you."

"I know," Morgan said sullenly.

Sighing, Meg said, "Well, it's dark stuff we're into now, anyway." She pivoted, crouching beside a small brazier where a pot sat. "Do you know what this is?"

"Soup?"

"Blood."

Morgan wrinkled her nose. "Blood of newt?"

"Blood of Meg," she replied lightly.

Crossing her arms over her chest, Morgan said, "Why not just use soup?"

Meg laughed and shook her head. "Soup isn't powerful. Blood is." She placed a glass rod into the stuff and slowly stirred. At the rim of the pot, small bubbles formed a beaded chain. "Every person needs blood to live and needs the blood of animals to keep on living. Good blood cures you, and bad blood kills you. Gods demand it in sacrifice, and warriors do too. Ask a Jew why he won't eat blood. Ask a Christian why he drinks it. Both will tell you the same thing: Because blood is life."

Morgan nodded, her eyes faraway. "We're not after life, but death."

Without replying, Meg gingerly lifted the steaming pot

from the coals. She poured the hot liquid onto a concave stone and watched it spread across the surface. Absently reaching to a line above her head, she pulled down a handful of dried leaves, crumpled them, and sprinkled them across the stone. With a blond stick stripped of its bark, she mixed the concoction. "Blood magic is powerful, but limited. I never use the blood of another creature, but only my own. Each spell is a sacrifice, a self-sacrifice."

Morgan watched her work. "How do you draw it? Do you cut yourself?"

"No. Violent blood makes a violent spell," Meg replied. She tilted her head. "There are some who draw their own blood, and they are powerful. But their spells only destroy. There are others who sacrifice creatures to the gods—priests making blood oaths. Some necromancers even sacrifice humans and use their blood to bring life to the dead, but that isn't my work."

All the while, Morgan had been shaking her head. "How do you use your own blood without cutting yourself?"

With the stick, Meg scraped the red paste to one edge of the stone and guided it into a second pot, where another liquid waited. She moved it to the brazier. "I'm a midwife. I bring babies across the tide of blood and into life. That tide of blood runs through every woman. Every month, it carries away the children that will not be born. Every nine months, it brings the children that will."

Something lurked in her words, something Morgan could not quite parse out. "What are you talking about?"

Meg stared straight into her eyes. "To be a woman is to be a mystery. The river of life runs through us. It pours from our hearts and washes through us and keeps us alive. Once a month the tides of life run so high they pour from us."

"Ughh!"

"It's one of the mysteries," Meg said. The mixture boiled, white spirits rising from the pot. They twined and danced on the air, and in a flurry they were done. She donned a glove, lifted the pot, and poured its contents, a gray powder now, onto a linen cloth. "The power of the river is unceasing. Sometimes it flows unto life . . ." she folded the cloth around the powder, making a bundle, ". . . and sometimes it flows unto death." When she handed the packet to Morgan, it was still warm.

It felt like a dead mouse in her hand. "This will not hurt Mother."

"No, but it will end the child in her. She must take it willingly."

Morgan put it in her pocket. "Or it will not work?"

With a warning flash, Meg said, "No, it will. But if you use it without her consent, I will never do another thing for you, and we'll no longer be friends."

"I'll convince her."

Mother sat in her sewing room. It was a small place paneled in walnut, with three embroidered chairs, a quaint fireplace, and the hoops and bolts and thread she needed for needle-point. It was the room where she would wait for Father when he was on a journey. He would come to that room to find her, would call her Penelope and catch her up in his arms. Morgan had known she would be there, working over her stitches as if Father would stride in at any moment.

Lingering in the doorway, Morgan said, "Mother?"

The woman startled, clutching the needlework to her breast and shooting her a haunted look. "Morgan," she gasped as if in relief, though she scooted higher in her seat, and her cheeks seemed to stiffen. "I wondered where you had gotten off to."

Where I had gotten?—she thought indignantly and gripped the packet of dead powder in her fingers. "May I come in?"

"Yes, child. Of course. I'm your mother. This is your castle."

Shyly, Morgan strode across the woolen carpet. "I wanted to tell you something."

"I wanted to tell you something too," Mother replied. Her smile was grown-up, a thing painted on. "I'm going to have another child."

Morgan blinked. "Yes, I know."

"How do you know?" Mother asked, alarmed.

Morgan saw no reason to lie. "I had a vision."

Fear faded, and Mother nodded deprecatingly. "Oh, yes, your visions."

"He will be a son, a strong son," Morgan went on. "Too strong. He has an antlered head and a great sword. He's the Son of War. The killing gods have put this baby in you, Mother—I've seen it—"

"Now, Morgan—"

"And he'll make war throughout Britannia and the whole world. He'll pour out blood on every land from here to Rome—"

"*Really, Morgan*—"

"And the garden of delights will never fill the world if he is born—"

"If he's *born! If* he's born!" Mother spat, at last silencing her. "Enough! Enough of your mad visions. Of course he will be born!"

"No, Mother. He mustn't be," Morgan protested. She brought out the packet of powder from behind her back. "Here. I've brought something from Meg. Just mix this with tea. It'll be bitter, and you'll be sick for three days, but then you'll be better. All better. There won't be any blood, any antlers. You'll be rid of the monster that's growing—"

"Monster!" Mother swatted the packet away. She stood, embroidery clutched in one hand and the other clenched in a fist. "My child *will* be born, and won't be a monster. If there's any monster that's come from me—" she broke off, mastering her rage. In a quiet voice, she continued, "I don't want you or that—that *witch* of a midwife anywhere near me. I'll bear this child and birth this child without either of you."

"Mother!" Morgan gasped, pale and amazed.

The woman lifted the needlepoint. "Look, Morgan! Here's a vision for you! Do you see it? Do you understand it?"

She did. The woman's worrying hands had worked a dreadful image into the simple cloth—King Uther standing beside his new queen, Queen Igraine, who in turn held the child of the king, the infant heir to all of Britannia. Of Morgan or Morgause or their father, there was not a sign.

"Get out," she said. "In eight months, when the child is suckling, you'll be my daughter again. For now, though, you are nothing to me. Stay away, and tell the witch to as well, or you'll both wind up in the dungeon."

4

As Misery Loves Company

Morgan paced slowly across the courtyard, an exile in her own home. For seven months, she had been a living shadow—driven from her mother's heart. The varlets and cooks could casually speak to Mother, but Morgan could not so much as glance her way. Lines of light might connect their eyes; lines of sound might connect their minds. What if Morgan were to breathe air into her lungs and warm it and charge it with the black poisons of her heart and then exhale it in the same room where Mother might inhale it and receive the darkness into her heart and let it slay the royal creature in her womb?

Fear was a disease. It had nearly killed Duchess Igraine and spread from her throughout the castle until everyone recognized its carrier: Morgan.

"That's her," someone muttered quietly. "An angel's face but a heart of murder."

Morgan glared at the man, one of Uther's meaty warriors. He had helped the king capture Tintagel, and now he and a hundred of his compatriots filled it. They had killed Father and raped Mother and banished Daughter. They hated Tintagel but dominated it and gathered to celebrate a royal wedding. Morgan pinned the man with her gaze.

He blanched and took a step backward. His lips moved in silent fear, forming the word *witch*.

Not yet, no, Morgan thought darkly. But every day, I get nearer.

She strode past more knots of soldiers, lingering to the last before going into the chapel. Morgan didn't dare wait. She didn't have an invitation.

The building loomed ahead, a fieldstone box set beside the great hall. Its second story held a line of small, irregular windows, above which hung a thatched roof. It wasn't a grand chapel, constructed by Celts rather than Romans. It was unworthy to host a king's wedding, but Igraine was too pregnant to travel.

Two guards flanked the doorway. The one on the right drew his sword and barred the entrance. "Invitation?"

Morgan stopped before the leveled blade. "I'm Morgan. I'm her daughter."

"We know who you are," the guard said.

The other man said, "She's her daughter. Let her in." He was middle-aged, with black curly hair and wise eyes. "By my order."

"Whatever, Ulfius," snorted the first guard. He withdrew his sword, waving it one last time significantly before sheathing it. "It'll be your head."

"It's always been my head," Ulfius replied.

Morgan said no more, only tucking her chin and walking between the two. They weren't all murderers. Somehow that fact was unsettling. It would have been simpler to demonize them all.

Morgan walked beneath the lintel and into the cave-smelling darkness. Candles glowed, and a quartet of fife, drum, rebec, and lute played in one transept. The benches were nearly filled already, and many of the soldiers outside would have to stand in the back.

Morgan headed for the back corner of the chapel, where a ladder led to a wooden balcony. She climbed. Dust sifted from the steps, and the whole platform crackled when she climbed onto it. A few folk sat on the three benches, but Morgan headed for an alcove at the absolute rear of the church. A statue of Saint James stood within the niche, and Morgan climbed up behind it. She hid behind the stone skirts of the brother of Jesus.

Outside, trumpets began a fanfare, and inside, the air changed. The king had arrived. He strode up the center aisle toward the altar. His subjects came to their feet, all except Morgan. They gazed on the man's face, his ermine and samite robes and the pendragon emblazoned on his chest. Morgan gazed at his back and saw right through the velvet cape to his hairy flesh, thrusting like the body of a bear. He carried a golden mace, as if to say he could smash any opposition—and smash it with gold. He had clubbed his way to the throne of Tintagel and to the bed of Igraine.

She came next. Trumpets echoed away to leave the lilting music of string and wind. Draped in white and enormously pregnant, Mother advanced up the aisle. She could have been any woman now, great with child, round and white like a comet.

There is a riddle in this for you, darling Morgan, said the wise voice. *A vision, if you can bear it.*

She muttered, "Any vision would be better than what I now see."

And the vision came: Mother hurtled through the skies among the wandering planets and bore within her life in its abundance. It was not a single life, but all life, as if the pearls sewn into her dress were in fact seeds folded into her flesh. Out of her body would grow everything. From a million folds emerged a million million beasts. Every animal born into being was her child. They lived awhile, spread across her body in their manifold splendor, and then returned, planted to rise again. Within her ever-fecund flesh, corpses became seeds. She was no longer Mother, but part of a great Female.

She has been called Venus, and Modron, and Baal, and older names. They crowded through Morgan, bearing her on their tide back to that first, ancient comet, that dragon who fell from heaven and crashed to Earth and gave birth to all living things from her violate and vaginate flesh—*Tiamat.*

Morgan swooned within the niche and clung to the skirts of James. She was glad she hadn't sat among the others. Sweat prickled her skin, and breath rushed in and out.

"'At last,'" the priest intoned, narrow and black between bride and groom, "'this is bone of my bone and flesh of my flesh, and she shall be called woman, for she was taken out of man. . . .'"

Morgan felt almost sick. Woman was not taken out of man, but man out of woman, and woman out of woman. All was taken out of her.

"'. . . and so a man will leave his father and mother and cleave to his wife, for they are one flesh. And they were both naked, the man and his wife, and unashamed.'"

Naked, and unashamed; a great bent back mantled in hair

and stippled in sweat, working as if against hard ground, and the knees lifted like the ridges of the furrow, the receiving earth from which would spring all that lives—

"'And unto the woman, he said I will greatly multiply your sorrow in conceiving and bearing children, yet your desire will be for your husband, and he will rule over you.'"

Slave of desire, slave to men, the ground forever to lie beneath the plow and be torn open and healed only to be torn again, and bear all in sorrow—

"'And to the man . . . saying cursed is the ground because of you, and you will eat of it in sorrow, and it will produce thorns and thistles unto you, until you return into the ground from which you were taken. And Adam called his wife's name Eve, for she was the mother of all living.'"

It is but another name for that great All-Woman, the sum of all mortal flesh, a simple woman and a compound goddess. The wise woman's voice was gentle. *Eve is Tiamat transformed, made to rise from Adam and be subject to him, made to be ashamed of her nakedness, and in sorrow to conceive and bear and bear.*

Mother turned around beside the king. They had spoken their vows and were man and wife. Mother was suddenly Mother again, caught between a man and a child and doing what she did only to endure the sorrow of her plight. On a single night, she had lost one husband and gained another, each by force, and had planted within her this antlered child, who even now waited to tear her open.

The trumpets began to peal, and the crowd cried its adulation. The sound was deafening there in the shadow of the saint. Morgan clutched her hands to her ears and trembled.

———

"Have you ever heard of Tiamat?" Morgan asked idly. She lay on a stony ledge in Meg's grotto, letting the cool of the place soothe her feverish skin.

Meg took a deep breath of the grainy brew in her cauldron. Tiny droplets clung like dew to her wispy bangs. "Can't say I have. Who is she?"

Morgan shrugged. "Some old dragon. She fell to earth and her body split open in a million places, and everything came out of her."

"Oh," Meg said with a sniff, "you mean Modron. She gave birth to everything, and she nurtures it, and she brings it down to death again."

Nodding, Morgan said, "She has lots of names. Tiamat is one of them. So is Eve."

"Eve?" Meg said. "You mean Adam's wife?"

"Before that, she was more. I think she was a goddess, but then they married her off to Adam."

Laughing, Meg stirred the pot. "It's always the way. A woman on her own's a dangerous creature. Marry her off and change her name, and she's safe again."

"Mother is called Queen Igraine now. She's not even 'of Tintagel' anymore. She's Queen Igraine of Britannia."

Meg shook her head. "There've been female dynasties, but they're lost because of the names. So are the goddesses. Call them what you want—Modron, Tiamat, Eve, maiden, mother, crone—they're all one." She shifted toward a small hearth, where a tray held shortcakes.

"What kind of spell needs shortcake?"

Meg smiled. "The festival of cakes and ale."

Morgan sat up and stared at the cauldron. "Ale? Is that what you're brewing?"

"Of course," Meg replied, drawing the shortcakes from

the fire and gingerly setting them on a grate to cool. "It won't be ready for a few months, but I put up a cask a few months ago. And these," she deftly slid a shortcake onto a cloth and handed it to Morgan, "are ready right now."

Morgan stared down at the round cake, pressed into a form that she knew—a woman, as round as the world. "What's the festival of cakes and ale?"

"It celebrates gladness. Coming together."

"It's like communion."

"Yes," said Meg as she retreated to a dark corner of her grotto. She grunted, and there came a sloshing sound. She appeared again, and a small cask rolled before her. "Except that this ritual isn't solemn and sad, but full of joy."

Morgan nodded and smiled and bit into the round cake.

Morgan lurched up in bed. She grasped the sheets, her hands wringing the cloth. What was happening? Her room was dark except for a blue triangle of moonlight spilling through her window. The air was still. A horse in the stable whickered, and the sea murmured restlessly.

Then came the second scream.

"Mother," Morgan gasped. She was out of bed and running toward the door before she had fully awakened. Realization stopped her: "Mother. . . ."

The woman's cries came again, agonized and desperate. "Help! Someone. Anyone!"

Morgan was someone. It was an invitation. Morgan grasped the knob and flung the door wide. "I'm coming," she said quietly, almost fearing her mother would hear. She descended the spiral. "I'm coming."

"Help!" Mother cried again, and her voice became an inarticulate shriek.

Morgan reached the landing and barged through Mother's door. "I'm here, Mother."

The woman lay on her bed, gasping in misery. Her hands clutched the mattress beneath her, and tears ran down her cheeks. Her belly, huge now, seemed as tight as a drum and ready to burst. She didn't seem to notice Morgan, but only screamed again.

Morgan ran to her and knelt by the bed. She caught the woman's hand in her own and squeezed. "I'm here, Mother. It'll be all right. You'll be all right."

The terrible seizure that had gripped her eased, and the woman took a few deep breaths. Her eyes opened, and she pivoted her face toward her daughter. "Morgan," she said breathlessly. "The pain is getting bad."

"I'm here," Morgan said.

"It's been on and off all night, but now it's bad." She swallowed. "It feels like I'm going to be ripped open."

Visions of the antlered boy came to Morgan's mind, but she said only, "I've learned some midwifery—"

Fear filled the woman's eyes. "I don't want you to do anything."

Morgan looked down and nodded.

"Kneel there and hold my hand," Mother said. "That's all."

"Meg is a great healer, and I've learned—"

"The child of the king won't be delivered by a pair of witches. That's what they've always said about her. That's what they're saying about you. She's corrupting you."

"I have no one else," Morgan blurted. "She's wise and has real power."

Lines deepened across Mother's face, as if it would shatter and fall off her skull. "She's dangerous."

An ache tore through Morgan. "Mother, you don't understand. . . ."

"Do you?" shot back her mother. "Do you? I had no choice in what happened to me. I started to choose the next day, when news came of your father and of the king. I could die or marry him, so I married him. I saved us both. What have you done? Making yourself a witch. They'll kill you, Morgan. That's what they do to witches—kill them."

"That's what they do to all of us."

Footsteps came up the stairs, rushing and frantic. Two nursemaids appeared, and behind them the royal midwives with their bags of implements. They rushed toward the queen, and one midwife shoved Morgan aside.

"You don't want her here, do you, Majesty?"

Mother's face hardened into a smooth mask. "No."

A guard arrived next, saw Morgan, and stomped angrily across the chamber. "What are you doing here?"

"Mother—"

"Don't hurt her, but take her out of here, and don't let her come back."

Morgan was numb as the man grasped her arm and marched her away. He muscled her through the door and started down the stair. "Let me go back to my room."

"The queen said to get you out of here. You won't be in the same building."

Of course not, Morgan thought. It was a mercy. She couldn't bear to lie in bed and listen to the cries. They were beginning again, pain in conceiving and pain in bearing. Morgan shook herself loose and walked ahead of the man. "I'm going."

It was a cool midmorning before the agony was done. For ten hours, Mother had cried out, and all the while Morgan had waited on a woodpile in the courtyard. She had even slept there against the faggots, imagining the villagers lighting her on fire. Then, there was a final shout of pain, and the cry of the child. Morgan sat up, smiling. No sooner had the child quieted, though, than Mother began to curse and protest and plead.

Morgan lurched up from the woodpile and ran across the courtyard, her nightshirt flapping. Stable hands and armsmen glared at her. Under their gaze, Morgan slowed and stopped, and her bedclothes settled around her. Mother had not wanted her before, when she was alone and in agony. She certainly wouldn't want Morgan now.

The shouts above grew louder and then gave way to a piteous weeping. It sounded as if Mother had been torn apart and would never heal the wound. Her sobs were punctuated by the rasp of metal-shod feet on stone stairs. Someone was descending the tower.

Morgan walked toward the sound, and in the arched door that led to Mother's room, she met a man.

"I know you," Morgan said, "Ulfius. You let me see the wedding." Her eyes narrowed. "And you were here that night. You were one of the imposters. I met you on this stair . . . Chamberlain Jordanus."

The man's eyes were intent in his black curly hair. "Morgan, let me show you your brother." He lowered the bundle and pulled back a fold of the swaddling. Within lay the face of a babe, indescribably beautiful despite blue-tinged eye sockets and traces of blood and vernix. He was the loveliest creature Morgan had ever seen, and from his brow emerged phantom antlers. "He is called Arthur."

"Named after Uther," Morgan replied flatly. "Not after my father, because he is the son of Uther, from that terrible night."

Ulfius drew the cloth over the babe's face and set his shoulders. "I must go."

She stepped out alongside him. "Where?"

"Arthur is going away. He's promised to someone who will care for him until he is king."

Morgan had a vision of him: a scuttling madman with white hair and beard and a baby wrapped in his arms. *This hobgoblin is powerful, a child-stealer who will miser the boy to death.* The voice was the warrior-woman's, fierce and harsh. *We will make sure of his death.* Morgan saw how it would happen. They were in a rowboat on a swollen river beneath a pouring sky, and the child at last died. Child and man and boat, all, went into the river. *No child should endure such terrors, not even the antlered one, but if Arthur dies, the Garden lives. . . .*

"He will take Arthur away from Tintagel and Mother?"

Ulfius nodded grimly. "Yes, I fear so." Clutching the child, he headed away toward the garden.

Morgan watched the man go. She couldn't have stopped him if she had wanted to, and as terrible as the child's fate would be, its death would save Britannia and the world from a tide of blood.

Pray for the babe, Morgan. Pray to Modron and Eve and Tiamat.

Murmuring to goddesses long dead, Morgan turned and ran. She reached the archway and charged up the stairs toward Mother's chambers. She didn't care whether she was wanted. The door flung back, and Morgan ran across the floor even as midwives scrubbed it, and she flung herself in her mother's arms.

Mother did not push her away. At least as misery loved company, Mother loved Morgan.

She will never bear again, said the ghost healer in Morgan's mind. *Your mother has been ripped open from within. She does not know this yet, and Uther will never know it. He will plow her for another heir. He will take her away to London, where the laying and ruling will be easier for him.*

Morgan blurted, "Will you take me?"

"What?" Mother asked blearily.

She will not. They will abandon you here.

"Oh, Mother," Morgan said, clasping her even more tightly and wishing that misery were love.

5

The Holy Flood

It was perhaps the last true embrace Morgan and her mother would ever have. Igraine, who had just lost her son, was about to abandon her daughter.

Two weeks after the birth, the aggrieved royal couple removed to London, leaving Morgan in the hands of tutors in Tintagel. It was just as well. Misery was not love, and the more Morgan had clung to her mother, the worse they both felt. Once she was gone, Morgan felt only emptiness instead of pain. The remedy seemed to work for Igraine as well, for she stayed away. By the time Morgan was eight, she had bested the best tutors her mother had sent. By the time she was ten, Morgan had become the undisputed ruler of the palace and the lands.

"Princess," the tutor said gently, disguising his intrusion with a cough into his wide gray mustache. "Did I cover that bit a little too quickly?"

Morgan looked up from the embroidery she had picked loose from the chair. She was a beautiful young woman with a dazzling smile, and she used it now on poor Dumarus. "Not too quickly. Too slowly. I'm not interested in Romans. I want to know about older people."

Dumarus lifted his brows, replicas of his bushy mustache, and he scratched a pate that was bald except for a few twisted white hairs. "I never had a student who wanted to know about the *older* nations."

"I never had a tutor who would teach me what I wanted to learn." He blushed a little at the praise. Dumarus was infatuated with Morgan, and he was brilliant and sweet. Otherwise, she would not have submitted to his training. "Tell me about Egypt."

"Egypt!" he said in surprise. He began to pace before the fireplace. Once, this had been mother's sewing room, but now the needlepoint was replaced with parchment. Blinking in synchrony with his words, Dumarus said, "Egypt . . . Egypt . . . Egypt . . ." He rolled up his scroll of Herodotus, which he claimed was but three hands from the original, and hefted the family Bible. He flipped absently through the front leaves, where five generations of Father's line were written. Igraine and Morgan appeared near the end, with Uther and Arthur last of all. "Most of what we know of Egypt comes from the first and second books of Moses. . . . Abraham first journeyed to Egypt during a famine, and he pretended his wife was his sister, that the Pharaoh not kill him. Instead, Pharaoh took Sarah into his harem and made Abraham rich—"

Morgan rolled her eyes. "Hasn't Herodotus got anything to say about Egypt?"

Dumarus's face fell, and he stared at his gnarled fingers. "Not in the scrolls I have. I remember reading some bits in my studies in Rome. He contradicts some of the biblical accounts—"

"Why didn't you become a priest, Dumarus?"

A fragile smile formed on his lips, and he looked into Morgan's eyes, asking permission to ignore the question.

She pressed. "There are two reasons young men don't become priests. One is that they fall out of love with Jesus."

"Oh, Morgan—"

"And the other is that they fall in love with a woman." She had used these same words on two other tutors and sent them packing, but she was sure Old Dumarus could pass the test. "So, which was it?"

Dumarus inhaled, thinking. "When you first fall in love, my dear, it's overwhelming, all-encompassing—a blinding mania. But love matures. It becomes quieter, patient and measured and deep. Some people think love is the blind mania, but true lovers love with open eyes and sane minds."

"Which was it? Jesus, or the woman?"

"Both," Dumarus said flatly.

"You don't know anything about ancient Egypt."

"No. Not much."

She got up from the embroidered chair where she sat and walked solemnly to the jangled scholar. "Do you know anything about ecstatic visions?" She loved that phrase, one used derisively by a previous tutor.

Dumarus nodded shallowly. "I used to have them, in that first blush of conversion. Some . . . seemed to prove true. Ecstasy means to stand outside oneself, and that's the problem. Sometimes when you're standing outside yourself, you see real things, and sometimes you're just out of your mind."

"Do you think I'm out of my mind?" Morgan asked, clasping his hand. "I have visions all the time, and they're always true. I'll tell you about Egypt." His hand was tense in hers, but he held on. Was it skepticism or secret desire that tightened his grip? These were two weaknesses in all men, and Morgan was learning to use them to her advantage. "Close your eyes, Erasmus." That was his Christian name, and she knew it thrilled him when she said it. "You will see what I see and hear what I hear."

Standing hand in hand with his student before the small fire of their room, Dumarus closed his eyes.

Morgan focused her inner sight on the vision plane and tuned her inner ear to the voices. The darkness of her mind began to transform. Blackness became brown, undulating in small and even waves. The sun sparkled on that wide, brown belly and glinted on the particles tumbling within the flood. A flood it was, reaching across the seared plains. It brought water and soil to the sands; it brought life.

Behold, the Great River. Her name is Nile. She is born in the heart of a continent, and she pours herself down through the golden hills of Nubia and into the kingdoms of Upper and Lower Egypt. She is Egypt. Without her, it all is dust.

The river receded, and the wide, brown plains around Morgan burst with wheat and barley. Green fields turned white, and workers scurried like ants among them, harvesting. Storehouses grew—reed and then wood and then stone—and around them sprouted huts and houses and palaces. Here, a city-state, and there. In the south they fused, and a king swept north along the river with a great army. He took the Lower Kingdom, and the gold of Nubia. The kings became pharaohs, and the pharaohs became gods.

The children of the Great River built works in stone—pyramids stacked on the plain and tombs carved into the valley. They chiseled names that are half god and half man, Amen-Hotep and Akhen-Aten, and another name: Hatshepsut. She was pharaoh, and she was goddess.

An ancient empire spread before Morgan, a people who had flourished for two millennia within the lap of the Nile. Hatshepsut was the Nile herself. She was Egypt. The power of life flowed through her and gushed from her in its season to make all the land bear fruit. For two thousand years, the god-kings of Egypt had straddled that great flood, but now the goddess-queen embodied it. She had wrestled the world from the hands of men and returned it to the arms of the goddess, who ruled before Babylon and Sumer, who would rule again now and forever.

"I am Hatshepsut," Morgan said, before the wise woman could speak again. "I have carved my name throughout the temples of the land, throughout the Valley of the Kings. I am the life of Egypt, and I will live forever."

From Morgan, a new flood filled the land. It was not the Nile but the River Brue and its thousand streams and rivulets. The waters poured across the Glastonbury Plains and rose, turning hills to islands. The highest hill, the tor itself, transformed from rock and rugged grass to an illimitable mountain. There, in the midst of apple blossoms, rose a different sort of tree, a wooden giant with its roots plumbing the Otherworld and its branches plucking the stars. A great serpent coiled around that tree, not in threat but in welcome, and the garden was green and bright.

"I am to rise like Hatshepsut and be the goddess-queen of Britannia. I am to bring the bounteous flood to her land, and spread the garden of Avalon throughout the world. My name will be remembered forever."

As suddenly as it had come, the verdant garden was gone, and only a dry valley of bones and dust remained. Tombs filled the rock, and wind filled the tombs. No one lived in this place except the royal masons and the grave robbers. Only the hieroglyphs told of the god-kings, of Hatshepsut herself. But even as she watched, workers chiseled her name from the stones. She was being obliterated. She would not live forever, and the return of the goddess was being wiped from the brow of the world. These were royal masons, and so her own son had sent them to destroy her.

They will carve your name from history, as they carved the name of Hatshepsut.

"No," Morgan said. "I will not be forgotten. I will chisel my name deep in every stone. I will live." She opened her eyes, and the visions flitted away. She still held tightly to the hand of her tutor, but now he knelt before her. He wore an expression of devotion, and he trembled.

Morgan smiled at him. "Am I out of my mind?"

Dumarus swallowed. "I don't know, Princess. But I may well be out of mine."

Morgan raised him to his feet. "Let's go see. Assemble a company of travelers. We march to Avalon."

At ten years old, the disowned princess of Tintagel seemed a queen. Her black hair gleamed in the afternoon sunlight, sharply contrasted to the crisp raiment on her shoulders. She rode a gray horse that was ten times her weight, fitted in royal livery. Utterly erect, Morgan kept her brown eyes fixed on the road. The reins of the beast draped decorously from its saddle, unused. The young princess preferred to twine her fingers in the creature's rich mane, as if she and the beast were old friends.

To either side of her rode stout retainers, Meg at her right and Dumarus at her left. They were a delightful contrast, the great fleshy woman who lived in the ground and the little wispy man who lived in books. The three rode abreast up a long, slow rise. Morgan's retinue followed, ten horsemen handpicked from among the fine boys of Dumnonia, a cook skilled in making meals on the trail, and a drover with a team of pack mules. The whole company sauntered along at the pace of the mules, but the going was easy. Sheep had shorn the land into a green lawn, and the company headed toward a shallow blue valley.

"The abbey is only the latest holy site to occupy the tor," Dumarus was saying. "We'll walk the ruins higher up the hillside, and you'll see the differences between pre- and post-Roman construction."

"You truly saw water across all this land?" asked Meg, as if Dumarus hadn't spoken. "It's the way Avalon once was, they say."

"It'll be that way again," replied Morgan serenely.

"Don't get your heart set on inland seas today," Dumarus said. "Aside from the Brue, there's only swamp water down there now."

Meg scowled across the neck of her dappled mare. "Her heart is different from ours, scholar. She sets her heart on something, and it happens."

Morgan looked slyly at him. "Don't you believe in me, Erasmus?"

He bowed his head, sunlight glinting off the top. "Of course I believe in you, Princess, but I'm not convinced by these visions."

"I am," Meg volunteered, reaching over to squeeze the girl's elbow. "You take Avalon by storm, child, and see if you can't spread it throughout Britannia."

The horses clomped up the last gentle rise and entered a

round valley above the Glastonbury Plains. They stopped, gazing out.

Rolling hills stretched down to a wide wetland, which encircled the tor itself. It was an ancient rock, chiseled by time and nibbled by sheep. It had a skeletal look, as if this were the bare scapula of the world. On a low ledge of the tor rested a small abbey, with a cloister and a cruciform chapel, little larger than Tintagel's own. Around the tor was a marshland, and beyond it the plains that held the town of Glastonbury. In the sheer distance lay the Eire Sea.

"It's lovely," Dumarus put in, "but it's no Garden of Delights."

Meg spoke quietly. "These are the barren remains, overworked and sterile. This is not the way Avalon once was."

"Do you know what I see?" Morgan asked, and both turned toward her. "I see the beginning of a new world." Her heels nudged the sides of the horse, and her fingers tugged its mane. The horse ducked its head and snorted, trotting into a fast canter and then a full-out gallop.

Dumarus and Meg watched her race down the shallow embankment toward the wetlands. They traded worried looks and then kicked their steeds into her wake.

Three horses thundered down the sloping belly of the land, and then ten more as the armsmen brought up the rear. The cook and the mule trainer remained behind to guard the mules and their supply train.

Galloping gladly, Morgan stood in her stirrups and whooped. One hand remained laced in the creature's mane, but the other flew free in the wind. Her legs guided the horse down across the swale, along the reed-choked marshes, and toward an isthmus. It was the only solid ground across the wetlands. Passage across it was blocked by a palisade, and two priests stood beside its gate, watching her approach. Morgan laughed.

The priests were small and worried behind their great wooden spikes. They drew their swords as if she were an army of Saxons.

Morgan's horse charged across the mound, heading straight for the palisade. She tugged gently on the horse's hair. His hooves churned the dust before the gate, and the beast halted, whickering.

"Who, in the name of all that's holy, are you?" demanded one of the priests. His sword twitched behind the barred gate.

Morgan stared past the slanting poles and into those worried faces. They might have been Dumarus but had never gotten beyond their divine infatuation.

Dumarus and Meg rode up, dragging their beasts to a halt. The dust from their hooves poured through the gate and made the priests cough. Next moment, the armsmen arrived with the same bluster and a bigger choking cloud. The priests sputtered and gagged.

"I am Princess Morgan of Tintagel, daughter of Queen Igraine of all Britannia."

The coughing ceased, and the priests stared, white eyes in dust-covered faces. "You're who?"

"Princess Morgan of Tintagel. Open in the name of King Uther."

Somehow, the priest's eyes grew wider still. Uther was more terrible than even an army of Saxons. The priests scrambled for the bar, and they heaved it from its brackets. The gate swung inward, opening onto that hill of pessimistic grass and angry stone. A dirt trail led up to the abbey, which crouched, low and irregular, near the base of the tor. The priests watched the faces of the visitors, as if accustomed to unhappy expressions.

Dumarus held his hand out toward the hill. "Well, Princess, lead us into your glorious garden."

Morgan didn't spare him a glance. She tugged on the horse's mane and clucked, and the beast plodded between the gates. Skepticism hung in the air all around her. Dumarus, the armsmen, the priests, and even Meg—they all had eyes. They could see that this place could not be less like a primordial garden.

Morgan had eyes too, and that was the whole problem. Giving the horse his head, she closed her eyes. She drew into her mind a vision of the Garden. It was easy to do. That wondrous place was more real to her than any plot of land anywhere. Lifting her right hand, Morgan gestured toward where the southern flank of the tor would be, and she called out, "Look there! Do you see the apple forest? What lovely blossoms! How they shimmer! Do you smell them, and the promise of fruit?" Without opening her eyes, she could see the glimmering wood and sense its ancient roots reaching beneath the turf.

Behind her, only the clatter of hooves responded.

Lifting her other hand, Morgan imagined the northern slope. "And there, the great tree Yggdrasil! Look how tall it is! The clouds are torn by its branches. And look how deep its roots are! It's older than any creeping thing. Do you see it? The world tree? If we eat of it, we will be like gods." It only became more real as she spoke of it, a great and rangy tree, as large as a mountain, as ancient as time itself. The bark of the tree held enormous valleys, and its leaves were the stars.

Still, only the dull thud of hooves followed her.

She extended both hands above her horse's head. "And,

look here, just before us. See that great waterfall? It is the wellspring of life, the immortal stream. Drink from that water, and your youth will return to you, your health, your life." She could feel the spray of the waters on her face, cold and invigorating. Her mind's eye painted a rainbow above the head of the cascade. At its foot, waters churned before coursing away down a riverbed and toward Avalon Lake. "Don't you see it? Don't you see any of it?"

When silence came behind her, Morgan opened her eyes—and she did see. It all was there.

The tor had transformed into a huge, verdant, and holy mountain. Its sides were robed in apple blossoms and mantled in evergreens. Wide and welcoming glades opened here and there, combining into rolling fields. On seas of grass, wild-flowers bloomed in vast rafts. To the north stood the great tree—the infinite world tree stirring its head among the stars. It seemed enormous even here, some hundred leagues away. Straight ahead, a waterfall plunged into a great basin of stone, the ancient and sacrificial cauldron of the Celts. Veils of mist draped the rocks and swathed the whole company.

Morgan turned toward her comrades. They were the only real-world things she could see, and their horses and provisions were as solid as the trees and rocks. "Behold, the Garden of Delights! Do you see it?"

At first, they only stared blankly ahead. At last, Dumarus answered for them all. "Yes, Princess. . . . Yes, we do."

6

Hearts in Avalon

Though Erasmus's horse stood still, he clung to it as if it were galloping through a firestorm. He had never seen anything like this. He wondered whether his horse had.

The rocky hill had transformed into a true island, huge and magnificent. The road had become a waterfall and pool. Even now, its gentle streambed washed the dust of the world from the horses' hooves. A moment ago, only a thin skin of grass stretched across the worn-down bones of earth. Now the ground was a thick tapestry of flowers: wild carrots and columbine, sundrops and yarrow, thistle and braewort, and on the slopes, heather as thick as snow. Instead of the occasional scrub bush, too rugged even for the teeth of goats, now oak brakes dotted the meadows. In the distance, they gave way to apple groves and stands of elm and mulberry, ash and beech. The mountain bore primeval forests that had grown without fire or ax since the world had begun. Greatest of all the trees, though, was that monster in the north, greater than the fabled baobab or banyan, higher than a mountain. Its highest boughs bore true snow, and its deepest roots must have reached the heart of the world.

"So you see it, just as I have said?" Morgan asked.

Erasmus nodded numbly. "Is this a spell, Princess?"

"If it is," butted in the witch, Meg, "I don't know it."

"Yes, it's a spell," said Morgan. "Older than any you know, Meg. This isn't a Celtic thing—sun and moon, cauldron and wand. This is deeper magic. I've always had it in me, and you have it in you, and every woman."

From the moment Erasmus had first seen Morgan, he had sensed the magic latent in her. Now it was flooding the world. "Are we . . . truly here, then? Or is this a vision?"

Morgan turned toward him. "What's the difference?" She tugged on the mane of her great gray horse, and it stepped forward through the churning water. "Follow me."

Erasmus urged his mount to cross the stream, and the witch advanced as well. The captain of the guard waved the armsmen forward. Hooves clomped on the stony bed, and waves rolled in their wake.

In the midst of the company, a man said, "You heard her! This is the immortal stream!" He swung his leg over the steed and slid from his saddle.

Morgan glanced over her shoulder.

The armsman fell to his feet in the splashing stuff and knelt, cupping the water to his mouth. He was suddenly gone. It was as if the water had swallowed him. His horse plodded on with the company.

"What happened?" Erasmus asked urgently.

Morgan gave a casual shrug. "He heard part of what I said, the part about the immortal stream, but he didn't hear it all. I said, 'Follow me.'"

It was a chilling pronouncement, and it still hadn't answered Erasmus's question. "But, where is he?"

"Back on the tor, in Glastonbury," Morgan said. "He's probably getting grabbed up by those two priests and asked where the rest of us went. They might even think him a witch and do what priests do to witches."

Erasmus blinked in amazement. "That's terrible. What should we do?"

Again, the enigmatic smile. "Follow me."

What a hypocrite, that stuck-up scholar! Meg thought. As if he had any sympathy for witches. Dumarus himself had almost become a priest, and he would've likely been a witch-burner. Even so, here he was, following Morgan, who had more natural power than any hundred witches.

Meg chewed on her lip, turning from Dumarus to Morgan. She was astonishing. She was only ten and still as straight as a stick, but she seemed a woman. Orphaned by a dead father and a living mother, exiled in the court of the king, Morgan was anything but abandoned. She belonged to herself, and to everyone.

The scholar didn't think so. He looked at her jealously as if Morgan belonged to him alone. Of course he wouldn't touch her until she was a woman—Dumarus wasn't that sort of hypocrite—but he would wait for her, years or decades if he had to. Meg might have called him a letch except that she herself was waiting for Morgan.

She would be a woman soon, perhaps within the year and certainly within five. When that transformation took place, Morgan would know what she wanted, and Meg would be there if she wanted her. Until then, she would follow.

Morgan rode her steed up a slope of high grass onto a wide shelf of spongy ground. The vegetation formed a thick mat that held the headwaters of a nearby stream. The horses shied on the sinking soil, but their riders watched Morgan and pressed onward. She rode past a thicket of briar, where the group had to go one by one. Meg muscled her horse up behind Morgan's, forcing Dumarus to ride after her. The thicket thinned and gave way, and Morgan began to climb along a sheer slope. The horses had traded one danger for another—instead of cantering atop a moor, they picked their way above a deadly fall.

"Where are we headed, Morgan?" Meg asked.

The girl nodded before them toward a jutting cliff. A gray slab of stone emerged from the green side of the mountain and extended like a worshiping hand toward the sky.

Meg felt suddenly ashamed of her jealousy. It was unworthy of Avalon. This was the glorious place where Celts, for ages of ages, had gathered to perform their sacred rites. It was not so much a patch of land but a place of spirit. Meg dispelled her sour mood and gave herself to the hush of the grasses and the narrow peril of the trail.

It was wonderful to ride along this cliff face, with the lake below and the heights above. It was marvelous to follow this born priestess.

Morgan was in ecstasy. All her life, she had seen visions, but never before had she drawn others bodily along.

The horse walked unfailingly to the stony precipice. He brought in his wake the whole company, even the beast that had lost her rider. Cantering slowly along the base of the stone, Morgan's mount reached a tuft of especially tender grass, and there he dipped his head to eat.

Morgan slid from the saddle, her arm gliding fondly along the flank of the beast. He had borne her as far as he could and carried her well. The horses would know what to do in a place such as this. Their instinct came from the Otherworld.

Morgan climbed the gently sloping stone. Each step bore her away from the shaggy hillside and toward the soaring sky. "Come, this way, out to the edge. Come sit with me."

Dumarus followed first, his eyes fixed on Morgan instead of the dizzy height. Meg came shortly after and struggled to pass the man. The armsmen were less eager to venture out on that dolmen, but they remembered the man who had vanished, and they straggled away from their horses.

Morgan reached a wide flat spot near the precipice. She sat, gesturing for the others to do so as well.

Some watched her intently. Others looked nervously to their hands or feet, their faces clouded.

"Come, and come gladly," Morgan said. "Do you know what this is? This is the beginning of a new world. For ten years, I've seen this place and others—some too far away to reach, others too ancient, and a few that never have been. Always, I've seen them alone. No more. Look." She swept her arms out, taking in the huge mountainside, the wide and glimmering lake, this distant Tree. The others looked, their eyes filled with stars. "You're the first ones to see this place. I'm going to bring everyone here, but you're the first."

"Where are we?" asked a bewildered armsman. His eyes were red, as if he had been crying.

"*This is Avalon. This is Eden.*" The words belonged to the wise woman, but they poured from Morgan's mouth. The ancient ghost and the young girl were one. "*This is the world as it was created to be. Bretons have called it the Otherworld, but it is the true one. The world you've known all your lives is just a shadow, and this is the real place that casts the shadow. All my life I'd been caught between the two. I thought this was the place I saw when my eyes were closed, but now I know this is what I see when my eyes are open.*"

A warrior rubbed his beard in irritation and said, "How do we get back to the real world, and when?"

Morgan stared levelly at him and said, "*This is how, and now.*"

Suddenly, from their midst, he was gone. His horse looked up from among the others nuzzling the hillside. Her ears rose querulously, and then she stooped to graze once more.

Morgan took a steadying breath. "*Are there others who want to leave? Christ had twelve, but one was a devil and another a doubter. I had twelve, and now we're down to ten. Are there any others who want to leave?*"

They sullenly shook their heads. Whatever questions waited on their lips fell to silence. Only Dumarus spoke: "Will we stay here forever, or return as they have?"

Morgan replied, "*We'll return to the world, to that place of ugliness, but you can't let your heart return. As long as it beats here, on this mountainside, nothing can harm you.*"

"Is it because of the Fall of Man?" asked Dumarus. "Is that why there's such a division between that world and this?"

"*There never was a fall,*" Morgan replied. "*There was only the word 'fall.' As soon as we heard it, we believed it, and as soon as we believed it, it drove the worlds apart. Once, everyone lived in this beautiful garden. Then came the word 'fall,' and we believed we had been driven out, that we must sorrow and labor and die, and since then that is all we've done. The Age of War began, when it was better to kill than to suffer. I'm going to end all that. I'm going to bring us all back into the Garden.*"

Meg said, "What about the world tree? What about the immortal stream. When do we eat and drink?"

"*Not yet,*" Morgan said. "*Not while the worlds are so separate. It's enough that your hearts will be here. You'll feel the storms of this place when the days are still, and the stillness of this place when there is war around you. You'll live in perfection while the world decays. That's enough. To have all knowledge and all life now, before the worlds are joined, would destroy you.*"

"What about you?" Meg pressed. "Have you eaten of the tree? Have you drunk of the fountain?"

"*No,*" Morgan said. "*But I will. When I bring the worlds together, I will.*" Her eyes filled with tears, and she suddenly understood who her voices were. "*I'm just a guide. You know that. I'm just the one who found this place and brought you. Other powers have been speaking through me, preparing you. Now, they want to speak for themselves.*"

Morgan shuddered violently and fell back on the stone. Her arms twitched, and her hands flailed. She felt like a stocking as it receives a foot, stretched and reshaped by the great, solid, living thing that entered her. Her flesh conformed to the new creature, and Morgan was transformed. She broadened at hips and chest. Her hair lengthened and turned a gentle brown. Even her clothes changed, becoming the simple handmaiden's tunic and apron. The mania cleared from her eyes, and Morgan sat up and then stood.

She was Morgan no longer. Her hands spread out toward the circle of believers. *"Welcome. I am Saint Brigid, once the sky goddess of Eire and still Mistress of Avalon. I am the mother of the Celtic people, called the queen of heaven by the priests of Christ."* She paused, her gaze resting on one after another of the folk sitting there. *"Normally, no one comes to Avalon except by my express will, but this girl—she has power, and she is implacable. She is a guide, as she told you, but a young one, and not immune to error."* Her eyes, already intense, grew piercing. *"Bringing you here today was one such error, but now that you are here, you will see what you will see."*

Morgan trembled again. She felt Brigid leave in a great rush. Moments before, she had been tall and strong, with the full figure of a woman, but suddenly, Morgan was a girl again. Her arms were thin, her chest and hips and legs. Another power was manifesting, this time emptying her. It felt as if her vital spark were being drawn out. She was no longer slender but gaunt, no longer smooth but stringy. Her back curved across the shoulders, and her knees bent. Jaw and nose and ears grew, and skin thinned and wrinkled.

She spoke with a voice like a crow's: *"You know me. I spend most of my time in your world. I am Badb, sister to Macha and Nemain. I am war, and they are death and destruction. We are the Morrigan, all too busy in the world where you live, and we'll be busier still. This Age of War is our age. Your sweet girl says you can be rid of us and live in this garden, free of want and fear. Believe her. It will make you easier prey. She says she will bring the whole world here. Good luck to her. War and death and destruction are immortal, but Morgan is not. . . ."*

Morgan wrenched violently, ripping her body from the grips of the Morrigan. She fell to her side on the stone. Every tissue ached, and the pain sank down into her bones. She gritted her teeth, uncertain she could bear the agony. Then it transformed, passing the threshold into pleasure. Instead of pain, she felt only numb longing. Her body seemed a loose garment hanging from her bones, and her hair was a golden mane, tangled and fiery. She was glad and sad all at once.

Lifting herself to one elbow, Morgan smiled crookedly. *"Hello. It's good to be in such a young body again, but I'm no princess. I'm a queen. The queen. I'm Maeve. I rule the passions of the people. I'm the one who lives in you when you get furious or drunk. I'm the one who takes you over when you give yourself to someone else and you only want to be eaten alive. Oh, yes, I am part of Morgan's perfect place, but even more a part of your world. As long as there is misery, there will be desire, and as long as there is desire, there will be me."* She blinked languidly like a lizard on the stone. *"I've got no use for bliss, and I'll be inflaming every heart I can against your little woman. I'll even inflame her own heart. We'll see who wins this war."*

Again, Morgan trembled. Other powers wrestled within her, struggling to take command. She wanted her body back, but how could she deny the deities that swept through her? These goddesses had been driven from the world by Jupiter and then by Christ, and they were hungry to live again. Morgan couldn't deny them.

"Enough!" cried Meg. She rose, breaking from the circle, and caught Morgan in her arms. The poor girl was convulsing horribly. "You can't have her. She belongs to us! She's one of us!"

Dumarus was there a moment later, and he wrapped his arms around both women. "In the name of Christ, I drive you out! You have no power over this child!"

The spasms grew only worse, and Morgan's teeth chattered until she bit her own lip. Blood ran in a red line from her mouth.

"What are you doing?" Meg demanded.

Dumarus still clung on. "I'm casting out demons."

"You're no priest, and these aren't demons."

"What else would take possession of a young girl's body?"

"You would, for one," Meg spat, trying to shove him off.

Dumarus growled back, "And you as well." He was smaller and weaker, though, and his wiry arms didn't reach around them both. Meg drove her elbows out to either side, flinging him away, but in the process, she lost hold of Morgan as well.

The girl fell to her side on the stone. She groaned, lolling back and forth miserably, but she no longer convulsed. The battle was done. The goddesses had left the poor girl alone. She curled up and cried, her tears dropping to the dusty stone.

Pushing Dumarus back once more, Meg gathered the girl in her arms. "There, there. It's over."

"I know," replied Morgan quietly. "That's why I'm crying. It's over." She gestured out beyond the circle.

Avalon was gone. They all sat on a ragged shoulder of rock halfway up the nibbled Tor of Glastonbury. Swamplands formed a ring around them, and at the pessimistic little abbey, angry priests stood, arms crossed over their chests. It had all been a delusion—mass hysteria.

"What's happened? What do we do now?" Meg asked.

Morgan looked into her eyes, and her face was beatific. "We go back to Tintagel, but we leave our hearts in Avalon."

7

Bloodstones

Sweating in the late sun of summer, Morgan knelt beside the goat and wrapped her arms around him. The creature did not shy from her. He knew Morgan: the gentle ruler of Tintagel. She had midwifed him into being, had raised him and set him loose to graze the baileys and courtyards of Tintagel. For a decade, Morgan had ruled the castle and was a friend to all the animals that lived there. But what she had to do today was not the work of a friend.

"Forgive me," she whispered to the poor beast.

He bleated once briefly and pulled away, reaching toward a nearby tuft of weed.

Morgan's arms tightened, and he stiffened as if sensing what was coming. At eighteen, Morgan was strong, and the goat couldn't get away. She drew a scroll from her waistcoat pocket and let it unroll. Already she had read the scroll dozens of times, and the words were memorized, but she had to see it one last time:

To Princess Morgan, Ward of Tintagel,

From Queen Igraine, bereaved wife of our late ruler,
King Uther,

Greetings.

I am returning to you, Daughter. London has grown
dangerous, and every day the roads are less secure. The
nation forged by my husband is falling to petty despots
and bandits, and I have neither the power nor the will
to prevent its demise. I long for the fastness of Tintagel, and so I ride in company with my personal guard
to my home

I, of course, am eager to see you, Daughter.

This message reaches you by advance rider, who
precedes us by a mere day. Have the castle prepared for
me, and a feast for me and my retinue. Slay the fatted
calf, as they say, for the prodigal mother returns home.

Fondly,

Queen Igraine

There was no fatted calf—Tintagel had never had cattle. Nor
would Morgan sacrifice any of the sheep, for their wool was
sacrifice enough. She had thought of raiding the chicken
coops, but even ten birds would not feed the queen and her
guard. So, it was up to this goat.

Tough teeth snatched the paper from Morgan's hand.
The damned message crumpled in the creature's mouth, and
he chewed contentedly. While the goat ate, Morgan drew the
small cauldron over beneath the beast and reached inside.
Her hand fastened on the hilt that waited there in the dark-

ness. These were ritual items, the masculine knife within the feminine cauldron.

Again, she said, "Forgive me." She lifted the blade, pressed it beneath the neck of the goat, and drew it rapidly across. The goat lurched in her arms. It kicked to get free, but the hot gush of its blood emptied its heart. Life poured into the cauldron, and the goat went limp in Morgan's arms. She clung to him, praying to the Morrigan.

"Triple Mother, I commend into your arms the life of our brother goat. Receive his blood as we receive his body. He lives on in our flesh and in your spirit." This was only the beginning of the ritual. The blood was too potent magically to be wasted. It was with the assiduous use of blood, her own and that of animals slaughtered for the kitchens, that Morgan had kept Tintagel safe this decade. Now, with her mother and her retinue cresting the horizon, the castle was in greater peril than ever.

Still clutching the knife, Morgan wrapped her arms around the fallen goat and lifted him. His head lulled across her elbow, and his hooves jutted stiffly before her. The last of his blood made a beaded path on the dirt as she carried him through the garden. The blood would only bring more life to that abundant place. Morgan did all the slaughtering there, that the earth might drink its due.

She rounded an ivied corner, passed through an archway, and approached the low wooden lean-to where the cook waited.

He was nervous, knowing the queen was on her way and the castle stores were meager at best. He barked at his assistants to sling the gutting hook. While the boys scrambled, the cook hurried to take the animal. "I'm to feed a queen and twenty armsmen with a single goat?"

"He's a big goat, and you have the milk from the she-goats, and eggs, and the vegetables—"

"You and your vegetables," the cook grunted as he took the goat. His eyes flashed in realization, and he said, "Forgive me, Princess."

"We're all nervous, Rafe," Morgan said, looking down at the line of blood across her clothing. "But you're just preparing a meal. I'm preparing a war." She turned and strode away.

While Rafe worked over the goat's body, Morgan would work over his blood in a complex but powerful spell. It would soften Igraine's heart, weaken her mind, and distract her eye. It would make her believe she ruled the castle and that Morgan was merely her wise, advising daughter. In truth, though, Morgan would continue to rule.

"Triple Mother, empower me to stand before her. Tintagel is mine."

The royal table of the great hall was ringed with men in armor. They'd ridden from London to Tintagel, confident in their arms against any petty king or warlord. At the gates of the castle, many of the warriors had ogled Morgan. Now, though, they sat with eyes averted and epaulets drawn in over sunken chests. They had learned they were no match for this girl.

"I know you're proud of your warriors," Morgan said quietly. Her eyes were fixed on the goat's skeleton, picked clean of all but ligaments. "But unless you've also brought the wealth of Britannia to feed them—let alone pay them— you can't keep them here."

"*Some* was all I said," replied Igraine through an unconvincing smile. Her eyes avoided Morgan's, instead wandering among the banners that draped the ceiling. "I said only that some would remain . . . enough to keep us safe in uncertain times."

Morgan lifted her face, beautiful and white beneath locks of black hair. "Uncertain times? I've survived an uncertain decade. I had no fortune, no personal army, and still I kept the castle safe. We don't need any of these men. Send them back to London."

Mother's smile grew more intense. "We won't give up warriors for witchery."

"What I do is not witchery," Morgan snapped, standing. The men nearby ducked away as if she were a Gorgon. "My magic is older than Dumnonia and Eire and druidry itself. It's older than Avebury, than the sea. I'm not a witch, but a filidh."

"Yes, yes. Sit down, Morgan—"

"It's beyond what Meg does, beyond even the works of mad Merlin—"

"It's very impressive, yes, Daughter. You go on trusting in it and using it to defend us," Mother said placidly, though all traces of the smile were gone. "But I need soldiers—"

"Soldiers need money. Where will you get money?"

Igraine nodded to Morgan's chair. "Sit down, and I'll tell you."

Morgan stared at her mother, eyes smoldering but curious. She sat.

"I'll keep half the men for half a year, and then we'll journey to Dor, to the court of King Mark—"

"Uther's been dead for only two seasons, and already you seek another husband?"

"I seek an *ally*." Igraine pounded the table. "If King Mark is our friend, his army can protect us against any land incursion—"

"Oh, yes, Mother—run to a man. Mark will protect you. And what's the difference between protection and possession? How long before he's forcing his way into your bed?"

"Morgan!" the queen said, jabbing a finger toward the door. "Leave my presence."

Without moving a whit, Morgan said, "I'm not done with my dinner. This goat was a friend of mine. I won't let his flesh go in the midden."

"Well, then, I'll leave, just as I would turn away from anything that disgusts me." Igraine rose, walking toward the double doors. "But know this, Daughter: I am going to King Mark, and you are coming with me."

Morgan stared sullenly after her mother. How could this be a softened heart, a weakened mind? Was she somehow warded against Morgan's spell? Had mother gained the protection of the Christ? "You go, Mother," Morgan said softly. "I'll stay, and we'll see if you can get back into Tintagel."

Igraine's armsmen stared after the retreating queen, but once she was gone, they averted their eyes to their laps. Not one of the twenty dared look at Morgan.

Her knife scraped the plate as she cut another piece of goatflesh. Staring straight ahead, she lifted the meat to her mouth and chewed. She had forgotten about the armsmen and even about mother, for a goddess was speaking to her again:

Don't be so quick to reject the journey to Dor, said the voice of the wise woman within her. *Your future lies there.*

"What future?" Morgan said.

Armsmen shot worried looks her way.

Your future.

"I have no intention of surrendering Tintagel to a man."

The chief of the armsmen blurted, "Forgive us, Princess. We don't wish to take it—"

"Leave me," Morgan growled. In the hasty clamor of scooting chairs and retreating boots, she said to the wise woman, "Give me one reason I should go to Dor."

As I said, your future. And your future is the future of the world.

That autumn, in the company of warriors, Morgan rode beside Igraine.

"Thank you for coming," Mother said, not for the first time.

Morgan only nodded.

Let the queen think she changed your mind. Let all of them think she leads the expedition. She is the Trojan horse that will bear you and your magic into Dor.

Morgan nodded again. Throughout the summer, the wise woman had counseled her to join the expedition, but in the end only an ominous blood scrying had changed Morgan's mind. If Igraine went without her to Dor, queen and princess and Tintagel itself would be destroyed. Morgan was determined to prevent it.

She reached to her neck, where she wore a bloodstone. The gem was small and round, polished by a patient river. Igraine wore such a stone too. Morgan had said these were signs of their reconciliation. In truth, they were amulets of protection, hollowed out to carry Morgan's own blood and a potent enchantment. If any man meaning harm touched the wearer, his ill wish would descend upon his own head.

Morgan raised the bloodstone from her throat and let it dangle from its slender chain. "Remember, Mother, keep it with you always—as a token of my love."

Mother nodded, lifting the stone at her own neck.

Morgan let the amulet drop within her chemise. It was the first of many enchantments she had prepared to make this trip a success.

An autumn wind swept along the road, laying down heads of grass, and Morgan took a deep breath of it. In the nearby woods, leaves argued in the treetops. Fall was her favorite time, the menses of the world. It was the sloughing time of the cycle of fertility, when old flesh fell away to leave barren ground.

Four seasons to the year, four weeks to the month, four stages to life—Morgan had become attuned to the power of four. It was more ancient than the cycle of three. Witches spoke of maiden, mother, and crone—spring, summer, and fall—but they had forgotten winter; they had forgotten death. Without winter, the cycle could not begin again. Death was the fourth stage, and it had power, and Morgan understood its power.

Ahead of them, Castle Dor gleamed in the autumn afternoon. It was formidable in stone and belligerent in line, just like King Mark. He waited within, doubtlessly hoping to make Igraine his thrall. Mother probably hoped no better, but if Morgan got her way, the king himself would become a thrall to desire. Morgan looked up to the wall of Castle Dor, looming large and tan above the faded grass. The company rode into its shadow, and the horses halted before the portcullis of iron and oak.

"Ho! Upon the tower," shouted the captain of Igraine's guard. "Open in the name of Queen Igraine of Britannia!"

"Britannia has no king nor queen," came the reply. "We open for no one but King Mark."

"Fortunately," a new voice shouted down to them, "I am he, and I welcome Duchess Igraine of Tintagel to my castle and my lands."

Morgan ground her teeth behind clenched lips, but Mother was all grace and gratitude. She bowed shallowly in the saddle, a meaningless smile on her lips. "My late husband, King Uther, always treasured your fealty, Mark."

Mark's face appeared above the battlements, his hair and beard shaggy and his eyes bright. His ears jutted like a horse's. "Alas he is dead, dear, for you and I both were more powerful when we clung to him. Now, I am but the king I was before, and you but the widow of Gorlois."

"And Uther," Igraine responded evenly. "I thank you for your hospitality and agree that we might find mutual benefit for ourselves and for Dumnonia by banding together."

"Let us hope we agree on that, yes," replied Mark. "But first things first. You sluggards in the winch room, up with this portcullis. Would you keep the duchess waiting until winter?"

The massive gate lurched upward in its tracks. It rose like a stage curtain and revealed an arched darkness replete with murder holes and armored men.

Morgan grasped the pendant at her throat. Two small stones and their cache of blood were all that protected her and her mother. They would have to suffice.

Mother rode forward beneath the sharpened spear-ends of the gate. They dripped dirty water on her veiled neck. Morgan nudged her steed up alongside Mother's, and found herself full of a sudden and strange admiration for the embattled woman. Igraine had no magic, and yet she boldly made her way through trap after trap.

The arch was blue with shadows, and the company passed through into a courtyard full of quintains. At its far side stood a wooden barracks and a long stable. Mark's men were quartered in much the same fashion as his beasts. Still, he had an impressive force.

The soldiers on duty stood at attention, but those that had been training or sleeping appeared in doorways in various states of undress. Some wore only breeches and a sheer shirt of sweat. A male scent rose from their tawny shoulders, and their eyes were equally naked. They stared with smug amusement at once-queen Igraine, now come begging to Mark, but when their eyes shifted to Morgan, a hungry look came. Every face betrayed desire, though some only faintly, and some in a wondering and worshipful sense. A few men had predatory eyes, and one of those advanced toward Morgan. He was middle-aged and meaty like Uther.

Dauntless, Morgan rode toward him. Weaving among practice dummies, she and Igraine reached the brick path before the stables. The man met them there.

"Welcome to Castle Dor," he said, an unwelcoming smile on his face. His arms spread to include both women, but he looked only at Morgan.

Morgan matched his fierce grin. "Please stand back."

Affronted, he reached toward Morgan. "I only want to help you down from your mount." An armsman behind him stifled a laugh.

"I know what you want," Morgan said coldly. "Now, move back."

The man lifted bushy brows and said, "You know what I

want? How is that? You cast a spell or something? Did you use goat guts to read my mind?"

Morgan stared down into his face. "I don't need goat guts to know your mind. Your thoughts are written on a goat's ass."

"Why, you," began the man angrily. He reached up to snatch her arm and wrench her from the saddle. The moment his bristly fist fastened around her wrist, the man shrieked and grabbed his crotch. He stared angrily at her, suspicion brimming in his eyes. "Why, you witch! I'll kill you—"

"Touch me again, and you die," warned Morgan levelly.

"Morgan!" Igraine said.

"I'm trying to save his life!" Morgan hissed.

"A witch! She's a witch!"

A crowd was gathering, five warriors of Dor for each one of Tintagel. The local armsmen held back their comrade, not so much to save Morgan from him but to save him from her. Morgan tightened her legs around her horse. At least she and Mother could dash away and perhaps clear the portcullises.

Through the jostling crowd came King Mark, shoving men aside. His beard and hair jutted in a wreath around his head. "What's happening here?"

"Nothing," Igraine replied lightly. "Just a misunderstanding."

"She put a curse on me!" the man said. "She sicced a devil on me!"

Morgan spat back, "If there were any curses, they were your own."

"I'm telling you, she hexed my trews!" the man roared, jabbing his hand down beneath the rope belt he wore. "Look, I'm bleeding!" He lifted red fingers. "I'm bleeding."

King Mark turned toward Morgan. "What about this? Are you practicing witchery here?"

Morgan smiled slightly. "Why would I practice what's already perfect?"

"Morgan!" her mother said.

"This is a Christian castle, young woman," King Mark said sternly, "and I will not have magic being cast here."

Morgan nodded. "I understand, King, but I cast no spell. My hands have been here all the while on the reins, and I spoke no words of magic."

"Don't believe her! She hexed me, and I'll see her struck down!"

"No," said another man—young, perhaps even younger than Morgan. He had golden hair and eyes like a summer sky. "She tells the truth. I heard it all."

The armsman whirled, swinging at the young man, who dodged aside.

"Hold, Rolus!" cried King Mark. "He's my nephew—"

"He's my squire!" Rolus protested.

"Let him speak." King Mark turned to the squire. "What did you see, Tristan?"

The young man took a considering breath. In a soft but steady voice, he said, "The good warrior Rolus approached these guests and greeted them. Morgan asked that he back away and give them room to dismount. Rolus did not, saying he wished to offer her a hand down. Morgan said she knew what he wished. Rolus asked her if she cast a spell to know it. Morgan replied that his wishes were all too obvious—"

"She called my face a goat's ass!"

This detail evinced laughter from the other warriors, but over the top of it, Tristan continued. "She warned him not to touch her. He touched her anyway and was wounded. She warned him not to touch her again or he would die, and he lunged at her, held back only by his comrades." Tristan blinked. "That about sums it up."

"How could she bloody me except that she be a witch?"

King Mark glanced between Morgan and Igraine, and he stroked his lip. Here was the deciding moment. The king could side with his warrior, and Morgan and Igraine would be slain for witchcraft, or he could side with his guests, and the warrior be flogged.

Morgan risked all with a muttered spell. She used the man's own blood, spreading ignominiously through his breeches, to cast a simple but effective spell of repulsion.

King Mark scowled at the man, and his nose curled. "How she could bloody you is an interesting question. But even more interesting is how you could thrice defy the request of a guest. The request of a woman—a child!"

"Thrice deny—?"

"She asked that you back away, and you did not. She warned that you not touch her, and you did. She vowed that if you touched her again, you would die, and if not for your own comrades, I would count you dead already. Whether she is a witch, I do not know, but whether you are a barbarous brute—!" Mark stared ferociously at Rolus, and then shot a glare at the men who held him. "Take him to the post and let the cat-o'-nine-tails scratch him until his back's like his groin."

Rolus bellowed as the men bore him away. He landed a punch on one man's jaw but paid for it when his own tunic was ripped from his back. More warriors closed in and kicked him toward the post.

Morgan felt faint. Her hands tingled, and her face

blanched. She glanced aside at her mother, whose eyes and mouth were cinched in a scowl. Morgan averted her gaze. The bloodstone spell had been fair, but this lashing would be brutal.

As if not a voice had been raised, King Mark nodded to Morgan and said, "I'll put you in the care of a young man who knows hospitality. He's not a warrior yet—only a squire—but he's my nephew and your savior. I give you Tristan."

The young man stepped forward, his posture regal but natural. He lifted his hand to take hers. She touched it before she even considered what might happen to him.

Unharmed by the bloodstone, Tristan smiled and helped her from the saddle.

8

Protectors

While King Mark conducted Mother around Castle Dor, Tristan guided Morgan. He took her to the garrison, the parapets, the cellars and kitchens, the grand rooms and the simple ones. He didn't lead her as if she were a woman, showing only sewing rooms and tea tables. Instead, he took her through the undercroft and the warriors' graveyard, though the smithy and the gardener's shack. Morgan loved to see it all. Castle Dor had more money, men, and power than Tintagel, and its walls were thicker and its gates heavier, but it was less beautiful. It had a man's soul.

Morgan's eyes shifted from the castle to Tristan. He was an uncommon man—soft-spoken but smart, dexterous but strong, young but respected. Warriors twice his age nodded when he passed. Yes, he was the king's nephew, but Tristan didn't trade on his lineage. Instead, his quiet reserve set him apart.

"The cistern gathers rainwater. It could see us through a year's siege, even in drought." Tristan's quiet voice rolled out across dark waters and reverberated from stony vaults.

His boot whispered on the floor. "Watch your step." He took her hand.

His touch, so natural and unafraid, had first won her trust. He harbored no ill will toward her, but did he harbor *good* will? Her hand tightened on his, and she followed him up the dark stairs. "How long before you're inducted as a warrior?"

Tristan ascended quietly. He wasn't ignoring her but carefully framing his response. "Most squires are made warriors by sixteen. It depends on one's skill and one's instructor." He topped the stairs, passing out the cistern door and into the yard. Torchlight striped his back, and a man's cries filled the night air.

Morgan emerged not fifty feet from the post where Rolus hung. The cat-o'-nine tails came down again, its lashes ripping open the man's back. Even as his face clenched, his eyes remained open and fixed on Tristan.

"I must get you to the banquet."

Morgan walked beside him, heading for the great hall. It glowed like a jewel box. "If Rolus gets to decide, you may never become a warrior."

Tristan nodded, his hair tawny in the torchlight.

"For me, you did that."

"For truth I did it." He came to a stop beside the great hall doors. "I'm not invited to this dinner."

Morgan looked into his eyes, spangled with torches. "Will you be all right?"

"He'll be too hurt to do anything tonight."

"Tomorrow, then, you'll have to take me out of the castle—someplace you and I both will be safe."

A smile lurked in his beautiful face. "I know just the place."

Morgan turned, unsure what to do. She slipped her hand from his and stepped away. "Until tomorrow."

"Yes."

Morgan passed from the cool night air into the fragrant and bright banquet hall. The room smelled of roasted boar with onions and leeks. A fife tooted and a lyre plinked to the roll of knuckles on a drum skin. It should have been the most pleasant place in the whole palace, and yet Tristan was outside.

Thoughts of him formed a nimbus around Morgan. In it, she floated into the great hall. Warriors and courtiers greeted her, and she replied, remembering not a single name. She reached her seat and sat and looked around in a daze of joy.

Of course she knew what was happening to her. It was the oldest magic, the inexorable tug of soul on soul and body on body. Morgan didn't fear love, but she wouldn't have expected it here. *Your future lies in Dor, and your future is the future of the world.* But, Tristan? He was pledged to the killing arts, a servant of death. Had Morgan believed only in Maiden, Mother, and Crone, she would have thought him the antithesis of all that was good. But Morgan knew of Death, the fourth state—a man among three women. Beautiful Tristan was he, winter to her summer. Together, they could spin the cycles of fertility.

And the cycles did spin. Morgan drank no wine that night, but throughout the courses and conversations, she sat in a drunken stupor. She declined every dance and, half asleep, walked alone to her rooms. Bolting the door behind her, she wandered through the darkness and laid herself down on the feather bed. True sleep eluded her. She clung to her pillow as if it were Tristan, wrapping her legs around him.

Desire was the most ancient magic, the gift of the goddess. It existed before the gods. They could not destroy it, so they had turned it to enslavement. Women had learned to suppress or dismiss or denigrate or die for their desire, but desire was not the foe. Enslavement was. Drawing long and wanting breaths, Morgan let the pillow become him, and she guided his hands to where she wished to be touched.

Morgan and Tristan rode the grasslands of Dor. Golden stalks rattled on the horses' knees and whispered on their hooves. "During the time of Uther, this all was grazed into short green lawns, but reivers are too numerous nowadays."

"Is that where we're going?" asked Morgan, nodding ahead of her. A great oak tree reached high into the morning sky. Each gnarled bough was a tree unto itself, and the grandmother oak was its own forest. All of the leaves were bronzen, but none had yet fallen.

"They say it's older than Rome," said Tristan. "They say an oak grows an inch every five years. That one is twenty feet through its middle. That makes it more than a thousand years old."

Morgan grinned and set her heels to the horse. He leapt beneath her and galloped toward the oak grove. His hooves pounded the turf, hurling the grasslands away. The sound redoubled, and Tristan's own horse thundered up alongside hers. His teeth were set in a smile, and he leaned low above the steed's pumping neck. He began to pull ahead, but Morgan nudged her beast along. They raced up the gentle hills toward that great oak. It crept slowly nearer, growing before their eyes.

Morgan gazed in wonder at the trunk and branches, losing track of the race. That tree was a whole world. She couldn't simply gaze on it; she'd have to climb it, to explore its boughs like winding paths and ascend its branches like twisted spires.

Tristan shot ahead and then reined in his horse under the umbra of the great tree.

Morgan slowed her beast to a walk.

"I won!" Tristan called out, his face glowing. It was an uncharacteristic shout for the quiet young man, and when he turned around and saw the reverent approach of Morgan, he looked chagrined.

She didn't comment. Instead, riding the horse slowly up beneath one great bough, she reined it to a halt. She lifted one foot to the saddle and stood up. Her hands fastened onto the branch, and she pulled herself up. Despite her fine dress, worn at Igraine's insistence, Morgan swung herself easily onto the bough. She walked along it, hands held out to her sides and dress draping around her ankles.

"I'm not sure you should do that," Tristan said, averting his eyes.

"I won't fall."

"It's a sacred tree. The druids used to worship this thing."

"That's what I'm doing," Morgan replied lightly. "How can a tree like this be worshiped from the ground? You have to climb through it, feel its bark, smell its leaves, hear it creak in the wind."

"The monks too," Tristan replied. "They say it was the rod of Jesse, planted when the ten tribes were lost."

"Oh, it's much older than that."

"I know."

"It's also more sacred." She grasped a mossy burl. It felt like velvet under her fingers. "Once, sacred things were all around us. The trees, the air, the ground, the creatures. We lived in a sacred world. But priests drove the gods out of nature. Now, God is the one thing we can't see, hear, or touch. I don't believe it. This tree is divine. I'm in it. I'm touching it. You can't convince me to come down."

Tristan's eyes remained on the trammeled track, and he blushed. "But, it's not the sort of place to be . . . in a dress." He glanced toward her, and the blush spread from temples to cheeks.

"That too is sacred," Morgan replied. She crouched and reached down toward him. "For your sake, though—"

"You'll come down?" he asked, reaching up to clasp her hand.

"No, you'll come up." She gripped his hand and dragged him up from the saddle.

Tristan kicked in protest, but then his fingers tightened on her hand and his eyes met hers. "You're strong."

"I've run Tintagel for ten years," she replied as Tristan got one boot onto the branch. "Building walls, birthing horses." She pulled him up beside her and held him as he gained his balance. "Once I even lifted a mastiff from a well."

Tristan peered at the ground, far below. He seemed less afraid of the drop than the embrace.

Morgan watched him. "You see what I've done? I've lifted you into paradise."

"Is that where we are?"

"Don't you recognize it? This is the tree God forbade. This is the Tree of Knowledge."

"Can we get down now?"

"Oh, Tristan," Morgan said. "You've just gotten to paradise. Don't you want a tour? Look here." She gestured to the bough. "Here is the golden road. Whoever walks it is granted irresistible beauty."

Tristan smiled and laughed. He looked into her eyes. "It's true."

"And there." Her hand traced out the corkscrew curve of a central spire. "That's the stairway to the stars." Tristan's eyes twinkled. "And do you see this?" she asked, gesturing to a spot where many of the limbs converged in a wide bowl. "What do you think that is?"

"I would call that the crotch," he said, and his face blossomed in red.

Morgan clucked quietly. "Accurate, perhaps even poetic, but I would call that the divine seat. Come." Without releasing his hand, Morgan climbed onto a nearby bough, and from there higher still.

Tristan came with her, and both were breathless before they reached that exalted spot. It had gathered moss over its millennium and was soft and cool. Best of all, no one could have seen them from the ground. In those velvety folds, beneath the bronzen leaves, they lay side by side and breathed the autumn air.

"Well, Eve, you've done it this time," Tristan teased.

Morgan smiled. "Did you know that she was the goddess?"

"Who? Eve?"

"Yes. She's the mother of all living. She existed before Adam, and the serpent is her son, her consort. She welcomes all to partake in the garden, in bounty, knowledge, and life."

Tristan folded his hands behind his head. "I always heard it that Eve brought sin into the world, and God cursed her."

"Of course that's how you heard it. The God of Abraham demoted Eve and her consort, making them subject to Adam. He also changed the tree so that, instead of being open to all, it was forbidden. He threw humanity out of paradise and into a world of domination, suffering, sin, and death."

Tristan's expression darkened, and he shook his head. "Rolus is going to kill me."

Morgan's reverie broke. She propped herself up on her elbows and looked into his eyes. "You're in real trouble, aren't you?"

"He's always disliked me, but now it's full-fledged hatred," Tristan said.

"But you're the nephew of King Mark. He'll protect you."

"No. Rolus himself is Mark's cousin, and look how he's protected him." Tristan shook his head. "Rolus will want me dead now, and he'll have his way. He has friends in the garrison."

Morgan reached to her chest. The bloodstone at her neck tumbled into her hand, and she began to smile. "I'll keep you safe from him." *Don't give up your protection, Morgan. You cannot do this.* Of course I can, she replied to the wise woman. You said it yourself: Tristan is my future. "If you promise to defend me and guard me while we stay in Dor, I'll keep you safe."

Tristan laughed. "Oh, thank you, mighty goddess."

"Here." She lifted the amulet from around her neck. The bloodstone gleamed. *Don't do it, Morgan! Only this stone protects you from Rolus.* "This is the magic that stopped Rolus before. It turns evil back onto evildoers. Whatever harm they intend against you is done to them."

Tristan stared at the stone, realization coming across his face. "The bleeding . . . the bruises . . . he wanted to rape you—?"

"He wanted to kill me," Morgan said. "He himself would

have died if he'd touched me a second time. Now, if he touches you with the same intent, he *will* die."

Tristan took the amulet in his hand. "I don't want him to die."

"But he wants you to."

"Wearing this would be tantamount to murder."

"No," Morgan said. "If he dies, it will be suicide." She pushed the necklace toward him. "Wear it."

Reluctantly, Tristan slid the chain over his head. "They'll suspect me of using witchcraft."

"They'll be wrong. This isn't witchcraft. This power is older than witches, older than God himself."

Tristan blinked. "Thank you, Morgan. And I do swear I will protect you."

"Yes, you will," Morgan said. *He can't protect you. Love is not all powerful.* "If ever I'm in trouble, I'll run to you. If I can't reach you, I'll send a bird messenger to bring you here, to this oak. You'll come and save me."

"Yes. I vow it."

She leaned in toward him, sliding her hand behind his neck. He didn't pull away. Her lips touched his, and he returned the kiss. It was chaste contact, sweet and brief, tingling with desire but at the same time shy. Leaning away from him, Morgan laid herself within the mossy bed.

"How long are you staying?" Tristan asked.

"Igraine planned for a week," Morgan said, "unless the talks don't go well. Then it could be a fortnight."

Tristan smiled. "Oh, Uncle Mark'll make sure of that."

Morgan and Igraine rode side by side beneath the dripping portcullis, warriors before and behind them. It would be a long trail home after a fortnight in a strange place, but both women wore smiles. They cantered away without speaking.

The standard of Tintagel now included the rampant lion of King Mark. It was embroidered in gold in the upper left quadrant of the shield, beside the purple pendragon.

Morgan glanced at Igraine. "You seem pretty pleased with yourself."

Igraine nodded. "I am. I've saved Tintagel, assured our protection, and retained our freedom."

"You swore fealty to Mark. You ceded the land to his son upon your death. You subjected yourself to him and gave him everything."

Igraine's lip grew stiff. "We're safe. We're protected. You'll be provided for into your old age. Without Mark, we could have lost it all tomorrow."

Morgan sighed. "Instead, we lost it all today."

It was Igraine's turn to scowl. "It's fine for you to talk. At least I made alliance with a king. What did you do? Dally with a mere squire."

"Tristan will someday be a great warrior," Morgan said. "And, besides, I surrendered nothing to him." It was true, though she had plans to surrender all. "And he protected me almost as well as I protected him."

Igraine glared at her daughter. "Yes—you and your black arts. It's a wonder Rolus ever got out of the sickroom."

Morgan shrugged innocently. "I think it's all in his head."

"You think the man could make himself bleed? Bruise himself and break his own legs?"

"It all comes down to desire. What he wants is what he gets."

Igraine could only shake her head. "You get stranger every year."

For a time, neither woman spoke. There was only the jangle of harnesses, the thud of hooves, and the explosive breaths of horses. The sun slowly rose behind them, its light like a hot hand on their backs. Morgan closed her eyes and remembered the blood she had foreseen from this meeting. At least Igraine and she yet lived. At least Tintagel would remain. Even the wise woman had proven wrong.

"It'll be good to be home," Morgan said, her eyes still closed.

The woman behind her said, "Yes, it will."

9

The Witches' Way

Morgan worked the mare's flank, the brush dragging furrows in her pelt. The oils of the horse's skin had begun to work across each hair, and their luster was returning. Lantern light gleamed from the follicles. Only an hour ago, this poor beast had been as dull as a dirt clod. Morgan had had to clip the clumps from her fetlocks and pound her pelt with an open hand, sending clouds of dust whirling. Then, it had been bucket after bucket, and mud gushing as dark as blood. The mare had been in a bad way when the warrior had ridden her in here—filthy, frothy, and pregnant.

Morgan shook her head grimly, working pig bristles across the creature's barrel. Her mind was a welter, thoughts whirling with the dust.

For two years, Tintagel had lived under the benevolent neglect of King Mark. Uther's money had run out, and so had all but a few of the warriors and servants. Mortar crumbled, but there was no lime for tuck-pointing. Smokehouses emptied, but there were no huntsmen to bring in game. Flower gardens went wild, more thistle than rose, and vegetable gardens became the overworked source of every meal. King Mark had kept Tintagel safe, yes, like a prisoner on starvation rations.

Of course Morgan resented the bad king and his purposeful oblivion, but she approved the results. Tintagel needed no warriors, for Morgan's filidh spells could repel all invaders, land and sea. Tintagel needed no huntsmen, for goat's milk and the flesh of plants were gentler food. Tintagel needed no masons, for wind and sea first had sculpted the fortress, and when they tore down what men had built, Morgan would merely retreat to the caves.

That thought brought to mind Meg, and a new storm of emotion.

Meg lay within her cave, in the niche where she had slept and wished to be interred. She had died in the depths of the last winter, cold and alone. Morgan had been so busy with her spells that she hadn't even noticed for a week. Poor Meg. Morgan still loved her, but they had had little dealing with each other. Morgan had outstripped her mentor in magic, and until she herself bore a brood, she had no need for a midwife. Now Meg was gone. Her body lay below, but her spirit still haunted Tintagel. It was Meg who had brought Morgan to this ill-used mare, and she coaxed her along even now.

"Yes, Meg, I know. Oats, though we can't afford them," Morgan muttered to the cool air of the summer night. She took a deep lungful of it. "She won't lose the foal. There's no swelling, and her ribs are full enough."

Still, anger kindled in Morgan. Some oblivious warrior had ridden this poor beast across the southlands of Britannia, had ridden her hard. She imagined the man—meaty like Uther, horsy like Mark, absent like Father—obliviously riding this pregnant mare. She had never known a worthy man. The good ones were weak and the strong ones were evil.

Except for Tristan. The mere thought of him was always enough to make Morgan's eyes slide closed and her knees grow soft. She leaned up against the mare and felt her warm solidity. The brush ceased its motion, and Morgan drew one of her long braids forward. She fingered it and thought of faraway Tristan.

They were in the same plight. While Morgan languished in Tintagel under the abuses of King Mark, Tristan languished in Dor under the abuses of Rolus. Tristan would be eighteen this year, and yet was still a squire to the drunken letch. Morgan and Tristan had traded many letters, her only bedmates, and he promised to flee with her after the harvest.

"When your foal is delivered," Morgan whispered to the mare, "I will be too." She dragged the brush across the creature's croup and onto the tail.

Footsteps came on the straw, and Morgan stiffened. She was used to a nearly empty castle, and she hated to be caught unawares. Turning, Morgan saw a barefoot young man in breeches and tunic. His hair was tousled and his face and hands smudged with dirt. He smiled, shy and not a little frightened—as well he should be. "Who are you?"

"I'm—uh, I'm new," the boy said.

Morgan shook her head, pulling the braid back over her shoulder. "There's no coin to pay you—"

"Oh, I don't need to be paid." He stepped farther into the lantern light. "See, I don't want to be a farmer, which is what Father is, and he said if I found a place to train to fight—"

"There are no armsmen to train you either."

The kid gave a cockeyed grin and glanced around. "Yeah, well, the whole place is kind of down at heel."

"That's the way I like it," Morgan said. She turned back to brushing and hoped the boy would take the hint and leave.

He did not. The straw crackled as he approached. "You like a castle without warriors? You like gardens gone to seed?"

"What's a garden for except seeds?"

"What's a castle for except warriors?"

Morgan stared at the young man. There was more to him than met the eye. He was perhaps five years younger than she and still had the big hands and feet of adolescence. Still, his face was handsome enough, his eyes a pair of bright promises. "What's your name?"

"Ar-Artemis," the boy said.

"Well, Artemis, go back to the farm. It's a much better life to swing a scythe than to swing a sword."

"Why?"

Morgan huffed. "Why? You wonder why it's better to cut grain than heads? You want to know what's wrong with being a warrior?" She lifted the mare's tail, displaying the flesh of fertility. "Look at this."

He blushed. "What am I looking at?"

"She's pregnant," Morgan said flatly. She flipped the tail down. "The armsman who rode her here didn't know or didn't care. Probably both. He thought the greatest thing a horse could do was carry him. No. The greatest thing a horse or any living creature can do is carry the next generation. This beast is performing a miracle, and the man who rode her was oblivious. He nearly killed her unborn foal and might have killed her as well."

Artemis's face darkened, and the promise in his eyes

dimmed. He looked almost like Tristan, a golden youth tarnished by drudgery and despair. "A stupid warrior."

"Not just one," snapped Morgan. "They all do it. King Mark has done the same thing to Tintagel, riding it rough and making it barren. Before him, it was Uther, and before him Ambrosius and Vortigern, and back to Caesar and Alexander and Nebuchadnezzar and Amen-Hotep—back to the beginning."

"You've studied," said Artemis reverently.

"Yes. Mostly on my own. It's all there for anyone who looks—history, healing, midwifery, magic."

"Witchcraft," he said beneath his breath.

"Wicca means only wisdom. Since when did wisdom become a dirty word? Since when did fertility become a thing to be despised?"

"It doesn't need to be despised," Artemis said. He caught the brush, stilling it and holding her hand.

"What are you doing?"

"This," he said, gathering her head in his other hand and leaning in to kiss her.

Morgan should have pulled away. She didn't want this boy—only Tristan, always Tristan—and yet Artemis was here and was so like Tristan, so young and golden beneath the patina of suffering. Morgan had spent two years caressing paper and ink, and now here was flesh. His lips were hot, and his breath sweet, and there was desire in them. This was not like Tristan's kiss, chaste and shy, but a wanting and wet touch.

Morgan pushed back. "No, it isn't right. You're so young. You don't even know who I am."

Artemis grinned at her. "You're a magic worker and a

scholar. What else is there to know? Besides, you don't know who I am either."

A chill of dread swept up Morgan's spine. "Who are you?"

"You may not believe this," the young man said, blushing again as he glanced at his feet in the straw, "but this rundown castle will one day be mine."

She couldn't have thought of more hateful words. Terror and anger roiled in her stomach, but somehow she managed to stand. "What are you talking about?"

"I'm the long-lost son of Uther. They say I am to be king and this is my birthplace. My name is Arthur."

Her hand flew, striking with red force on Arthur's face and flinging him back. Emotion amalgamated into fury. Morgan stood above him, trembling and unable to speak. When at last the words flowed, they came in a flood. "Arthur! Bastard son of Uther! Your father killed my father and raped my mother." She spat on the straw. "The taste of Uther is in you. He came to her in disguise and tricked his way into my mother's arms, and now you, my *half-brother*, have done the same to me. You're the warrior who rides and rides the world into sterility, the Son of War, and the next dominator of Britannia!"

"What?" he asked, shrinking away and wiping the blood from his lips. "What?"

"I'm the daughter of Queen Igraine. I'm your half-sister, Morgan."

He stopped moving, stop speaking. What could he say or do? A look of amazed dread filled his face, but he didn't know the half of it.

Morgan was being traded into more male hands—these five years younger and illegitimate. She was becoming her mother, sold by degrees until she would eventually even desire to be dominated.

Arthur lay there, staring up at her in stupefaction.

Morgan turned. She dropped the brush by the horse's hooves and strode out of the lantern light. Her sandals crackled on the straw. She would leave tonight, taking what little she needed. No longer would Morgan reside in the shadow of her mother on a cliff above the sea. Now she would live in no shadow, not even her own, would shelter beneath no hovel but the naked sky.

She was giving up Tintagel but gaining all Britannia.

Goatskin shoes bore Morgan soundlessly from her room and down the stairs. Meg had made these shoes, had chewed the skins and sewn them together with fullered wool within. Meg also had spun and woven the shift that Morgan wore, "as brown as good dirt." Its color and the rag cloak around her shoulders would make Morgan nearly invisible—the twin of the earth.

I knew you'd need to run, Meg said in her mind. *Every woman someday's got to give up or run. . . . I just wish I could go too. . . .*

"You will, Meg. . . ."

The Morrigan won't let me. They've got me tied to Tintagel.

"I *am* Tintagel." At the garden, Morgan crept between the rose briar and wall. She passed the postern gate; it was the first place they would look. There were other ways known only to Meg, ways beneath the bedrock, through the caves, and to safety.

Morgan stole across the bailey. She glanced back, but

only her braids followed. Ahead lay the door to the spring cellar. How many times had Morgan descended through it to Meg in her antediluvian chambers? Now, the home had become her tomb. Morgan lifted one door, and its hinge mewed like a drowsing cat. She slid into the blackness beneath it and closed it over her head.

Without light or hesitation, she rushed down the stony stairs, past the slough, down more stairs, and into the main chamber. Reaching the place where the woman lay, Morgan slid to her knees. She couldn't see Meg but didn't need to. The days had done their work. What had been her skin was now a sack drawn tight around bones. Morgan had not come for the woman's body, but for her soul.

"Meg, help me," she said, breathless. "I need your wisdom." A distant thud came above, and voices raised in worry. Morgan breathed, listening. "Morrigan, I know you three sit vigil for my Meg. You've tied her spirit to Tintagel, but I am the soul of Tintagel. Bind her to me. Let her go with me and guide me."

An answer came, not in a divine voice, but in the wild, warning bray of a ram's horn. Arthur must have reported what had happened. They must have gone to her room and found it ransacked. They would be looking even now. The castle dogs added their hue and cry, terriers in the lead. They would go to ground after her.

Down deeper, to the darkest place. I'll show you the witches' way. Even if they'll not let me go, you'll get out.

"Hear me, Morrigan!" Morgan said. "Bind Meg to me!" She stood and ran.

The main chamber led down to two cellars and a third. Bottles rang on their shelves as she surged by. Hanging sheaves brushed her shoulders like dry hands. Something cracked off her forehead, and Morgan wrenched down garlic cloves. She stooped, dragging the bundle on the ground behind her. It would mask her scent so even the dogs would lose her. Down another stair, she stopped.

The escape is just here, up the stone.

Panting in the darkness, Morgan lifted the garlic and shoved it down the front of her shift. She carefully set one foot on the blind slope ahead of her, and then the other, scrambling up. At its peak was a great boulder that had fallen from the ceiling.

"Where now?"

Grab the top of the rock and get up on it.

Reaching blindly up, Morgan found the pointed pinnacle of the wedge, set her feet, and pulled herself up. Her weight on the great lever tilted the stone back. Morgan surmounted the boulder and felt the cold air of the space beyond. Only a crescent-shaped passage opened above the rock. Morgan slid through it.

The moment she passed the arch, her weight shifted the stone. It pivoted into place, sealing the escape and dumping Morgan within.

It was the point of no return. Morgan sat in the inky darkness and listened for the dogs. She heard only her own breath echoing from the black walls. The air was growing close. It was time for some light. She reached to her knee, skinned when she knelt in Meg's chamber, and daubed the stinging spot with her finger. Lifting it, she breathed the ancient name of light.

Her fingertip glowed. Tiny points beamed in the red spot, and they leapt up and away to swarm through the cave. They pasted themselves on walls, ceilings, and floor, outlining the chamber.

It was small and irregular, its upper reaches following the cave's lifeline. The floor was solid, and the walls and ceiling. There should have been a passage, the witches' way, but the chamber was sealed tight. Morgan stood up—difficult in the narrow space. She felt her way along the walls, seeking a crack, a shifting rock. Her hands left desperate prints all across floors, walls, and ceiling. There was no escape.

Beyond the boulder came the scratching sound of canine claws.

Falling to her knees, Morgan whispered, "Morrigan, let us go. You want us both to die down here?"

The dog in the main chamber yipped its discovery. Claws rasped on stone. Men would come and find her, and she would be the prisoner of Tintagel. Worse, they wouldn't find her, and she'd be a ghost. . . .

Blood seeped from beneath her knee. It spread in a small pool, glowing brilliantly. Every corpuscle shone like a tiny lantern. Motes rose from the pool, drawn into the air as if along a vertical shaft. A pathway was forming. It bisected the little chamber, reaching from the floor to the cave's lifeline in the rock above.

The witches' way . . . a ley line.

Morgan had heard of these lines, of course—Otherworld roads that crossed points of power. Wizards walked them, and druids, even the fey Tuatha dé Danann, but Morgan had never thought she would.

Reaching out, she parted that blood-red path as if drawing apart a curtain. Magic unfolded before her, a pathway up out of the cave and across the wide lands of Dumnonia.

I go with you, Meg said. *You are Tintagel.*

Morgan sighed deeply. "Thank you, Morrigan, for releasing us. Let no creature on earth or under it know where we walk tonight."

While the dog scratched beyond the boulder, Morgan stepped onto the ley highway. Its red walls folded around her, and she and Meg were gone.

10

The Second Eve

Morgan put Meg away with all the others. Though she bore a tribe of wise women within her, she would walk this road alone.

The ley highway was carrying her to Tristan. She willed it to, and it would. At each intersection, Morgan turned toward him. She walked the sanguine way, feeling neither fear nor pain but only the surety of her love at the road's end. She would join him, and they would flee together and make a home for each other.

At last, Morgan reached the road's end. She stepped out of the sky and into an oak grove in Dor. The great tree stood before her just as it had two years ago—bronze leaves tinged in gold. Around it spread grasses bleached with autumn, thistle and ragwort and beggar-ticks. Beneath a cloud-cluttered sky, they wore their wintry aspect, knowing what was to come.

The fey road had borne her through months as well as miles. It knew she sought Tristan in fall, and it brought her there. Still, it would not be fit for him to find her amid all these dead things. This was not a time of death but of new life.

Morgan pivoted. It would take much magic to transform this grove, but she had it in her.

"You, for instance, flower of the north," Morgan said gently, cupping the down-turned head of a thistle, "you'll have another night to live."

Her fingers tightened, and tiny spines pierced her skin. Morgan closed her eyes. The blood in her hand began to glow. Red particles of power soaked through those dry spines and poured into the thistle stalk. Up toward the bloom and down toward the root it went. Withered flesh filled out, and the blossom lifted its head. Dry stamens turned purple again, and leaves that had been days away from falling now were as verdant as at Midsummer.

Morgan turned. "And you, flower of the south," her other hand tightened on a thorny rose, "gather your petals from the path and your fragrance from the wind." Vitality rushed through the briar, enlivening the flower above her fingers, and a hundred others throughout the thicket. "Grow to hem this garden in, that it will be safe from the violent world." The rosebushes spread. Their branches creaked as they reached around the grove, and their roots crackled up from the dry ground.

Morgan strode gently through the blooming grove. Droplets of blood fell from her fingertips, and flowers bloomed in her path—clover in purple and white, violets and lavender. Grasses joined them, making a fine green carpet.

She touched a wild apple tree, and its craggy branches burst with round fruit. She caressed a single ivy vine, and it spread to drape the oak like ribbons around a maypole. Never had she worked such magic, and it weakened her. Still, this was only a foretaste. Someday, she would transform the whole world.

When all in compass of the tree was green, Morgan turned to the grandmother oak itself. She walked slowly toward it and laid her hands and head on its rugged bulk.

"You, Great One—I need you most. You will be the Tree of Knowledge, for in your lap we will have knowledge of each other." She felt weak, and if not for the tree, she would have fallen. "I haven't enough blood for you. If you'll be what I wish, you must become it yourself."

Boughs twisted blackly beneath a crown of leaves. Beyond was a sky in white cerements.

"It will have to be enough," Morgan said. She kicked off her kid-skin shoes and climbed. The vast body of the tree was rumpled and worn, and it gave knobby footholds for her. She pulled herself up to the first great bough and rested there awhile. Her skin was as pale as porcelain. She had very little magic left, but when Tristan came, she would need only herself.

Morgan reached the exalted lap of the tree. Even its mossy carpet had gone gold with autumn. Morgan crawled onto it and lay down. She was warm, safe above the green grove and beneath the rattling sky. She breathed. How long did it take a body to make more blood?

"Tristan. . . ." She had prepared this bed but had forgotten to call him. "Oh, Meg, oh Morrigan—you've delivered me this far. Don't leave me stranded. Bring him. Call Tristan."

"Call," said a voice, sharp and fierce. "Call." A crow perched on a nearby branch. It was a sinewy bird, its eyes like ink-drops. The crow cocked its head and jabbed its beak into the bark. "Call."

Morgan smiled weakly. "Thank you, death mothers. You are still with me." She held out her hand, blood covering her palm. "Come to me."

The crow leapt, spread its wings, and lighted on her hand. It looked into her face, black feathers above white flesh. "Call."

"Yes," Morgan said. She stroked its plumes, leaving bead-like droplets along its back. "Morgan calls."

"Morgan calls," it replied. "Morgan calls."

She nodded. Closing her eyes, she evoked an image of Castle Dor and willed it into the animal. With a flick of her wrist, she tossed the crow into the air.

"Morgan calls," it said, flying off toward the castle.

She smiled, lying back down. Tristan was coming. He would join her in the lap of this great tree, and then they would be one. Their lives would begin anew, bound in desire.

Morgan would sleep until he came. She drew off the robe of rags and the shift that was like good earth, and let them fall to the ground. She removed every thread, even the twine that bound her hair. He would find her naked and unashamed.

She slept in her garden. Tristan was coming, and in the season of dying, they would begin a new life.

Tristan struggled beneath a load of armor. At eighteen, he should have been wearing the armor, but his uncle and his master were in collusion.

"Not a spot, lad!" Rolus bellowed, his breath bitter with ale. He had learned not to touch Tristan, but had discovered other ways to punish him. "And then fashion me a new lance. I left half of the other one in young John!" He laughed, gesturing across the infirmary to the cot where John lay. He was only Tristan's age, and this had been his first joust. The scent of sepsis told that it would be his last.

Careful not to drop so much as an elbow cop, Tristan carried his master's armor through the infirmary. Half of Mark's men were here, getting their wounds dressed and filling their heads with ale. They'd spent the morning killing each other and would spend the afternoon drinking and feasting.

Perhaps Tristan didn't want to be a warrior after all.

A black beast winged in through the window and circled the room.

"Get away, harbinger!" shouted one man, swinging a sheet at the crow.

"She's a witch," said another, crouching at the head of his cot. "If she circles you, you'll lose your soul."

"Morgan calls," the bird cried eerily. "Morgan calls Morgan. . . ."

Tristan halted, his spine tingling.

"You hear that?" Rolus said, rising from his cot. He jabbed a finger at the bird, and a bandage trailed his elbow. "It's that witch, Morgan! The one who cursed my—"

Laughter erupted, and someone shouted "Get her, Bloodypants!"

Rolus ambled after the bird. "I'll murder you!"

"Murder calls. . . . Murder calls. . . ." The crow flapped its wings just above Rolus's fingers.

Tristan gathered himself. He knew what this meant. Morgan waited for him in her Tree of Knowledge. She was in trouble. He would go to her and save her, but he dared not let his master know. With tentative steps, Tristan headed toward the door.

"Squire!" shouted Rolus. "Put down that load and come catch this bird!"

Tristan let the grimy armor slide from his arms onto an empty cot. He blanched as he faced the violent man.

Rolus leapt from a stool, overturning it but getting a fistful of black feathers. He crashed atop a man with a broken arm, and they both spilled to the floor. "Get that damned bird, or I'll have you on the black list."

Every day for the past two years, Rolus had threatened the black list—excommunication and forbiddance to wear armor and bear arms. Always, it had been enough, until today. "No," he said with quiet reserve. "Let the bird alone."

"Murder calls Morgan," shrieked the crow. "Morgan calls murder. . . ."

Rolus rose from the ruined cot, and blood filled his fuming face. "Are you defying me?"

"Morgan calls murder Morgan calls murder Morgan."

"No. I'm resigning. You'll have to find another squire."

A predatory smile split Rolus's red face, and he surreptitiously gestured to a pair of men behind Tristan. "Quit, and you'll never be a warrior."

"I already am a warrior," Tristan said. He could sense the men creeping up behind him, but knew that they dare not lay hands on him. "Do what you must, Rolus, and I'll do what I must."

"Is that a threat?" Rolus roared.

A loop of rope lashed down around Tristan's head. He ducked his chin, protecting his throat, but the thick hemp cinched around his mouth. Someone jerked on the rope, and he fell backward. The floor struck his shoulders, driving the air from him. As Tristan twitched and gagged, the man wrapped his ankles and yanked the rope tight. He pulled Tristan's feet up to his buttocks, tied the line in the center of his back, and looped it over his arms, one at a time. All the while, he touched only the bristling cord. When he was done, he stepped back. Tristan kicked to get free but only managed to tighten the line around his hands.

"Hog-tied," Rolus said, leaning over him. "I did what I had to do, Tristan. You're out of your mind. Maybe time in the ropes will bring everything back. Meanwhile . . ."

"Murder Morgan. . . . Murder Morgan. . . ."

Rolus strode out of the infirmary and returned with a bow and arrow. He sighted on the crow, his fingers quaking. The bow thrummed, and the shaft whistled away. It caught the crow's tail, ripped feathers free, and sailed on to strike a rafter and shudder there.

The beast screamed, "Murder!" one last time, and flew out the window.

"Meanwhile, I've got a witch to kill!" Rolus tucked the bow under one arm, snatched a tankard of ale from a wounded man nearby, downed it, and cried, "To the horses!"

Every man who could rise did so, bloodthirsty shouts in their drunken throats. They ambled after Rolus, who had already charged from the room. The clatter of arms and the shriek of a startled horse told that he was already on his way.

Tristan wriggled, his teeth sawing through strand after strand of hemp.

Morgan awoke in a delirium of desire. She had dreamed of Tristan, that he had come and lain with her, that they had joined and would never be separate again. It was only a dream, of course, but it had left her languid and glad.

The sky was dark, but the leaves above her were lit with the last light of the sun. They gleamed. Boughs, half in shadow and half in light, reached to the golden dome. She was alone, except for one familiar beast.

He sat on a nearby twig. His feathers jutted as if he were cold, and he said simply, "Murder. . . ."

"What?" Morgan asked blearily. "Not murder. Morgan. Morgan calls."

"Morgan calls murder Morgan calls murder Morgan. . . ."

She felt the tree tremble, and she sat up. Hands gripped her ankles, and more grabbed her shoulders. They pulled at her, callused fingers. Men rose around her. They were only shaggy shadows against the gold leaf. Their breath plumed down with the smell of ale, and they laughed.

Morgan wrenched one way and then another, but there were too many hands. Men pinned her against the dry moss. She screamed for Tristan.

They said Tristan was welcome to whatever was left.

Their hands crushed her wrists and ankles. Her bones ground against each other. She screamed, but one of them rammed a sodden rag down her throat. They pried her legs apart, and a man drove himself up between them. He tore her open.

A man hangs pierced on a tree as his own people and the foreign soldiers, his own friends and the scribes who cursed him, all stand below, all guilty. It is mass murder, not the one killing the many but the many killing the one. He was the Second Adam, undoing the sin of the first.

You will be the Second Eve. . . .

Even the sunlight had given up on her, and the leaves turned from gold to rust. She could not have seen who this was, his face black amid tangles of beard and hair, but it didn't matter. This was Uther and Rolus and Arthur and every man except Tristan. Only he could be sinless in this, for she had given herself to him, but this was not he. Violent, vicious, bestial, spitting above and below . . .

Morgan hadn't thought there was any blood left in her until the man was done. Then the next one climbed up where he had been, and the others held her and waited for their turns.

Was this how Mother had awakened on that terrible night? Had she been dreaming of Father when the monsters came?

Morgan wished for magic. With all this blood, she should have been able to burn these beasts to the bone. She cried out to the Morrigan, but even their crow was gone now. She cried to Meg, but what could a ghost do against flesh?

The third, and the fourth, and the fifth, sixth, seventh, eighth . . . tenth . . . fourteenth . . . twenty-third . . .

They weren't raping her. They were killing her. They were murdering her with the single most violent weapon they owned, the progenitor of every knife and sword and spear that had ever been.

Yet your desire shall be for your husband, and he shall rule over you.

She spat out the sodden cloth and gasped a breath. "Modron . . . Epona . . . Brigid . . . Mary . . ." Their names rolled out of her, but none would answer. They all had abandoned her. Only the ravenous pack remained, eating her alive.

Morgan gave up the ghost. She hovered above herself and those jackals and watched them feed.

Bloodied at mouth, wrists, and hands, Tristan rode bareback on a pony. The horses had all been ridden or were too well guarded to steal. It was just as well. The pony was surefooted in the black fields. Its hooves stabbed into the tangled grass and lifted from burrows that would have lamed a horse. Still, the journey had shaken Tristan, yanking away each tear as it emerged.

"Why?" he asked the staring stars.

The tree hulked ahead. Tristan dug his heels in the pony's sides. He hoped the warriors were still there so he could bury his stolen sword in one or two of them before they killed him.

The stout little pony bore him up the gentle rise. It slowed and stopped before a thicket of thorn. Tristan dropped down from the beast, drew his sword, and hacked. He smelled fresh roses, and felt petals and thorns drag across his arm. In moments, he could clamber through.

The grove within was trammeled like spring earth. Horses had been here and left their piles. The beasts were gone, now—horses and men.

"Epona . . . Modron . . . Brigid . . . Mary . . ."

Oh, she was still alive. He'd hoped she hadn't survived.

Tristan sheathed the sword and climbed. His fingers felt along the rugged bark, and his feet followed on burls. He climbed to the first bough, and scrambled up others until he reached the crotch.

There Morgan lay. Starlight traced jagged figures across her. She was bleeding, and she was breathing. "Brigid . . . Mary . . . Epona . . . Modron. . . ."

"It's me," Tristan said, struggling to keep his voice from cracking. He pulled off his shirt. "You're bleeding. Use this to stop it."

She shook her head blearily. "Nothing can stop it. . . ."

Tristan blinked, paralyzed. "Morgan . . . I'm sorry . . . but I'll have to touch you to stop the bleeding. . . ." He climbed up beside her, folding the shift and setting it into place. Pushing her legs together around the cloth he lifted her, one arm under her shoulders and the other under her legs. "I'm sorry. . . ."

She sighed into his hair as if she would never breathe again.

Tristan shook his head violently. "No, Morgan. Don't give up. I'm going to carry you down, somehow. I'm going to take you back to Tintagel."

"Not . . . Tintagel. Avalon. . . . Bury me . . . in Avalon."

Tristan swung his feet onto the first branch. He balanced Morgan on his lap and eased downward. "There. See. We can make it."

"Avalon . . ."

"I don't know where Avalon is."

"Glastonbury," Morgan sighed.

Tristan's tears dropped onto her. "I swore to protect you."

"Your oath . . . could not undo . . . mine. . . ." She slumped against him as if dead.

Tristan allowed his tears to roll freely now, and his curses too. He swore to avenge her, to slay his former master—but first, he would carry her to Glastonbury.

To Avalon.

11

At the Gates

For three days, Tristan carried her on their doughty pony. It was agony. They were outlaws—Morgan the witch and Tristan the horse thief. He stole other things: sheets, salves, clothes, food, a blanket, a knife, a saddle. That first morning, he washed her in a creek and dressed her wounds as best he could. Oats from a feed bag gave them their first breakfast, and raw eggs their only other food that day. Next day, he killed a cat and cooked it on the end of his borrowed sword. Even so, Morgan was unable to eat it. She had not awakened for hours.

Now—for days. Dressed in a peasant's tunic and skirts, Morgan curled in his arms. Against his neck, her forehead felt like hot iron. When he pried at her eyes, the pupils were as wide as black buttons. Morgan clutched her hands in tight fists against her chest and tucked her knees up beneath her chin. Worst of all, though, were the constant visions and voices. She had always been able to glimpse the future and hear the goddesses, but now she saw and heard only the horrible past.

"Where are you, Tristan?" she blurted suddenly, her eyes clenched. "Where?"

"I'm right here," he said, holding her more tightly.

She shivered despite the warm winds from Glastonbury. Within her blanket, she began to buck. "Do you know what they're doing?"

"I know, Morgan. I know. But it's over now."

"They're killing me . . . killing the Garden. . . ."

"Hush, now. It's over."

"They're making me mortal . . . maculate. . . . I'll never be the same. . . . I'll be bleeding forever. . . ."

"I've stopped it, Morgan. You're not bleeding. The fever's burning all their filth away. You'll be fine."

"They've begun the Age of War. . . . They've cast us from the Garden. . . ."

"Hold to me. I'll keep you safe."

"I'll cling to you . . . and you'll kill and steal for me. . . ."

Tristan stared bleakly down to the Glastonbury Plain. The River Brue coiled across it like a worm. He clucked to the pony, nudging its flanks, and it trotted down the swale toward the Ponter's Ball. "We're almost there. Almost to Glastonbury."

"The new garden . . . ," she said. A great sigh poured out of her, and she slumped against him. Her hands eased, and the hot tension that had possessed her fled away.

"No, Morgan! Hold on!" He kicked the pony to a gallop.

She breathed in small gasps, and dots of perspiration speckled her brow.

"We're almost there. Hold on. We'll claim sanctuary. They'll heal you."

"No . . . sweet Tristan. They'll try to kill me. . . ."

"I'll protect you. I'll kill them before they can harm you." His scabbard slapped the pony's haunch. He'd slain a cat with that sword, and now he'd slay a priest? "I'll force them to help us."

The pony frothed at the bit. It wheezed as it ran toward Glastonbury Tor.

On three sides, the great hill was encircled by the wetlands of the River Brue. The fourth side connected to the Ponter's Ball, an isthmus from tor to plains. It was the only land route across the impassible morass, and the pony headed straight toward it. A palisade gate blocked the farther end of the isthmus, and on the near side stood a huge monk, as muscular as a headsman. He wore a black hooded robe and a sword at his belt.

Tristan drew the reins and clucked, slowing the beast. "You're sure we have to go to Glastonbury?"

Morgan didn't reply, lying limp against him.

The pony cantered across the isthmus and approached the palisade gate. It slowed to a trot, and then halted before the ominous priest. He was a giant, a Christian Goliath.

"Open wide. Two refugees seek sanctuary."

The monk's eyes glimmered darkly in the shadow of his hood. "I know who you are. You cannot enter."

Tristan set his jaw. "What of sanctuary?"

"This place is closed to you, now and forever."

Tristan shook his head slowly. There would be no help from anyone, mortal or divine. They were outcasts and would have to live by tooth and steel. Lifting Morgan, he said, "Give me a moment." He slid his leg over the pony's rump and stepped down from the saddle, with Morgan cradled in his arms.

The heaving beast clomped lightly aside, relieved of its burden. It chewed on swamp grass and cast a wary eye toward the humans.

Tristan knelt, drew off his stolen cloak, and laid it on the road. He tenderly lowered Morgan to rest there. She curled up on the hard ground. Tristan kissed her cheek and stood, gazing piteously on her. To the priest, he said, "She's dying. You're letting her die."

"The wages of sin is death."

"She has done nothing wrong!"

"She is a witch, the mother of harlots and abominations of the earth."

"She was raped and is dying."

"It is written, 'And the beast with the ten horns shall hate the whore and shall make her desolate and naked, and shall eat her flesh and burn her with fire. For God hath put it in their hearts to accomplish his will.'"

Tristan quietly said, "God damn it." He drew his sword. This would be his first real battle. He looked up at that bulwark of muscle, whose long sword gleamed. Tristan raised his own rusty blade. "Let us through."

The monk came on like a hammer blow, in one smooth arc of power. His black robes billowed out to eclipse the tor and then the very sky. His sword roared down like lightning. It struck.

Tristan braced his paltry blade in the sword's path. Steel crashed on steel, and Tristan's sword was cut like paper. He whirled away from the colossal blade, but its impact shoved him over. With riven hilt in hand, Tristan tumbled sideways off the Ponter's Ball. One foot jabbed out but slid in muck. His legs collapsed, and he pitched into the black waters. It slapped over him and engulfed him in ignominy.

Flailing, Tristan struggled to his feet. His hair flung filth as he turned back toward the giant.

"Morgan! No!" he gasped.

She rose from the cloak, arms to her sides, and stepped toward the monk. She was tiny and plain beneath his black bulk, and a grim smile spread across his teeth. He lifted his blade for a second blow.

Morgan woke at the gates of the Garden.

It was a glorious mountain, white at its peak, purple in the reaches beneath, and then green in verdant slopes. Trees grew in primeval tangles lower down, and wildflowers filled the lowland grass. Creatures grazed there, gentle and primordial before all were turned on each other.

Morgan knew those slopes. This was the Garden she would open to the world.

But it was closed to her. A tall gate stood before her, forged from quintessence. Those bars were unbreakable, impassible, and deadly to mortal flesh. Deadlier still was the angel who stood there.

He was huge, a man all in white with eyes like stars in his skull. His face was fair but utterly cold, and he bore in his hand a flaming sword. He looked at Morgan where she lay. "You cannot pass. Not now or ever."

Morgan pushed herself up from the ragged cloak where she had lain. Her peasant clothes straightened. She had to face him and throw him down. Morgan strode toward him. "Stand aside and let us through."

He retreated until his back was against the gate. His eyes glimmered with uncertainty. "Stay back, or I'll strike you dead."

Morgan approached. "You have no power over me."

Someone cried out, a voice of despair. Tristan. He pleaded for her to stop, to join him, but Morgan was done with despair. She walked toward the angel with the flaming sword.

He raised the weapon in massive arms. His serene expression shattered with grief. "You are forbidden!" His fiery sword descended on Morgan. The keen edge cleft the rags she wore, and the skin and bone beneath. It carved a horrid path through muscle and organ, passing through her as if she were simply air.

Tristan watched the sword cut her in two. One shoulder fell away from the other. The sword sliced right through her ribs and belly, emerging between her legs and clanging on the hard-packed road. Morgan dropped in severed halves to the ground.

No, not Morgan—the peasant rags she had worn. The sword had cut through them, front and back, but Morgan stood whole and unbloodied.

The great sword rattled as the monk drew it back across the rocks. Beneath his hood, his eyes were as wide as moons. "Y-you! Y-you *are* a witch!" He hefted the sword, readying another blow.

Morgan advanced.

"Your sword was forged against mortal flesh," Morgan said, sky-clad before the angel, "but it can no longer harm me. Your God threw me down once, but I have risen. I will enter those gates. I will take back my lands. I am the Second Eve." She rushed him.

He lanced his sword into her belly. Metal separated tissue from tissue but cut none of it. It slid through every divide, ruining not a cell. The angel ripped his sword free, but she was inviolate. He stabbed again, and her flesh received the blade without harm. Behind the retreating steel, her body closed like water. A fourth stroke, and a fifth. Still she stood, ever-penetrated but ever-virginal.

Morgan grasped his hands and pried them from the flaming blade. It fell to the ground, tumbled across toothy stones, and splashed into the swamp. Black waters closed over it. The metal hissed as it sank, its flames extinguished.

Morgan gripped the angel's sword hand and rammed her shoulder into his waist. He was nearly twice her height, and the blow tipped him over her back. He was also enormously heavy. She roared and hurled him to one side.

The great messenger of God crashed to the earth and bellowed.

Morgan flung herself on his back. She slid her arms under his and around his neck. Lacing her fingers, she flexed her arms.

Bedeviled, the angel struggled forward on his belly. He rolled, getting one knee beneath him, and then the other. He rose, dragging Morgan up from the ground.

She swung to one side, wrenching his shoulders and neck and head, and hurled the angel down.

He skidded on his face in the dirt. Gasping, the angel lunged to get away, but Morgan landed on him again.

Tristan had not moved a whit from where he stood, thigh-deep in the swamp. Only his jaw had shifted, hanging low.

Morgan was ruthless and relentless. The monk who had

seemed so powerful was now a gibbering monkey. He was panicked to escape this naked woman, this witch who climbed all over him. Bleeding from a broken nose and scraped hands and knees, he moaned in terror and outrage. Whenever she pinned him—which was whenever she was not throwing him—he looked toward the abbey in dread.

It was magic, assuredly. She had been getting her blood up for this fight, and now she was a human badger, ferocious and implacable.

The monk landed on his back and flailed, unable to catch his breath. Morgan pounced on him. That seemed to awaken his lungs, for he bellowed, "Release me, witch!"

Morgan smiled. The angel's eyes were no longer stars, distant and imperturbable. He had learned mortal fear.

"I know who you are, Michael, guardian of the gates. You are the banisher, but now *you* are banished. No one will ever guard these gates again. They'll be open to every creature, mortal and immortal."

"Release me!"

"I'll release you only if you promise to flee and never return."

"I swear it, witch! Get off me."

Morgan opened her fists, releasing the twisted fabric of his shift. She stood up, stepping gracefully back and gesturing for the archangel to rise and depart.

At first, he didn't, only staring in amazement. Then, the archangel rose and loped away. He gained speed as he went, terror driving him across the land bridge. In moments, he had reached the far side and tore along it like a madman along a heath.

Tristan watched the priest go. He deserved what he had gotten, striking an unarmed woman. Still, the wrestling match had unhinged him. Madness showed in the high strides of his knees and his ginger tiptoes, as if each step was into the mouth of a devil. He never would return to Glastonbury or to the abbey—that much was clear.

Morgan might never leave it. She stood on the Ponter's Ball, untouched by sword or fist. Her flesh was radiant and whole, clothed in light and magic. She was no more naked than the blazing sun.

Tristan trudged up from the muck. It coated him, thickest below the knees. He came to her and knelt, dropping his face to the dirt. It was the most natural motion, the reflex of mortal flesh in immortal company. All he could manage to say was her name, and it seemed a prayer. "Morgan."

She looked down on him. Her gaze was so bright it felt like sunshine on his back. "Tristan," she responded simply, "now for the gate."

Her hands lifted slowly above her head. Light gathered in the arc of her body and intensified, pouring from her. Overhead, her fingers bent, grasping air. She dragged them down and said simply, "Fall!"

The wooden gate erupted in flame. Its great metal hinges cracked, and its iron bolts shot out like arrows. It dropped to its base and slowly began to topple. Flames roared across it as it fell. With a sound like thunder, it crashed to the ground.

Morgan watched placidly as the quintessent gate dissolved before her. She stepped onto it and crossed between the crumbling walls. Beyond them lay her beloved Avalon.

Clover spread from her feet out to ancient oaks and apple trees, along the blue shores of the great lake, and up to the chanting waters of the eternal spring. She gazed beyond the snowcapped peaks to that mountain-sized tree in the sheer distance.

Pointing to a stone ledge that jutted from one steep slope, she said, "There is where I was first possessed by the goddesses."

Tristan had watched her walk across the burning gate and wondered if he should follow. Beyond it, Morgan pointed up the side of Glastonbury Tor and spoke, but the fires drowned out her words.

Tristan climbed to his feet and ran after her. He crossed the burning gate—fearful of fire but more of losing her—and came to her side. He immediately dropped to his knees beside her.

"No," she said, catching his hand and lifting him. "You needn't bow to me. This is our world now, yours and mine."

He swept his hand out toward the rumpled hill, wondering what she could possibly mean. But it was no longer the stony hill, so pessimistic beneath its thin skin of grass. Suddenly, it was verdant and wide, surrounded by a great and deep flood and filled with life.

Dumbfounded, Tristan clung to her hand and said, "Avalon. . . ."

12

In the Cottage of Brigid

Yes," she replied. "Avalon. Let the vision pour into you. It will fade and be gone, but you have to know that it was true."

Tristan gaped at the beautiful island. It was vanishing already, its flowers replaced by weeds, forests by shrubs, glory by squalor. "What's happening?" he asked, turning toward Morgan. His shock only deepened when he saw her—bruised and burned, pale and trembling. "What's happening?"

Morgan went to one knee. "You saw me drive off the angel at the garden gate. . . . I won the battle of spirit. . . . The battle of flesh continues. . . ." She slumped into his arms, as light and helpless as a child. "The abbey . . ."

Tristan shot a glance over his shoulder to the pessimistic little group of buildings near the base of the tor. "They'll not treat us well."

"One . . . will. . . ." Her head lolled against his shoulder.

Setting his jaw, Tristan lifted her from the ground and strode toward the abbey. Morgan's body showed every sorrow she had suffered. Her feet were blackened from the fiery gates, her legs bruised from the wrestling match. She bled from old injuries and new, but her face, ringed by Medusa-braids—her face was beautiful.

Tristan looked away. He stared hard at the abbey. It had been built of the very stone of the tor, natural shapes stacked and cemented into uneven walls. Within irregular windows lurked figures—monks, nuns, perhaps the abbess herself. They had seen everything and wouldn't be kindly disposed.

Tristan no longer had a sword, not even the pony, but he felt ferocious. "Just let them deny help," he muttered under his breath. "God help them." Reaching a footpath that curved up the final contour of the hill, Tristan walked to an iron gate that let into the cloister.

A crowd had gathered beyond the ironwork, and their eyes were baldly defiant. Most were nuns but one was a monk, and he quickly withdrew the key he had just used to lock the gate.

Ascending three stone steps, Tristan halted. "Let us in. We seek sanctuary."

"Go," said the monk. He was slender and sour in his brown robes. "There's no sanctuary in Christ for such as you."

Tristan's nostrils flared. "I'll break down the gates."

"You wouldn't dare."

A woman interrupted, "Oh, yes, he would. 'The kingdom of heaven is taken by violence, and violent men bear it away.'" Through the crowd trundled an old woman, hunched in her homespun robes. Her face was as lined as weathered stone, but her eyes twinkled brightly. She looked Tristan up and down. "You saw what they did to our other gate, and we'll have to rebuild it without Jeremiah to do the hauling." Nodding with decision, she said, "Let them in."

The monk lifted the key between two fingers and dangled

it as if it were a dead thing. "I disagree, but as always, defer to you, Mother Brigid."

"As always," she echoed, snatching the key. She fit it into the lock, and many of the nuns drifted to safe corners. With a metallic click, the lock opened, and the gate whined inward.

Tristan stepped to the threshold. "Thank you," he said to Mother Brigid. The fury had left him, and he felt only frantic. "We need help. She's terribly wounded."

"I know just the place," said Brigid with a wink. She laid an old but strong hand on his arm and gave Tristan an encouraging pinch. "Come with me." Turning, the old woman strode away at a surprising pace. Her colleagues moved aside, lining the walls of the cloister.

Tristan followed, wondering about the deliverance he was receiving. Once he had passed the others, he said, "Mother, she was raped."

"I know," said the woman.

"Not by me," he added breathlessly. "By a host."

"I know."

There was something in her tone that made Tristan trust her. "We're fugitives. This is the third day since the rape, and I've given her whatever I could lay my hands on—steal, that is—but she's worse off than before."

Brigid nodded, striding toward a door. She produced a different key from her pocket and fit it to the iron lock.

"She's no ordinary girl—woman . . . person. She has visions, and when you're with her, you have visions too. She hears voices, and she's got power, and God wants something out of her. That's the best way I can say it."

The latch clicked, and Brigid turned toward him. "You love her."

Tristan flushed. "Um. Well—"

"It is all right. You should. Many others will. You're right about her, and you were right to bring her here." She pushed back the door, stepped across the threshold, and gestured him to follow.

Tristan passed through the door into a different world.

He left behind the dour abbey, with its walls of fieldstone and its scent of mildew, and entered a sweet little cottage. Spices hung to dry in the rafters, and their fragrance mixed with the scent of rushes on the floor. A small fire burned on the hearth, and above it hung a kettle that steamed with cider. A round table, two rough-hewn chairs, a straw pallet in one corner—there was not much more the little cottage could have held.

"Where are—" Tristan glanced back to see that the doorway no longer led to the abbey, but to emerald hillsides above a sapphire sea. He gasped, almost lost his balance, and pulled the door closed behind him.

"Lay her there, on my bed. The linens are clean," Mother Brigid said. She went to the fire, pivoted the iron from above it, and set the kettle of cider aside. Lifting a different kettle from its hook, she filled it with water from a nearby bucket. Her hands darted to the rafters, and she began dragging down dried herbs. She crushed them above the water and stirred the fragrant brew.

"Where are we?" asked Tristan as he laid Morgan onto the straw mat. He pulled a sheet up over her battered form.

"You know where we are."

Tristan nodded. "What can I wash her with?"

Brigid pointed to the water left in the bucket, and she tossed a rag into it. Then, stirring her brew, she pivoted the kettle out above the fire.

Retrieving the water, Tristan wrung out the rag. He knelt

and tenderly washed the dirt from Morgan's pale face. "And who are you?"

The old woman sat back on her heels and smiled. "I am Brigid."

An eldritch prickle of dread touched Tristan's spine. "You're more than that, aren't you? You're not just an abbess. You're another . . . magician—what's the word?—filidh? You're like Morgan—a kind of g-goddess."

"A very perceptive young man." Steam wreathed Brigid in a fragrant cloud. "A goddess, once, yes—sky goddess of the Isle of Eire. Now I've become Saint Brigid." She pivoted the kettle back from the flame, grasped its handle in a cloth, and carried it to Morgan's side. Kneeling beside Tristan, Brigid dipped a rag in the stingingly hot brew and began cleaning each of Morgan's wounds.

Tristan shook his head, overcome. He stammered, "An-and Morgan? That's what . . . that's what she is? A goddess?"

Brigid paused, staring at Morgan. "No. She's different. Morgan was born mortal, like everyone else, but she's making herself divine."

Tristan breathed deeply. "I don't understand any of this."

With a laugh, Brigid said, "None of us do. There's never been anyone like Morgan."

Tristan stared levelly into Brigid's wise, ancient eyes, and his nervousness melted away. "She talks about the Age of War, about the Second Eve. What does any of that mean?"

Brigid breathed deeply. "It's a long story."

"We have time," replied Tristan. He shifted to Morgan's feet and began to clean the burns. "I want to know."

Nodding, Brigid said, "For the last four thousand years, the goddesses have been dying. It all began in Sumer, between the Tigris and Euphrates—"

"The land of Eden."

"Yes. Even Yahweh remembers the beautiful bounty of that land, before the first great cities were built. In that time, all people tended the land. Fertility and growth were the greatest powers in the world, the powers of the goddess. Gaea was her name. She invited all humanity into her garden to tend the plants and animals and live with her. She invited them to the tree of knowledge and the eternal stream."

Tristan wrung out the cloth and drew it gently across Morgan's sooty feet. "I thought God made the Garden of Eden."

"The gods came later, lesser divinities of war. Yahweh and Elohim were among them. Once cities were built, it was suddenly profitable to gather men in armies and march them to kill and conquer and steal. The Age of War had begun. The powers of domination and death became greater than the powers of fertility and life. The gods, once the sons of the goddess and her consorts, attacked her and threw her down. Eve—the goddess whose name meant "Mother of All Living"—became a mere woman. Her divine consort became a mere serpent, and both were put under the dominion of the First Adam, who was in turn under the dominion of Yahweh."

"The Fall of Man. . . ."

Brigid nodded. "It was a true fall, but not as Saint Paul imagined it. It was loss of the garden and Gaea, banishment into a world of war. Before that time, humans were part of nature and lived with her. Afterward, they fought the goddess and her world. Men fight everything, even themselves. By cleaving from Gaea, we cleaved to misery."

They continued dressing Morgan's wounds. At first, Tristan was ashamed of her nakedness, but now she seemed a savior, torn and bleeding upon the shroud.

"Gaea fell, and her story is Eve's story. She shattered into thousands of lesser goddesses, who dwelt on for millennia before they too were cast down." Brigid said. "Tiamat in Babylon, Isis in Egypt, Baal in Canaan, Juno in Rome . . . and eventually Brigid in Eire. Some were killed outright. Some became mortals or devils. Some were married off to the gods who had conquered them. That was the way Jupiter took control. He was perhaps the most merciful. I found my own way, becoming a saint." She whistled in amazement, staring down at Morgan. "Do you know what you're looking at, Tristan?"

He flushed, and shook his head.

"Here's a mortal woman who is doing what immortal women fear to do. Morgan is fighting the gods. She's taking on the heavens."

Tristan swallowed. His hands trembled. It was good that he was done washing her, because he could hardly hold the rag. "When she said she was the Second Eve, I thought she meant she was a savior like Jesus."

"That's one way of seeing it," Brigid replied with a shrug. "But it's not whole truth. No, she means the goddesses are being reborn in her. She's destroying the Age of War and bringing Gaea and the garden back to the world."

Tristan sat by the cottage window and looked out on Avalon—vast and Otherworldly, too verdant to be real. He'd lived all his life in a world at war, but here was the Garden of Peace. He feared to venture into it.

"Why don't you take a walk?" Brigid said. She sat on a stool nearby and spun wool on a hand wheel. "She's resting now. Go see Avalon."

Tristan rose from the window seat, ventured to the door, and even pushed it slowly open. It was like opening floodgates. The fragrant air of Avalon poured across him, bringing visions of ancient trees and fey beasts—fauns, centaurs, fairies, the Seelie and Unseelie Courts. . . . He felt their eyes on him. All of Avalon watched. Tristan pulled the door closed again and retreated to the window. It offered just the right amount of paradise.

I'll be a warrior someday, he thought. I'm a son of Yahweh and Jupiter, product of a dying age. I'm a stranger here.

"It's just as well," Brigid said. "She's coming around."

Tristan startled and hurried to Morgan's side.

"Easy, now. She won't be able to talk much. She won't be truly well for months."

Tristan padded softly up to her and knelt. "Morgan. How are you?"

The sheet rose and fell with breath. "I'm . . . where . . . ?"

"Avalon," Tristan replied with quiet intensity. "You were right. One person helped us."

"Brigid," Morgan breathed.

The old woman only sat and spun.

"We've cleaned you up. Brigid made a poultice. We bound your wounds. You'll be better now. You won't die."

"I feel like I already have," Morgan replied.

Smiling bitterly, Tristan leaned over and wrapped her in his arms. He felt her breath on his neck. Something jabbed his breastbone, and he eased her back down, catching the object. It was the bloodstone she had given him two years before. "If only you had been wearing this in the tree—"

"It had to happen this way," Morgan replied. "The sacrifice cannot escape the knife."

The image was terrible. Tristan sat back on his heels and stared blearily at the wall. "At least you didn't die."

Morgan shook her head. "I couldn't die. I had to live, to bear this worst misery and go on and undo it for everyone else."

The spinning wheel grew still in Brigid's hands, and she set it gently aside. "There's more to it than even that, Child."

Tristan glared. "What? What else could there be?"

"You must, indeed, bear this misery. . . ."

"You don't mean?" Morgan struggled to sit up. Her face grew very pale, and her eyelids fluttered closed. She slumped. A prickly sweat broke out across her forehead.

Tristan stroked her face. "It's all right. I'm here. It's all right. I'll keep you safe."

"You can't," Brigid said quietly. "Just as you couldn't protect her from the rape, you can't protect her from the child."

"The child—?" Tristan began. Realization hit him. He lay down beside her, his arm draped across her. "It's all right. I'm here. I'll keep you safe. It's all right."

13

On Separate Roads

*Y*ou'll take care of her?" Tristan asked. He stood just within the cottage door, his hand on the latch.

"Of course," said Brigid. She poked a stick into the bank of embers, watching two tiny sparks circle each other and flee up the chimney. "But you said you'd stay."

Tristan blinked. "I *did* stay. I stayed a month. I don't belong here."

The old woman glanced out the cottage window. Avalon was stormy with late summer. Woolen clouds tumbled above the hills. "It's winter in the world."

"Snow, ice, sleet—I've got enough anger to melt them. I'll still be blazing when I get to Dor."

Brigid waved her hand. "Go if you must, but don't pretend you're going for her. She doesn't wish it. Revenge won't do her any good."

"It'll do me good," Tristan said. "Life is growing in her, but death is growing in me. What Rolus did to her that night he did to me every day. He's turning them all into monsters. If I strike him down, a whole garrison of them will fall."

Brigid shook her head. "Death and killing, killing and death."

"I'm not like her. I'm a warrior. This is how we settle things."

"Yes, I know."

Tristan lingered a moment more. "Look, I want to thank you for all you've done, and all you'll do—"

"Your pony's in the stables, well tended. They'll let you take him, and enough feed to get you to Dor. We can offer you no arms or armor—"

Tristan held up his hand. "I'll get what I need, just as before." He looked at Morgan, sleeping on the old woman's pallet. "Tell her good-bye for me, and tell her I'll return."

"I'll say good-bye, but I'll not lie. I'll tell her that if you survive, you'll return." The old woman poked the fire.

Nodding grimly, Tristan clicked the latch of the cottage door. It opened onto a chilly hallway of stone. He could still see Avalon out the cottage windows, but a mere step brought him to the abbey hallway. He closed the door behind him. The mildew was somehow even sharper in the closed-up winter, and the hallway seemed a cave.

Tristan knew what he was doing. As cruel as the world was, it was *his* world. He had always hoped to be a warrior, and he would become one only by avenging Morgan.

"I should tell her myself." He clicked the latch and swung the door inward. Beyond lay a small, stony cell. There was only a cot, a side table, a candle burnt to a nub, and an inkpot beside curly pieces of parchment. Brigid's cottage was gone.

Slowly, Tristan closed the door. There was no turning back now. He was on the warrior's road. He released the door handle and strode down the hall toward his pony and a death-duel.

Morgan couldn't bear it any longer. Tristan would have understood, but he'd been gone for a month. Who knew how long that might have been in the world outside? During that time, Morgan had healed much, but she was ready to make herself sick again.

The knife cut shallowly across her thigh. She had the cup ready and watched the blood run into it.

"Violent blood makes for a violent spell," said Brigid darkly.

Morgan didn't look at her, eyes intent on the metal cup. Firelight flickered across her face. "What choice do I have? There's no monthly blood for either of us." She wrapped a bandage around her leg. "Besides, it is a violent spell."

"It is," agreed Morgan, sitting near the window. Fall was deepened across Avalon, the grass turning the color of parchment and the oaks the color of rust. "It's your right. Who could contest it, least of all the men who put the child in you?"

Morgan gritted her teeth. "Least of all them." Holding the metal cup in a pair of tongs, she positioned it atop a bed of coals.

"But it is a choice. You've started down a path, Morgan. You've endured great misery, and there's more to come. No one can blame you for ending it now, but you would be ending it. You'd be making all the suffering meaningless. If instead you bear the child, you'd make meaning of it."

At the edge of the cup, bubbles formed. Morgan lifted the stuff out and poured it on a shallow dish. She snatched up a dried herb and crushed it, letting the pieces fall. "It won't stop me. I've wrestled the angel. I've broken into the Garden. I'll bring the world with me."

"But why not have this child be the firstborn of the Garden?" Brigid looked up from whatever it was she worked on, her hands going limp in her lap. "You're free to choose, Morgan, whether this was a child of rape or not, but to drink that cup is to take the warrior's way. It's to destroy life rather than nurture it."

Morgan scooped the clumpy mixture back into the cup and returned it to the blaze. The blood-soaked leaves crackled. They gave up their moisture with fitful little bursts of steam. Soon, the concoction had reduced to ash, and Morgan pulled the smoking cup from the fire. She poured the gray powder into a cup filled with cider. The ashes floated on the sweet liquid. Morgan stirred. "There has to be some recompense for what was done to me."

"Let the child be recompense. Let Tristan be recompense." Brigid stood, and the small cloak she had been knitting fell to her feet amid the rushes. "Don't drink this cup."

Morgan stared at her over the steaming cider, ashes in its golden flow. "I've decided."

On his stolen pony, Tristan rode across the frozen grasslands of Dor. Icicles hung from the pony's fetlocks and jingled with each step. This was a sturdy creature, and Tristan had named him Stoutheart. He had carried him through driving sleet and across frozen roads. His sword was sturdy too, the blade of the vanquished priest. Tristan had retrieved it from the icy muck of Glastonbury and the same day had used it to slay a brigand. The man's mismatched armor had become Tristan's own. He also carried a crude lance, fashioned from a sapling. Its butt rested on his foot.

Castle Dor loomed up before him, defiant on the snowy

plains. The fortress wore its winter habiliments, ice hanging from every cornice. Men sat by the arrow loops, their breath sending up little white flags. It was sloppy discipline. If Tristan had had a bow, he could have slain them from the road. Dor had degenerated around the degenerate Rolus.

Clucking to Stoutheart, Tristan brought him to a halt. He stared up the golden road to the portcullis gate, the black mouth of a monster. "Ho, in the castle, Tristan has returned!"

"Tristan Deserter or Tristan Horse-Thief?"

"I come to avenge Morgan of Tintagel! I challenge Rolus to battle me on this plain this hour."

The monster himself had been listening, and he responded with a derisive laugh. The steam of Rolus's breath made a yellow cloud above the hoardings, but he kept his face hidden. "Morgan of Tintagel? That witch deserves to die. The only wrong I did to her was leaving her alive."

"This is a challenge of honor!" Tristan declared.

"Honor? You come in shambled mail with a twig for a lance and call it honor?"

"Yes! I call it that. If you've not enough honor to meet me with your polished blade and war horse, then let it be a battle of dishonor!"

The snickering that followed was aimed at Rolus. As slick as an eel, he reversed his course. "I'm full of wine. Come fight me when I'm sober."

Tristan stood in the saddle, holding out his arms. "Full of wine! At midday! On duty? What dishonor! And if I waited till you were sober, I'd have to fight you a day after they put you in the grave." Rolus's cronies jeered him. "I'll put you there myself, today! Who wants to see this death-match, and now?"

Cheers came from the walls.

"Lest anyone say I cheat, bring out a skin of wine, and I'll drink it, and we'll both be full."

There was a moment's silence, as if Rolus considered or conferred: "Get an eyeful of the sun, Tristan, for it's the last sun you'll see." The other warriors shouted in bloodthirst. Some began calling out wagers and odds, and others vied for the best spots to watch the slaughter. There came a rhythmic clang as Rolus descended from the parapets. He shouted for his horse to be saddled and lanced.

Tristan twitched, so used to obeying that shout. Apparently, Rolus's new squire was slower. To keep Stoutheart warm, Tristan rode him before the wall, marking a jousting lane.

At last, the gates rose in their grooves, and Rolus rode forth. His horse made Stoutheart seem a large dog. Astride it, Rolus wore plate armor, gleaming and thick, with chain beneath. His lance was a third longer than Tristan's, and steel tipped, and he bore a bilateral shield. Tristan had no shield at all. Deadliest of Rolus's provisions, though, was the wineskin he clutched in his hand. Riding across to Tristan, Rolus lifted the skin and chucked it over to him.

"Drink up," he called as Tristan caught the skin. "To the dregs. Then you'll have in you what's in me. And it'll be that much more red when I lay you open."

Tristan felt the hefty sack and stared at the cork, rammed on askew. Rolus himself had prepared this skin. What had he put in it? Piss? Poison?

"These were the conditions—fight now, with a skin of wine in us both, and to the death," Rolus said. "If you back out, I win, and you'll be my captive, and my boy again. Now *drink!*"

Tristan pulled the cork from the lip of the skin. He'd ridden a week to come here this day. He'd chosen this wine, and he would drink it. It was red wine, as bitter as myrrh, and he poured it down his throat. His fingers squeezed into a fist on the sack, and when it was empty, he tossed the thing away. Only at the dregs did he taste the grit, something undissolved in the wine.

Rolus turned in the lane, ready for the charge.

Perhaps Tristan could kill the man before the wine killed him. With sanguine lips set in a grimace, he rode to his end of the lane, spun Stoutheart, and prepared the sapling for the charge.

Rolus bellowed. He dug heels into the poor beast beneath him and hurtled toward his hated squire.

Tristan yelled too, and Stoutheart leapt. Horse and pony, man and boy, roared toward each other.

Morgan lifted the cup. In the cider, ashes swam like minnows. She tipped the drink and drained it. Sweet cider and bitter poison rolled across her tongue and down her throat. It burned. The liquid reached her stomach and splashed through it. She shook, fire racing to her hands and feet. Her fingers tingled. She tried to put the cup down, but it fell from her grip and rang bell-like on the hearth. It rolled into the fire and sputtered.

"It's done," she said. Then she was on her knees on the stone, doubled over. She held her face in trembling hands and saw a vision.

He rides in tattered armor, a pole for his lance and a pony for his steed, bent in frantic fury in a charge, eyes keen and hands steady. Something like blood stains his lips and sloshes hot inside him. . . .

"I see Tristan. . . . He rides against . . . the rapist. . . . He's bent on killing him."

And suddenly, she was within the vision, the red stuff dripping from her lips, the heat churning her belly. She bore forward with that implacable speed, driving her crude weapon to the heart of her foe, her child.

Riding aback Stoutheart, halfway to Rolus, Tristan suddenly remembered the bloodstone at his throat. He wanted this fight to be fair. With lance leveled in his right hand, Tristan released the rein, grabbed the rock, and ripped it from his neck. The rein flapped loose as Tristan grasped the creature's mane instead.

Rolus's lance soared toward him. It bobbed erratically, impossible to judge, but the arm that held it and the horse that propelled it were beefy enough to kill. The tip dipped low, too low to reach Tristan. He wouldn't need to swerve or duck. Roaring, the drunken man swept his lance aside, from Tristan to Stoutheart. The head of the weapon drove into the horse's breast, between its heart and its right shoulder. The pony didn't scream, only bearing on as the shaft rammed into it.

Tristan too roared. His own lance met its mark. The sapling nosed past Rolus's shield and plunged into the seam between his breastplate and pallette. Tristan had cleaned that armor enough to know its fatal flaw. The sharpened tip pierced chain and shirt, burst ribs, and impaled Rolus's chest before emerging from his back.

All of that happened in an instant. Then the two steeds

tore past each other, the riding man and the dying man exchanging places. Tristan drew back on the pony's mane, unwilling that the wounded beast run on. It slowed, its legs curling easily beneath it. Tristan swung one leg over the pony's rump and leapt free, rolling in the snow to spare the poor beast. He needn't have. Stoutheart turned a tight circle and trotted toward him, plumes of steam shooting from his nostrils. Despite the lance, his breast was unbloodied.

Tristan gaped, and then saw the reason. The pony's mane glinted where the bloodstone hung, tangled on its broken chain. The fiendish blow Rolus had meant for Tristan's horse had pierced Rolus instead. Whirling about, Tristan saw that it was true.

Rolus flopped in agony, a lance jutting through his chest. He had no breath and arched like a speared fish. He was dying.

Tristan staggered toward him across the snow. All those years of torment scrolled through him again, but they seemed nothing now—paper thin. Rolus painted the snow in sunbursts of red. His eyes were imploring.

So this was what it was to stand over a dying foe. It felt base, vicious, horrid.

Above his head, the warriors of Gore cheered. He would be one of them soon, would take Rolus's place among them and steer them from degradation to honor. Still, it wasn't enough to justify this slaughter.

Rolus kicked his last. Even imploring eyes had been better than dead ones.

Tristan turned aside and vomited. It probably saved him. The wine gushed from his belly and hit the snow. It bore black specks of poison and clotted tissues from his stomach lining. The stuff steamed and smelled sepulchral. Again he vomited, and again until none of it remained. He couldn't stop, crouching as if in defeat.

Someone approached. "Well done, Tristan. I'd wondered when you'd finally up and kill the old drunk." It was King Mark. "Welcome back. You're a warrior now, lad. A warrior!"

"Brigid had said you would return," Morgan said quietly. She lingered near the window and gazed at winter in Avalon. "She said you'd return, if you lived, and that you'd be a warrior."

Tristan gave her a shy smile, leaned forward on the stool, and nodded. "Brigid knows much."

"So," Morgan said, studying his bearing. "Rolus is dead, and you've taken his place."

"Yes." He looked down at his feet, shod in steel. "Listen. I wanted to ask you—that is . . . I know you might not be comfortable there, at first, with all the warriors—"

"Oh, Tristan, I don't need a man to save me."

"No. That's not what I mean. I just thought, with the child . . ."

Morgan's hand strayed to her gently rounded stomach. "This isn't your child, Tristan."

His face was beautiful, his eyes clear. "It's not really for the child. It's for me. I'd be honored to have you as my bride."

Morgan left the window and approached him. "We're on separate roads now, Tristan. We have separate destinies."

His face darkened, and he stared at an empty space beside the hearth. "Well, I . . . I suppose Avalon would be a better place to . . . have a child. . . ."

A rueful look filled Morgan's eyes. "I can't hide here. I want my child to be born in mortal places. She or he will be the first in a brood of new believers."

He reached out to her, his hand hovering above her stomach. "May I?" he asked. When she nodded, he placed it above the baby. "Brigid also said you'd tried to get rid of the child."

"Yes. You saved it. I was watching your joust. I was overlaid on you—felt what you felt and did what you did. When you vomited, so did I. You confirmed yourself in the way of the warrior, and I swerved back in the last moment. Now, we're on separate roads."

Tristan blinked in thought. "Yes, separate roads. Still, Morgan," he looked into her eyes, "I never loved anyone before you."

"Nor I before you," she said. She bent down and kissed him, a parting kiss. "I'll be heading out just behind you. But from here on, our feet carry us apart."

"I know."

"The roads are opening. Spring waits at the door."

"Where will you go?"

"North, to Traprain Law and my sister, Morgause. I have the mysteries of Gaea to teach there." She glanced around the little cottage. "I'll miss this place. And I'll miss you. Goodbye, Tristan of Dor."

He nodded, and his voice was husky. "Farewell, Morgan le Fey."

14

Traprain Law

Morgan crested a hill and reined in her horse. The lowlands of Lothian spread before her, a patchwork of pastures, fields, and woodlands. Hedgerows bounded each plot, and where river and road crossed, villages were stitched into the fabric of the earth. Walls of fieldstone or wattle and daub rose to roofs in thatch, or the occasional church topped with slate. These settlements were far enough north of Hadrian's Wall to escape the border reivers, but far enough south of the highlands to be warm and rich. Nestled in the center of it all stood the castle Morgan sought—Traprain Law.

"At last," she breathed, rubbing her stomach.

It had been a long road, and perilous. At six months, the babe in her was visible to all. A lone, pregnant noblewoman in the wilds had been too succulent a prize for brigands to resist. Morgan had taught them restraint. For blood magic, she kept a small wound ready on the back of her hand. A quick bite would bring blood into her mouth, and with it she could spit fire on the attackers. Only one man had been immolated entirely—the first man. Then rumors spread of the dragon woman who rode alone on a phantom steed. Her belly was full of serpent's eggs and her mouth of brimstone. The kinder wags had called her Melusine, the poor, fated half-faerie dragon who fled her beloved. They were close to right. The unkind ones had said she was the Mother of the Beast. Those rumors brought companies on horseback, with lancers and archers and even exorcists. To escape them, it had been better simply to slip the world away and linger awhile on the red roads of fey.

Still, Morgan had feared to stay long. Time twisted on the ley-line highways, and for a babe in the womb, time was life. She didn't want this child so horribly conceived to be horribly born. So, she had ridden, pregnant through a pregnant land. The ground swelled with crops, and the towns with news of a king: Arthur. He had been declared at Canterbury and was to be crowned at Caerleon. Arthur. Bastard brother, the get of a rapist, as her own child would be. Morgan had fled the southlands just in time. In Traprain Law, she would be safe from Arthur, safe to bear her babe.

She bent down to stroke the bay gelding, a gift from Mother Brigid of Glastonbury Abbey. He had been a good beast and seemed to know her state. "Have you a final gallop in you?" she whispered in his ear. "Surely, if I can bear it, you can." She clicked her tongue, and the gelding set off at a run.

Morgan stood in the stirrups, her face forward and bright as she drank in the morning air. Hedgerows rolled past her, and the land opened like a blooming flower. It was good to ride this way, fast and carefree after months of skulking. She dashed through the town below Traprain Law, passing a cooper's shop and startling two men off their haunches. They shouted something after her, but she fled away, across the river and up the thistle-thick hillside. Palisaded earthworks ringed the castle, though their gates stood open in this time of peace. The horse galloped over the humpbacked road and slowed to a stop at the castle gates.

A guard emerged from the conic house nearby. He sucked his fingertips, and remnants of food hung in his beard. "What're you after?" he asked, eyes squinting in a red face.

"I've come to see Queen Morgause of Lothian."

"Petitions are Thursdays."

"I'm her sister."

The man laughed, wiping his hands on his trews. "Her sister's a witch! Better come up with a different story."

Morgan bit the back of her hand and spat fire, setting a bush aflame. It crackled as it burned.

The guard goggled. "Uh, I'll let her know you're here." Without turning his back, he retreated into the guardhouse, grabbed a horn, and blew. Morgan recognized the tones as a royal summons, though it was played with such urgency it seemed an alarm. Dogs in the bailey took up the cry, and men began to shout.

"Open the gates," Morgan commanded quietly. The guard pretended not to hear, intent on his playing, until she added, "Or else."

"Open the gates!" he cried. "Open in the name of the queen's sister!" He strode to the portcullis and gripped it as if he could lift it by fear alone. "Open in the name of all that's holy!"

Morgan smiled. She was not often equated with "all that's holy."

With the horn in one hand and the gate in the other, the guard played and yanked and cursed. At last, the portcullis slid skyward, and Morgan rode placidly beneath. Even her horse seemed to enjoy the moment, stepping high through the dark passage.

They emerged in a courtyard aboil. Armsmen ran down from the parapets, dragging swords from their sheaths. Porters fled from the wagon they had been unloading. A priest emerged, a great cross gleaming in his hand like a dagger. Best of all were Queen Morgause and King Lot, who ran from their breakfast in the great hall. Lot had a piece of egg clinging to his trews.

They were a stately couple, nearly twenty years older than Morgan. Lot's severe face was framed in black hair and beard, salted with gray. He wore a samite shirt and trews and a vest of wool. Beside him, Morgause might have been beautiful under her piled brown hair if she weren't scowling. Her anger was bolstered by bowstrings drawn all around.

Morgan held out her hand and said pleasantly, "Hello, Sister."

"What are you doing here?" Morgause asked.

Morgan pulled her cloak gently back. "I need help," she said quietly.

Her sister stared at the spot and pursed her lips. "Really, Morgan, you parade around as if it were something to be proud of."

"I was raped."

Morgause blinked. "Breathing fire. Blighting crops. Dancing with demons. . . ." She shook her head. "It was bad enough when we thought you were just a she-dragon. Now we know you're my sister."

There was no sense disabusing her. Fear had gotten Morgan into the castle, and fear would keep her here. "I've come to stay and wait out my pregnancy."

Morgause blanched, her mouth dropping open. "Oh, you must be fooling."

Stepping down from the horse, Morgan bowed her head and bent her knee. "Sister, I'm asking sanctuary. Were I your worst enemy—"

Morgause muttered under her breath.

"—you would have to take me in. But I'm your sister. Do you dare spurn the ancient rites of hospitality?"

Morgause grew paler still. She must have heard the implicit threat. "Do I dare spurn the Gospel of Our Lord and share my house with a—" she stopped, fear hemming in her words.

"A what? A whore? I was a virgin until I was raped. How has the sin committed against me become my sin? And if you think I am a witch, you are wrong. And if you think me a she-dragon, you are mad. What were you going to say, Morgause?"

The woman's stony face cracked, and she reached to her husband, who supported her.

"Now, that's enough," Lot said, seeming to speak to both women. "We will of course not spurn the rites of hospitality nor the Gospel of Christ. You may stay, Morgan," Morgause's fists tightened on his jacket, and she looked pleadingly in his eyes, "but you will abide by the Word of the One True God while you remain here."

"Yes," said Morgause, seeming to find her voice. "That means no magic, no fornication or adultery, no stealing or cursing—"

"I know the commandments," Morgan said. "I swear to you, King Lot, I'll abide these rules while I stay."

Something changed in Morgause. She stared with new

eyes at her prodigal sister. "Oh, Morgan, I've prayed for you for years, that you would turn from your wickedness. Maybe this is the right thing, the will of the Lord."

"I feel I've been drawn here," Morgan replied placidly. "There's much to be done."

"Yes," agreed Morgause. She walked to her sister and laid hands on her shoulders. "Much to be done."

Morgan's room was amusing, a little-used chapel with a fresco of Christ calming the waters. The castellan had placed her cot beneath it so that Morgan would look up into that beatific face and those upraised hands. Perhaps the hope was that he could calm her as well. The chapel had a door, thankfully, but no bolt, and whatever implements of silver might have adorned the altar were gone before Morgan was allowed in.

Dinner was even more amusing. Morgause sat at one end of a long table and Lot at the other. Morgan sat equidistant between them, as if they had positioned her chair using a ten-foot pole. Directly across from her sat the four sons of Lot—Gawain, Gaheris, Agravain, and Gareth—two of them older and one younger than she. Agravain was the same age.

"Strange that Mum and Grandmum were up to the same thing at the same time," he quipped above a plate of river prawns.

"What was that?" Morgause asked shrilly.

"Just talking about hobbies, Mum," Agravain said with a wry smile. "Seems Grandmum likes to knit as much as you do."

Morgause gave a stiff smile. "She does more needlepoint, but she taught me what I know. We're both good with our hands."

Agravain hunched down, pretending to choke on a prawn, and pounded his chest. Morgan liked this jokester. She liked all her nephews. Gawain was proud, and rightly so, of his arctoid body and leonine mane. Gaheris was slight and a natural flirt. He'd been nudging Morgan's toes throughout the first course. Agravain was the jester, and Gareth the starry-eyed dreamer.

"Knit one, pearl two," Agravain muttered, wiping back his tears.

Lot sniffed. His fork and knife lurked like a pair of vultures above his lamb shank. "Have you thought of any names yet, Morgan?"

Swallowing a chunk of apple, Morgan said, "I haven't thought that far."

"It's difficult when you don't know who the father is," Morgause said.

Morgan nodded. "Yes. Our mother said the same. Of course, eventually she found out the rapist was Uther and named her son Arthur."

Agravain's eyes flew open, and he shot a look at his mother, not wanting to miss her expression. It was a rare sight. Her mouth had dropped open with food still in it. Her hand quivered, tossing droplets of sauce from her vacated fork. Agravain grinned and looked the other direction to his father, who scowled.

"That bastard's no brother of my wife," Lot said. "Not even a half-brother."

"Don't be embarrassed, Mother," Agravain broke in, pretending to soothe. "Mary did the same naming Jeshua after Jehovah."

Morgause dropped her fork, and it clattered to the floor. "That's the sort of blasphemy I feared you'd bring under my roof, Morgan—"

Gawain said, "It's not her fault. Agravain's been saying worse for years."

"I gave up murder. Blasphemy seems tame," Agravain replied.

As Morgause and her sons launched into what was clearly a longstanding debate, Morgan considered Lot. He fumed, his eyes focused on no one in the room. Here was a potential ally, and a way to solidify her position in Lothian.

Morgan said, "I don't mean to speak against Arthur, brother or no, but how can he hope to hold the throne without an army?"

"That's it," Lot said, pointing at her as though he could gather her words on his finger. "That's just it. Arthur can *claim* the throne, but can he hold it? Any man can steal something that's not his, but not every man can hold onto it." His teeth locked fiercely.

"Look at these four strong sons," Morgan said. "Here's more army than Arthur has."

"That's no exaggeration," Lot replied. "Each is a fine warrior, each could lead a legion. That'd be twenty-four thousand!"

Agravain stared openmouthed at his father. "Where are you going to get twenty-four thousand? You'd have to enlist every troglodyte and termite."

Lot gestured dismissively. "There's a legion worth of footmen in Gododdin, and a few hundred cavalry."

"Some of them would have to ride pigs," murmured Agravain.

"And from Dalriada and Rheged—there's another legion. We bring the highlands and the islands in, and there's the rest."

"The great kings of the north," Morgan tossed out casually, as if flinging oil on a fire.

"The Great Kings of the North," Lot repeated.

"You'll never do it," Gawain said. "Gather an army and march it down there."

"He has to march down there anyway," Morgan broke in. "He has to go to Caerleon and pledge fealty. He'll be taking treasure to give the new king—and a large enough force to keep the treasure safe. . . ." Silence descended around the table. "One way or another, your father will be marching an army to Caerleon." She turned to pin Lot with her eyes. "The question is what he'll do with that army once he gets there."

Lot had nothing to say. His gaze was focused beyond the stone walls of Traprain Law.

"Enough of this monstrous talk," Morgause said. She wore a mask of calm. "First blasphemy, and now treason."

Agravain said, "He's not king yet, Mum. It's not treason until he's king—if he's ever king. And what's the harm in gathering the Great Kings of the North to go together to the coronation? Until the parade of fealty, it could go either way. Da wouldn't have to know what he would do until he was standing right there before Arthur, doing it."

"Eat your prawns."

That night, Morgan ascended the highest tower of the castle. She wanted to see the moonrise. It signaled the gathering of her inner village—the wise woman, the warrior, the healer, midwife Meg, and all the other goddesses within and around her. All her life, Morgan had heard their voices, and now she was their priestess. They had guided her on the trail—they and the child within her—and she needed their counsel to-night.

Morgan climbed a dark spiral, the arrow loops spilling their slim trails of moonlight across the steps. The hatch above hung open, and Morgan climbed through to an empty lookout. Traprain Law was at peace, though it would not be so much longer.

Morgan went to the eastern window and saw the moon—a waxing gibbous, great and oblong. It was shaped like Morgan, going through the same swelling cycle. She smiled to see it, and sensed the smile of the village within her.

"It's me again, my friends," Morgan whispered, gazing on the great orb. "We've quit the trail and come to roost." The castle spread below her, rectilinear and masculine beneath the round heavens. "It's no home, but a refuge, for now. I need your counsel to make it more. King Lot has voiced a—"

Someone ascended the dark stairs. Morgan drew a quick breath and pressed herself against the wall. She closed her eyes, struggling to see the leys as they passed this place. Not a single red strand came through. The wound on the back of her hand ached, as if sensing what would come.

"Who is it?" she hissed.

It is a man, answered the warrior woman.

A dangerous man, said the healer.

All men are dangerous, the wise woman added.

In the stillness beyond Morgan, the only answer was the creeping tread of boots.

"Who is it!" Morgan said in a clear voice.

A man's head poked through the hatch, black hair and beard framing it. "It's me, Morgan," said King Lot. "I fol-lowed you here."

Morgan's heart pounded. *Why would he follow you?* asked the healer. *Rolus followed you to a tree,* said the warrior woman. *Don't let him near you.* "What do you want?"

Lot paused, taken aback. "To talk." He climbed into the room.

Morgan stayed by the window. "Then talk."

The king wrung his hands in the darkness. "Is it true what they say . . . about your magic?"

"I'm no devil."

"No, I don't mean that. I mean about your power—that you can do things no one can do, see things, know things. They say you're like Merlin."

The voices in her head snarled in derision. Morgan snorted. "Merlin is mad."

"He's making a king of Arthur," Lot replied. "He's making a bastard boy without an army into a king." He moved to the southern window and stared out toward Hadrian's Wall. "I'm a man, and legitimate, a king with army—but I don't have a Merlin."

She breathed more easily. *Desire makes men dangerous,* the wise woman said. *Now you know his desires.* "I'm not a Merlin. I'm Morgan."

"Yes, yes," Lot said impatiently. "But can your magic do what Merlin's does?"

"It can. And some things he can't do," Morgan replied. "But I've sworn I will do no magic while I'm here."

Lot smiled. In the darkness, his teeth looked like pearls. "I release you from that oath, on one condition."

"Name it."

"That we can speak more about the Great Kings of the North."

15

Deliverance

Summer came, bringing morning fog and afternoon heat. Through them both, Morgan labored.

Sweat stippled her skin and soaked her nightshirt. Muscles clenched, and hands and teeth. For thirty-six hours, she had endured false labor—painful but unproductive. Now, the labor was true.

"Anwyn," Morgan whispered to the maidservant. She was only six, the same age Morgan had been when Arthur was delivered. "It's time. Get the midwife."

Anwyn ran out the door.

Morgan flopped on the cot. Arching her back and rolling from side to side, she laughed miserably. She knew what poor Anwyn was thinking: Will this happen to me? The answer, of course, was yes.

Meg, where are you? Her spirit was never truly far away. She had been there during the violence of conception and was here now for the violence of birth. Meg couldn't ease pain or prevent atrocity, but she could watch, and Morgan longed to know that she watched. Meg, do you see?

The contraction eased. Enervated, Morgan lay supine on the cot. She stared up past her knees to Jesus. He held his arms up in an encouraging way, but his eyes were wide with dread.

Morgan rolled to her side. Christ's watchfulness was less comforting than Meg's. Any man's attention would have been like sun on a sunburn. Morgan closed her eyes, but her mind's eye saw shoulders against rusty leaves, avid faces looming above her, bodies moving in that repeated stabbing motion. She blinked away the memory and stared at the chapel wall. There was something demonic in men. They had cheered. It had been sport to them, hounds on a fox. They had done the same to Rolus—applauded as he twisted and died on the impaling tree. Men were simultaneously demonic and childish, like a pack of boys setting fire to a chick.

Over the last few months, Morgan had fostered that demonic childishness. She had helped Lot foment war against Arthur. Lot had gone out to visit his neighbors, the Great Kings of the North. He took along blackberry wine, a specialty of Lothian, and gave a bottle to each ruler. They did not know that each glass held a drop of witch's blood, but as they drank, they became thirsty for more. Bloodthirsty. They swallowed and listened, and through mouth and ear, war was conceived in them.

Morgan cringed at the thought. Yes, Arthur would champion the Age of War. Yes, he would keep Avalon locked away. Yes, he was her foe, and only his death would allow her vision to bloom into being. Still, these were only elaborate justifications for murder. Arthur was a mere boy, her half-brother, and yet she wanted him dead.

Desire is the culprit. It drives men and women both. Divine and demonic, desire is the best and worst of humanity.

Before Morgan could answer the wise woman, a needling tightness began in her sides. It felt like a rash at first, though in moments it spread across her belly. Her muscles snapped taut, and a terrible ache set in below. It was the next contraction, and she would be dilating. After assisting Meg in so many deliveries, Morgan knew what these things meant, but it was different to feel it all.

Footsteps came down the hall, leather shushing on the stone floor. The chapel door flung open, barking on a shrine near the wall. In strode a midwife who could not have been more different from Meg. She was short, gray, and slight, with eager hands and strides too long for her wiry legs. If she hadn't lifted the hem of her skirt, she would have ripped it. Despite her age, she moved with amazing energy. Behind her came a passel of lesser women bearing the sheets, spirits, and implements of the procedure. An efficient finger jabbed toward the altar, the benches, the baptismal font, the lectern—and women fanned out to prepare the room.

"No . . . baptism . . ." Morgan growled.

The midwife glanced at her. She had accomplished all these arrangements with silent insistence and now strode up to Morgan. "How are you?"

In the grips of a strong contraction, Morgan couldn't respond except by shaking her head.

The midwife nodded sternly. "I'm Roena." She turned away to snap small commands to her darting troops.

Meg, why couldn't it have been you?

Roena looked at Morgan. "Are you comfortable? Do you need pillows, a broom to bite, anything?"

A broom to bite! Morgan thought bleakly, but she simply shook her head.

Roena gave the same perfunctory nod. She opened a

leather bag, beginning to draw implements from their slots. "By the way—Meg says hello."

Morgan blinked. "What?"

"Meg," Roena replied casually as she dug into the bag. "She says hello." Roena nodded toward the corner of the chapel, beside a Madonna and Child. "She's just over there."

Despite the contraction, Morgan forced herself up on her elbows and craned to see the corner. She so wished for Meg to be towering there, big like a bear. A misshapen shadow fell beside the statue of the Nativity, but it might have been simply the play of light. "You can see her?"

"Feel her," Roena responded.

"How do you know her?' asked Morgan as the contraction finally eased.

"I trained her," Roena said. "I was Morgause's midwife, and I trained Meg before I came with Morgause to Lothian."

"Then you're a—"

"Not in this house I'm not," Roena whispered with a knowing wink. "I seem to have been converted. I seem even to baptize babes when a priest is not near. Water is water, after all, even if it comes from a Pagan spring." She smiled. "Now, lie back down and stop looking for Meg. You won't see her, only feel her."

Morgan lay back down, comfortable for the first time in months. "I always call her, but I'm never sure she's there."

"She is. Or one of us. We have to be quiet. Wise women aren't well tolerated."

Spreading her hands on her swollen belly, Morgan said, "I know. That's why I'm here."

"Yes." Roena quietly circled to examine Morgan. She washed her hands, dried them, rubbed rye spirits across them, and gently began the check. "You may not realize it, but there are a number of us watching you. There's someone in every city, and in most towns."

"What are you talking about?"

"We want what you want. We've tried to bring it about one bed at a time. Did you know the Athenian women stopped a war by denying their husbands? We rule the bed too, but it isn't enough."

"I still don't know what you're saying."

"We seek the goddesses," Roena said. "We haven't magic, and all our efforts have come to nothing, but you, Morgan, you have magic—" She withdrew her hand. "You're at five fingers. Nine means it's time."

Morgan felt another contraction begin. She tensed, bracing herself for the pain. It came like thunder, and in its loud grip, she had a vision:

The skeins stretch taut, the warp of time. Between them moves the weft. She is a single thread rising above the warp to arc awhile in the tapestry's face, and then returning beneath it to arc awhile in the darkness. Always, she rises again, the same thread, the same fibers and colors but in a new position in time.

As the contraction cased, Roena leaned toward Morgan and took her hand. "Don't you have magic to dull the pain?"

Morgan shook her head. "Blood magic needs blood, and violent blood makes for violent spells." She breathed deeply. "No, I have no actual spells that will help. But even without blood, I have will, and magic is mostly will. It can remake the world."

Roena patted her arm. "I've never heard it put that way."

"I'm glad you're here," Morgan said. "And I'm glad Meg is too. I don't feel alone anymore."

The old woman looked pleased. "Tell me more of your magic. . . ."

When she heard Anwyn rush by, calling for the midwife, Morgause rose quietly from her knitting chair and strode out into the hall. Her gait was always stately and self-assured, especially when she headed for the crypt beneath the old chapel.

At the hall's end stood a door of banded oak. Morgause reached into a pocket on her bodice, drew out the large iron key, and opened the lock. With no more sound than a rustle of samite, she slid into the musty space. She pulled the door closed and locked it again before descending the stair.

The crypt was cold and dark, but Morgause knew the way. To either side opened niches where lay the long-dead ancestors of Lot. All had gone to bones, with the occasional hunk of hair or set of fingernails. Morgause was not interested in the dead, but in the living.

She came to the groin vault where the center tile had broken through, where even whispers in the chapel echoed plainly. There, among the moldering dead, Morgause stood and listened to her sister and the midwife.

"Oh, Lord in heaven," she murmured.

Morgause fell to her knees on the floor and leaned over, heaving breaths into the dust. Still she could hear the demonic rituals, the Christ-hating harlotry. Such sins could not go unpunished.

The sounds of labor intensified. The woman-monster was giving birth to a child-monster, and all the while Morgause lay dying below.

———

"Once more, now, Morgan," Roena said. The old woman seemed to be sweating in sympathy with her, hands slick with blood and water.

Biting on the broomstick, Morgan set her heels on the pallet and gave a final great push.

"The head is out!" Roena cried. She held on gently and pulled.

The rest of the baby followed in a sudden gush. Its hair was pasted to its head, its skin was purple with white patches, and blood crazed its body. The baby's arms and feet drooped, no longer contained, and it wailed.

Morgan laughed.

Roena pulled the child to her belly and wiped him. It was a boy, the scrotum swollen and purple beneath the kinked umbilicus. With one hand, Rocna wrapped a leather thong around the cord and cinched it tight. Then she cut just beyond the thong. She dropped the umbilicus and most of the afterbirth into a waiting bucket. With another swift motion, she wrapped the shivering child in a swaddling cloth.

"He's a boy," Roena said, smiling. She brought him to his mother, who lay weeping on the bed.

"He's beautiful," Morgan said, seeing past the mottled skin and conic skull, past the vernix and blood.

Roena peered gladly at mother and child. "What will his name be?"

Taking a deep breath, Morgan replied, "Mabon."

"Ahh," Roena said. "The eternal youth, firstborn of the sky-goddess, Modron."

Morgan nodded. "The firstborn of goddess worshipers."

———

Mabon changed everything. All Morgan's life had driven toward his birth, though she hadn't ever known it until she held him in her arms. She had been torn apart by Mark's men, and then by this child, but now she was whole.

Mabon shared Morgan's cot, her warmth, her milk. They slept at the same times and woke at the same times. Mabon needed her, but Morgan needed him even more.

Lot's family came to see the new child. Morgause said an unwanted prayer over the baby's head. Gawain approved his heft, and Gaheris cooed that he wanted ten such sons. Agravain, in his usual fashion, said he was more interested in planting babies than harvesting them. Gareth merely smiled, a child himself. Even Jesus seemed to lift his arms as if to say, "Well, why not?"

Out of horror and destruction, Morgan had borne a perfect creature into the world. Here was true power. Nothing mattered except him. Morgan was in bliss. She had found her Garden of Delights—anyplace that she and Mabon shared.

Only at night did she fear, dreaming he was gone. She would lurch awake and claw out to find him. When she did, Morgan would nurse him until they both fell back to sleep. I'll never be alone again, she would tell herself placidly, timing the words with each draw of milk. The words would slow and taper to nothing, and mother and child would rest together on the cot.

Morgan drifted slowly up from sleep. She let her dreams flit away like fleeing fish. Her body was buoyed on wakefulness, and she surfaced. Overhead, the chapel roof creaked with nighttime wind. Morgan sighed. She moved her arm to find Mabon, but the spot that should have held him was cold and empty.

"Mabon!"

Morgan sat up, heart thundering, and told herself this was just another dream, but she knew better. She searched the blankets, the cot, beneath it. There was no sign of him. She crawled through the chapel. Not beneath the benches, not among the vestments, not with the cup and plate of the Eucharist. She shoved back the altar, overturning anything that might hide a baby. He was gone as if he had never been. Her whole world was gone.

"Mabon!" she sobbed. "Mabon!"

Morgan clawed a jackstraw from the case and lit it in the embers of the fire. She carried the flame to an oil lamp on the wall. Light poured across the mess she'd made. She tore through it again, but he was not there. The voices in her head argued, but none knew where the boy had gone. Morgan stared bleakly at Christ above the stormy sea, and he lifted his hands in a shrug.

She rushed to the chapel door and threw it open. "Help me," she cried, hardly remembering who lived in this castle. "Someone help me! Mabon is gone!"

16

Torches

Delirious, Morgan staggered down the hallway. Terror still drove her, the spasms of panic amalgamated into this single trembling stride. She was going to get help. "Someone," she muttered, trying to assemble the scraps of thought that tumbled in her mind, "someone who lives here . . . Sister . . . Morgause. She'll help . . . and King Lot."

That's where I am, in the castle of King Lot in the North—in Traprain Law, in Lothian. But where is Mabon?

Dark windows flashed past, the panes splitting starlight and throwing it on the floor. Morgan stomped through it. The moon wouldn't be out tonight, trysting with the sun beneath the world. Tonight of all nights!

"Morgause! Morgause, help!" Morgan shouted. She had reached their bedchamber and gripped the deep-carved door. For a moment, her fingers probed the wood, as if the relief might hide her son. Then she found the handle and flung the door open. The room beyond was black and fresh with night wind. "Morgause! Help!"

The woman let out a yelp, and linens rustled. "What? What is it?"

"Mabon," Morgan blurted, and she dashed tears from her eyes. "He's gone."

"What do you mean, gone?" Morgause hissed. "From magic, you mean? A spell gone bad?"

"No! No spell. I swear it. I slept with him in my arms, and now he's gone."

More rustling, and footsteps on creaking wood. "How could that be?" A jackstraw flared at the hearth. Morgause's face was a yellow ghost lingering near it. She lit a candle and set a glass chimney over it. "Have you checked beneath the cot?"

"Everywhere. The cot, the altar, the closet, the benches. . . ."

"He can't have just disappeared," Morgause said, approaching. She was beautiful, even fresh from bed, and her eyes were feverish in the candle light. "Unless an incubus came to you—"

"No incubus!"

Morgause shrugged in apology. "They say Merlin was born from an incubus. I just thought maybe magic people—"

"What's happening?" growled Lot groggily.

"Mabon is gone," Morgan said, passing her sister and rushing to the bedside. "We have to wake the castle, search everywhere. Someone knows something."

The king sat up, gathering the bedclothes around him. "Morgan, I'm naked."

"I'll round up the staff and question them," Morgause said decisively. She lit a second candle. "Someone will know something. Morgan, you go look again. We can't wake the whole house if it was just a nightmare. If you don't find him, come to the kitchens. Lot, get yourself dressed and meet us there. You might have to rouse the garrison if we end up searching beyond the castle—"

"Beyond the castle!" Lot groused. "Morgause, don't you think that's a little too far—"

"No. We have to take care of this tonight. Whatever my sister needs from us, we'll give. Whatever it takes to resolve this—"

"To find Mabon, you mean."

"Yes. To find him." Morgause lit a third candle and handed it to Morgan. "Go, now, so my husband can dress."

"Yes," Morgan agreed, taking the candle. "Anything. Just hurry! If someone took him—" She couldn't finish.

A dread burned in Morgan. What if the Unseelie Court had taken her son, a changeling or a hostage? Would true baptism have stopped them? Was this repayment for all her dabbling? Who would've wanted Mabon? Someone had taken him, someone or something. . . .

Numbly, Morgan headed out the door. "In the kitchen, then. . . ." She staggered down the hall. With each breath she softly sobbed, "Mabon . . ."

King Lot watched her go, and he shook his head sadly. "What do we do for the poor creature?"

Morgause slowly closed the door, its black bulk eclipsing her sister. "All her life, she's been playing with fire. Now, it's burning her up."

"So you think it's her magic?" the king asked, crossing to his armoire.

"Of course. What else?"

Pulling on a chemise, Lot said, "Poor child."

"Yes. I fear she's lost forever."

Under a moonless sky, the group trudged across the bailey. Cooks and maidservants followed King Lot and Queen Morgause, who in turn followed Morgan and Roena, who followed a stable boy.

"Right here's where I first spotted 'im," the boy said excitedly, pointing to a wedge of light cast by the stable lantern. "Crossin' here, big billowy robes and gray hair. I never saw a fellow like that so I stopped soaping the reins and went out after. He was fast, coming down along here," he continued as he followed a track the castle dogs had worn down to a rain puddle. "He was kind of half-shadow, and it was hard to follow him along the ivy. Then he came here." The lad stopped beside the postern gate, a great round stone that could be levered aside to let folk escape the castle.

"The postern gate," Morgan growled, glaring at the spot. The infant Arthur had been spirited away through a postern gate.

"Did you see the baby?" asked Roena.

"No," the stable boy said, "but the man had big robes. He could've had a baby in there. I'd've tried to stop him if I knew he had a baby."

Through clenched teeth, Morgan said, "Merlin."

Roena placed her hand on Morgan's arm and whispered. "Is that how it really feels? I don't sense magic in this. Do you?"

"I don't know," Morgan replied, shrugging off the hand. "But Merlin could have done it; he would have done it if Arthur asked him to."

"Rouse the garrison," Morgause said to Lot. "Horses and torches. We'll scour the countryside. Maybe he's still nearby."

Morgan nodded grimly and turned from the group. She

stalked back along their trail, passed the wedge of light that had betrayed the kidnapper, and strode into the stables. Her favorite gelding waited in the third stall. Snatching up halter and rein, Morgan gently slapped the beast's rump to wake him up. She fit bit, blanket, and saddle, and pulled the drowsy horse from his stall out into the night. She mounted.

Morgause shouted, "Open the gates for the sister of the queen!" and she and Lot approached from behind. They had gotten torches somewhere and handed one to Morgan.

She took it without a word and rode from their midst toward the yawning portcullises.

"We'll bring the garrison," pledged King Lot. "We'll scour the countryside and find your boy."

Stiff-backed, Morgan cantered beneath the gates. Her torch lit the throat of stone, and then she was swallowed in voracious night.

A yank on one rein sent the gelding off the road and along the footings of the wall. Without kicking him, Morgan brought him to a gallop. The tight pressure of her trembling legs had conveyed her urgency. Around the buttresses they went, beneath guard towers where men argued about what went on, and to the postern gate, where she drew the horse to a stop.

This was the castle's anus, tucked up between walls, a dark and unmentioned hole in otherwise impenetrable stone. A man had emerged there, living filth. His boots had wiped the dew from the grass in a straight line from gate to woods.

This time, she did kick the gelding. Her torch fluttered flaglike above her head as she bore down the path. Still holding the reins, Morgan bit the back of her hand. In the last two months, she had let the wound heal over, using Lot's blood for most of the works of war. Only a scar had remained until that brutal bite. A flap of skin came loose, and blood ran, cupric, onto her tongue. She lifted her hand and painted her forehead with the stuff, thick so that it would run down and fill her eyes. Unblinking, she let the rivulets gather. This was not a spell so much as an act of desperation. Blood scrying. It should show her whatever magic was at work hereabouts.

Morgan and her horse burst into the forest along the trodden path. Her sanguine vision showed faerie rings here and there—perhaps a dozen. Power glowed from the mushroom circles, the rising soul of whatever dead thing lay below. But even if Mabon lay in a shallow grave—oh, she gasped to think of it!—the toadstools would not yet have risen to feed off him.

Morgan rode on along the trammeled way. More magic lurked in a hollow tree ahead, home to a colony of sprites. They buzzed up to see who came, and Morgan would have thought them only gnats except for her scrying. The tiny faeries swarmed her as she passed, tasting her skin and knowing her grief, but their gnat-song held nothing of Mabon.

She was missing something, something about all of this. Why would Merlin walk all this way? Why not fly or simply vanish one place and appear another? Wouldn't his breath have left a glow on the bark? Wouldn't his magical trail be clear before her?

Ahead stood a sacred grove of oaks, whose dryad souls were older than Rome. They had survived the millennial fire that had leveled the wood two hundred years before and now were giants among dwarfs.

"Mabon." Morgan rode up between their knees and halted. "Mabon, my son, the Eternal Youth. Have you seen him?" They shook their shaggy heads and whispered behind leafy hands. "Merlin, then. Did he pass this way?" To that, the spirits of the wood were silent. Morgan rode on.

The land dipped, a carpet of humus down to a wide-running river. There was more magic here: naiads in their eddies, selkies and their otter kin, and the river's own spirit. Morgan lifted her torch and charged down the slope. Why would he come here? The gelding splashed into the stream, and water rose, cool and clear, up to his shoulders.

"I need you, spirits of river and wood," Morgan said. "My son is gone. Stolen. His kidnapper might have passed here. Have you seen him?" Only a watery chortle answered. These fey were her people, and she wielded their power, but they did not yet trust her. "Won't you help me?" She held out her bleeding hand. "What must I do?" Not a soul responded. Even the river grew silent.

Tears washed away the blood and her scrying sight. The woods lost all their red tracers of magic. Morgan let her torch slump and fall, and it hissed in the river before floating away. All was blackness.

"He's gone," she told herself. "I'll never find him now." She sat her horse there in the tide and wished to die with Mabon.

In the terrible distance, lights appeared among the trees. They were not faerie fire but yellow flames on black torches. The other searchers were coming. They called out his name and her name and the names of Merlin and Jesus. Lot had been true to his word. They would scour the forest, but Mabon would not be found. He had been stolen from her as surely as Arthur had been stolen from Igraine.

Morgan waited for the searchers and the sun. Her heart, for three days full, was barren now.

"It's all right, Sister," Morgause said gently. She wrapped a white bandage around Morgan's hand. "We don't want to lose you."

Late sunlight stabbed through the chapel windows, and red light bled on the floor beside her cot. Someone had put the furnishings back in order. "I'm already lost." Morgan lay on her back and clutched the edges of the cot as if it were plunging.

Morgause seemed almost pleased. "There's hope for the lost, Morgan. You can find your way back. Find your way back, Morgan."

Morgan closed her eyes, shaking her head.

Her sister leaned over her. "Look at you." She stroked her forehead. "You've painted yourself in blood."

"I was looking for him," Morgan said. "It was a spell. My blood showed me magic in the air." She stared accusingly at her sister and saw herself reflected in the woman's troubled eyes.

"You've always had visions, Morgan, I know that. They've always been completely real to you. If I had visions like yours, I would probably believe what you believe—"

Morgan nodded, gripping her sister's hand, "Yes, you would!"

Gently, Morgause patted the bandaged fingers. "But the truth is that no one has the visions you have. No one believes them except you."

Morgan's eyes narrowed. "That's not true. For one, there's Meg—"

"Meg?"

"Yes, the midwife at Tintagel."

"Oh, yes, Meg. Mother wrote about Meg. She said you

kept referring to this person who didn't exist. There was no midwife at Tintagel, Morgan. There never was a Meg."

Shaking her head, Morgan laughed bitterly. "Of course there's a Meg. Roena trained her. Ask Roena."

Morgause's face dropped. "Oh, now you're just being cruel."

"What are you talking about?"

"Didn't you hear? Didn't you know? She died last night, out searching for you. She fell off a ledge and broke her neck."

Morgause went very white. "No!"

"Yes. Another of your mad escapades. Mother complained bitterly of them. She said you would climb naked through the caves, would slit the throats of the castle animals, would cut yourself and scream at all hours."

"You're lying."

"Shall I show you the letters? I have them all. Twenty years of them. She spoke to me more in writing than she spoke to you face to face, and why? Because of these visions and voices . . . these delusions."

Morgan's eyes grew watery. "How could you be so vicious?"

Morgause shifted, as if to stand, but then settled again on the stool. "No, it would be cruel to show the letters."

"Letters prove nothing. Mother has her own delusions— too frail to see through a disguise, too deluded to admit she's been raped—"

"You're fixated on rape!" Morgause interrupted hotly. "You think everyone's raping everyone. Couldn't father have had a last night with Mother? Couldn't Arthur be his son? Does it all have to be so sinister? Everyone else saw Father, and only you saw Uther—"

"Only I see the truth!"

"Yes, and only you see antlers on Arthur's head—Mother wrote me about that. He doesn't have horns, Morgan. He's not a monster!" Morgause softened her tone. "Listen, we all see what we want to see. The difference is, you want to see horrible things."

Morgan set her jaw. "Avalon isn't horrible. I've taken people there—a host of twenty people."

Morgause shook her head slowly. "Not according to them."

"What about Tristan? He saw Avalon. He avenged my honor, and he loves me."

"Then why isn't he with you?" Morgause asked.

"He chose the warrior's way—"

"No. He's not with you because he thinks you're mad."

Morgan stared at her. "That's not *true*."

"There never was a rape, Morgan. Tristan found you in the tree, bleeding, claiming you'd been raped. He did everything you asked, even took you to Glastonbury, a three-day journey. He waited by your bed while you languished in coma, spoke to you though you were delirious. He even rode back to Dor and challenged his former master, saying the man had raped you. They fought to the death, and Tristan prevailed, only to learn that Rolus couldn't have raped you."

"What do you mean?"

"Rolus had been a Roman slave. He was a eunuch, Morgan."

"What? What about the others?"

"There were no others. No one raped you."

Clutching her head in misery, Morgan said, "If I wasn't raped, where did Mabon come from?"

"Precisely," Morgause said. "Where?"

Morgan gaped. "What are you saying?"

"You've been claiming to be pregnant ever since you came, Morgan, but the pregnancy never showed. It had been ten months since the supposed rape, and still nothing. At last I sent Roena in to talk you out of it, but you went into labor and pantomimed the whole thing. It never happened. There never was a pregnancy. There never was a Mabon."

"If there was no Mabon, why was everyone out in the woods looking for him?"

"We were all looking for you, sweet child. You ranted at us, woke the whole castle, led us all over, and then hopped on a horse and rode out in the middle of the night."

"You yourself called for the gates to be opened!"

"No, Morgan. You did. They thought your voice was mine. Haven't you ever wondered why you're alone? Haven't you ever wondered why people turn away from you? Mother, Father, Uther, Tristan . . . me? It's too hard to be with you, to battle your delusions. They're killing you, Morgan, and everyone around you. You have to wake up to the truth."

"I can't wake up!" Morgan said despondently.

"Not on your own, no, but there's a way. Sit up," Morgause said. She placed her hand under Morgan's trembling shoulder and lifted her. She gestured toward the chapel's altar, where the Eucharist waited. "All things are possible through Him who loves us."

"You want me to . . ."

"Yes, Morgan. Your own blood can't save you, but His can. Go. Go to Him, Morgan. Receive and believe and be made new."

Shaking, Morgan sat. She called out for the goddesses within her, but they were silent. Were they powerless against this Christ? Were they mere delusions? Tears gathering in her eyes, Morgan stood. She took a small step toward the altar, not even trusting her own legs anymore. She shuffled slowly across the chapel. Oh, it would be good to be done with all of this. Of course it was a lie. People don't steal babies from their mother's arms. They don't rape girls in trees. They don't live in caves and make spells from their own blood. Her whole life had been a waking dream, a living nightmare.

All she had to do was drink the blood of Christ and eat his flesh and she would wake up.

Morgan stopped before the altar. She stared at the loaf and imagined a man made of bread nailed to a tree. The people of the world flew in to peck his flesh until it was gone. Even now, wild visions plagued her. Beside the loaf sat the cup, brimming with wine as red as blood. Figures moved across its surface. There was a young warrior—the boy Arthur become a man. He had an antlered head and a sword like a hunk of lightning, and with it he killed and killed. Blood poured out across the nations—not the blood of Christ, but the blood of people.

Arthur was the Son of War in the Age of War.

Morgan glanced back at her sister.

"And on the night Our Lord was betrayed, he took bread, and when he had given thanks—"

"No," Morgan interrupted. "You're the liar, not me. None of what you say is true. Meg was real. Mabon was real. My power is real. I'll save myself and you and the whole world. I *am* the Second Eve!"

Morgause's face fell, and her temples turned gray.

"I know what you're going to do. You'll forbid anyone in the castle from mentioning Mabon ever again, from even acknowledging that he once lived. You'll tell them that I'll hex anyone who speaks of my child, and no one will." Morgan said. "But I'm not mad. You cannot make me mad!"

Shaking her head, Morgause stood up and strode from the room.

17

In Another's Skin

As dawn approached, Morgan sat alone in the chapel. A single candle pushed the darkness into the corners.

She wasn't deluded. They'd removed all trace of Mabon from the chapel and the castle, but they couldn't take away the stretch marks and lactation. You made those marks with your fingernails, Morgause said, and triggered the milk. No. What of the stitches? What of the suspended periods? Minds can be mad, but not bodies.

Morgan stalked toward the altar. On it waited the bread and wine of Christ. She was hungry.

Take and eat, said the wise woman.

Morgan took them down and carried them to her cot. The bread seemed only bread, and she pulled off a hunk and ate. *Drink all of it.* The cup was certainly not filled with blood, and she drank. It would be full again soon.

Scry for him, using the very implements of your foe.

Morgan rooted through her pack to find the knife. Making a small puncture in her wrist, she gathered the vital fluid.

True blood mixed with false. When the cup brimmed, Morgan set it aside and bound her wound. Then, staring into the cup, she spoke an invocation:

"Modron, Mother, you know the one I seek. My child. My Mabon. He was stolen from me as your Mabon was stolen from you. They took even the memory of him, but I remember. Show him to me, Mother. Show me Mabon so I might save him."

The blood trembled from her touch. She set the cup on the stony floor and eased her fingers away. The cup shook even more. In planes and folds of blood, she glimpsed running feet, a burlap sack, the moonless night, and stony stairs.

Robes flash, and a gold cross on a braided cord. The man shows the sack to a woman, and she peels back the opening to hear the baby cry.

"They took him. The church spirited him away!"

The man strips him bare and plunges him into a cold bowl— once for Father, once for Son, and once for Holy Ghost. He screams all the while and chokes on the water.

"They baptized him," Morgan said bleakly.

Then, there is a hayrick, the child swaddled and lying like Christ in the hay or Moses in the bulrushes. The farmer sets out, and Mabon rides away into the night. In place of his mother's finger, he clutches that same metal cross.

"Where, though?" Morgan pressed. "Where did they take him?"

The chalice shuddered. Its base rattled on the stone floor. The blood, once contained, spilled red blots all around it. The eye of the grail was failing.

"Why? Is it because of the baptism? Is it because he's wrapped in Christ?"

As if in answer, the cup flipped. Blood spattered the chapel floor. The chalice rolled away, its metal chattering. It came to a halt beside a leg of the cot, and all was silent.

"They've hidden him. The blood of Christ is stronger than my blood," said Morgan grimly. She stared at the sanguine mess and saw something else:

A beautiful thing hovers above the Lake of Avalon—a glorious, jewel-studded scabbard. It holds an elegant great sword, but the scabbard is the thing. It shines. Anyone who bears it cannot bleed. Here is an item of great goddess power, hiding a sword that is the weapon of Christ. Just as the eternal youth is wrapped in Christian power, the Sword of the Spirit is wrapped in goddess magic.

Morgan wanted that scabbard and sword. "What is its name, Mother Modron?"

The name came to her as easily as her own: Rhiannon. It was the name of a goddess whose son was stolen when three days old. The name of the sword came too, though Morgan had never heard of it before—Excalibur.

A hand reaches above the waves and snatches up that sword and scabbard—the hand of Arthur. He has them already. With these two great weapons, he will be invincible. Here is the sword that will carve its way across Britannia and the continent. Here is the scabbard that will keep Arthur alive and unharmed

"Without them, he'll fall. With them, I'll find Mabon," said Morgan quietly as the blood-pool drained away to nothing. "Thank you, Mother. Thank you, Modron."

In the crypt below the chapel, Morgause had to stifle a cry as blood poured blindingly into her eye.

———

For two months, Morgan lived alone in a crowded castle. Soon, she would be just plain alone.

They had made all the preparations without her. Lot had mustered his retinue for the march to Caerleon and the coronation of Arthur. Morgause would go with him, and their four sons, all of whom were expected to swear fealty to the new king. None would.

All of Britannia would be at Caerleon, all the great kings of the north. Some were bringing more retinue than they precisely needed. Several hundred here and there would alarm no one until they reached the city and were several thousand. By then, it would be too late.

On the night before the company rode, a knock came on the chapel door. "Morgan, it's Lot, the king. I must speak with you."

She lay on her cot, arms empty. "Enter."

Lot pushed the door open. He was a tall black silhouette in the doorway, watchful and somewhat apologetic. Morgan did not rise, and a line of anger formed along Lot's jaw. He clenched his fists and released a long breath.

"Tomorrow, I go to start a war," Lot said without preamble.

"Good luck."

"It's your war as much as mine," Lot pressed. "You have no love for your brother."

"Half-brother," Morgan corrected.

Lot nodded, lips tight in his black beard. "And you pledged to help me with your magic, help make me king."

"I did help," Morgan replied. "The 'Great Kings of the North,' remember?"

"Yes, but the job isn't done. There's still the coronation and the battle. Your services are not complete."

"You need me." Morgan smiled sadly and sat up. "I wish I could help you, but I've gone mad."

"Your sister is the one you should speak to about that."

"Poor King Lot has lost his voice. Only his wife speaks—!"

"I speak for myself."

"Then speak for yourself. Do you remember my baby? Do you remember seeing him? Do you believe he was real?"

The king was red-faced and sorrowful. "Morgan, this isn't the time—"

"Of course it is," she snapped. She stalked angrily toward him, her finger jabbing his chest. "If you want my help, my magic, you must believe in it. You must believe in my baby. Say it, Lot."

"What should I say?"

"Say you remember Mabon. That he was real and here."

"All right," Lot hissed. "I remember. He was real and here."

Morgan studied the man's face, framed in black hair. "Morgause told you to deny it. She told you not to discuss the baby with me—"

"Of course. . . ."

"Not because I'm deluded—because she wants me to think I am."

"Yes, whatever."

Morgan ground her teeth together. "Do you want my help, Lot of Lothian?"

"Of course."

"I give it on one condition."

"Name it."

"Arthur bears a holy scabbard and sword. You must promise to capture them and grant them to me."

"Give you Excalibur?" Lot roared, laughing. "That sword's taller than you are. How are you going to wear it, let alone wield it? I'd not give up Excalibur to a little slip such as you."

She let the demeaning comment pass. "Then promise me the scabbard only. You will do all you can to gain it and will bring it safely here."

"Yes," he said with finality. "I promise. Now, will you aid me?"

This time her smile was genuine. She retreated to the cot. "Yes, though Morgause would not allow me to come."

"Of course not."

Morgan lifted a bag, set it on the cot, and drew from it a number of enspelled items: a dagger with a deep blood groove, a few vials of smoke potions, a horn that could deafen foes on the battlefield, and a ring inset with a tiny blade. "These are only trinkets of magic, small items with limited effect. The true magic will come from me, here in Traprain Law."

"How will you know what's happening? How will you direct the spells?"

"This ring," Morgan said, holding up the golden band. "This ring will tell me. Put it on and wear it always, but don't fidget with it. When you wish to call me or consult me, turn the ring gently once. The blade within will nick your finger, and the blood will link you to me." She raised her hand, showing the same sort of ring on her finger. "These will allow us to speak, and they will form a conduit through which I can shunt spells. You will be at the center of the fight, and all spell effects will emerge through you."

"What sort of effects?"

"On that score, you must trust me," Morgan replied,

refilling the bag and handing it to the king. "After all, I'm not crazy anymore. Suffice it to say, you'll have what you need when you need it."

"I will have victory over Arthur?"

Morgan shrugged. "You'll have every chance to achieve it, but you'll still have to beat him."

Smacking his fist into the opposite palm, he said. "I'll have to kill him."

"As I said."

Morgan had the run of the castle. They hadn't left her in charge, but she had taken charge. In the absence of Lot's family, Morgan was the nearest thing to royalty. She moved into their quarters, wore her sister's clothes, pored over Lot's books, and waited during the month it took the retinue to reach Caerleon.

The wait was over. The armies were encamped all around the city, seemingly in separate locations, though all the great kings of the north had massed near the Gloucester Road. Lot had gathered them already and shaken hands with each in turn. Through his ring, Morgan poured the touch of rage into them. Men who a moment before had been nestling mice now were lions in pride, prowling for a kill. That was her first spell.

Next day, when Lot had mingled among the retinue of Arthur, he shook hands with the famous mage Merlin. The spell she insinuated beneath his skin was subtler in effect but far more powerful. A malaise rose before the old man's eyes, slowly peeling his sight from the world and turning it inward. The spell numbed his body, dulled his ears, and in every way severed his slender anchors to reality. Merlin was set adrift within himself, and there was no deadlier place for him to be.

The stage had been set. Mad Merlin convalesced in his chambers. The great kings of the north gathered in the royal hall of Caerleon. Lot and Morgause stood next in line to approach Prince Arthur.

Two hundred leagues north and east, Morgan was ready. She had thrown the bolt of the royal bedchamber lest a knave interrupt her spell. She then had arranged the room to match the royal hall. In a grand chair sat an effigy of Arthur, fashioned from King Lot's clothes. Morgan stood in front of it, in Lot's position, wearing clothes like those he wore. The ring on her finger matched the ring on his. Through them, she could take control of him—speak and hear and see and act. It would not be Lot but Morgan who confronted Arthur.

She closed her eyes and saw through his. With a frisson of delight, Morgan sent her soul into his body and took it over. She felt the tall solidity of his frame, musky and muscular, the hair everywhere, as if he were half-beast. One hand held to Morgause, and Morgan tightened her grip. The ring bit into her finger.

A breath brought the scent of perfume and warm bodies in close quarters. A glance showed samite and lace and Britannia's elite. There was steel here, too, the ten great kings and she, dressed in true armor and armed to kill young Arthur.

The time had come. The previous couple had cleared away from the throne of Arthur.

Morgan stepped forward, dragging her sister along. The joy of her spell was overwhelming, and she couldn't restrain herself. "Do you know who this is, Arthur?" she snarled.

The prince had every right to look shocked by this ferocious question, but instead he smiled placidly. Blond and cocky, handsome and full-grown at sixteen, Arthur had changed much since that kiss in the stables. He'd changed much, and not at all. Arthur looked on Morgause, his half-sister, and said, "So beautiful a woman should be known to me, but she is not."

Here's a man who kisses one sister and flirts with another! "Of course you don't recognize her!" Morgan raged in the voice of Lot. "She only happens to be your sister!"

Arthur's eyes lit up, and his syrupy smile dripped only the more. "No wonder you're so lovely! We're kin! Mother told me of you, Half-sister. I met Morgan once, another beauty, but not you. And this must be your husband, the lucky King Lot."

Morgan trembled with barely concealed rage. "You are no legitimate son of Uther or Igraine, conceived in rape and born into abduction, raised who-knows-where and returned out of oblivion to lord it over all of us!"

One of Arthur's warriors—Ulfius in gray-black curls!—stepped forward to gabble, "I have proofs, elaborate and well-demonstrated proofs of the lineage of this man, traced back through Uther and Constantine and even to Caesar himself!"

"Another rapist—Caesar, who fathered ancestors for every man in this room and every sheep outside. Proofs mean nothing!"

"What of Excalibur?" blurted Ulfius. "What of the contest with the anvil and stone?"

Yes! What of it? She saw the glorious scabbard Rhiannon and the glorious sword Excalibur glinting at Arthur's back. Now to incite him to draw the blade: "I was never allowed a try at the sword, nor these men with me. None of the eleven outlying kings were given the chance to draw the sword."

Arthur stood from the throne—predictable puppet— and stared into Morgan's eyes. Reaching to his shoulder, he grasped the hilt of the sword, ripped it from Rhiannon, and held it high. He must have thought he was a Saxon, must have thought she would shrink away as if he would use the blade on her. Then, with an almighty heave, he rammed the sword down into the marble slab beneath the throne. It sparked and sank deep, only the hilt jutting forth.

"There," Arthur said petulantly. "Draw it! Just try. Anyone else here who thinks he can draw it is welcome to have a go. Then I'll take Excalibur throughout the land and let every king try. It's futile! No one can draw this sword except me! No one can wield it except for King Arthur."

The chamber fell silent, every eye on King Lot. Within his body, Morgan stared at that sword. This, at last, was her moment. No one else had been able to draw the sword because Merlin had prevented it. With Merlin in coma and Morgan's magic in these fingers, she would draw the sword and slice the head from this usurper. Then, King Lot would be declared the new sovereign of Britannia, and Morgan would be the power behind the throne. The Age of War would be done, and the Age of the Garden would begin.

Morgan stepped forward, holding onto her sister with one hand and reaching for Excalibur with the other. Morgause whined, twining her fingers more tightly around Lot's. Morgan tried to slap her hand away, but there came a sharp, scraping sensation—the ring slipping loose!

Morgan fell out of Lot's body. She tumbled to the bed-chamber floor, and her face slapped the cold stone. Her spirit had retracted across two hundred leagues, and she could barely breathe, let alone stand. . . .

It had been but a moment away—the sword, the scabbard, the death of Arthur and realization of her dreams. Now, Morgan was cut off. Lot wouldn't willingly don that ring again. He had regained his body and would not give it up. Still, the fate of Rhiannon and all Britannia could not be left in his inept hands.

There has to be another way. . . . Rhiannon will be mine.

18

Rhiannon

For over an hour, Morgan lay on the bedchamber floor, her body compressed against stone. She felt boneless, a living wineskin. In time, she had the strength to rise. Shaky and winded, Morgan struggled to her feet, clung to the bed-post, and laughed bleakly.

She'd gathered her body; now to gather her mind.

Without Lot's ring, you can't track him, but still you can track Rhiannon.

Morgan worked her own ring free, its blade harvesting a slender slice of skin as it came loose. The metal band bounded across the floor. She hardly had the strength to stand, but another journey called her. Morgan staggered to the bedchamber door, unlocked it, and stepped out into the hallway. The gelding who had borne her on the night of the abduction would bear her again this night.

On her way to the castle stables, Morgan realized she still wore the comically oversized clothes of the king. She had nei-ther the time nor the strength to change. The stable hands would whisper about crazy Morgan; let them. She might

even laugh with them. That would give them a scare. If only
the leys crossed in Traprain Law. . . .

Morgan marched into the drowsing stables, a single
lantern glowing at the far end. The horses stood asleep. Their
tails twitched fitfully with dreams of flies. Morgan took
down halter, bit, and rein—no time for saddles either—and
woke the lovely bay. She spoke gently about the midnight
ride. Morgan knew these creatures, and they knew her,
united by instinct.

She backed the beast from his stall and led him out beneath
the stars. Climbing the paddock, Morgan straddled him and
rode toward the portcullises. A whistle and yell woke the gate
guards, and they scrambled to the winch room. In moments,
Morgan rode out across the rumpled hills of Lothian.

Stars cluttered the sky. Cassiopeia bid farewell to the
Great Swan as it flew the Milky Way; the Mother Bear and
her Cub danced lightly around the coiling Serpent; Cepheus,
the house of the king, bled meteors into the night. Morgan
had always known the constellations. Their lines were etched
across her mind. The leys were the same way, points of
power in grand conjunction, and Rhiannon was a planet
wandering among them.

Ahead, in a great black forest of oaks, the leys crossed.
The intersection occurred in the midst of a millennial glade—
nine oaks that had grown from a single ancestor. Long ago,
the forest giant had drawn down lightning and was killed by
it. It was gone, but the trees that had risen from its root ball
now were giants themselves. They had survived the fire that
leveled the rest of the forest two centuries before and were
sentinels left from ancient days.

Morgan and her gelding knew the spot, a place of medi-
tation. Tonight, it would be a place of transportation.

The woods loomed up before the galloping bay, but he did not slow. He rushed eagerly along a deer trail, startling the harts from their sleep in the grass. The woods stood ahead, fat columns in a natural basilica. Morgan rode in among them. The gelding's hooves drummed the ground and sent echoes through the forest vault. Star shadows confused the path, but not the horse. He took a winding way to the heart of the wood.

There gathered the ancient trees, nine who were one, each a thousand years old. In their midst, the forest glowed red, an Otherworld conjunction.

"Take me there," Morgan whispered.

The horse leapt among the boles, his flanks scraping on rugged bark. Morgan's heart thundered in time with the gelding's as they arced through the air, legs and minds reaching for ground. They never found it. The horse floated above a red road. Feet and hooves were useless here, but hearts could gallop. They bore Morgan toward the scabbard.

"Rhiannon." Morgan could sense it in the sheer distance, as bright as Vega and as fiery as Arcturus. The scabbard even bent the leys toward it.

Beyond the crimson tunnel, Britannia scrolled away, as thin as paper. Here and there, it was tacked down by sidhs or standing stones, and every forest held a few magic folk. Aside from them, though, the world seemed unreal.

The scabbard was very near now. She could make out its linear shape and even the back of the man who wore it: Arthur. He was dark and small in the midst of boiling armies. His great sword, Excalibur, clanged brightly on the blade of another: Lot.

Here was the showdown, king against prince, man against boy. Morgan didn't care who won. Just now, she wished only for the scabbard. "It is mine," she told herself, and she and her bay soared down the ley-line way.

Below them, Arthur and Lot grew larger, their steel dancing and deadly. To them, she would be as insubstantial as a gust of wind, but after she had passed, the scabbard would be gone. Wrapping the fingers of one hand in the gelding's mane, Morgan leaned down and reached with the other hand. She was the Morrigan, swooping to snatch her own from the battlefield. "It is mine!"

Arthur seemed to hear. He turned.

Morgan snared the scabbard only a moment before it slipped loose. Still, her grip was enough to snap the strap and fling the scabbard away.

Morgan growled in frustration, the gelding mounting back up the sky. She brought the beast to a rearing halt and turned him around to make another lunge—but Lot snatched up her prize. If he thought he could hold Rhiannon anymore than Arthur had—!

A blazing light appeared in the south. It seemed the sun had abandoned its underworld journey and stared down on midnight. A man sat in the sun, and Morgan knew the man: Merlin.

The battle of king and prince had become a war for wizard and witch. Oh, if Morgan had come with spells prepared, if she could do more than spit fire on this man—who was already robed in flames! She would gladly fight Merlin, but that was a fight for another day.

For now, Lot had the scabbard in hand, and Morgan would have him in hand, too.

Wheeling at top of the sky, Morgan's gelding dashed down a red hill. She charged toward Lot, who stood amazed. Merlin filled his eyes and cast his shadow large behind him.

No one saw Morgan, wreathed in fey. She flashed down, caught Lot in one arm, and pulled him up across the gelding's back.

"Come with me."

"Who! What!" gabbled Lot.

Morgan smiled at the poor man. "Do you believe now?"

The king could only stare as the ground fell away beneath him. Even bright-beaming Merlin diminished into a distant star. "Yes."

"Hold onto the scabbard," Morgan said. "It is mine."

Wearily, he handed it to her. It burned in her grip, its jewels emanating power. The touch was not killing but healing.

"What now?" gasped Lot. "What about my men, my wife . . . your sister?"

Morgan shrugged, her eyes locked on the scabbard. "They'll come. Morgause is smart. She'll know to bring the army back to Traprain Law. They'll flee the field and regroup beyond. They'll be back by the turn of autumn."

"But Arthur lives."

"Yes, for now. With Merlin at his side, we can't destroy him . . . yet. But we have the scabbard and its power. Now that Arthur can bleed and die, we'll make sure he does both." Shifting the scabbard to her reins hand, Morgan grabbed the king's waistband and hoisted him up onto the gelding's back.

He sat before her, his back bent above the pumping head of the horse. "Why are you wearing my clothes?"

Morgan laughed. "You're offended? You might have asked why I was wearing your body."

He didn't ask. They didn't speak another word as they galloped away through red skies. Behind them, Caerleon and the failed coup boiled away to nothing.

At dawn, they reached Traprain Law. The gate guards

were so stunned to see their master, by all accounts in Caerleon, that they refused entry. They feared some new witchery. Morgan and Lot might never have gotten in except that she spat fire at the guards. They decided they would rather put up with her inside than die outside.

At the stables, Morgan woke one of the boys and instructed him to water the gelding and feed him oats, to brush him down and wash him and sing to him sweetly until he slept. The boy set about his work, dutifully fulfilling all except the song. One stern look from Morgan evinced a pained melody.

Smiling, Morgan marched toward her chambers. She was having fun. Rhiannon made her bold. She didn't even fear Lot's reaction when he found his bedchamber in shambles, at its center a dummy of Arthur on a false throne.

Still, Morgan was tired. The preparations, the possession, the journeys by spirit and body across Britannia, the ecstasy of holding this wondrous scabbard—all had taken their toll. She entered the chapel, set the bar across brackets she'd installed, and stripped off her disguise. She bathed at the baptismal and, clean and cool, lay down with Rhiannon wrapped in her arms.

Morgan drifted. Her body felt logy. A few more breaths, and she dissolved into water, the deep flood of Avalon.

Her surface dances with spirits. Her deeps hide troves of jewel and coin, sacrifices made throughout the centuries. She encircles the isle of Avalon and guards her secrets.

But along comes a sword, a violent and terrible secret that must be hid. Excalibur is a Christian sword, though the madman who bears it has no idea. Merlin is desperate, fleeing the Saxon god Wotan. He comes to Morgan—no, that is not her name, but

Brigid, who presides over lake and sky both—and begs her to take the sword.

Brigid says, Give it to me. This sword should not be. Sacrifice it to me, and I will sink it in my deepest pool.

Merlin hurls the sword, and it flies and falls. It penetrates the water and sinks through her. It is a painful sword, cruel, but Brigid is glad she had taken it into herself. It passes through light-less regions and down to utter chill, and comes to rest atop a hoard of riches. There, like scar tissue encasing a splinter, the jewels and coins encase Excalibur. She shapes them gently, making a glorious scabbard. Its purpose is to protect Brigid and all Britannia from the Sword of the Spirit.

Invagination. It is one certain way to contain male power. The scabbard is called the "Great Queen," for she forms herself around the king of all blades. Rhiannon is her name.

Brigid gazes down on that scabbard and is pleased but not sat-isfied. Rhiannon is powerful, yes, but strait, formed as a negative image of the masculine sword. In the end, her power and her very existence derive from the sword. She is sterile and sterilizing.

Brigid's power is great and wide. She is not the singular sheath but the all-receiving lake. She is the ever-fecund world, opulent in jewels but even richer in soil. Brigid—and Morgan too, for she was regaining herself in the dream—*is not made to be a singular sterile receptacle for a singular male energy, but rather the all-welcoming earth that is pierced by innumerable seeds and brings forth according to her fertile bounty. The power of the seed is tiny but ubiquitous. The power of the earth is im-mense and singular.*

Morgan opened her eyes, but her hands remained clutched on the scabbard. She could hardly catch her breath, the vision was so strong. She was becoming a goddess, growing into that immense power, and her first duty was to reclaim her firstborn son.

"I'm coming, Mabon," she whispered fiercely. "They can't hide you forever from me."

She would dress and eat and pack and ride out with the scabbard on her back, intent on finding him. And all along the way, her powers would grow. In time, no Arthur, no Merlin could even imagine standing before her.

The women had gathered at the river. Baskets full of the week's wash waited on the shore while the women waded to the center, where boulders broke the surface. There they pounded out the grime. Over centuries, those toothy stones had been rounded and bleached by cloth and water, and the women too had been rounded by their labors. Backs stooped under gray tunics, and tongues wagged with talk.

". . . I don't think there *are* real witches anymore," said a woman, younger, straighter, and more slender than the others. Her eyes were sky-blue under rafts of blonde hair. "Surely they've all been baptized."

An old woman clucked and shook her head. "Just doing the wash doesn't mean you're baptized, Lydia."

Another said, "What about the witch at Traprain? She stinks of brimstone and spits fire."

"You stink of brimstone."

"Not out my mouth, I don't." They all laughed. In their labor, they'd found a place to gather, and when the day was warm and the water clear and the talk good, it might take them awhile to do the wash.

Lydia said, "Imagine all those years and years they spent praying to the Devil, not even knowing there was a God."

She shook her head and clucked, as if practicing to be like the others. "And then imagine them finding out and not giving up the Devil after all. Who'd do such a thing? And why?"

"I hear the Devil gives it to them." The old women snickered.

Lydia shook her head, "Gives what to them?"

"His horn."

"He pokes them with his horns?"

"Not with his horns! With his horn."

"How many has he got?"

"Two little and one big."

While the others laughed, Lydia blushed and looked uncertainly at the stained shift in her hands. "Now you're just teasing me. I don't think you know anything about witches or the Devil."

The oldest woman, whose face looked like wrinkled sackcloth, said, "Live with a man for a year, and you'll know something about the Devil. I lived with old John for seventy, God rest his soul, and I guess that makes me pretty much a witch."

They laughed in reply, their voices sharp against the dull thud of clothes on the rocks. A sudden silence fell over the group, and horse hooves sounded on the wooden bridge upstream. Someone muttered, "Speak of the Devil—" and was hushed as Morgan le Fey rode a bay gelding over the archway.

She sat straight upon the horse, a black robe draped over her shoulders and an empty, jewel-decked scabbard on her back. Her face was pallid and elfin, beautiful beneath long black hair. She slowed the horse to a canter and brought it to a halt at the edge of the bridge. Her eyes swung slowly about and fastened on the women.

Their hands stilled on the stones, clinging to the tattered

rags they called clothes. Under her breath, one woman said, "I bet she's never washed a thing in her life."

As if she had heard, Morgan turned the horse's head toward them and clicked. It reached the bank and slowly descended, nostrils flaring.

The women began again to scrub. They hunched their backs like shields against the witch. Perhaps she would ride on when no one greeted her.

"Good day, friends," Morgan said. Her voice was strangely quiet. "Could you tell me if there is a church hereabouts?"

Eyebrows rose among all the women, but most kept their faces averted.

Lydia did not. She looked up, meeting eyes so deeply brown they seemed black. "A church? Why do you want a church?"

Someone muttered, "She plans to convert."

Morgan stared levelly at Lydia. "My son. He's been kidnapped. He was taken to a church and baptized and carried away. I'm trying to find the church he was taken to."

When she stopped speaking, the women were silent. The snide comments died on their lips. Lydia gazed in amazement. "How old was he?"

"He was three days old," she replied quietly. "He'd be two months old now."

Heads shook and tongues clucked. One of the old women said, "What's his name?"

"Mabon," Morgan replied.

"Who would steal a baby from its mother's arms?" Lydia asked. "Steal it and baptize it?"

With a snort, the oldest woman in the group set a hand on her hip and said, "I could name half a dozen, starting with that new priest in Abercorn—son of a bitch."

Lydia blanched, putting her hand to her mouth. "Clare, he's a priest!"

"Aye," Clare replied as she trudged out of the water, "but seventy years with old John made me a witch, and a witch can call a priest a son-of-a-bitch if she wants to." To Morgan she said, "I'll take you there if you don't mind a walking pace. He might not've done it, but it's a place to start."

"Thank you," Morgan said.

Lydia also strode out of the water. "I'll go, too. My load's done, and Abercorn's on the way."

"It is not."

"Shut up."

A third woman and a fourth stepped up out of the water, and one of them said, "How's it you know a priest took your baby?"

Morgan pressed her lips together, and she seemed very sad. "It was from a vision."

"One from God, or from the Devil?" Lydia blurted, and the others all bristled, fearing Morgan's response.

She swung her leg over the gelding's rump and stepped down, and she was as short as the bent old crones. "That's the funny thing. God and the Devil don't seem to care much about kidnapped babies. But I'll tell you who does care."

"Who?" Lydia asked.

"Did you ever hear of a woman named Rhiannon? Her baby was kidnapped when he was three days old, too. The servants were so afraid they'd be punished that they killed a dog and left its bloody bones in the crib and accused Rhiannon of eating her child."

"Oh, no!" Lydia gasped, hand over her mouth.

"In punishment her husband Pwyll made her go to the city gates and work as a mule, carrying visitors in on her back."

Clare patted Lydia's shoulders. "What'd I tell you about men—they're just a couple horns shy of devils."

"Actually, three horns," Lydia said, and they all laughed.

The group set out, leaving their laundry by the river and walking with Morgan le Fey. She told them of her vision, of her child, of how her sister claimed he had never been born, of Tristan and the things in Dor and Avalon. In time, most of the women wandered away, but Clare and Lydia walked until they reached the doors of the church at Abercorn.

"It isn't the same as in my vision," Morgan said sadly.

"No harm in asking around, though," Clare replied. "You go on in. We'll wait here."

Morgan smiled at the two women. "You don't need to. You've shown me to the church."

Lydia said, "Aye, but there are other ones. We could show you to them."

A questioning look filled Morgan's face. "You would come with me?"

"Old John's dead," Clare said flatly, "and Lydia's not found any John at all, yet. We're at life's rough ends. Of course we'll come, if you don't mind our pace."

Morgan laughed. "No. And I'll certainly not mind once I buy you a pair of horses."

The priest at Abercorn was not the one from her vision, though he did sell her the horses she needed. Morgan, Lydia, and Clare rode them to the center of town, past rows of wattle and daub houses and onto an avenue of half-timber shops. By the creek stood an inn, its three chimneys bleeding gray smoke into the descending dusk. Stabling their horses in back, Morgan and her friends entered. Lot's silver bought them a room, and Morgan's reputation bought them privacy.

As she lay there that night, an old woman snoring on one side and a maiden feigning sleep on the other, Morgan sensed she would never find Mabon. She would always seek but never find. Tears ran down her temples, and Morgan clutched the scabbard all the tighter.

Mabon is your true reason for the journey, but you will have to find other reasons too—in these women and the thousands like them.

Morgan would begin with them, the widows and maidens, adrift without guardians. She would teach them to be guardians of themselves. Clare and Lydia had left all they had had, which could not have been much, but Morgan would give them more. She would travel with them and bear the scabbard to all women, rich and poor. . . .

"Mabon," she muttered miserably.

Your boy is gone, the firstborn of a new generation of believers. But you can bear more like him—thousands of second-born believers. . . .

19

Convergences

Next day, the sun peered down through the cool air of evening as Morgan, Clare, and Lydia rode into Tyningham. They passed a row of shanties that stood along the river. Each had a dory leaning against it, with nets strung out for repair, buoys and poles lying along the walls. The road descended toward the docks, where the town bustled. Men labored on dozens of piers that extended into a deep, wide wash. Some fishers hauled their boats up to overturn them on the grassy banks, while others rowed out into the channel. There was only one other woman on the docks, and she staggered from man to man, pleading softly with each before moving on.

Morgan led Clare and Lydia to the riverbank and dismounted. She laid the reins across her horse's withers and let the gelding nose forward for a drink. The other two women watered their steeds as well.

Lydia crouched beside Morgan, looked out across the river, and sighed wistfully.

Morgan studied her, young and quiet, with lovely blonde hair drawn back over her shoulder. "What is it?"

"Oh, nothing," Lydia said, shrugging. "Rivers and roads, you know? Stand by a river or a road, and you wonder where it goes. You wonder who else is on it." She looked down at her hand, idling in the water. "I wonder if my hand is touching the water that's touching your son."

Morgan stiffened. She set her hand atop the current and closed her eyes. "There are rivers in our blood," she said. "They run through us." A nimbus of red formed around her hand, the water dragging away small curls of it. "Our skin keeps the rest of the world out and keeps us in." Crimson tendrils reached downstream. In time, Morgan shook her head and lifted her fingers from the water. "My son isn't in this river, but another child is."

She stood up, her eyes focused just upstream, in the eddy beside the largest dock. Morgan strode into the water. It lapped around her skirts and then rose to her waist.

Someone pointed at her, and fishermen raised their eyes to stare.

Water engulfed her neck, but still she strode. Brown liquid closed over her head. For a few moments, a rippling wake showed where she moved, but then she was gone.

Lydia and Clare stared in amazement. On the docks, fishermen laughed and traded speculations.

Only one person understood what Morgan was doing: the woman who had been frantically searching the docks. "Oh, no! She's found her! She's found my daughter! She's drowned!"

The agony in her voice hushed everyone, and the men craned to see.

"She's coming up!" someone shouted.

A fold appeared in the dark waters, and then the wet mound of a head pressed through it. Morgan's eyes rose above the surface, and her nose and mouth followed. She gasped as silty water poured off of her. Two more steps brought her shoulders and arms up, and water gushed from the limp figure she carried.

It was a girl, her eyes stuck wide open and her mouth filled with a brown pool. Mud fell from her blue skin. The girl's hands and feet dragged across the river's surface as Morgan marched to the banks.

The mother wailed. She ran, breath shrieking in and out of her. Men rushed from the docks toward Morgan and the child.

Morgan knelt, turning the girl over her knee and pounding on her back. Water poured out of her mouth and gushed across the ground. It foamed with whatever last breath had remained in her lungs. Morgan pounded again, and a final rivulet cascaded out.

The mother fell to her knees beside Morgan and grappled the limp child. She turned her over and stared into unseeing eyes. The girl's lips were purple. Her hands hung down like rags. "She's dead?" the mother asked, amazed and outraged. "I turn around a moment, and she's dead?"

"Give her to me." Morgan said it with such force that the woman handed the child over. Morgan knelt, laying the girl facedown on the grass, and then lying beside her. She wrapped her arm over the girl's shoulder and set her face in the ground and said, "Mother, this one came up out of you, but it's not time for her to return. She hasn't even bloomed. Give her back."

Blood from Morgan's palm oozed across the girl's sodden shirt, but still no breath came. Fiercely, Morgan said, "Give her back!"

Breathe in her the breath of life.

She flipped the child over, catching the girl's face in her hand. Blood smeared across her blue skin and lips. Morgan drew a great breath, clamped her mouth over the child's, and blew. Air shot from the girl's nostrils. Morgan pinched them shut and blew again. The child's chest swelled, and she shuddered, but the air just rushed back out. Morgan blew again, and a third time. The girl convulsed, coughed, spewed water and blood, and took a breath of her own. Blue skin began to become pink again.

"She's alive!" the mother cried, gathering up her child.

The crowd cheered—not just fishers but also fishwives and washerwomen and weavers. It seemed half the town had gathered to witness the miracle.

"She brought her back to life!" someone said.

"She saw her at the bottom of the river."

"It's a miracle."

"God led her."

Morgan rose in their midst. "No, it was not God."

"The Devil, then? Are you a witch?"

"No," Morgan said. "I am a priestess of Gaea."

The people blinked, uncomprehending. "Who is Gaea?"

"You're standing on her."

"The earth? You're a priestess of the earth?" A number of the people laughed.

Morgan scooped up a handful of mud. She sculpted it into a crow, muck mixing with blood. "That you might know the truth," she said quietly, detailing the last plumes with her fingernail. "Gaea, Great Mother, bring this beast to life." The crazings of blood flared and widened across the mud. It transformed into black feathers. Vitality spread through the mud. It shook itself awake, cawed once, and flew skyward.

The crowd watched in amazement as the bird winged away. "How?"

"These are the Gaean mysteries—fertility and life."

A tall fisherman said, "Teach us."

Morgan shook her head. "I will teach your daughters and sisters, wives and mothers."

Scowling, a different man drew his woman up next to him. "I'll not let my wife be a witch."

"It's not up to you," Morgan said, turning toward the woman. "It's up to her."

The man insisted, "It *is* up to me."

Morgan shrugged. "Make your choice. The other wives of Tyningham will know the mysteries of fertility. They'll be giving their husbands children and filling their nets with fish and their gardens with the bounty of the earth." She gazed at the whole crowd. "Here is your moment, men. Empower your wives, and they will bring you blessing, or lock them away . . . and I will bring you cursing."

Some stormed off. Others only turned white and stared, unsure what to do. Many women remained, though, the mother and daughter first among them.

"Teach us," the woman said. "Teach us the mysteries of Gaea."

While Morgan and her retinue swept through the northlands, Arthur and his army swept through the south. He proved himself a man of blood. When a king did not submit, Excalibur took his head, and for each rebel king, Arthur killed a thousand rebel peasants. He was murdering Britannia. His armies marched into villages and made war. They marched out, piled high with pillage and leaving a graveyard behind. The Son of War paraded down a red carpet that flowed from ten thousand throats.

Morgan's road was different, paved with dry dust and walked with women. They did not establish dominion but broke it, did not kill but gave new life. In shanties and royal houses, Morgan turned fear to love. Her battlefields were beds, and she taught women how to win those battles. By degrees, she returned to them what had been stolen, beginning between their legs and ending in the heavens. The voices of the goddesses, which had spoken to her since childhood, now spoke to everyone. Just as Lot led the men of the north, from Rheged and Gododdin to Dalriada and the Hebrides, Morgan led the women. She didn't even need money; she was the guest of the world.

A year later, on a bright morning in late summer, Morgan, Lydia, and Clare rode side by side toward Lothian. In companionable silence, their horses clomped along the Roman road. It rose up a hill between fieldstone houses and then turned sharply south, down the center of town. From the street ahead spilled the rumble of commerce.

"A new marketplace?" wondered Morgan aloud.

Clare shook her head. "Doesn't sound like selling. Sounds like trouble."

"What does trouble sound like?" Lydia asked.

"Sounds like a mob with a rope," Clare replied. She lifted an old eyebrow toward Morgan. "You ain't exactly popular with the king."

"True enough," she replied, volunteering no more. She rode up the hill, turned her gelding at the corner, and then stopped dead, staring.

Before her lay a road draped in cedar boughs, their fragrance sweet on the wind. To either side stood the people of Lothian, looking expectantly toward her. From the windows of homes and shops along the way, heads poked and smiles formed. A cheer rose, and fife and drum began to play. Folk danced.

"A year ago, they reviled me," Morgan said grimly. "Now, this."

Even King Lot stood there atop a podium. Morgause clung to his arm, and squires held his standard high behind him. He applauded his sister-in-law and cried out, "There she is, our own Merlin!"

Morgan smiled wryly and clicked her tongue. Her gelding edged forward over the cedar boughs, and Morgan rode toward the king. Her friends followed.

"We've heard of the miracles you've performed," he said above the roar of the crowd. "We know how you've made the kingdoms of the north into a single people. And now, in our hour of greatest need, you return to us." He smiled, an unaccustomed expression.

Morgan rode up to the platform and kept on going.

The applause faltered. "Battle looms with Arthur!" Lot called after her. "He has his wizard, but we have our wi—filidh! With you, with the scabbard of Arthur, we'll defeat the tyrant of Caerleon!"

The crowd's adulation dropped to silence, and all the people heard her say, "Of course I'll go with you. But first, I want to rest." The horse plodded on down the road, toward Traprain Law.

Lydia followed, saying, "She's just a little tired."

"Give us a week," Clare added, "and we'll march."

The crowd stared after them in stunned silence.

"Did you hear that?" cried Lot in feigned gladness. "She marches with us! Hurrah!" The people of Lothian picked up the shout, and they yelled it after their savior.

It was a very different reception in Traprain Law. Morgan had to depose the traveling monk who had taken over the chapel. She and Clare then lugged three beds into the room, and set the heavy bar in the door brackets. They had hardly gotten undressed and washed and clothed in their nightshirts before the door barked against the bar, and on the other side, someone crashed to the ground.

"Aghh!" Lot growled, scrabbling to stand. "Morgan, it's the king. Let me in."

She stared angrily at the door. "Do you remember Mabon?"

"What?"

"Do you remember my son, Mabon?"

The king paused, gathering his will. "Of course I remember him, Morgan. Now let me in."

Morgan walked patiently toward the door. "Stand back!" She lifted the bar and leaned it up against the doorpost. "All right. It's open."

The door swung slowly inward, pushed by the trembling hand of Lot. He tried the smile he had worn in town but then wiped it from his face. "I thought we should discuss the coming campaign."

"I thought we should sleep," Morgan said, "and I made that clear."

Pressing inward, Lot glanced at her nightshirt, loosely laced at the neck. "This may not be the best time, but—"

"Then get out—"

"But our hatred of Arthur unites us."

Grudgingly, Morgan said, "Go on."

"I've mustered five armies, one for me and one for each of my sons. We'll drive straight south to the channel and cut Arthur's kingdom in half. Then we'll side with the Angles and Saxons in the east and sweep westward, destroying Arthur." His eyes glowed maliciously. "Like it or not, we're counterparts. I have military might, and you have magical might. You have the scabbard, and I have the sword—"

"Arthur has the sword," Morgan interrupted.

"You know what I mean."

"But you don't know what I mean. You aren't my counterpart, Lot. Arthur is. What he's doing, assembling a nation from all these disparate pieces, is what I'm doing. He's trying to create a new Britannia, and so am I."

"He's our enemy!"

"Yes," Morgan agreed. "My opposite, my enemy. We're striving against each other to reach the center."

"Enough splitting hairs."

"This is no small distinction. You think I am your Merlin, your kingmaker, but I want no man to be king. I'm working toward a very different nation. I side with you, Lot, only because you side against Arthur."

He snorted angrily. "I'm glad we're clear on that."

"Let's be clear on a few other things," Morgan said. "I accompany the army but I'm not under your rule or anyone's. I take suggestions, not orders. I have my own tent, my own guards, my own porter, absolute privacy, and utter freedom. I'll use my magic to bring down our common foe, not for digging latrines or any of the thousand other tasks you need done."

Lot nodded distractedly, glancing to Rhiannon. It leaned against her bedpost.

"I keep the scabbard with me at all times except when you enter battle. It's my scabbard, but I'll lend it to you to fight Arthur."

Lot scowled, his jaw flexing. "What else?"

"My friends remain behind—Clare, who is a midwife, and Lydia, who is a priestess. They'll be afforded every courtesy you would pay me—with food, clothes, room, protection, and freedom. They'll be allowed to work unobstructed with the women of Traprain and Lothian, performing rites and ceremonies."

"You want to turn the castle into a den of demons!"

Morgan smiled placidly. "And you want my power. I'm glad we understand each other."

Shaking with fury, Lot said, "One week, and then we march!"

"Oh, that's the last thing. I stay here with Rhiannon until Arthur's army approaches. I'll know, and I'll appear the day before he does, with scabbard and magic to tear him down. You'll have my tent ready, equipment in place and guard posted, when I arrive."

Lot couldn't even speak. He pivoted and stomped out the door.

Morgan closed it behind him, set the bar in its brackets, and turned toward her friends.

Lydia looked frightened, but Clara wore a bemused grin. "He's not used to taking orders."

"He'd better get used to it," Morgan said. "They'd all better."

———

After so long on the road, this reclaimed chapel was a haven. Even Christ welcomed her, lifting his hand in congratulation. From her bed, Morgan smiled back. Yes, she had done as well as Arthur—traveling as far and gathering as many. He had made the south a land of men, and she had made the north a land of women. It was inevitable they would come together.

Her half-brother, her counterpart.

Morgan's thoughts calmed, settling around her like dry leaves. In their chance positions, she perceived a new thought—or a very old one.

If Arthur truly is your opposite, said the wise woman, *perhaps he is your perfect consort.*

No, not Arthur. There was no one in the world she hated as much as him—not Uther, not the men of Mark. Arthur murdered anyone who didn't submit and dominated anyone who did. He was her antithesis, and her half-brother! It would be like lying with Satan.

You've been accused of that before. Gaea had mortal consorts who were her lovers and sons, both. Fertility knows no taboo.

Morgan turned onto her side, determined to get some sleep, but the thought of sleeping with her half-brother lingered, and it made her ill.

In a week, Lot and his troops marched south, laying waste to the same lands Arthur had ravaged.

Morgan meanwhile wandered the red road of fey. She could step across leagues in a moment or hover unseen for hours. She spent most of her time spying on Arthur and seeking weaknesses.

He had none. Smart, muscular, handsome, decisive— Arthur filled any room he entered. It didn't matter who else might be around him or what anyone else said, Morgan's eye and ear forever went to him. He listened to his advisors and then made up his own mind. Though his troops were limited, he made one man count for five. Though his coffers were small, he paid his people in praise—a coin they gladly received. His ingenuity, resilience, and style were flawless, and they made her hate him all the more. Still, she couldn't tear her eyes away.

Only when Merlin came did she flee. He had seen her once, lurking within the red stitching of a banner, and leapt after her, chasing her across the sky. Her blood wards failed, and he might have caught her except that she hid in a labyrinth of lines above an ancient barrow. After that, Merlin was vigilant, and she could catch Arthur only in quiet moments.

Tonight, veiled in red mist, she hid herself in the glare of a lantern just within the garrison tent of Arthur's army. All around her, cots were full of sleeping warriors. Some men lay in the rushes on the floor. Only one still worked his armor—Arthur.

He could have had anyone do it, but the future king instead blackened his own nails and cramped his own fingers. A few months ago, Morgan would have said it was because he was suspicious, a perfectionist, a warmonger. Now she knew better. Arthur did all his own work, from dressing to hosteling. It was another damnable virtue.

With a rag, he applied a thick gray substance to the armor, and then with a separate rag, worked the plates until they shone. His arms rippled beneath the chemise he wore, and his legs jutted, strong and lean, from beneath his shift. He worked systematically, moving piece to piece until the whole elaborate breastplate gleamed. Tuille and tasses, gorget and helmet, his touch transformed the battle-scarred metal. He was beginning to sweat, and droplets sheened his arms.

He was beautiful, and she hated him.

A sound came beyond the tent flap, and Arthur looked up. He smiled slightly and nodded. Polishing again, he said, "I don't want you on the march tomorrow. Go instead to the white cliffs and see if you can sense where our reinforcements are." The person beyond responded in a low voice, and Arthur said, "Yes. Meet us in Bedgrayne by week's end. We'll pin them down beyond the hill fort and cut them to pieces."

Through the flap stepped Merlin. She glimpsed but a tip of his white beard, and she was gone, soaring across the air. Her heart thundered with fear and desire. Damnable and unreasoning desire.

Morgan knelt in her tent at Bedgrayne. Night breathed across the canvas, and Arthur was out in it. He and Lot would do battle tomorrow, but he and Morgan would do battle tonight.

Arthur stalked through the forest toward her. She sensed his approach, and more—she had sent for him. If he was indeed the true consort of the goddess, as hateful as that idea might be, she had to find out tonight. Tomorrow, Arthur would be dead.

"Keep coming, young prince," whispered Morgan darkly as she stared at the makeshift cauldron. Before her, nestled in the sandy floor, was Lot's own helmet, overturned and filled with blood. Morgan had chosen the helmet because it bore the masculine power of the head even as it served the feminine role of the cauldron. This helmet gave her views into Lot's mind, and gave her power over the mind of Arthur. He didn't know she summoned him, but only followed his feet. "You're almost here."

The cauldron performed a secondary function: guarding Rhiannon. Mist rose from the blood and whirled into the air, holding aloft the scabbard and shielding it from scrying. Merlin could not know where the scabbard was, and nor could Arthur until it was too late. Wrapped in veils of magic, Rhiannon began to hum, and then to sing. She was calling to her counterpart, Excalibur, just as Morgan was calling to Arthur.

He was very close now. The dancing mist around Rhiannon thickened, taking on the ghostly semblance of maiden, mother, and crone. Morgan was the fourth personification of feminine power—death.

She still wasn't certain she would lie with him tonight, or kill him afterward, or give him over to Lot. The night would have to unfold as it unfolded.

Rhiannon emitting a moan of desire. Circling mists encased the scabbard in light. It was time. Morgan reached through the spell forces, grasped Rhiannon, and quelled her swelling song. She swung the scabbard over her shoulder and lashed it around her body. Now, she was ready to meet Arthur. Even with Excalibur, he could not draw her blood, and if union would be, it would be.

Arthur was right outside the tent.

Morgan's guard leapt up—she had forgotten about him!—and drew steel. He was too slow. Excalibur was already hissing through the air, and then through the guard. He fell heavily against the tent and slid down. His head toppled between the flaps, eyes wide with surprise. The killing stroke had caught the man's brow and sliced all the way through to the back of his head.

Staring down at that horrible vision, Morgan held her

breath. This was the true Arthur—a killer. Morgan and Rhiannon both held still as the vicious prince stalked away. Arthur had come, yes, but he left a dead man in his wake. How could Morgan ever have desired him?

"Rhiannon," she whispered in sudden realization. It could be scried. Merlin could appear in this very tent. She turned back toward the helmet, but saw that it had flipped and spilled.

The guard, said the wise woman. *He protected you in life. Let him protect you in death. . . .*

Gently pushing open the tent flap, Morgan saw the uppermost bowl of the guard's skull, lying full of blood. Tears came for the poor man, but she knelt and pulled the gruesome thing into the tent.

Let your tears honor him. Let them mingle with his blood, and the spell will be even stronger.

Weeping, Morgan unstrapped the scabbard, held it over the bone bowl, and began an incantation. White mists rose from the blood and tears. They enveloped sword and sorceress. Rhiannon would survive the night, and Morgan too.

"The question is, who will survive the day?"

20

Bloodlust

It was a night of turmoil. Morgan crouched alone in her tent and stared at the blood bowl. She felt sick. Had she really hoped Arthur would find her and climb on her like Uther on Igraine? She shook her head.

In the center of the dark space, Rhiannon hung imprisoned in guardian ghosts. They churned around her like doubt and dread and doom. Within Morgan's head, the council of women argued, wisdom berating reason berating desire.

Morning stole up the sky. At last the sun stared on the atrocity, and no one could deny it.

Morgan peered bleakly out the tent flap and saw a desolated camp. Her guard was not the only man slain. At every second or third tent lay a body with a dark-red puddle beneath. The flies had known for hours what the army was only now discovering—that the Son of War had visited them, and his name was Arthur.

Heavy boots approached. "The goddamned bastard! The monster! The demon!" A man flung back the flap, and sunlight stabbed Morgan's face.

She winced, covering her eyes. The afterimage of his silhouette was emblazoned on her mind—the lean armor and jagged hair of Lot.

His rant had ended when he saw her, craven and confused. "I thought you'd be untouched by this. I thought you'd be in here fiddling with your spells, smiling over your potions, happy." He spat in the dirt. "I'm glad you're not. Welcome to mankind."

Squinting, Morgan said, "How many dead?"

"Maybe three hundred, maybe four—but ten times that have deserted. And Arthur killed horses, too."

"Killed horses," Morgan echoed angrily, shaking her head. She latched onto that emotion. Anger was the antidote of fear, and already it solidified her churning stomach.

"We still outnumber his troops by ten thousand, but not if more men flee."

"They'll stay," Morgan said. "They'll each fight like two men."

Lot crouched, his face jutting into the tent. Sweat beaded across his forehead, and his eyes were wide and wild. "You have a spell?"

"I'll make a spell. A bloodlust spell." Already, she devised the ways to do it, to harvest blood and lust, to make men ache to kill.

"Excellent," Lot said feverishly. "But what about Merlin? How are you going to stop him?"

A summonation. There is an old beast beneath this land—the Red Serpent of Nottinghill.

Morgan clenched fists on her knees. "I don't need to stop him. I need only wake a divine ally. She's a jealous creature, and she'll eat Merlin alive."

Lot grinned viciously. "Good. Start your spells. I'll go rally the men.

"Take your helmet," Morgan said, pressing the sanguine thing into his hands. "Don't clean it. With the residue of my blood, I'll be able to hear whatever you say—give suggestions, not orders."

"Not orders," he said solemnly, but his smile burst forth again. "We fight today, and Arthur dies today!" Standing up, Lot stomped off. His steps were no longer anxious but eager.

Morgan pulled the flap back down and sat for a moment, gathering her thoughts.

Look behind you, Morgan.

She turned, seeing the blood bowl and the coruscating spirits. Lot had forgotten to take the scabbard. It was just as well. Morgan might not have given it up. She would keep it safe and would know if Lot needed it.

There were more pressing matters—awakening the Red Serpent and infusing the warriors with bloodlust.

Morgan crawled past the scabbard to an empty stretch of sand near the back of the tent. Pressing the fingertips of one hand together, she traced a summonation circle. While her flesh displaced particles of earth, her mind displaced particles of spirit. The moment she completed the circle, a well opened between world and Otherworld. Now, it was a simple matter of calling down into that echoing place.

"O spirits of the ages, heed! I call the Red Serpent of Nottinghill, the snake-woman who once haunted the Bedgrayne. Answer me!"

Though the sand circle seemed solid, it emitted a hiss with the low clangor of underworld chains.

Morgan nodded. "You hear but fear to speak." The hiss

grew suddenly louder, and Morgan knew she had the beast. "And well you should fear. A new power has come to Nottinghill, and he claims it for his own. He has called you a myth and will fell the sacred forest."

A fierce feminine voice said, "His name . . . ?"

"His name is Merlin. He is a great power—not as great as you once were, but far greater than you are now. Stay below, Red Serpent. Do not wander your lands, lest Merlin find you and slay you—"

Chains rang like bells, and giant scales rasped. The serpent gathered to leap. In fury, she surged up, intent on emerging through the circle.

Morgan idly dragged her hand across the line, breaking it and closing the well. The Red Serpent would find another escape and be angrier for it. She would stalk Nottinghill and seek Merlin and at least detain him. Perhaps she would even tear him to pieces.

Morgan didn't dwell on that thought. Already, she worked through the permutations of her bloodlust spell. What single image would encompass blood and lust? Several flitted through her mind: the menses, the moon, the engorged phallus. . . . None were quite right. Her mind perseverated on another image, bathed in blood and lust both.

Arthur.

"What happens?" Morgan demanded, staring into the blood bowl. Beyond the tent, the air was a solid roar of fury, but Morgan listened to her inner voices. "Wise woman, tell me what happens!"

Your spells work perfectly, but the creatures you employ are unworthy.

"The army?" Morgan gasped.

You stoked the fires of their hearts, but they have such small hearts. These men slept while Arthur murdered their comrades. They fight with twice their native valor, but twice nil is nil. With a smaller force, Arthur has surrounded them.

"At least that way they can't run," Morgan said through gritted teeth. "What of Merlin, though? He has not come to Arthur's aid. Surely he has fallen to the Red Serpent of Nottinghill?"

Huge and ancient, she should have been a match for Merlin. Indeed, she found the man and wrestled him to the ground in a near-kill, but was snagged by a water spirit and shunted to the Otherworld. The serpent is gone. Merlin is shaken and gasping, but he lives, and soon he will join the fight.

Morgan hunched, her mind reeling. "A viper would have slain him more surely." Her hands clenched on the sand. "Still, we might win the day. Lot is strong—"

Before the wise woman could speak, another voice resolved itself from the clamor of battle. Lot's voice echoed through his helm and into Morgan's mind—

"A man who learns of swords would be a fool not to learn of stanching wounds. You were a good man, Arthur, yes. And if I can keep you alive a few moments more, you will be yet a good man—and perhaps a great king."

Morgan shook her head slowly. "What is this? Lot hates Arthur. They are sworn foes."

Men have hearts of war, hearts made and unmade by it, the wise woman said. *Arthur is victorious, and no man can resist joining a victor.*

"Better yet, I will summon my scabbard Rhiannon to heal you. Its sorcerous protections are bound to me—my helmet become a cauldron. I need merely call on my sister-in-law, your half-sister—

Look! We have her in common as well!—and she will bring me my scabbard, and the king of all Britannia will be saved."

"Oh, no, Lot," Morgan murmured, eyes tracing out the bloody bowl that warded the scabbard. "I'll not bring you my scabbard. Not to heal Arthur. Not to surrender it to him."

Lot couldn't hear her, but she could hear him: ". . . *Come, sister Morgan. Arthur will die without the scabbard. I cannot be king now, and Britannia must have a king. . . ."*

"No, Britannia must not have a king, and Arthur must die." Only then did she realize her victory lay at hand. Arthur *would* die, and Lot *would* fail to unite the people. There would be no king, and Morgan and her brood would rise.

Victory.

". . . the helmet. Yes, she's supposed to hear me through this helmet. . . . Your half-sister . . . no, the other one. . . . She has your scabbard, and I've ordered her to bring it. . . ."

Morgan laughed. The kings of the world had lost their power to command. She sat and listened avidly as Lot babbled and Arthur died. It was an absurd scene—tens of thousands of warriors slain so these two could sit down and become friends.

". . . and don't pretend you don't hear me, Morgan! I order you to bring me my scabbard. . . ."

Morgan shook her head bleakly. Women were not so impressed by war. Perhaps it was because they had spent millennia losing every battle but remaining unvanquished.

". . . here they are! Wonderful. . . . Come, quick, Guinevere! He lies just here. . . . Yes, a belly wound. . . . My sword, actually, though I tried to get Arthur's healing scabbard from the witch who's watching it. Or should I say, the bitch. . . . Yes, Merlin, she's nearby. A runner could show you the tent—"

Morgan listened no more. "You've failed me, Lot. . . . I'll take my scabbard and find a new warrior-king who can bring down the great Arthur." She reached up into the whirling column of mist and snatched Rhiannon. "Or better yet, I'll kill him myself." She gingerly stepped into the blood bowl, and the spirits shot up. They formed a mystic cocoon around Morgan, and she vanished from the tent.

Let Merlin seek her. Let him chase the ley labyrinths and send his Seelie hounds sniffing. Morgan would not be there.

She had no home now. She couldn't return to Lothian, for it was loyal to Arthur. Instead, Morgan would have to wander Britannia as she had wandered Caledonia. It would be no hardship. Morgan traveled light. She would skip down out of the air into peasant hovels and the courts of kings and would do her work. While Arthur busily subjugated subjects, Morgan would busily liberate them.

Eventually, the king would be vulnerable. Morgan would stoop down on him like a falcon on a hare, and Arthur would be dead.

Six months gone, and the Battle of Bedgrayne was a fading memory. The dead lay in their mounds under blankets of snow. Arthur was king, and all Britannia rejoiced. Or some of Britannia. A few pockets, anyway.

Morgan avoided such pockets. She'd spent the autumn among migrant farmers and the first half of winter in a tinker caravan. They were fine folk, and they believed in the old powers. It was a simple thing to reveal to them the oldest power of all. Now they believed in Gaea. Their feet would carry them throughout the land, and carry their faith with them.

Still, Morgan was done with sleeping in hay bunkers and eating from feed bags. She wished for meat and a featherbed. It was time.

She stepped onto the leys near Gloucester in the west and stepped off near Bexhill in the south. She'd seen a Saxon wedding, and she wanted to be a part of it.

Despite piles of snow, the company had gathered outside. The groom, a giant of a man, danced rhythmically in their midst, circling his bride. His furs made him seem a wolf preparing to gulp down a lamb. Smiling, the bride watched him, and the brooches that hung from her tunic gleamed like coins. The two clans clapped in quickening time to the man's dance. They were tall, blonde, and barrel-bellied—bluff folk who spoke loudly in their strange tongue and laughed even more loudly. The whole group began to turn in opposition to the groom, those on the outside running to keep up. They chuffed, their breath making white blooms in the air. It was a merry group, and Morgan could use some merriment.

She appeared beside a fire pit where three pigs turned on spits. "How much longer?" she asked one of the spit men. Her father had taught her the rudiments of Saxon, though between accent, stature, and complexion, she had no hope of passing as one of them.

The man looked up at her, his brawny arms bare to the shoulder and his shirt bloodstained. "Another hour." He blinked at her, and then lifted a drinking horn that hung at his neck. "But the beer's ready now."

She declined, thanked him, and wandered toward the dance circle.

Morgan paused before flinging herself into the fray. The outer folk ran at full speed. They were young men, eager to race. Judging her moment, Morgan leapt in among them. It was all she could do to keep up. Hands pressed momentarily on her back as a faster runner rushed by. She migrated inward, among the middle-aged dancers. They moved well, but with none of the frantic energy of the young. They smiled at her as if she were a child, so small, with that strange black hair. Some whispered, trying to place her with the groom or the bride. Morgan only glided farther inward, trusting to familial anonymity. At last, she reached the inner circle, old and rich, unwilling to run and unneeding to. These were the families who had paid for it all, and they stared baldly at her. She ignored them, her eyes on the bride and groom. They were locked in a kiss that brought a mounting roar from the crowd. As they broke apart, Morgan applauded and cheered with the others.

The bride and groom turned to smile at their guests. Their eyes came to rest on Morgan. Within his mane of golden hair, the groom's face creased in confusion. Others were looking her way now. One older man touched her elbow and said in Saxon, "Have we met?"

Morgan shook her head. "No, we haven't."

His eyes were sharp above an unconvincing smile. "Are you with the bride or the groom?"

"Neither," Morgan said flatly. "I am with the goddess." She had spoken the words quietly, but was sure that most of the people had heard. She would shortly need to flee.

Crumpling his old face in a deep scowl, the man said, "Which goddess? Joerd? Sif? Nanna?"

Morgan couldn't hide her smile. They still had their goddesses. "No, Freya and Frigga."

"Of course!" The old man said with a smile. He turned and held his hands out. "Listen, all of you—a sign! The goddesses of love and marriage have sent us their priestess to bless the wedding of my son!" A cheer rose, and the man pressed Morgan toward the couple.

She went, her heart pounding gladly. How long had she been called a witch? Among these Saxons, though, she was a priestess. Striding reverently to the couple, she set her hands on their shoulders and said, "May the goddesses dwell in your hearts, that you may love, and in your home, that you may live, and in your land, that you may prosper."

A joyous roar ended the blessing, and Morgan was swept up in it. She rode along in the arms of the old and the young, her feet falling into the rhythm of hands and drums. All her fears fell away, and she drifted in bliss.

This is a foretaste of the world I am bringing into being, she thought as she circled the bride. It is a world with a woman at its center and a man in orbit about her, and a community set in motion by it all.

Morgan had come here to feast and teach, to open hearts to the goddess, but these people had opened her own heart, too. They weren't merely followers but allies.

"Thank you, Priestess Morgan," said the groom later as they feasted on roast boar. "You'll always be welcome in the home of Alle of Sussex."

At Midsummer, Morgan went uninvited to another feast. King Arthur was founding his capital city in the hills of Cadbury, a city he would call Camelot. He had summoned the people of Britannia for the groundbreaking celebration, and Merlin had summoned the powers of the Otherworld. In throngs of flesh and spirit, Morgan could move undetected. Just now, nothing of Camelot existed except a few foundation stones, but all the pavilions and tents, all the mingling creatures, made the city seem real already. It was a bright, loud, brash place, and joy was in the air.

Morgan wondered if she had the courage to do what she had come to do.

Beneath a starry sky, she meandered down a grassy lane. At the corner of one tent gathered a crowd of revelers. They were common laborers who'd stolen a keg and were making a party of it. Morgan edged quietly by. She didn't belong with them, in her dress of black samite with lace at bodice and wrist. She'd even piled some braids on her head and held them with a hairpin, letting other braids fall to frame her face. She'd dressed for the state banquet, but hadn't fit in there, either. No other noblewoman had been unescorted, and Morgan ducked out before she would be noticed. Now, she lingered on the fringes, catching glimpses of Arthur and hoping for a chance to meet him alone. So far, though, he was in the center of it all.

All your life, you've been on the fringe—neglected, shunned, feared, abhorred.

It was the warrior woman, and Morgan bristled. "I prefer to be alone."

All his life, Arthur has been desired, nurtured, promoted. . . .

"Of course he's at the center of everything," Morgan murmured. "He embodies the age. I'm its antithesis."

It's merely a matter of changing the age.

Morgan reached up and touched the long hairpin that held her coif together. That single slender spike would do it, strong enough to punch through skin and muscle, poisonous enough to kill instantly. All she had to do was seduce him, get him alone, and kill off the last great king of war.

Returning to the nobles' pavilion, Morgan glanced in. Past a luffing wall of canvas and a line of servants sat King

Arthur, with the priestess Guinevere at his side. She was an important piece of furniture for him, a sort of living throne. Whenever he sat to receive dignitaries, his foot rested in her lap. This signified that the mortal king ruled only because of the power of the land—the divine goddess. Somewhere, the goddess had been demoted to a priestess, and the priestess to a piece of furniture. To make matters worse, Arthur had fallen in love with his footstool.

Even from this distance, Morgan could tell that she did not return his feelings. He whispered something to her, and she turned away. He touched her lightly on the arm, and she withdrew it. He said something more, his eyes glistening, but she shook her head and left, stranding him among his subjects.

It was perfect. Morgan couldn't have hoped for better.

Arthur slumped. He tried to put on a brave face, distractedly greeting the folk who approached him. At last, he quit the throne altogether.

Morgan moved quietly, wanting to follow. He would go alone. She knew by the wounded pride on his face, the very look she herself so often wore. Arthur plunged from a side flap of the pavilion and strode out into the night. He walked with his eyes down, brows furiously clenched. It made it easy for Morgan to follow without being seen.

Beyond the reach of the lanterns, Arthur crossed the starlit grasslands. He strode straight for the foundations of the city gate. It was as if he planned to flee his city before it was even built.

Morgan stalked him, a hunting cat. He was working himself into a fit about his beloved—the sort of anger that made men do regretful things. Morgan paced silently across the grasslands, coming within an arm's reach of him. Perhaps she wouldn't have to do any seduction at all, but would merely sink the pin now, as he sat. She reached up to her hair and felt the metal head, warm and hard and ready.

"She said no," he muttered, hurling a handful of rocks.

"Who?" Morgan blurted.

Arthur startled, standing up and turning. He had grown, fully a man. She smelled bath oils on him, but also the scent of muscles and tan skin and clean hair. His shoulders were broad and his eyes piercing even in this dark place. "Who are you?"

Morgan dropped her hand, the pin clutched between her fingers. "I'm a Briton. You're the king of Britannia." She stepped toward him. "I wanted to speak to you about your kingdom."

He shook his head in the darkness and sighed. "Tomorrow. There'll be time to talk tomorrow."

Another step, and she would be able to ram this thing through his eye. "I know. You grieve your foot-holder. Your . . . virgin foot-holder."

"What?" Anger lit his eyes. There was something else there, too—desire. "What do you know of it?"

"I know your kingdom needs the power of the land. There are other priestesses who aren't bound by vows of chastity. . . ."

He studied her. He was breathing hard, like a stag taking in the scent of a ready doe. Arthur took her suddenly, his arms around her and his lips pressed to hers. For a moment, he clenched her, but then he let go, as if terrified of what he had done.

Morgan drew him back into her arms. It will help me sink the pin, she told herself, but she held the metal piece carefully away from his skin.

It was wrong to do this. Even if he were the perfect con-sort, it would be wrong to enjoy it this way.

I'll kill him when we're done. She knew it was a lie. As he covered her neck in kisses and pulled wide the bodice of her dress, she tossed the pin away into the nighttime grass.

21

Feminine Wares

By morning, Morgan walked the Foss Way north of Cadbury. She could have wandered the red roads, but just now she needed to feel her feet beneath her. There were plenty of others on the road this morning, staggering away from the Carnival of Camelot. Half-drunk and all-sexed, they were no better than Morgan. Still, they laughed at her. She was silent and alone, sober in samite and lace. Despite their debauchery, they looked at Morgan with the wrong sort of eyes and saw a woman of little or no virtue.

Let them berate you, said the wise woman, one voice in the cacophony. *If they knew you seduced your half-brother, they would hate you. If they knew you tried to kill King Arthur, they would stone you. Barbs and jests are better. At least they won't kill the baby within.*

The child of Arthur was growing in Morgan. Meg had listed the signs—fever and itch, hunger and dizziness, mania and sadness. New humors pulsed through Morgan. She hadn't felt this way since those first days after the rape, when Mabon was growing.

O Mabon! For nine months, he had been at her center, and now she had no idea where he was or even whether he was. She would never forget her firstborn son, but this baby brought new hope. For the first time in two years, the emptiness in her was filled.

"I intended none of this," Morgan said quietly to the council within, "but I regret none of it."

This is life. It starts small, in silence and deep darkness, needing much, enduring patiently and growing. In time, it is magnificent. Only death is quick and decisive. Life is slow and full of days.

For the last hour, the road had risen. After Bath, Roman stone had given way to rutted earth, and it to trammeled grass. She was getting beyond the crowds, in sheep pastures without a farm in sight. No one passed this way except vagabonds such as she, looking for a quiet place to sleep. Morgan felt safe here, but shouldn't have.

In the distance behind her, a horse sneezed and a whip cracked. Morgan glanced back to see a wagon moving up the road. It had high sides, a wooden roof, and a single door. Its lock swung like a pendulum as the wain jolted along. On the seat crouched a thin man, the reins paying out from his hands and slapping with regular fury on the haunches of the horse. The man was tall and wiry, his hair dragged back tightly to gather behind his head. His waistcoat and breeches seemed to have been tailored for a shorter man. He spotted Morgan and half-stood on the footboard.

Sighing wearily, Morgan stepped off into the taller grass and kept walking.

The leather slapped twice more, and the horse wheezed as it dragged the wagon up the rise. It rattled up alongside Morgan and slowed. The horse stomped his hooves and strained against taut reins. The tall man stood on the footboard, reins in one hand and hat in the other. He smiled beneath a wide black mustache.

"Greetings, wayfarer!" he said, bowing as the horse paced her. "You seem footsore."

She kept walking. "Not really."

"You've marched all the way up from Bath, and you're not sore? You, alone, without husband or horse or even provisions?"

"I don't need husbands or horses or provisions," she replied flatly.

The man winked at her. "Oh, I understand. On the run, are we? Get ourselves in trouble in the city, and now we're marching God-knows-where."

"God does not know where," Morgan replied. She folded her arms over her chest and stopped walking.

Beside her, the wagon bounced on a few yards more before it came to a halt. The man slung the reins on their post and leapt off to approach her. "You misunderstand me," he said, rubbing lanky hands together. "I'm in a position to help."

Morgan took a step back. "You aren't in a position to do anything."

"Allow me to introduce myself. I am Delgut, dealer in feminine wares."

"I don't need any feminine wares."

"But I do," he said, and his fist flew.

Morgan spun instinctively away, but the leather sap in his hand crashed against the back of her head, and she crumpled in the grass.

Inside the shuddering wagon, five women stared down at the newcomer. She lay between their feet, another body for Delgut to sell. She was different, though, with real lace and no visible sores. Beautiful skin and hair. A rut in the road pounded the wagon, and the benches bucked. The newcomer rolled back and forth, and her chains rattled, but she didn't wake.

"If she's a runaway, she ran away from money," said Daedra. At thirty, she was the oldest and largest of the women and mother to the youngest, who was fourteen. She had skeins of glorious red hair, and her face was a mask of freckles. "What kind o' woman runs from money?"

"Not you, Mom," said Rachel, smiling beneath her blonde hair.

"Not her, neither," replied a brunette with a poxy face. "She's a thief. That's why she's got such nice clothes."

"Yeah," mocked Daedra. "She stalks women her size and steals their clothes."

"Maybe a murderer," suggested another woman.

"Well, whatever she was, she's a whore now," Daedra said sourly.

Rachel sighed. "Anything would be better than being a whore."

"Yeah? Like what?" Daedra asked. "Say she was a queen. What's a queen do? Get done by the king."

"A queen's not a whore. She's a wife."

"Then go find yourself a husband, Rachel. But I bet you'll find your duties don't change," Daedra said, "except you got to cook and clean, too."

Rachel shook her head sadly. "It just seems like they ought to have more use for us than that."

"If you were a man, what would you do with you?"

"Probably what they do with me."

Daedra's tone softened. "Look, it's just that they got everything and we got nothing except ourselves, and so the only way we can get something is to give them what we got."

The brunette said, "She's waking up."

They stopped talking to watch the woman, her head rolling side to side. Her braids snaked like Medusa's hair. The wagon jolted again, and sunlight slanted through a barred window to rake the woman's face. She opened her eyes, wide and brown, and blinked at the ceiling. "Where . . . where am I?"

Daedra leaned toward her and spoke with quiet authority. "You're home. Your spot'll be in the front corner on the right, above the tambourines and drum. Usually you don't get the floor unless it's your shift to sleep." She grasped the woman's shoulder and tugged on her. "Now, get up and get in your spot."

The woman didn't get up, instead staring at the shackles on her wrists and ankles, and then pressing at her groin. "Did he . . . ?"

"No. He doesn't do that," Daedra said.

"Just everybody else does," added Rachel. "And what are you, anyway, a queen or a thief?"

Rubbing the back of her head, the woman said, "Neither, at the moment."

"Get up," Daedra repeated. With one powerful arm, she lifted the newcomer and propelled her toward the corner of the wagon. Amid jangling chains, the newcomer fell onto a bench beside a mousy woman with gray hair. Across the narrow aisle, the fifth woman slumped and began to snore.

Rachel pressed, "What were you?"

Absently, the newcomer sat up. "I'm a priestess. I'm Morgan."

Ahs and amazed nods came all around, and Rachel whistled.

"Well, priestess," Daedra said, "you're one of us now. You'll get your food and a spot to sleep on, clothes, perfume, face paint, protection—"

"Everything a girl could want," Rachel said.

Morgan shook her head, hands clenched. "What are you talking about?"

Daedra stared levelly at her. "You're a whore now."

With a disbelieving laugh, Morgan replied, "I'm not staying here—"

"He'll keep you on a pretty tight rein at first, just until he knows you'll do it and won't run. And you can work like that. Some men like the chains."

Morgan shook her head slowly. "You have no chains. Why do you stay? Why not run off?"

With a heavy sigh Daedra said, "Didn't you hear what I said—food, clothes, perfume, a place to sleep—"

"You don't need this—this Delgut to get you those things."

"Maybe you don't—or didn't—but I do. I been doing this for sixteen years. It's all I know. And who's going to take me now?"

Morgan's eyes were strange and wide. She hadn't yet learned to look down at the ground, to avoid locking onto anyone's gaze. Daedra growled and began to get up, but Morgan said something amazing. "*I'll* take you."

The lines of anger on Daedra's face solidified in a red mask of rage. "You? You're a kidnapped whore in chains. You can't even take yourself. How're you going to take me?"

Morgan shifted her hands and seemed to bite the back of one of them. A red spark came between the wrist rings, and then a metallic clink. The shackles fell off, and the chains snaked between her legs and clanked to the floor. "I'll take all of you."

Rachel gasped excitedly, clutching her knees. "Take us where?"

"I'll take you and make you great," Morgan said. "Delgut tried to make a whore out of me, but I'll make priestesses out of you."

"Priestesses?" Daedra said. "Who do we worship?"

Morgan shifted her feet, and the metal that had held her ankles cracked loudly, sending small red bolts of lightning across the planks. "Gaea. You'll be her priestesses."

"You mean her witches. That's lower than being a whore."

Shaking her head, Morgan said, "Did you know there was a time when the words whore and priestess were the same? Did you know there were temple prostitutes who did what you do, but not for money or for a meager roof and a set of rags? They did what they did because it was the holiest, most powerful act in the world." Her eyes shone. She stared into a bright world, and the women glimpsed it reflected in her eyes. "All life comes from us! It arises from the earth herself, the ever-fecund goddess whose womb is the ocean. She gave birth out of her abundant fertility, and gives birth again and again. Every living thing is born of her and dies to return to her and be born anew.

"Don't you see? Earth is the great harlot, offering her abundant life to any who would pluck it. From first to last, the battle of God has been against the world he wishes to conquer. He has even told his men to fill the earth and subdue it, taking dominion over all things. But she who was chained and trampled, ravaged and dominated, is returning. She'll take back what is hers and take all of us with her."

Gazing into those bright-beaming eyes, Daedra fell to her knees. "I don't know. I don't know. I don't deserve to see such things. How can I be a priestess?"

Morgan stepped to her and lifted her gently to her feet. "How can you not?" Her eyes showed a glorious garden. She looked down at the others, who knelt also. Even the fifth woman had awakened to stare. "The garden is before you, friends. Have the courage to shuck the old world and receive the new."

Clinging to Morgan's arm, Daedra said, "What do we do?"

Morgan gave a strange little smile. "Follow me." She swept her free arm out toward the door. A galvanic charge rushed through her body. The beam gathered across her fingers, twined into a cord of power, and stabbed out through the door crack.

More metal failed. The lock thudded to the ground, and the door swung slowly open. Morgan stood in the doorway, her small figure outlined against golden grass.

"Can you run?"

Daedra said, "We're prostitutes. Of course we can run."

"Then follow me," Morgan responded with a laugh. She leapt out of the moving wagon.

Daedra was second, her heart making her face beam. Rachel leapt third, and the other women bounded afterward.

They had expected Morgan to run away from the wagon, but she didn't. She ran alongside it, her samite dress hiked to her knees. Her legs flashed like a little girl's. Daedra tore out after her, red sinews and braids working in unison. Ahead, Morgan leapt onto the riding board and pulled herself up.

She disappeared around the corner, just as the reins lashed the horse.

Daedra surged up to the board and clambered on.

Delgut was beating Morgan in the face with his bare fist. Daedra shoved herself between the little woman and that all-too-familiar fist and kicked Delgut in the groin. He doubled over, and she kicked him again, this time in the shoulder. He fell off the speeding wagon, hit the ground, and rolled in the grass. Even when he stopped rolling, he didn't stop squirming.

Daedra whooped as she turned to grab the reins of the horse. She pulled with even pressure, calming the beast. The wagon slowed, and Daedra drew the horse to a stop. The other women caught up, their eyes wide and their hands covering open mouths.

"I can't believe you did that, Mom," Rachel said. "So much for 'once a whore, always a whore.'"

Daedra shook her head and laughed, staring back a quarter mile to where her former master lay in the dirt. "I can't believe I did it either."

"What do we do now?" asked the brunette woman. "Like, for money and food? And how can we ever get far enough from Delgut that he won't just come and kill us?"

Morgan wiped blood away from her enigmatic smile. She scanned the horizon, her eyes stopping on a great ring of ancient oaks. "Just follow me."

The red road carried them up out of the oak grove and over the rooftops of Withington. Wheels spun on the rutted air, narrowly missing a chimney here and a spire there. Morgan clutched the reins, guiding that canny horse through uncanny spaces. Had anyone in the tiny town looked up, he would have sworn the carriage of the Morrigan was sweeping by overhead. He would have been nearly right.

The priestesses clung on for their lives. None had ever left the ground except in dreams, and to fly this crazy way made them gape and shudder and scream. Rachel was the main screamer, for joy instead of terror. Beside her, standing on the running board with arms hard around her, Daedra could only laugh. "God damned! God damned!" The others had worse responses, vomiting onto the scarlet road, weeping to be released, or simply scrabbling back within the wagon to hole up in the darkness.

Morgan paid them no heed. Her teeth were clenched in a wind-filled grin, and she watched the lands scroll away. The women couldn't doubt her power now. She had saved them from what they had been and made them new and carried them across the sky. Leaving Withington behind, they soared above the Midland Plains.

As the sun dropped below the world, they crossed the winding Severn above Worccster. Windows below gleamed with candle light, making the city seem a cluster of lanterns. The wagon rolled on as evening swept its arm beneath it.

"Where are we going?" Daedra shouted, pushing Rachel up onto the footboard.

Morgan searched the darkness. "Someplace."

Daedra laughed. "Well, it's not like we could go noplace."

"Oh, it is." Morgan turned red eyes on the woman. "If we're not careful, we could very easily go noplace."

Daedra's jaw grew gray as she clenched it. Beside her,

Rachel leaned back and studied the sky. Blue stars winked in the heavens. "What kind of place are we looking for?"

"A home," was all Morgan said.

Those two words swept around the women like a warm blanket. Morgan made room for Daedra on the driver's bench. Between sky and soil, the three rode side by side.

22

Alone No More

Soon, the moon emerged, a great white plow tearing through the horizon. It furrowed the distant hilltops and dragged through the Lake of Grass and the Lake of Wind.

"I'd love to live there, in a cottage by the water," Rachel said. "Stone walls around green pastures. That would be a home."

Morgan shook her head. "Our home will be a place of power, where magic is already on the move." She took a deep breath of the red winds. "Someone is calling me. We'll be there soon."

Britannia slid southward below the rushing wheels. The horse whickered on its way. Puffs of steam from its nostrils dragged through the spokes and dissipated behind. The moon arced overhead like a killing blade and began to tumble from the sky.

Then, she saw them—the three witches. In an ash grove below, they gathered for a midnight ritual. Torches stood in a circle around them, casting triangular shadows across their backs. They faced the center of the circle and shouted into the darkness.

"They're calling me—a summonation," Morgan said.

"Calling *you?*" Daedra asked. "How do they know you?"

"They're calling for a magic servitor. They think I'll do their bidding."

"Those are real witches?"

"Yes, but I am more than they."

Daedra shook her head. "Don't go down there. It'll be three against one."

"They'll wish it had been nine against one." Morgan clicked her teeth and drew on the reins.

The horse nodded in the traces and turned down a narrow cutoff. It plunged on a path formed by the witches' incantation. The trees rose, no longer soft plumes but raking hands. Hooves thrashed through the peak of an elm, and wheels shredded its leaves. The wagon drove through foliage and rushed down into the circle of torches.

As soon as wheels touched ground, Morgan stood on the footboard, dragging at the rein. The horse shrieked as it dug its hooves into the soil. It turned within the fiery circle. The wagon slewed, knocking down three of the burning brands before it came to a stop. Dust rolled into the nighttime air, enveloping the wagon and its riders. Through the thick cloud, Morgan glimpsed the witches scrambling to outflank her.

"Get inside the wagon," Morgan ordered Rachel and Daedra. "Don't come out until I say." The two women nodded and hustled off the footboard.

Slinging the reins on their post, Morgan leapt from the wagon. Her feet landed in the churned earth. She bit her hand and spat on the ground, and fire gushed up from the spot. It burned in a tall pillar and cast Morgan's shadow toward one of the witches.

She was fair and young, eyes wide and hair standing like flames on her head. "Evil spirit!" she called in a tremulous voice. "We've brought you here, and you are ours to command!"

"I'm not evil, nor a spirit," Morgan said, "and I am no one's to command!"

Behind Morgan, a blonde woman began chanting in the language of the Saxons. She claimed the power to bind "this demon" to her service. Slowly approaching, she drew a handful of blue powder from her pocket and threw it at Morgan. As it struck the air, each mote came alive, and the whole gnat swarm rushed to envelop Morgan.

With a wave of her bleeding hand, Morgan turned the blue motes red and sent them whirling back. Burning meteors sank into the woman's clothes and pitted them. "Your kobolds won't work on me," Morgan said.

The third woman cried out, "By the triple goddess, I bind you." From outstretched fingers lashed strands as gossamer as spiderweb. They shot to the other two witches, forming a triangle around Morgan. The sides of the triangle snapped shut, trapping her.

Morgan stared down the strands.

The woman who had cast the spell smiled under slender black brows. She tightened her grip, and a pulse of grayish light rushed down the strand to jolt Morgan. "You can't escape. These aren't physical bonds, but lines of will. They bear our desires and demands to you as if they were your own. While you wear these lines, you are our captive."

Morgan sighed. "Lines of will run both ways." She grasped two of the strands, and bolts of red force lit them.

The witches suddenly had handfuls of flame. Fireballs smashed into their chests and flung them backward.

Morgan whirled, grasped the final leash, and discharged another bolt. The third witch dropped her cord and stumbled away, knocking over a torch. A huge ball of fire split the end of the cord and rolled, burning, into the underbrush.

Morgan yanked all three lines up in one fist, their ends sputtering. She whipped the magical scourge down on the women. It crackled and sprayed fire. The women rolled to escape that devilish cat-o'-nine tails. Morgan snapped the whip to one side and then the other, driving the women together. Soon, all three cowered in the same space of scorched earth.

Morgan strode up and towered above them, coiling the whip around her hand. "Who's the captive now?"

The redhead wailed, "Forgive us, demon!"

"I'm not a—" Morgan reached down with the rolled whip, snagged the woman's sooty chin, and lifted her face. "You have power, you three, but no vision. Summoning evil spirits . . ." She clucked and shook her head. "What's your name?"

"I can't," she said miserably.

"Fine. I'll call you Icant." Morgan glanced to the other two. "And you'll be Idont, and you Imustnt."

The blonde scowled. "I'm not Imustnt. I'm Hilde, queen of Eastlund. And this is the queen of North Galys, and you've got the chin of the queen of the Outer Isles."

Morgan nodded approvingly. "You are rulers here?"

"Yes," replied the queen of Eastlund. "We rule through puppet husbands—handsome and harmless kings."

Morgan's free hand went to her belly, still flat and tight, though it would be showing soon. "That would seem the perfect sort of mate. . . ."

The queen of North Galys said, "Not perfect, but serviceable."

Serviceable. That is one thing neither Tristan nor Arthur were, the wise woman said. *You need a puppet husband to make your son legitimate. Your baby needs a home, as do you, as do your priestesses. Perhaps you've been looking for the wrong consort all along. . . .*

"Won't you please release us?" asked the queen of the Outer Isles.

Morgan stared levelly at her. "No." The women trembled, their eyes going dark. "No, because I'm going to train you, teach you the new magic. There'll be no more spells of bondage and domination. We have greater spells to work."

Despite the fear in her eyes, the queen of Eastlund stared in amazement at Morgan. "You would teach us?"

"On one condition," Morgan said. "That you take me to another husband like yours."

King Urien stood on the parapet of his castle and stared out. The sun was setting in red and golden majesty across the Eire Sea. Shadows flooded up to engulf his once-great kingdom.

Before Arthur, Rheged had been strong. It could stand against the Bernician Saxons and King Lot in Gododdin. Then Lot enlisted the aid of Urien and the other so-called "Great Kings of the North" to go to war against Arthur. The campaign had emptied Rheged's coffers and laid its best and brightest men in the grave. As if that weren't price enough, Lot betrayed them all in the end and became the favored servant of the new king. Urien and Rheged were left to dangle and die.

"Since before the Romans, since before history, we've

ruled Rheged." Urien's gray beard bristled as he chewed on his words. He stuck a thumb into his waistband and rested his fingers on his belly. "Now, the nation will pass out of being."

He needed something, desperately needed an infusion of power. . . .

There came a sound below the castle—a jangling sound, strange in the iron stillness. Urien turned toward the noise. His gaze swept past the walls of Mureif Castle, past the streets of Gore City, and to the island's shore. Anyone who would enter Gore had to cross the Sword Bridge, a wooden span that stabbed out from the mainland. Just now, a wagon rolled across, five women sitting atop it and playing tambourines. They waved scarves in the air and seemed to be singing.

Urien shook his head. There was an ages-old prohibition against tinkers in the city. These women would be turned back like all the others. Lifting his hand like a visor above his eyes, Urien squinted toward the wagon. It seemed that a woman was driving—a strange little beautiful woman.

The king ached inexplicably. He'd been a widower for fifteen years, and all that time had not felt this sort of longing. He was suddenly, unutterably lonely.

The wagon rolled up to the near gates and came to a halt. Even the music ceased, and the scarves stilled their glad dance. A gate guard was walking out to speak to the driver.

"No," Urien muttered, "let them in. Don't turn them away. Let them in." This was what he needed. That wagon would save him from Gododdin and Bernicia. The woman on that wagon would save him from solitude. "Let them in!" he shouted desperately, though the guard couldn't have heard. "Let them in!"

His own son, wearing the armor of his trade, strode out

into the bailey and looked up at Urien. "Father, what do you wish?"

"Ride to the Sword Bridge, Pascen! Order the guard to let those tinkers in!"

"Tinkers, Father?"

"Hurry. Escort them personally, Pascen! Here's our chance!"

"Our chance for what?"

"Hurry!"

Morgan listened for the third time to the gate guard's reasoning, but all the while she watched King Urien. The witches had been right about him. He needed her. A simple spell had sent longings to Urien across the sanguine sunset. They would be enough to bring her in, to grant her audience. Then, they would fade. Morgan wanted Urien to choose her knowing all—except the truth of the baby. He had to be ignorant of that, or he would be no father to her unborn child.

The guard ceased his quibbling, turned, and snapped to attention. He stared stiffly toward the gate.

A young man stood behind it. "Open up, I said!"

The guard swallowed. "Yes, Prince Pascen. Yes!" He cupped hands around his mouth and bellowed: "Open for the prince!" A rivulet of sweat rushed down the guard's temple, and his throat tensed for another shout, but the portcullis began its lurching ascent.

The young man beyond it ducked and hurried forward. He was lithe and lovely in trews and brocade. He wore at his slender hip a sword shiny enough to be ornamental but heavy enough to be deadly. On his face was written confusion and a little irritation. He approached the vagabond wagon and eyed it critically. When his eyes reached Morgan, though, they contained more desire than derision.

"I am Prince Pascen," the young man said, bowing. "My father sent me here to bring you to him."

Oh, yes, Prince Pascen, said the maiden in Morgan's mind. *Another Tristan. Another young and all-encompassing love!*

She can't afford that now, the wise woman said.

"I'm Morgan le Fey. I've come to speak with your father."

Nodding, the prince turned. "Then, follow me." He strode toward the open portcullis, waving the wagon after him.

Morgan urged the beast forward. "There's more to us, Prince Pascen, than meets the eye."

Under his breath, he said, "I certainly hope so."

By the time Urien had primped, changing his waistcoat three times, the tinker wagon had rolled through the gates of the castle. The heralds sounded their trumpet even as he hurried down the stairs. The women were waiting. He fetched up just inside the main door. They could wait a moment more. He didn't want to arrive all panting and sweaty. Urien grinned. How long it had been since he had panted and sweated for a woman. A tinker, no less! But her face, her eyes, her figure!

"Well, King," he muttered to himself, "on with it."

Striding purposefully, Urien marched through the double doors and out beneath a cold night sky. Four lamps shone warmly beneath the myriad stars. He held his hands out to his sides. "Welcome, entertainers, to Castle Mureif, the jewel of

Gailhom." His hands spread to indicate them all, though his eyes looked to their leader.

No lovelier creature had ever walked the world. Petite and pretty, with skin like porcelain and sable-black hair, she wore a gown befitting a noblewoman. And her eyes were as brown as good earth! Urien had never dallied. He'd never even spoken with a tinker, and yet all his desire was bent on her.

The woman descended from the footboard and lighted on the bailey stones. She bowed gracefully. "Thank you, King Urien, but we are not mere entertainers. We are much more than we seem."

Urien's heart pounded at the promise in those words. "Forgive my assumption. Whom do I have the honor of addressing?"

"I am Morgan le Fey, half-sister to King Arthur and late princess of Tintagel. Now, I am a priestess of ancient mysteries."

King Arthur! Urien's cheeks blazed, and he knew he looked a fool. Perhaps here was his hope for favored status from King Arthur!

"And here," said Morgan le Fey, gesturing to the wagon door, "are more royal sisters: Queen Hilde of Eastlund, Queen Cerewyn of North Galys, and Queen Bernicia of the Outer Isles." As each woman was named, she emerged.

Nodding in dumb amazement, Urien recognized them all. He was too shocked to be diplomatic. "Well, what are all of you doing in a tinker's wagon?"

"The wagon, too, is more than it appears," Morgan responded, her hand caressing one battered wall. "It is a moveable temple full of priestesses." From within emerged the same women he had seen sitting atop the wagon.

Urien had gone from astonishment to stupefaction. "Wh-why have you come?"

"I've come to make you a proposition." The word sent a thrill through Urien. "May we speak in private?"

His face split in an avid smile, and he offered Morgan his arm. "Yes. I would like that very much."

Morgan stepped solemnly forward and laid her diminutive hand on his arm. What a sensation, the touch of her flesh!

Urien walked her toward the main hall of the palace. "We'll speak in my audience chamber." It was right near his bedchamber, but he would not mention that. The lovely young priestess clung to his arm, gentle but firm. Through the double doors, past the great hall, and up a flight of stairs, they reached the audience chamber.

Urien ignited a jackstraw, carried it into the dark chamber, and lit a waiting lamp. Light swelled to show walls in red velvet and deep carpets from Kashmir. He could light more lamps, but he preferred to keep Morgan in a small compartment of light.

"Let's sit here," he said, gesturing to a pair of brocade chairs beside a small lamp stand and desk. She held his arm all the way to the chair and settled down sweetly. Urien smiled and sat in his own seat. "Now, what is this private proposition?"

Morgan reached her hand up before him—so lovely a hand—and she seemed to pinch a cobweb out of the air. She drew her fingers aside and pulled down. "There," she said. "Do you feel the difference?"

Urien's face fell. Desire had become dread. He'd been under an enchantment. The same beautiful woman sat before him, but no longer did he feel the overwhelming want to bed her. "What did you do?"

"I'm a priestess of ancient mysteries," Morgan repeated.

"Magic. . . ."

"Yes. I inflamed your desire so that I could enter the castle and meet you, but I've removed the enchantment because the matter I must discuss is business."

"Business," Urien said in a long exhalation.

"Your kingdom is in peril," Morgan said. "Threatened by its neighbors and collapsing within. You need allies. I will be your first."

Urien shook his head, trying to understand. "Alliance with Arthur? I'm already sworn to him. Or do you mean Tintagel?"

"Alliance with magic. I'll marshal the magical forces of world and Otherworld to make Rheged great again."

Scratching his neck, Urien said, "How do I know you can do it?"

"You've seen the other queens. You know they have used their magic to make their nations strong and prosperous. I'm offering you the same arrangement. We're equal partners in rule. You conduct all matters of state and politic, and I conduct all matters of magic and commerce. We share the throne, we share the risks, we share the coffers."

"You're proposing marriage?" Urien asked.

"Yes, as a business transaction. I gain a home and a nation, and you save a home and a nation. I make you powerful, and you make me secure."

Even without her enchantment, his heart was pounding. He needed something just like this, some*one* just like this. She was so beautiful. "I can't treat marriage as a business proposition."

She blinked. "If you mean that we share a bed, that is also negotiable . . . as a business proposition."

He returned her gaze. "I need . . . proof that you would be willing to include such things in our arrangement."

Morgan thought for a time. Purposefully, she stood and crossed to his chair. She placed her hand fondly on his cheek, and bent to blow out the lamp.

23

Queen of the Basilica

Morgan walked beside King Urien of Gore. He clutched her arm, his middle-aged hand strong on white samite. At last, here was a human being who held to her, a man who needed her and knew it. She held him too. The aisle was long and white, the benches full of great folk: kings and queens, dukes and duchesses, priests and priestesses and warriors. These were the folk among whom Morgan and Urien would succced or fail. They clung to each other, bound in need.

At last, Morgan had discovered the true relation between men and women: not the politics of passion and possession, but the safe and sterile association of business. This was what Mother had been doing with Uther and Mark. They weren't lovers but contractual associates, pledged to mutual protection and support. There need be no love in such unions, only utility. Neither partner had claim over the other, and every aspect, even sex, was negotiable.

Morgan let a laugh shush from her nose. Without even

having intended it, she had found her perfect consort, a man as solid, useful, and familiar as a saddle.

Urien gazed at her lovingly, his eyes misty above his coifed beard. He played his role perfectly. Glancing toward the congregation, he nodded to his three sons—Riwallawn, Run, and the beautiful young Pascen.

Morgan, meanwhile, traded smiles with the three witches—Hilde, Bernicia, and Cerewyn. They and her priestesses formed a powerful bloc near the front of the basilica. Soon, they would be even more powerful, when Morgan sent them throughout Gailhom and Rheged to initiate more women in the Mysteries of Gaea. The queens and duchesses in the congregation may have been strangers now, but soon they would be friends, and then followers, and worshipers. Soon, this basilica would belong to Morgan.

It was a great round building with a wide dome and four transepts. Today, the cruciform floor plan reminded worshipers of the cross. In days to come, it would be the quatrefoil seat of Morgan's rule. She would take the apse, just before the altar, and the three witches could each have seats in transepts and nave. Then, Morgan would be queen of the basilica, and Rheged would be the new capital of goddess worship.

All it would take was two words.

Morgan and Urien stopped before the priest. Beside him stood Rachel, thought by most to be maid of honor though known by bride and groom to be a priestess of Gaea. This would be a marriage between the ancient goddess and the newborn god.

The priest spoke, and then the priestess. At last bride and groom said those two all-powerful words: "I do."

Three months later, Queen Morgan and her priestesses traveled Rheged, doing the work of Gaea.

Morgan stepped down from the wagon onto the footman's stool. Beneath her elegant gown of black, her pregnancy was just beginning to show. The footman helped her to the cobbles and then caught the hand of Rachel. She too was beautifully dressed, and carried a basket overflowing with bread. Behind her came Daedra, a leather valise held beneath her arm and glass vials ringing in their straps. Together, the three women strode away from the wagon and to the front entry of the manor.

Unlike the trim and tightly walled townhouses of Gailhom, the country estate of Duke Johnstone was open. Its gates swung in the wind, and its hedgerows were as gappy as an old man's teeth. Dogs ran loose across the tall grass, and the front doors hung open.

Morgan stopped and stared into the entryway. It seemed a cave.

"Greetings to the house!" Rachel called. "Queen Morgan has come for her audience with Duchess Mary." No response came. "Who guards the door?"

There came sounds within, muffled voices raised in anger—a woman's and a man's. Rachel was about to call out again, but a serving maid skittered into view and gave a pasty smile. She bowed low before Morgan and said, "My mistress sends her apologies. She will be ready shortly. I am to take you to the music room, where I will play for you."

Morgan nodded wordlessly, hearing a faint thump and crash.

The maidservant bowed again and gestured for the

women to follow her. She retreated into the house. Morgan, Rachel, and Daedra followed through a wide parlor, down a hallway of exposed timbers, and into a small room well removed from the main house. Worn tapestries hung on its walls, and chairs and a couch stood in a cluster in its midst. The maidservant guided each woman to one of the chairs, blew hair back from her eyes, and rapidly picked up a rebec and bow. Without preamble or introduction, she began to play, a sad and sonorous tune. The sound of horsehair and catgut drowned out all other noise.

Morgan listened, eyes grave. Beside her, Rachel's fingers fidgeted on the basket at her knee. Daedra only ground her teeth.

When the first song was done, there came a second, and a third. At last, Duchess Mary arrived. She was impeccably dressed, her back held stiffly erect, and white powder covered her face.

The maidservant let her bow scrape to a stop. She stared for a moment, set down the instrument, and excused herself. Still, she made no move toward the door, which was blocked by her mistress.

Duchess Mary bowed. "Forgive my late arrival, Queen Morgan. I had an unexpected matter to tend to." She sniffed, drew a kerchief, and dabbed at her nose. A tiny spot of red remained on the cloth.

Morgan solemnly stood and approached the woman. She had meant to greet her in the name of Gailhom, present her with the gifts of bounty and knowledge as she had done with dozens of noblewomen. This time, Morgan silently lifted her hand to the thick powder on Duchess Mary's face. One gentle stroke across her cheek revealed a fist-shaped bruise. Morgan took another step, embracing the woman. Into her ear, Morgan said, "Remain here. My priestesses and I will return."

Morgan nodded to Rachel and Daedra. They stood, leaving their things behind, and followed Morgan into the manor house.

It wouldn't be hard to find him. They followed the trail of powder across wood floors, up a carpeted stair to Duchess Mary's room. Then the telltale drops of blood led to where her husband was.

He was sitting on the bed, doing up his trews. He wore no shift, and his shoulders glowed red. Whistling to himself in a drunken way, the duke looked up only when the three women in black swept through his open door and slammed it behind them.

"Who are you?" he slurred.

Flanked by the other two, Morgan stared baldly at the man. Her eyes seemed like hard-boiled eggs and her mouth like a cut in her face. "You had better never hit her again."

The duke's face grew livid, and he stood. "I ask again. Who are you?"

Morgan bellowed, "I am the one you are hitting. I am the one you must answer to. There will be no more!"

At first, he winced back from her shout, but then the duke gathered himself and lunged.

Morgan flared red, power pouring from her skin. Flame enveloped her, hurling back the man's hands, and white smoke curled from his blackened fingers. He bounced off the fiery aura, fell to the floor, and clutched his hands between his legs.

Above him stood Morgan, inviolate in flame. The surge of magic eased and ceased. Anger drained out of her but left pitiless eyes. "My midwife will bind Mary's wounds, and my priestess will open to her the feminine mysteries. I will put my mark on her, if she will have it, and any harm you do to her will happen to you instead."

The duke hissed and writhed on the floor, black hands trembling. "What about me? What about my fingers?"

"Find a sausage maker," Morgan said. She turned, flung open the door, and stormed out. Daedra and Rachel followed.

They could hear the man whimpering as they passed through the hall and descended the stair. Heading straight to the music room, they found the door bolted against them. Morgan leaned an ear to it and listened. She rapped lightly. "Duchess?"

A gasp came from the other side, and the bolt was shot back. The door opened to show the maidservant's anxious face. "We thought it was the master."

"No," replied Morgan simply. The servant opened the door wide, and Morgan passed through.

Duchess Mary looked like a ghost—a white face and scarlet eyes. She wrung her hands. "Did you kill him?"

"No." Morgan sat down on one chair and invited Mary to take the other. "Do you want us to?"

"Not yet," Mary replied immediately. A sad smile crossed her face, and she laughed. Shortly, the sound turned to sobs. "What will happen when you leave?"

Rachel knelt to one side of her. "Nothing will. You aren't defenseless."

Mary stared back, uncomprehending. Daedra brought a pitcher and basin from a nearby room and began to wash her face. "There are ancient powers that watch over us and will watch over you, if you wish them to."

Beneath the powder and the bruises, Mary's face was aglow. "I do."

The "Great Kings of the North" were becoming less great by the month. Since Lot's betrayal, all of them had shrunk. Their armies had been reduced to straggling bands of deserters, their taxes to chickens and carrots, and the kings themselves to belligerent boys.

"Please! Please, all of you!" Urien shouted, pounding his hand on the table. "Enough squabbling! That's how Arthur and Lot have bested us. They've hanged, drawn, and quartered us, and we're coming to pieces! We have to stand together."

"*Stand* together?" the king of Dalriada said wryly. "We can't even get off our arses."

Prince Mador of the Hebrides smirked. "Instead of a standing army, I've got a lying-down one."

"That's called a graveyard," said his brother, Prince Patris.

Their jokes met with angry laughter from the men around the table.

"Let's be serious," Urien pleaded. "If we band together, we can—"

"Die together!" interrupted King Moffat of Annandale. The others laughed, lifted their mugs in salute, and drank deeply. This time, no amount of pounding from Urien could bring silence to the group.

Until Morgan walked in. Even five months pregnant, she was gorgeous. As she appeared in the east door, laughter died in the kings' throats. They straightened and wiped the irreverence from their faces. Innocently, Morgan wandered toward the table. "What's funny?"

Blushing happily, King Moffat replied, "Just something your husband said."

Morgan lifted an eyebrow. "He *is* clever, isn't he?"

Muffled affirmations came around the table.

"He's the best man for beating my half-brother at his own game."

"King Arthur already has our fealty, Queen Morgan," Patris pointed out.

"Let him have your fealty, but not your hearts. Your hearts are here in the north. Our nations must favor each other in trade and war. We must make our kingdoms the envy of Britannia, and then declare ourselves free." Morgan walked toward the western door. "Just because you didn't win doesn't mean you have to lose." Pushing her way through, she said, "But what do I know of such things?"

She left, but her words lingered. The Great Kings of the North looked at their hands and studied the foam on their tankards.

"Your wife's got something there," said the king of Dalriada.

The others nodded in agreement.

Urien stared toward the door where she had disappeared. "She surely does."

Morgan stood with the three witches at the mouth of a cave. Below them, the Tember River shone in glittering expanse, flowing to break around the isle of Gailhom. Only the sword-shaped bridge joined the isle to the mainland—Urien's bridge. It was time for Morgan to have a bridge of her own.

She pricked her finger and squeezed it until a pearl of blood stood on the tip. Then, reaching above the cave, she drew a quick figure in red—a Sheila-na-gig, Goddess of the Open Door. Blood spread across the black stone, sank in, and began to blaze. The image etched itself in rock. In time, its fire died, and ribbons of smoke poured from the crevices. Morgan and the three witches could still see the Sheila-na-gig clearly, though it would be invisible to the uninitiated.

"Spread the word about this place," Morgan said gravely. She rubbed her belly, as if scrying the baby within. "Anyone who needs escape, who needs safe and silent passage, must come this way." Morgan ducked her head, stepped into the rocky hollow, and descended into the throat of stone.

Behind her, Bernicia asked, "Shall we put stores down here—food and weapons?"

"No, this isn't a hidey-hole. This is a passageway." Morgan descended farther still.

"To where?" asked the woman.

"To Gailhom."

At the base of a long downward passage, Morgan led them into a strange new light. The cave opened beneath the blue-green river. A log floated by overhead. Fish snapped at insects on the surface and then dived to troll the depths. Only a gossamer tunnel of magic kept the mighty Tember from pouring down upon them. Currents murmured and chattered against the magic field, but the ground beneath Morgan was bone dry.

"Astonishing," Bernicia said.

Morgan nodded. "Urien has his bridge, and I have mine. His is for the many and mine for the few."

The other witches goggled in amazement. "Such power you wield, Morgan."

The queen only nodded. "The power of Gaea."

Morgan strode in stately grace down the same aisle she had walked eight months before. Everything had changed.

Instead of a slender white gown, she wore a voluminous black robe. No one walked beside her. This ceremony was not about joining her to anyone but separating her from everyone. Only her child came along, huge within her belly. It would be born any day now, and the people waited for the child as for the son of Mary.

It was only fitting. Morgan had become the spiritual leader of Gailhom, Gore, and Rheged, admired as far north as the Hebrides. She was loved and revered, though her own faith was a mystery to most. Since a married woman could not be a nun, the people called her "Queen of the Basilica." She would officially receive that title today.

Morgan smiled serenely. To either side stood followers and friends—women mostly, but also men who couldn't tell lust from devotion. Through miracles and initiations, she had gathered these hundreds. They were faithful and strong believers. Many stood beside male keepers—fathers or husbands or sons—but a time was coming when they would stand alone, as Morgan did.

Urien himself waited in the first row, proud of his wife and the kingdom she had revitalized. Gailhom thrived, the envy of her neighbors and the terror of her enemies. In Gododdin especially, home of King Lot, Morgan was maligned as the "Witch-Queen." Stories of her kept the armies of Lot away. By contrast, her own people called her the "Faerie Saint."

Up three steps for Father and three for Son and three for Holy Ghost, she reached the altar. She halted before the priest.

He gazed lovingly at her, knelt, and intoned, "Beloved Morgan, queen of Gailhom, with joy we welcome you to your basilica." He lifted a golden scepter shaped like a key, the cross of Christ at its end. "We are your servants, now and evermore."

She received the scepter and turned, lifting it above her head. Small though she was, Morgan was great with child, and she seemed an effigy of Gaea herself.

"Behold, my beloved people," cried Morgan, "this new image of divinity. You have seen the crucifix, emblem of death. See now the sphere, emblem of life." Magic surged up her arms into the scepter. It crawled in red lightning over the hunk of metal and then arced out above the congregation. Galvanic charges whirled into a great blue sphere. It spun majestically, its surface covered in white swirls. "She has waited millennia to return to you, but now she comes."

The initiates knew instinctively what Morgan meant. All the others only stared in wonder and wished they knew.

"You rise from her and descend into her; she is the source of all life and the end of it. Every creature is her child, every god her son." The image changed, the cross of Christ over-laying the sphere, cutting it into quadrants. "In endless cycles of four, she gives life, fertility, age, and death—and life again."

All the congregants gazed in awe, the sons of Christ see-ing the cross and the daughters of Gaea seeing everything else.

Morgan lowered her hands, and the vision unwound, energy returning into her. She wore a tight expression. "Thank you, my people. The Queen of the Basilica thanks you. As you belong to me, I belong to you, now and ever." She set down the scepter and held onto her abdomen. "Now, though, you must leave me." She took a staggering step and sat down on the stairs. "All of you except the midwives."

Urien ran to her. He whispered urgently, "Is it time?"

She only nodded.

Clutching the sides of his face, the king turned toward the people and said, "You heard the queen! Get!"

24

Pangs

After Urien dismissed the crowd, Morgan dismissed him. She said she wanted to give birth in the center of the basilica. That woman! What she wouldn't do for theater.

Urien slapped his leg and smiled in admiration. He stifled a laugh of excitement and sat down on a bench in the basilica's antechamber. He would gladly guard the door and await the news.

Since the night Morgan had rolled into his life, everything had changed for the better. She was his opposite: young, charismatic, beautiful, driven, magical, wise. She had arcane power, and with it had saved Rheged. Marrying Morgan had been the best decision Urien had ever made, and though this was supposedly a business arrangement, he couldn't deny it any longer: He loved her.

Tonight, the queen was even bearing him a son.

Urien stood up and tiptoed to the double doors, barred against him. He peered through a slender crack. By swaying side to side, he could see the queen and her entourage. Morgan sat in a strange, tilting seat. It held her knees apart, and there was a place between them where the baby would come. She clutched the armrests of her birthing throne—Urien's child would be born on a throne!—and her face clenched.

"Don't push yet," said one of the midwives sharply.

"I know," Morgan spat back. "That's what I'm doing. Not pushing."

Urien smiled and murmured, "That's my girl." He swayed farther, taking in more of the group. There were four initiates in the so-called "Mysteries of Gaea," her girl's club. They wore white robes and stood at her feet and hands, mumbling rituals. Sometimes Urien was jealous of these women. They spent so much time with his wife he wondered if they engaged in . . . unspeakable delights. Morgan's drives seemed strong enough, but Urien had successfully negotiated only three exchanges. Perhaps she was spending herself on women, a tantalizing thought!

But there was a man there—two men! Urien bristled. He pressed the doors against the bar, widening the gap, and stared angrily at them. Realization struck: These were Morgan's eunuchs. They'd been Christian hermits living in revilement of their own flesh when Morgan converted them. Urien himself had inspected the men to make sure they were harmless. He laughed. His jealousy was getting absurd!

"Think of something else," the midwife instructed as she wiped Morgan's brow.

Morgan curled forward and gritted her teeth. "What else?"

"Think of the baby's father."

"I'd rather not," Morgan growled.

Urien blanched. What did she mean by that? He pressed his ear to the crack and listened.

"Do you know what that idiot did two weeks ago?" Morgan asked, panting.

Idiot? What did I do? What did I do?

"He asked Guinevere to marry him."

I did not! Who's Guinevere?

"Of course, she said no."

What are they talking about?

"Of course?" echoed the midwife. "Guinevere would've been queen of Britannia! I'd've said yes. Besides, Arthur is handsome."

"That's all he is," Morgan replied.

"Do you think he realizes?" the midwife asked. "About the baby, I mean."

"Who? Arthur or Urien?"

"Either of them."

"No. Merlin might have told Arthur, but otherwise he's in the dark. As to Urien, well . . . he hasn't an inkling."

"Just hope the child doesn't have Arthur's blond curls."

Morgan laughed. "Then even Urien might get the idea."

They all laughed, all but Urien.

He got the idea. By God did he get the idea! He wanted to break down the doors and storm in there and accuse her of adultery—of incest! No, he wanted her to recant it, say that everything he had believed and hoped was indeed true and everything that now threatened it was a lie. If only he hadn't heard! This was betrayal on every level. Morgan had fooled him about the child, about her allegiance, about their future together, about love. . . .

No, she had never lied about love. She'd made it clear this was business, even the sex. Oh, but that was part of the betrayal, to make him believe the baby was his!

Urien gritted his teeth. He wanted to rip her apart and throw the baby in the sea. He would, too, if not for this bar and those eunuchs and her magic. . . . He slid down the door and went to his knees, rocking in a cold sweat. He was impotent, a eunuch himself. She'd made him think he had power and love, the two things every man wants, but in fact he had nothing and could do nothing.

"No, I can do something," he hissed feverishly. Urien stood up, brushing the dust from his knees and his waistcoat. "I can write to Arthur. He'll want to know about this incestuous, monstrous bastard."

The child was already screaming as its head emerged. It spat the mucous plug from its throat, and Daedra used a pig's bladder to suck the nose clean. "Last one."

With a final, exhausted push, Morgan bore the baby into the world. It emerged on a tide of blood and water. The umbilicus dragged the afterbirth into the base of the birthing chair.

"A boy!" cried Daedra, lifting him high.

Rachel and her initiates subtly changed their chant.

"Another boy," Morgan said, weeping wearily. "You see him, don't you?"

Daedra gazed at the child—long and lean, mantled in blood, a bluish piece of placenta clinging caplike to his head. "I'm *holding* him, Morgan!"

"But you see him, all of you," Morgan pressed. "He's really here."

"Yes," they chorused.

Morgan closed her eyes, and tears streamed into her hair. "Not like Mabon."

With a level and loving gaze, Daedra said, "He was real, too, Morgan. The marks of him are all over you."

He was suddenly in her arms, this slick and squalling

creature. "My beautiful boy," Morgan said, kissing his mottled head. He had thick black hair like her own, and he was almost gaunt. "Welcome to the world, Mordred."

Daedra worked him over with a warm cloth, cleaning away the remnants of his former world. She lifted a knife from the bath of rye spirits, shook it once, and handed the wet blade to Morgan. "It's time to release him."

"Yes," Morgan said quietly. Then, to her son, she said simply, "Once, we were one. Now, we must be two. With this knife begins your separate life. May it be long and lovely, and at the end of your days, may you return to Mother Gaea, from whom you were born." Morgan lifted the knife and slashed, severing the cord just beyond the string that tied it off.

Mordred wailed, his legs kicking against the air.

"Yes," Morgan cooed. "It hurts me too."

Daedra lifted the child and wrapped him in swaddling. She delivered him into the hands of Rachel and the three initiates, who would present him to the four corners of the world. The sun was rising beyond the eastern windows.

"He's in your hands now, Mother Gaea," Morgan said, and she drowsed in the birthing throne.

Morgan was in bliss. For two days, Mordred and she clung to each other, slept together, ate together, and were never separated, not even when she bathed. This child wouldn't be another Mabon. Morgan ordered her eunuch guards to allow no man except Urien near her chambers, and only Daedra and Rachel among the women.

Urien had come, of course, and he was given a chance to hold the child. He shook strangely, an agonized smile on his face and tears running down his cheeks. It seemed almost as if he would drop the boy. Morgan took Mordred back, and Urien murmured, "I'm not much for babies. They're so fragile. You can break their necks so easily." He left and did not return.

The third day and night were agony. To escape the fate of Mabon, Mordred must survive these long hours. No one could be trusted. Morgan banished even Rachel and Daedra from the basilica. Only the queen and her prince remained. They stayed alone in the center of the sanctuary, the doors barred and the windows shuttered. Using the birth blood, Morgan poured a warding circle around them on the floor and enchanted it to slay any creature that crossed it. The warding worked. A cricket that violated the ring died in midleap and was just a husk when it hit ground. Within that deadly circle sat the Queen of the Basilica in her birthing chair-turned-throne. Her son clung to her breast, and the slops bucket waited nearby. At her fingertips were spells ready against all comers.

No one came.

By the dawn of the fourth day, Morgan was exhausted and famished, but Mordred was still with her. She broke the warding circle and emerged, carrying her child and herself to Daedra and Rachel. The initiates cared for mother and son, and they rested and grew strong.

Still, for a fortnight, Morgan kept Mordred with her always and allowed only Urien and her closest comrades near. In time, she permitted others, by written request. One by one, they would enter the heavily guarded basilica and approach its queen on her birthing throne, the boy cradled in one arm. They came to adore. Morgan's absence had only kindled the people's desire. Christian faithful knelt as before the Madonna and Child. Pagan faithful knelt as before Gaea.

"Approach the throne," Morgan said.

The young woman, little more than a girl with the first budding of breasts, rose from the floor. She wore a clean but threadbare smock over a too-large dress. The girl's hair was tied up beneath a veil, and her wide eyes seemed old. She strode up the nine steps and did a little curtsey that she had outgrown.

Morgan stared gravely at her, Mordred reclining in her arm. "You understand how terrible a thing this is?"

"Yes."

"I sit here with my newborn on my arm, enthroned on the seat of fertility. Every day, women come to me, women twice your age who hope for half of the fecund strength that you have, and you ask me to take it away?"

"Yes."

"Come closer." Morgan reached out and cupped the girl's jaw. "Would it be so terrible to bear, truly?"

The girl tried to look down, but Morgan held her chin. "The child will be my grandfather's."

Morgan stiffened, a sad smile on her bleak mouth. "Go with Daedra. She will teach you what you must do. She'll teach you other things, too, ways to stop children and grandfathers both."

The girl's face brightened—how dark her world is, that this would be light to her!—and she thanked Morgan. She descended to Daedra, and both of them withdrew to the north transept.

Morgan took a calming breath and called out. "Bring in the next petitioner."

A page nodded and disappeared into the narthex, returning with a familiar man beside him. "King Urien to see you, my queen."

"Urien!" Morgan stood and descended the stairs. She clutched Mordred against her and held her free arm toward the king. "You can come to me and Mordred any time."

"Can I?" he asked. His tone was both brusque and pleading. He bustled up the aisle and fell to his knees. "Can I, Morgan?"

Morgan hurried to him and knelt. "Of course. You're my husband—"

"Am I?"

"You're Mordred's father."

"Am I?" he reached for her and desperately gripped her arm. "Can't we go back to the way things were, Morgan? When it was us, you and I together, when we shared a bed instead of you and Mordred."

Morgan shook her head in disbelief. "We never shared a bed."

Beneath his gray beard, Urien's chin shuddered. "All right, then, not how things were. How I thought things were. How I wished they were."

"You're not making any sense."

He stopped and straightened. The fit was over. "I'm sorry. I just thought . . . I just thought it was worth trying."

"Yes, Urien, of course," Morgan said. "It's always worth trying."

The man stood up. He shook out his arms, turned, and walked away.

"We'll eat together, then, tonight," Morgan said to his retreating back.

He didn't turn or look back, and the doors slammed behind him.

———

Urien didn't meet Morgan for dinner, taking it instead in his own chambers. From then on, he avoided her. Morgan went to see him, but he was always indisposed, his guards unwilling to let her pass.

She guessed at what had happened: Urien had fallen in love with her. Despite all their talk of business and political partnership, he had turned the whole matter into love—a one-sided, obsessive, tragic love.

Mordred shifted in her arms, and his soft brown eyes fixed on her.

Morgan smiled down at him until his eyes closed in sleep. She then peered out the lofty window of her room. Beyond was a five hundred foot drop to the Eire Sea, which shimmered at the end of day. The sun spread its golden veil across undulating waves.

Poor, lovesick Urien. I pity him.

"I can pity him, but not love him."

He feels betrayed. . . .

"He betrayed *me!*" Morgan insisted. "He changed the conditions of our partnership."

It was foolish of us to think it could be just a partnership.

Mordred woke up and twisted his mouth. A couple small sniffs, and he began to cry. Morgan shushed him, drawing open her robe and offering her breast. He latched on.

"I can't worry about Urien now, not with Mordred here and so needy." In two months, he had come far—losing the last black remnant of his umbilicus, doubling his weight, focusing on his mother's face. . . . Morgan loved her son, and he loved her too. It was a perfect circle, and Urien was only intruding.

Now you are being cruel.

Morgan glanced out the window. There were four great

ships on the golden sea—large ships with bellied sails and prows pointed toward Gailhom. They were black against the sunset. Had this been any other harbor, their speed would have been perilous, but Gailhom's western edge dropped sharply into a deep basin. Even so, these ships cleft the billows in a great hurry.

An urgent knock came, a key in the lock, and the door flew open. Urien charged in, gray hair standing from red temples. He slammed the door and locked it again.

"Urien!" Morgan said. "What are you doing here?"

"Did you see the ships?" he asked, striding toward the window and craning to see. The four vessels reefed their sails, and the ships slowed against the river's current. "Warships."

"Whose?"

"Arthur's."

Morgan sat up, her breast slipping from Mordred's mouth. The baby reached for it but couldn't latch on, his head lulling. Morgan lifted him and helped him fill his mouth. Urien watched, his face despondent. Only when the child was suckling again did Morgan look to those ships. "Why would Arthur send warships?"

"Why?" Urien almost barked. "One reason—Mordred."

"What?"

"The king wrote me, demanding I give Mordred to him. He said Mordred was his son—"

Morgan's face grew white. "No! He can't have Mordred."

"Of course not," Urien said. "That's what my response was. He said if we didn't hand over Mordred, his soldiers would take the island and snatch up every male baby and bear them all away."

Morgan's jaw dropped. This was a manifold horror: not just Mordred but every baby boy in every house of the capital. She knew those mothers—initiates, most of them. Arthur was coming to steal all their babies.

"Close the docks! Close the gates! Sound the alarm," Morgan gabbled out. She stood up. "We can't let him take them."

Urien caught her by the arm, and something small and sharp jabbed into her skin. "You're right. Not all the babies. Just one."

Her eyes widened in realization, though the rest of her body seemed suddenly sluggish. "What've you done?"

"You started this with a spell," Urien spat viciously. "Well, here's a little spell of my own."

He pulled Mordred from his mother's nerveless hands. The moment the baby lost hold of her breast, he began to squall. Urien laid the child on the floor and turned back to his wife. With a strength that belied his age, he lifted Morgan. She couldn't move, stiff in his grip. Urien carried her to the bed and ripped her shift open, exposing both breasts. He stared like a hungry predator. "I'm your husband, damn it. I shouldn't have to poison you to do this."

As the baby lay, screaming, on the ground, Urien knelt and drank.

There was nothing Morgan could do but lie there, seeing, hearing, and feeling it all. He did not stop at the breasts, but took all of her. She had not thought it could be worse, but when Urien finished, he went to Mordred, wrapped him in his swaddling, and carried him out the door.

Naked and paralyzed, Morgan listened as the warriors of Arthur burst into home after home and dragged away the little boys.

25

To Save Mordred

Whatever poison he had chosen carried Morgan through that awful night, a prisoner in her own body. If only it had made her insensate! She would not have to hear the clash of steel and crash of doors, the mothers and babies screaming. She would not have to see the fiery bellies of the midnight clouds, or the door guard who watched her all too much. If only she were asleep, she would not have to be naked and ashamed, torn up and unable to put herself back together.

Arthur and Urien were doing the same thing, performing the immemorial rite of man in the face of defiant woman. They took what they wanted and established forevermore their power to do so. Partnership between the sexes could not survive such masculine spasms. It was time for a different arrangement.

By the agony of degrees, the sun returned to ravaged Gailhom. Its light drove Arthur's raiders onto their ships and spanked the ships out to sea. All that while, Morgan was returning to her body. Patiently, she tested each limb, using minute movements to avoid alerting the guard. When fingers would move, and lips, she used both slowly and silently to cast blood magic on herself, healing the damage done by Urien. She gathered herself for an all-out strike.

Morgan rose suddenly, landing on bare feet on the floor. The guard turned, but she hurled her hands up. The air before them grew red. It rolled like thunder and struck him, lifting him off his feet and hurling him against the corridor wall. He crashed and crumpled, a man asleep in a pile of metal.

Grasping the ties to her gown, Morgan did them up. She was naked no longer. This simple robe would be her battle armor. Barefoot, she strode down the hall. Her nose led her on, the scent of herself carried away by Urien. He would be easy to find—cowering in his chambers, barricaded and guarded. It would not be enough.

Morgan rounded the corner and saw the soldiers: twelve hearty men. They had been leaning against the walls and conversing, but as soon as they saw her, they snapped to attention in two rows of six.

Morgan didn't even slow. "Stand aside."

"We would, my queen," the guard captain said in a tremulous voice, "but the king—"

"You've chosen." Her hands bludgeoned the air, and it roared in red waves into the men.

All twelve came off their feet. As one, they rammed into the walls and doors. Wood splintered, and hinges cracked, and the whole mass of man and door shoved inward to push over the barricade. Guards crashed down amid tumbling splinters, and there came the long, ominous moan of a wardrobe toppling. It fell on its face, a thunderbolt, and came to pieces around the king's ruined clothes.

Beyond the chaos of destruction, Urien huddled in his bed. He held his blankets in a paltry shield before him.

Morgan marched over groaning guards and ruination. "Listen, all of you. You're alive because I need witnesses, so—witness and live." Her eyes were pinned on Urien. "As for you, Husband—King—you have a choice. Swear your absolute and unconditional obedience to me, or die on the spot."

Urien released a tight whine, like a deflating sack. Morgan stomped toward him. He slid from the bed to his knees and then his face. "I swear! I swear! Forgive me, Morgan. I was mad. I did what I did for love!"

She stopped, rooted in place. Her eyes blazed, and her hands wrung blood out of the air. "For love! For love of what?"

"You, Morgan," Urien said abjectly, speaking into the stones. "For love of you! Everything for you."

"You rape me for love of me? You steal my son for love of me?"

He could only weep piteously.

She had no pity left. "Where is he? Where is Mordred?"

Urien shook his head. "I don't know. I gave him to a soldier, one of Arthur's soldiers. They took him and all the newborns."

Morgan lunged for Urien, hauled him from his face, and hurled him toward the shattered doors. Guards scooted back to let him land.

Urien whimpered, "Help me! Help me!"

The guard captain glanced from Urien to Morgan. "We serve the queen," he said. "And you do, too."

"Excellent response," Morgan said, shoving Urien into the guard captain's hands. "Take him to the dungeon, clap him in irons, and lock him away. Then send a special detail to the crypt below the basilica, to the deepest, darkest grave, and transform it into an oubliette—"

"An oubliette, my queen?"

"Yes, an oubliette. I want to forget about him. Put him in there. Feed him and water him as you would a dog you hated but wanted to live."

The guard captain took hold of the king.

Urien pleaded, "You can't do this to me!"

"I thought the exact same thing last night." Morgan motioned to send the guard captain away, and the warriors winced from her hand. "The rest of you—anyone who can stand, help those who can't. Battlefield curatives. Take any man who can't fight to the infirmary, but the rest of you, head out into the city and help. While you protected this rapist, a thousand others went through every house in Gailhom." Her eyes were red, not with fury but with checked tears. "This will never happen again—not to me or to any woman in this city."

The guard captain nodded grimly and led Urien away. Others extricated themselves from the wreckage and began checking on their comrades. Morgan marched out past them. Her mind already whirled through what she must do.

The ley conjunction in Gailhom ran straight through the basilica. It had been a site of power from the foundations of the world, occupied by tell, tomb, cairn, shrine, and temple. There, she would seek her son.

Morgan retrieved the keys to the basilica and descended to the castle yard. She flung open the door, startling the guard, but plunged on across the grass as he gaped behind her. "Open the gates, in the name of the queen!" she shouted.

A helmeted head poked from the guardhouse window. The man's eyes grew wide, and he withdrew. There came a curse, the clatter of spears falling from a rack, and the soldier bolted from the door toward Morgan. He held no weapon, his hands open and imploring. "Highness, surely you don't mean it—with the invasion and all. Who knows if they're gone—"

"Open it!" Morgan shouted.

The man dug in his heels, skidded to a stop, and pelted back toward the gate.

"If the babies are gone; the soldiers are gone too. Open it, and get out into the city!"

With more curses and the strain of muscle against mechanism, the gates edged up their tracks. Morgan marched out beneath them. A dark tunnel of wet stone gave way to streets in chaos. She stopped, mouth dropping open.

Every door had been kicked in. Every tenth house had burned. Folk wandered in shock and terror, kneeling beside others who had not survived the night. The air was filled with the scent of blood and sepsis, smoke and despair.

Morgan stared. These had been her nightmares, but now her terrors were true.

The basilica hulked at the height of the road, round and impregnable. Arthur's men hadn't smashed its doors or windows. Perhaps they thought it was still a place holy to Christ. Morgan headed toward it.

She approached a man who lay facedown on the cobbles. His back had been torn open by a sword stroke. Three crows sat there, beaks red from pecking him. The blood would be a conduit for Morgan. She reached three fingers toward them and said, "Come with me, Morrigan. I have better work for you."

The biggest crow cocked its head and launched itself up from the dead man. Black wings battered the air, and it soared to Morgan's shoulder. The two other crows landed opposite the first. Their sanguine beaks exploring her hairline and ears as she strode on.

Near the basilica, a preternatural hush filled the air. The crows sensed it too, hopping on her shoulder and riffling their wings. Morgan climbed the steps to the double doors, lifted the key—the iron hot from her fist—and turned it in the lock. The mechanism released, and she pulled on the bronze ring. The doors shifted slightly before rattling to a stop, barred within.

"Open in the name of the queen," Morgan commanded.

Through the crack came a multitude of anxious whispers. They combined into the voice of one woman. "Please, Queen Morgan. Don't be mad!"

"Open!" Morgan shouted.

The bar shifted and dropped, bounding loudly on the flagstones. Morgan yanked on the rings, and the doors swung wide.

There before her stood perhaps a hundred women, each holding at least one child in her arms. Many had their hands clamped on their babies' mouths. The foremost, a mere peasant with roseate cheeks, said, "We're so sorry. Them soldiers was breaking in everywhere, but leaving the church, so we come and brung whoever we could. We used the crypt door, and they didn't know. We're so sorry!"

Morgan held out her arms as if to block their escape, and her face reddened. She shook her head. "Oh, my dear mothers, you can't know how right you have been. This is your haven, now and always. That you've saved these . . . hundred children. . . . Thank you!" She walked into the mob and wrapped her arms around as many as she could. The crows squawked, prancing down her arms to avoid weeping faces. "Let your children cry. It's a day for crying."

One by one, the women peeled their hands from the mouths of the babes, and a chorus of blessed screams filled the air.

"Stay here, if you wish, or go home. The soldiers are gone. We must begin again." They looked in fearful hope at her until she repeated those four critical words. "The soldiers are gone."

Then, they flooded out past her. Morgan dropped her arms and waded through the throng. In their haste, the women jostled her, and the crows took wing. They flew through air that was hot and stale. Circling and laughing, the birds waited for their mistress to get clear of the crowd.

Morgan stepped past overturned benches and makeshift beds, reaching the central aisle of the basilica. The red road ran right through her. She could feel its sinews plucking at her heart. Lifting her hands, she called to the crows.

They banked and dived and lighted on her hands.

"Beautiful children, listen: I need my friends now, Queen Hilde of Eastlund, Queen Cerewyn of North Galys, and Queen Bernicia of the Outer Isles. Find them."

The crows cawed gladly and took flight. Their wings gripped air for only a moment before gripping magic. Scarlet power traced every plume, gathered across the shoulders of the beasts, and closed over their bloody beaks. Then, they were gone, winging through the Otherworld.

Morgan didn't wait for their return. She raced up the

nine steps and reached the baptismal. She had filled it with Avalon water, useful for many rituals, but today, she needed something thicker.

She bit the back of her hand and thrust it into the bowl. Blood spread in ropy lines through the water. Though she held her hand perfectly still, ripples formed. The water was troubled, churning. Waves took shape, a net of white foam linking peak to peak.

The sea rolls before a westering wind. Sleek fish dart beneath the billows, and white birds soar above.

"I don't want the sea. I want Mordred. Where is he?"

Waves tumble on the wide sea, toying with a tiny thing in their midst—a ship. Its sails are bellied full, its decks awash in flopping fish. No one mans the tops or the decks, and the helm is tied to run with the wind. The ship breasts green waves on its flight from shore.

"Where's the crew? Where is Mordred?"

Those are not flopping fish but babies. They've been laid out across the decks, side by side, the children of Gailhom naked beneath the sky. Mordred is somewhere among them. The men of Arthur have the heart to steal away a generation of boys, but not to put them to the sword. They set them adrift on the waves, depending on sun and sea to kill them.

"No," Morgan whispered incredulously.

"What is it?" asked Hilde of Eastlund. She stepped out of the air, the power of the Otherworld clinging to her.

Without turning, Morgan said, "Mordred and hundreds of others." She stared at the ship and the bounding waves, seeking a ley line convergence. "They're dying of exposure on the deck of a ship."

On the other side of the baptismal, Bernicia assembled her body from scraps of magic. "Who would do this?"

Morgan shook her head sadly, "Who else? Mordred's father . . . Arthur."

Cerewyn ran up behind the other two. "What will we do?"

"Get cloth," Morgan said. "Vestments, altar cloths, anything you can find. And Bernicia, find pure water, something we can give these poor ones until they're back with their mothers."

As the witches ran off, Hilde asked, "What am I to do?"

"You'll have to sail the ship."

"I don't know how to sail a ship."

"You're a Saxon. You have to know how to sail a ship!"

Hilde's eyes were wide with fear. "Why don't we just walk the red way with them?"

Morgan shook her head. "The ship will cross it only momentarily. We can't carry hundreds of babies away in a moment."

Cerewyn returned with a set of drapes she had pulled down from the southern windows. "I also found a ritual knife."

"And here are skins of Avalon water," added Bernicia.

Morgan nodded to them both. "Excellent." She pulled her bleeding hand from the water and spun about. "The ley line conjunction is ten seconds away. Come with me." She ran down the aisle. The three witches of Cumberland hurried behind her.

In midstride, Morgan vanished. Her foot rose from the world and set down in the Otherworld. One by one the other women leapt into the leys. Each step carried them over dozens of miles. They crossed an intersecting ley and veered down it. The ocean rushed past beneath them, and the ship nosed across the line.

"Now!" Morgan shouted. They slid down onto a deck

full of screaming, riling babies. The women stepped gingerly. Their eyes were wild with the horrible scene, their hair charged with magic. "Hilde, get to the helm. Untie it and turn the ship around."

The Saxon woman sighed heavily. "I'll do my best, but how do I sail *into* the wind?"

"*Change* the wind!" Morgan said. "And you two, gather up the children. Get them below and wrap them and give them water. If you find Mordred, call out!"

The three witches hurried to their tasks, and Morgan began her own: searching for her son. She studied the faces below her, burned by sun and wind. Some babies squalled, some slept, some stared in mute dread at the blue heavens. None were Mordred. She stepped over a group of kicking boys and searched more faces. It pained her to straddle these dying children and offer no help, but first—

"Mordred . . . Mordred . . . Mordred . . ."

The mainsail swept by overhead, and all the other sails followed. "I've brought her about!" shouted Hilde gleefully. Her blonde hair shot up in a ragged halo around her head. "I'm shifting the winds. We'll drive to shore."

"Good!" shouted Morgan. She stared into every helpless face amidships, but none was the right one. What if they had killed Mordred outright? What if Mordred had fallen overboard?

Some of these babies were already limp on the planks.

Even if Mordred survives, said the warrior woman within her, *Arthur will die for this. In the fullness of time, we will kill him and his Guinevere, and his court, and Merlin too. Camelot will be razed and erased from the memory of the world.*

Then, the one cry that was Mordred's—the nonsense language spoken fluently, child to mother—came to Morgan's ear. She stepped over two more boys and found him, lying beside the capstan, his face in its shadow. "Mordred!" She scooped him up. His flesh was hot and red. "Mordred!"

"We're heading for shore!" Hilde called. "Another few moments, and we'll be there."

"Gailhom?" asked Morgan, staring toward the helm.

"No! Of course not. I couldn't get us back to Gailhom! Just land. Any land!"

Morgan panted blearily, pulling her robe aside and drawing Mordred into it. "Water! I need some water!"

Bernicia climbed up from the hold, where she and Cerewyn had carried many of the babies, and she brought a water skin. She stepped lightly across the deck and passed the skin to Morgan. Child and mother drank.

"How many do you think we'll save?"

"Maybe forty. Maybe fifty."

"Have so many died already?" asked Morgan.

"No," Bernicia replied, nodding toward the rocky shore. "But they will when we crash."

The word had hardly emerged when the hull shrieked and the ship listed and the women were thrown to the deck among screaming babes.

26

Return

They carried babies away from the wrecked ship, forty in the landing boat. Morgan and the witches waded in chest-deep waters with four-foot waves, guiding the craft. Then, back again for forty more, and to the shore. The rest hadn't survived sun and sea. Their grave would be the foundering wreck.

At last, Morgan and the witches beached the boat and fell to their faces on the sand. Forty of the little ones lay swaddled in the heavy hull. The others lay under the shade of an ancient cedar. She couldn't save them all, but how could she choose?

Panting, Morgan gasped, "How many can you carry?"

Hilde stared wearily at the children. Freckles stood out across her fair face. "Five, perhaps. I'll tie my belt tight and put two of the stronger ones in back of my shift and three where I can hold them in front."

"What about you two?" Morgan asked. She got up, went to the cedar tree, and lifted a sleeping Mordred into her hands.

Cerewyn shrugged. "Maybe five each, maybe six if we made a hammock out of our robes and held it between us."

"Do it," Morgan said. She gently laid Mordred in the boat. "That still leaves most of them behind."

At the bow, Morgan fell to her knees and set her hands on either gunwale. She left sandy prints on the rough wood. Her palms moved slowly atop the grit, and then faster. It grew hot against her skin. Sand abraded her hand, tearing tiny holes. Blood smeared the briny hull. She anointed the prow, and then rose to press her hands along the starboard gunwale, the stern, and up the port side. At last, she stood in front of the boat.

"I will take these." Lifting her hands to the skies, Morgan said, "O Brigid, Sky Mother! These are your children. Lift them to your breast. Bear them to their mothers."

All around the boat, the bloody handprints shifted as if alive. They gripped the rims and dragged them upward. The boat leveled, standing on its centerboard, and then rose from the ground. Sand sifted from the hull into the wet valley it had cleft. The blood-hands strained harder, and the boat bore along the rocky coastline. Morgan followed, walking in a serene trance.

The three witches watched in awe. Then they scrambled to the tree to save the other children of Gailhom.

A year before, these strange women had come to Gailhom aboard a tinker's wagon. They had been unwelcomed and suspected. Now they came with a floating boat, and shirts full of wailing babies. They were no less strange, but they were saviors.

When word came that the Queen of the Basilica and her

witches had bested Arthur and won back the kidnapped boys, the city poured out to welcome them.

Terrified mothers went woman to woman to find their babies. Others testified how their children had been saved in Morgan's basilica or hiding in the watery bridge beneath the Tember. Morgan had saved them all.

No, not all. Some had perished, and even more of the fathers and mothers who had fought for them. The joy of Morgan's return was tempered by many sorrows, and a new hatred for King Arthur.

Urien crouched in the rancid darkness of the oubliette. The cell was deep but narrow, its floor too small to lie down on. No part of it was out of reach of the offal grate. A month before, Urien had been king. Now, he was the lowliest prisoner, hated or—worse—forgotten.

He assumed it had been a month. They brought food once a day, and he made a mark on the wall each time. Thirty-nine marks—too many to count in the brief time that the lantern shone. Today, Urien would write the fortieth mark with a slash through it, the fourth bundle of ten.

Forty days in the pit while Morgan reigned in light and adulation.

At first, Urien had hated her. She'd administered this sentence spitefully, usurping his control of the guards. Surely they wouldn't remain faithful to her. Surely one of them would kill the witch and release Urien. Each time a meal came, though, Urien knew that Morgan still ruled. Hatred gave way to grudging admiration. She hadn't needed him after all. She could have imprisoned him months before the invasion. . . . Thoughts of the invasion brought paralyzing guilt. Morgan hadn't done wrong. Urien had. He deserved to die alone in a dark pit. The more he turned it over in his head, the more he felt thankful to Morgan for his punishment. It would pay for his evil. That's what was happening. He was paying. Morgan wanted his transgression to vanish so that he could be released and they could be together again. Urien's imprisonment was an expression of her love.

Such had been the tortured logic of the pit.

Lantern light came, fitful above the metal grating. It was the wrong time. Urien had learned to count his breaths and pile them in his head, twenty to a minute, a hundred twenty to an hour, twenty-eight hundred from meal to meal. He was still in the middle nine hundreds. Who was it? His liberator? The light glimmered off the bars, making even the rank water seem like diamonds.

Urien scrambled to his feet. The grating above sliced the light into parallel shafts, which swept down across him. His hands were crepuscular, and his face would be too. He had become a hunk of offal, but his eyes were full of his beautiful visitor.

"Morgan!"

She stood above the grate. Beside her, a servant held a lantern on a pole, her own private sun. It made her face glow and outlined her foreshortened figure. In one arm, Morgan carried a baby—her baby, Mordred.

"You saved him!" Urien said in delight and shame.

Morgan didn't reply, but only stared down into the darkness. She lifted her other hand, which held a wooden goblet. Its contents must have been hot, because steam gushed toward the vault above.

Coughing to clear his voice, Urien said, "Aren't you going to speak?"

"You took my son away from me," she said coldly. "But I got him back. Now, I've come down to take your son away from you."

Urien gaped. "What? What have you done with my sons?"

"Not your sons," hissed Morgan. "Your son, or daughter, or whatever else you got inside me."

"Whatever I . . . ?" He'd nearly forgotten what he'd done. "Oh, no."

"Oh, yes. I would have given you children, Urien, but not like this. We were business partners, and children would have been part of business. Not now." She lifted the cup as if making a toast, and tiny bubbles leapt and popped around its rim. "You poisoned me to get this creature inside me, and now I poison me to get it out."

"Do it!" Urien cried miserably. "Drink it! I despair that you would, but perhaps the child will buy my redemption."

Morgan's eyes flared in the lantern light, blank but ferocious. "Your redemption? *Your* redemption?"

"All I want is to be back with you—"

"You'll never be back with me—"

"On whatever terms. I'll be your servant. I'll be your slave. Only let me be near you again. Kill the child if you must—it'll rip out my heart, as I deserve—but let me be redeemed!"

She shook, clinging tightly to the baby in her arms. Some of the potent mixture spilled down the cup, and it hissed on the wooden edges. She lifted the goblet, set her lips on the brim, and tilted her head back in a howl. The cup flew, bounding off the grate and flinging its poison down on Urien.

He clawed at his eyes. The liquid stung them. By the time

he could see, Morgan was gone, and the golden light vanished down the stony hall.

Urien slid back into the forgetful muck and rocked, howling. He hated or loved her more than he could bear.

Six months pregnant, Morgan sat her throne. Mordred dandled on one knee, and the scepter of Gailhom on the other. She was Queen of the Basilica, renamed Castle Charyot, and undisputed ruler of Rheged. She had fortified her nation, suspended taxes to Camelot, and raised a strong army. Her priestesses had been to every household in the north and won many women to the secrets of Gaea. Her witches had been to every court in the east and won many allies.

The work went on. Today, as on every Wednesday, Morgan received petitions from her people. From highborn to low, they filled the basilica, waiting to approach their giving mother. Morgan adjudicated fences between swine yards, dispensed remedies for boils, and settle arguments between spouses. In rectifying such mundanities, she made the people her people.

"—just that he knows I got a prize bull and he's been wanting it to stud his cow, so all it takes is knocking down the wall one night and—"

"I told you I didn't knock down that wall!"

"Then who did?"

"It fell down! If you'd not've slapped it together that way, then I'd not've had that bull smashing in my barn door—"

"My bull didn't smash in that door. It was falling apart, a rotten hunk of wood!"

"I built it myself last year!"

"That's what I mean!"

Morgan held up her hands, silencing the men. The throng hushed, eager to hear Queen Morgan's pronouncement. "You two are incapable of resolving this issue."

They nodded cautiously, and one said, "That's why we've come."

"Right," Morgan replied. "So I turn the decision over to the other two parties involved." She closed her eyes, and her face gained the serenity of a woman in a mystic trance. A susurrus moved through the crowd. When the murmur reached a peak, Morgan's eyes popped open, and she said, "In the opinion of the cow and the bull, no harm has been done."

"What?" chorused the farmers. The crowd roared with laughter.

Morgan's hands patted the air, quieting them. "They go on to warn that if you leave your barn door and your wall in such shoddy repair, they'll do it again."

While the rest of the petitioners cackled, the aggrieved farmers traded angry glares, growing redder by the moment. Then one laughed, followed by the other. A punch to the shoulder precipitated a slap on the back. The two neighbors shook their heads, cussed each other, and turned away from the throne. They retreated among their country folk, cheered and jeered in equal measure.

Morgan lifted her scepter and called out, "Who'll be next?"

Before anyone could respond, a voice boomed down from the vault: "I would speak with the queen." It was a man's voice, with a thick Saxon accent.

Searching the stony dome, Morgan glimpsed movement—the sollerets and jambeaus of an armored leg, wreathed in the red aura of the ley lines. "Who are you?"

"I am King Alle of Sussex," replied the voice. "You danced once at my wedding, great priestess."

"I did, indeed." Morgan smiled. She'd been watching this young king, had grieved for him when his first wife had died in childbirth, and had even played matchmaker for him. She was pleased to see that his mate descended the Otherworldly stair beside him.

"We are newly wedded, King Alle of Sussex and Queen Hilde of Eastlund."

Statuesque, blond, and freckled, Hilde stepped down out of clear air onto the cut-stone floor. On her arm was a giant of a man, even taller and more muscular than she, and somehow more blond. They were a pair, she in an elegant gown and he in shimmering armor. Both smiled infectiously. Strangest of all, though, the arriving rulers went to their knees before Morgan.

"To what do I owe this honor?"

Alle raised his eyes. "You have healed my broken heart—"

"*Our* broken hearts," Hilde corrected.

"I owe you service for that alone," Alle said. "And I owe you a second service. All my life I have been devoted to Wotan and Frigga, but my new bride has taught me of Gaea, and told me that you are her new incarnation."

Morgan struggled to keep shock from her face. She had never heard herself described that way and wasn't sure she liked it.

Alle went on. "I've begun to mass an army of Saxons and Angles in the east. It would take decades to gather a force the equal of Arthur's, but now I find you are massing your own army here in the north. We both wish the same thing—to be rid of Arthur and his Christian God, to bring about an age of High Paganism."

She hadn't heard those words either, though the Saxon pantheon was nearer to Gaea worship than Christianity was.

"I pledge myself to this task, though it take the balance of my life," Alle said. "I will bring war to Arthur and destroy him, and I ask your blessing and alliance in that regard." He stopped, his eyes beaming.

Morgan turned toward Hilde. "Is all this true?"

The witch nodded deeply. "All true."

Morgan rose from the throne, bearing Mordred with her but setting down the scepter. She reached to a compartment within her throne, removed the enchantments on it, and drew out a shimmering treasure. "Then I have a wedding gift for you." She held up the bejeweled scabbard Rhiannon. Reverently, Morgan walked down the stairs to the kneeling queen and king. She held Rhiannon out across one arm. "If you swear to guard this scabbard and use it to destroy Arthur and Camelot, I will grant it to you."

The smile at last was gone from Alle's face. With utter gravity, he said, "I swear it upon the halls of Valhalla. I will not rest until Arthur is dead."

Nodding with equal solemnity, Morgan gave the scabbard to him. "While you wear it, you cannot be slain, or even bleed. Your bride will teach you all about this great treasure— its powers and origins. Wear it well, good ally," she said, lifting first Queen Hilde and then King Alle from the ground, "and slay the tyrant Arthur."

Urien had lost all count of breaths and meals and days. He had given up hating his wife or loving her, or even realizing she existed. Nothing existed except the foul darkness. He was sick all the time—filthy, hungry, despairing, mad. He had died already and was simply waiting for his body to notice. Uncounted, the breaths went on.

The light came. It would be food—hardtack, spoiled meat, fish bones. He didn't even rise. Let them drop it through the grate onto the floor. He would eat it if he found it, and let the rats eat it otherwise.

Golden columns swept down the wall and spread across the floor. The warm shafts felt like leaves settling on Urien's shoulders. With his head bowed, he waited for the food to fall.

Instead of food, words: "I thought you'd want to see him." The voice was a woman's—familiar, almost beloved. What was her name?

"Who? Who do I want to see?"

"Your son."

"Who? Pascen? Riwallawn? Run?"

"Owain."

"I don't have a son named Owain."

"Now you do."

Urien looked up past the black bars of the pit and into the golden lantern. He squinted and shielded his eyes. He glimpsed his wife—Morgan was her name! A one-year-old boy stood beside her. "Owain?"

"No," Morgan said gently. "That's Mordred. This is Owain." Her arm shifted. Lantern light outlined everything in gold ribbons. She held a swaddled baby in her arms. "Your son. Ours."

Urien stumbled to his feet and craned his neck. He reached grimy hands toward that perfect, clean baby. The king began to cry.

"Owain needs his father," Morgan said. "You won't be my equal, but you will be free, and my nominal husband as well." Morgan cupped Mordred's head, gently guiding the toddler back from the grating. Two guards stepped up into the light and set metal pry bars down to grip the grate.

Urien didn't know what to say. He hadn't even conceived that this moment would come. It was as if a slug were lifted from the muck and crowned king.

The grate tipped away from the hole.

"Thank you, great goddess. Thank you!"

27

Generations

S ons grow faster than nations.

On the shores of Sussex stood Morgan, small and dark above the pitching sea. To one side was five-year-old Mordred and to the other was four-year-old Owain. They were brothers, but they could not have been more different.

Mordred was tall and lean, with hair like the riffled wing of a raven and skin as white as chalk. He was intense, brilliant, morose, and sarcastic. All his mother's best traits were exaggerated in him, honed to a razor's edge—and fragility. Mordred's flesh was haunted by the incest that had given him birth, with too little muscle and too much brain. His mind was haunted by other things. Morgan had tried everything short of magic to glimpse the shadows that lurked there, but Mordred kept them secret, as if they were treasure.

Owain, on the other hand, was short and stocky, red-haired and freckled. He had a bluff if shallow demeanor that made him immune to Mordred's sapping moods. Owain loved hunting with his father, and at the tender age of four he had already killed five squirrels, three conies, a pheasant, and a yearling deer. Urien bragged that his son would become as great a warrior as Cuchulain, and Mordred replied this was certain as long as the war was against hedgehogs.

War had brought Morgan and her sons to Sussex, to the docks of Bexhill. There, they stood beside King Alle of Sussex and Queen Hilde of Estlund and watched the fleet of long ships head out to sea.

"How many can each hold?" Morgan asked dubiously.

Alle rubbed his blond beard. He had outgrown his lean, youthful body, and the fires of idealism had been stoked and banked to furnace heat. "A hundred per ship, but you must account for ten crew. Perhaps fifty households, some single men and some families."

"Fifty warriors times ten ships is five hundred," Morgan said. "This seems the least efficient means to build an army."

"They'll go again, and it'll be a thousand," Alle said. "And then fifteen hundred, and two thousand."

"While Arthur has twenty." Morgan shook her head.

"But each of these will have sons, perhaps four, perhaps five. That will be ten thousand more."

"In twenty years, when Arthur's twenty thousand have become a hundred thousand." Morgan stared bleakly at the fancifully carved sterns.

Alle's eyes narrowed, and his jaw worked beneath blond whiskers. "What would you have me do?"

Morgan shook her head and turned away, leading her sons from the shore. "It isn't what you will do, but what I will do."

At the crown of the hill crossed the ley line that had brought them. A step, and they returned to it. The shoreline fell away below them, and the thatched roofs of Bexhill, too. Morgan and her sons walked above the world, their feet striding on air.

"Do you see how beautiful it all looks up here?"

"Yes," said Owain in astonishment. "The people look like bugs."

"They do close up, too," Mordred said.

"That's my point. It is beautiful here, traveling so high and fast, free of bandits and kings. Free of bugs." She rested her hands on their shoulders. "It's our curse to live forever outside of society. It's the curse of the rest of humanity to live forever in it."

They walked in silence, the sun unmoving in the sky. The plains of Sussex gave way to the forest of Bedgrayne, where Lot had capitulated to the *enfant terrible*. Across the heart of Britannia they walked and to the hills of Cadbury. They cast faint shadows down on Camelot. It was a city in alabaster among emerald hills. Merlin and Arthur had created it almost overnight, gathering folk to build it and live in it and die for it.

"We're above the heart of the enemy," Morgan said quietly.

Owain stared down, amazed, at the figures frozen below. "It don't look so bad. Looks kind of nice."

"Like a termite mound," Mordred said. "White and beautiful in its buggy way. They burn, don't they, Mother—termite mounds? That's how Æthiopians eat, isn't it? They burn a mound and eat the termites like prawns?"

"Yes, they do."

"That's what you want to do: set Camelot on fire and eat them all up."

Morgan lifted her gaze beyond Camelot, some twenty leagues away, to Glastonbury Tor. "Camelot is a hive of warriors breeding war."

"Aren't we getting ready for war, too?" Owain asked.

"We're fighting fire with fire."

"And then eating them like prawns afterward."

Morgan snorted, clutching her children's arms and stepping out of the sky. Her foot set down in Avalon.

"Ohh," said the boys.

They stood on a mountainside beside a glimmering waterfall. At its base lay a mirror pool that poured through smaller cascades into a river. It plunged down the rocks among heather and brae and made its wanting way toward the wide lake of Avalon. Before them, the mountain was steep, shelves of rock jutting from its side. Behind them, the slope grew gentler, allowing apple trees to thrive. Their white blossoms set a sweet fragrance in the air.

"Does Da know about this place?" asked Urien.

"Most men do," Morgan responded quietly. "Though they don't believe in it. Women know and believe. They feel it in their hearts, the primeval garden we all seek."

"This is Eden?" asked Mordred.

"A part of Eden. There are pieces of it in every land, veiled in the Otherworld. Some day, they'll be veiled no longer."

Mordred nodded, stepping up toward the river. "So, you can come here whenever you want, but still you stay in Gailhom?"

"Yes."

Mordred crouched down by the water.

"Don't drink that!"

He looked at her, his eyes black. "Why?"

"It's the immortal stream. You don't want to stay young. You want to grow up." She walked to him and knelt. Her hand scooped the water, cold and alive on her skin, and she drank. The draught burned and chilled her at once. It remade her belly and her gut, sieved into her spleen and heart, and enlivened every faculty they provided: desire, fortitude, temper, courage. The water reached her mind and rejuvenated it, sank into her bones and made them young, perfused muscle and skin. In moments, she seemed twenty again. "I want to stay young while I train you—and hundreds of others here on Avalon."

"Here?" Owain said. "Why here?"

"Because here you can learn and grow one year for every month. Here, the witches and my initiates and I can rear generations of children before Arthur can. This is how we build our nation, not with conquest, but with bounty."

"They grow so quickly," Urien said, gazing out across the practice grounds of Mureif Castle, where Mordred and Owain sparred with wooden swords. "They look too old to be ten and nine." Urien drew the shawl tighter around his shoulders; October's winds were especially biting this year. He lifted his teacup and cradled it in his hands, letting its heat sink into stiff knuckles. "It seems every time you go off on one of your little excursions, they come back a few inches taller."

"They do," said Queen Morgan.

He loved her. All of Rheged did. She had saved them from the tyranny of Arthur and was saving them from the tyranny of themselves.

Urien quietly began to cry but hid the tears in his tea. He reached up with a cloth: Morgan would think he was dabbing his lips, not his cheeks. "They know their languages, their sums, strategy and tactics, and they're a head taller than their peers."

"They have no peers," Morgan said sharply.

"Of course not," agreed Urien.

Her tone softened. "At least not here in the castle. There are a number of children in the city who grow as fast. And many throughout Rheged and the Saxon lands."

He hated when she mentioned the Saxon lands. King Alle, that twenty-stone phallus, had designs on her, and she might have designs on him, too. It wasn't Urien's place to tell Morgan what to do: He was only her husband. Still, the less she messed with that man, the better. "I won't have them going off to fight for Alle."

"You won't have . . . ?"

Urien whimpered, ducking his head. "I-I just mean th-that I would rather they stayed here until they're fifteen."

"Five years," Morgan said, considering. To Urien's surprise and relief, she nodded. "Five years will be about right."

Emboldened, Urien ventured, "It's just that I love them so dearly." He shook his head. "I can't imagine what might happen to my boys in Alle's meat grinder."

"Only one is yours," Morgan replied, her voice holding no reproach. "But you are right. I'll hold them back. There will be enough warriors to fill Alle's lists. Two fewer will not hurt anything."

Urien wept openly, falling to his knees beside her chair. He clasped her hands and said, "Thank you, Morgan. Thank you." He kissed her hand. "I love you so much."

"I know," she said, patting his head fondly. "I know."

Mordred and Owain wouldn't fight in Alle's army, but Morgan would.

She didn't fly to Sussex or march up the Thames. She swung no sword in the sack of London, nor cheered the meeting Saxons and Angles at the city center. Even so, Morgan led them all the way. She commanded from within Rhiannon. It was no mere wedding gift, but a jewel-encrusted geis that gave her power over Alle. He didn't realize it, but his great, muscled body was merely a puppet. With it, Morgan had won victory all up the Thames Valley and even enticed Arthur out to Liddington Castle on Badon Hill. Soon, she would destroy her brother and his army forever.

In the highest tower of Mureif Castle, Morgan stood alone, swinging an invisible sword and straddling an unseen horse. This spell was among the strongest she had ever cast. At wrists, elbows, shoulders, hips, knees, ankles, neck, and brow, Morgan wore a mixture of her blood, Alle's blood, and the filings from a lodestone. Each spot linked her to the Saxon king. Just now, the both of them made a twilight charge on the fourth palisade gate of Mount Badon.

Morgan buried her great sword in the neck of one of Arthur's knights and felt the blade sever flesh and bone and grate on the hauberk. He managed to slash her leg, but Rhiannon healed the wound instantaneously. Morgan yanked the steel from the dead man and bore on up the hill. Her steed had not even slackened its gallop—a great warhorse for a great warrior.

Ahead, Saxon troops crowded the palisade gate, hacking with swords at the hinge-beams. Morgan whooped a war cry, the voice emerging as Alle's—and her blade gleamed like a red banner. Saxons shouldered aside to let their king pass.

Morgan leaned down on the neck of the great warhorse and slid Rhiannon so that it lay flat against the beast's sweating flank. At full gallop, the great steed rammed the gate. Wood shattered and flew inward. The horse's neck snapped, but still it ran on. Hooves bore down the ruined hunks of wood, flattening the soldiers trapped beneath. A halberd jagged in and sliced Alle's neck but slid harmlessly out the other side. Healed in the midst of death, horse and rider thundered up the hill. The rest of the Saxon cavalry followed at a gallop.

Ahead, the fifth palisade gate swung wide, and a tide of defenders poured out. Who led the charge but Arthur himself! How many years she had fought to reach him, to slice his throat, but the wards of Merlin were too strong. Now, Morgan came to him in the flesh of Alle. Now, she could kill him at last.

Knights pelted down the hill ahead of their king. Morgan would have to carve her way to Arthur through flesh. So be it. She and a knight rode past each other. Their swords simultaneously punctured each other's breastplates. Morgan kept her saddle and charged on, unharmed, but the knight took a bloody spill and was trampled under the Saxon charge.

The main wave of horseflesh crashed upon them. Morgan's steed rammed another, pole to chest, and flung it and its rider to the ground. The warhorse bounded on over the fallen forms, and Morgan cleft another man in half. She shouted in exultation.

It was different to be a man. Men had muscles built for fighting, minds that craved death—dealing it and being dealt it. Battle was exhilarating, the reason to be. How strange that this meat puppet would have such a hold on its master!

Suddenly Arthur was there. He was small next to Alle, but his eyes were lit with the same hungry light. With teeth clenched in his bearded jaw, Arthur lunged aback his steed and rammed Excalibur into Alle's side. It ached to have that sword in her, but Morgan knew its touch was not deadly.

With a gauntleted hand, Morgan reached down and seized the end of Excalibur. Anyone else would have lost fingers, but Alle wore Rhiannon. His hand clasped the sword in the wound, and Morgan said, "I had Rhiannon, and now I have Excalibur too." She wrenched the blade.

Arthur's arm was no match for Alle's. Excalibur tore free of its master's grip. His hand hung open in astonishment as Morgan whirled the blade around and caught the hilt. There was no blood on that shimmering metal, and an arc of energy coursed from it through Alle's arm to the scabbard on his back.

Beneath her breath, Morgan whispered, "Good-bye, Brother."

She brought Excalibur down in a killing stroke. It would split this singular man in two, but at the last moment, he dodged. The blade caught his shoulder instead of his head, and laid it wide as if he were made of butter. Through clavicle and scapula and ribs it went, grinding to a halt in the middle of his lung, inches shy of his heart. Morgan hefted the blade up out of the wound.

Arthur reeled back, eyes wide with shock.

Again, the sword fell. This time he couldn't escape.

"Mother! Mother! Open up," came the shout of Owain beyond the hatch. It bounded with his pounding fists, nearly rattling the bolt loose. "Open up!"

Arthur was gone. The hillside, the swarming Saxons, the killing stroke. The spell was broken. Trembling, Morgan fell to her knees and wailed. "Owain! I told you not to interrupt me!"

"It's important!" he shouted back, still pounding.

Morgan could only pant and shake her head. What could be more important than the death of Arthur?

"Ships, Mother. Warships from Camelot. They've sent their fleet to take Gailhom!"

Her shallows breaths became deep. Morgan lurched to her feet and ran to the window. Indeed, on the moonlit seas, a score of warships floated, loaded rail to rail with soldiers. The bastard Arthur had known she would aid Alle. He hadn't done this to take Gailhom, but only to distract her from Badon Hill.

Gritting her teeth, Morgan stalked to the hatch. Alle would have to finish Arthur. He was already mortally wounded and had lost Excalibur and Rhiannon. Alle couldn't possibly lose now.

Flinging back the bolt, Morgan barked, "I'm coming! I'm coming!"

The queen of Rheged and her two warrior sons strode from the main gates of Gailhom and out along the docks. Torches had been tied hastily to posts, and they sent their torrid light across the crews that scrambled there. They were boarding the twelve ships at dock: four fighting galleys owned by Gailhom, two dragon boats from visiting Norsemen, three fishing boats pressed into service, and two merchant barges that would have to be pulled by asses onshore. All the ships were preparing to set sail and meet a fleet of twenty warships—fully manned and armed and closing fast.

"Who's in charge here?" Morgan shouted.

One mate paused long enough to say, "The warden of waters."

"Where is he?" Morgan asked.

"There," the man said, hitching his head toward an armored warrior.

The warden of waters had hair as black as midnight and a gigantic frame. He stood facing the ships, his hands cupped around his mouth as he bellowed orders. By the set of his jaw and the flames in his eyes, it was clear he relished the coming battle.

Morgan knew that feeling all to well. Tonight it would lead to destruction.

She, Mordred, and Owain stormed up to him. "What are you doing?"

"Who do you think you are, coming over here—?" The warden spluttered to a stop and bowed before Morgan. "Forgive me, Your Highness."

"What are you doing?"

He gestured toward the water. "Launching our counterattack."

"No," Morgan said. "That's not the basis of our defense. We've commissioned no fleet—"

"We have four ships, and the Norsemen are eager to help. If we don't go, we'll be sacrificing the ships anyway—"

"But not the crews. It would be suicide."

"The Norsemen don't care. They love a fight."

"I'm talking about our own crews." Morgan shook her head. "Order the crews onto the pier. Order them to torch the ships, the docks, the Sword Bridge—"

The warden of waters listened incredulously. "You can't be serious."

"Deadly serious," replied the queen. "If bridge, docks, and ships remain, Arthur will use them against us. If they're gone, the wall, cliffs, and sea will hold him at bay."

The warden shook his head. "I beg of you, Queen, don't—"

"You're relieved of command," Morgan said summarily. She turned to her sons, chronologically teenagers, but in form and mind men. "Mordred, Owain, go. Order them in my name. Tell the Norsemen we'll replace their ships. Tell them if they set sail, they do so without our aid."

"They'll do it anyway," Mordred said. "They're Norse."

"Then, Gaea help them. Tell them they'd best shove off before the fires get them." As her sons ran off on their missions, Morgan shook her head and said, "Arthur, you have your stalemate, but time is my ally. You're mortally wounded, your sword and scabbard are gone, the power of Merlin is sapped, and your defenses are breached. You can't win. . . ."

Two Norse long ships sailed away from the burning dock and into a midnight war. From the walls of Gailhom, Morgan and her sons watched them do battle. Firelight showed arrows leaping ship to ship, grapnels and men following, swords flashing and bodies falling. A luffing sail caught fire, and flame ran the lines to the reefed main. Soon, both ships were engulfed. A Norseman ran, head on fire, and leapt into the careless sea. More splashes came, men choosing to drown instead of burn.

"They should have stayed with us," Morgan said grimly.

Mordred replied, "They love war too much."

How true. Morgan couldn't destroy the Son of War by making war.

The other long ship unfurled its sail to bash through the blockade. It struck a war galley side on, staving it but also snapping its own prow. Even as both boats sank, their crews leapt across to kill each other.

The Norsemen were gone to their Valhalla, where they could slay for all eternity. Arthur's men, no doubt, went to their own warring heaven and were marshaled in among the armies of Michael.

Morgan shook her head bleakly. "We've given him what he wanted. War."

Already, the eighteen remaining galleys set their prows toward Gailhom and her burning docks.

"Of course we gave them war," said Owain. "How else do you stop Arthur?"

The same way we've stopped tyrants for ages, Morgan thought. Not from without, but from within.

On the thirty-first day of the blockade, news came of Alle's defeat and death at Mount Badon. Arthur was victorious, Excalibur and Rhiannon were his again, and he ruled all lands south of Hadrian's Wall.

North of it, Morgan remained. She would be Arthur's next target. His ships kept Gailhom penned in even as his army marched north toward renegade Rheged. Morgan could not hope for military victory, but she would not submit to defeat. She had a new, deadly plan.

28

The True Consort

A nd so, Arthur, my brother," Morgan said, standing before the opulent throne of Camelot, "I sue for peace. Let us have no more war between us." She bowed low, her black gown spreading across white marble. Her eyes never left the bearded king and his Queen Guinevere.

Arthur nodded slowly. "I'm heartsick of war too, but Rheged must return to the kingdom. You and Urien will swear fealty to me."

"Of course," Morgan replied, rising again. "And the taxes will be paid."

He smiled at that, and the mistrust slowly drained from his face. He sighed, "To be done with war. . . ."

"Yes, my hope exactly," Morgan replied. She held her hands out to her sides. "And as my greatest show of union, I present to you my two sons, Mordred and Owain."

From the archway behind her came the two young men. They were only sixteen and fifteen, but seemed ten years older. Mordred was knifelike in white and black, and Owain big and bluff in blue and red. Side by side they approached their mother and knelt next to her.

"I humbly submit them to compete for seats at your Round Table. When the scions of Rheged serve Camelot, we will be joined, indeed."

Arthur rose. His face was red with hope, and little candles gleamed in his eyes. Leaving Guinevere on the throne, he descended the stairs. He shook his head sadly and spread his arms. "Sister, we have been too long at odds." He wrapped Morgan in an embrace and clung to her.

She could feel his heart pounding in his broad chest. How close she had come to slicing that heart open, and now there was not a sign of the blow. Still, she had found her way near enough to strike it again.

Arthur released her and turned toward Mordred and Owain. "Sons, I would have you fight for me, not against me." Actual tears gathered in Arthur's eyes. "This is a day of joy! We accept your terms, Queen Morgan of Rheged. At last, there will be peace."

Morgan smiled and nodded. *Peace, yes, under your iron fist. It is the only kind of peace you understand. But now that war is done, the upper hand will be mine.*

Morgan remained with her sons in Camelot. She stood on a balcony of the castle and looked out over the nighttime city. It was truly beautiful. Tile, shake, and thatch gleamed silvery beneath the smiling moon, and shop windows and pubs glowed like gold. Cobbled streets thronged with revelers in the Feast of the Pendragon—the celebration of Camelot's victory over Britannia. The bronze Fount of the Bountiful

Weirds ran with mead, the castle was festooned with flowers, and the bells of the basilica hadn't ceased their paeans of triumph. Joy filled the city, joy like wine—strong and sweet, bitter and deluded.

For days, women had sewn banners and woven wreaths to welcome home their heroes. So potent were their men that the hegemony they enjoyed over the city had become hegemony over a nation. They were truly the great dominators. What woman would not swoon before such a man?

Morgan would not. Her nation had fallen to them, and she had seen what these heroes were capable of. They had stolen her babies and raped her women and killed her men. They were her enemies.

Mordred arrived behind her. "What are you looking at, Mother?"

"What am I looking at?" She turned toward him. "Nothing, Mordred. Lots of loud and lovely nothing."

"Oh, Mother," he said, laughing as he slouched against the rail. There was wine on his breath. "You're too bound up. Sure, it's *their* party, but," he paused, lifting a leather wine jack and taking a swig, "it's a party."

She loved this violent child. That was the problem with men. They were utterly antithetical to all that was good, and yet they were everywhere—sons and brothers and lovers. "Is it wise to get drunk the night before the contest?"

Mordred snorted. He pantomimed the joust, one hand holding invisible reins and the other cradling his wine jack as if it were a lance. With eyes fixed and mouth snarling, he made as if to gallop. A screech, and he smashed the wine jack to his chest. Red wine sprayed across the balcony.

Morgan shook her head in disgust.

"It's just a party," he repeated, letting the ruined leather fall to the ground.

"You're a mess."

"Aren't we all?" Mordred sighed gustily and withdrew. "Well, I'm sure our host has another shift I could stain." Rummaging through the chest, he said, "Ah, ha!" and ripped the wine-stained shirt from his shoulders. He mopped himself with it and threw it dramatically out on the spattered balcony. Dragging the new shirt on, Mordred headed for the door. "I'll leave you with your thoughts—such dark company." And he was gone.

It is nice to imagine a world without men.

A moment later, the wise woman was belied.

A man rode down the abandoned parade route. Amid piles of spent ribbon and bough came a young warrior on a white horse. His head was fair, his eyes keen, his face strong. He wore old armor polished to a high sheen, and his horse strode more like a wild thing than a trained beast. None of these facets were the man, though: He was the diamond within them.

"How he shines!" Morgan murmured. She leaned over the rail, watching with naked want.

Desire is your prison. If only you wanted women the way you want men. . . .

The man did not see her but rode past her balcony.

Morgan could hardly bear it. She shouted suddenly, "What's your name?"

The horse pulled up slowly beneath him, and the man turned to look over his shoulder. "What?"

Blushing in the darkness, Morgan repeated, "What is your name?"

"Lancelot," he called back.

"Lancelot," she repeated quietly as he turned and rode on.

From a different balcony the next day, Morgan watched her sons wrestle, duel, and joust—and watched Lancelot, too. Mordred's gift for taunt had pushed many opponents off guard, and he had risen rapidly. Owain's brute strength and indefatigable aggression elevated him as well. But Lancelot—oh! What she'd sensed in him the night before proved only the barest glimmer of what was. Every blow struck true, every foe fell honorably. Lancelot was quick, mighty, precise, gracious. If there was virtue in any man, there was virtue in this one.

As he rode in the lists—eyes and arms and lance in parallel—Morgan rose from her seat. She hadn't meant to, but all the others in the royal box did as well, so she wasn't conspicuous. She gripped the wooden rail and clutched a breath around her heart. Steeds and lances and men concatenated. Armor failed, and horses like muscular comets rushed past. Lancelot rode on, lifting his pristine spear. The other man ended in a gasping heap on the ground, flung down but unhurt, as Lancelot did to them all.

Morgan cheered with the crowd, but those nearest her turned questioning eyes. Only then did she see who lay thrashing on the ground. "Owain!"

He struggled to sit up and shook his head dizzily.

"He's all right," a man said to Morgan. "And he's already won his spot at the Table. I suppose that's why you cheered."

"Yes," she said, nodding shallowly. *What's happening to you, forgetting your own son while this lovely Lancelot rides by?* "Owain. . . ." she muttered, watching him.

He was fine, rising to cheers. Dust sloughed like a jacket from him, and he limped from the field, waving.

He was fine, but not Morgan. She backed up and sat down. It suddenly struck her. There was only one reason why Lancelot would have such an effect on her: He was the one in one million, the perfect consort. This was not a matter of love, but of husbandry. For every thousand bulls born, only one remained a bull, and all the rest were castrated. Only one bull was needful, one rutting violent beast, and the others were pacified. So too it was with men. Only one in a thousand was needful, one snorting and fearsome beast, and the rest could be made eunuchs. And only one in a thousand thousand would be worthy of a goddess—and this was he.

"Lancelot's going to joust again, for the final!" the man beside her said.

Morgan's breath caught, and she slid to the edge of her seat. "Who could beat him?"

"Your Mordred, let's hope," said the man. Indeed, on the opposite side of the field, Mordred arrayed himself.

Morgan stood again. Now there was reason for fear. Lancelot had not harmed a single man he had ridden against, but Mordred had killed four. Would he kill Lancelot, the one in one million?

Mordred's horse champed, jabbing its hooves into the dust. Across the field, Lancelot's white steed stood steady and alert.

Mordred yelled and dug his heels into the flanks of his beast. It hurled itself into a full gallop, neck straining against the reins. Mordred lowered his lance and raised his shield and bore forward like a hound of hell.

Lancelot charged from his side, a white flash.

The spears came together. Mordred's slid just above its

mark, barking from the pallette and hurtling on over the shoulder. Lancelot's hit square on the shield and stove it, ripped the metal back and Mordred's hand with it. Tearing and popping sounds came as Mordred's arm shattered and stretched out unnaturally behind him. Lancelot let his weapon fall. He had taken Mordred's arm but would not take his life. That hit, still, was cruel. Mordred tumbled in the air, dark and weightless like a dead leaf.

Morgan was standing and screaming. She flung her legs over the rail of the royal box and dropped among the peasants. Shoving through the throng, she reached the lower rail, beyond which lay the lists.

Mordred had risen. He stood on the far field, his shattered hand dripping blood beside him, and his good hand brandishing a sword.

"Mordred, no!" Morgan shouted. "You've won. You're part of the Table Round! Lay down your sword!" But her words were lost in the bellowing air.

Mordred and Lancelot came together, their swords flashing. A brutal overhand blow by Mordred was clanged aside, and the follow-up stroke sliced shallowly across his throat. Mordred staggered back, a thin line of red blossoming beneath his smiling teeth.

"Mordred, no!"

The warriors hurled themselves together again. Mordred's blade was fast and first, but his stroke to the neck flew back. Lancelot muscled through the block and rammed his sword into Mordred's face—not the blade but the crosspiece. It destroyed his nose and brought fresh blood. Mordred wailed and fell back, dropping his sword and lifting a hand to his ruined face.

The crowd roared, a breaking wave that swept Morgan

over the final rail. She ran through the dusty lanes and fell to her knees beside her son. Her arms wrapped around him. She cradled him and moaned his name—her son, second born but first grown, Mordred with the ruined hand and face. "I'm here, Mordred. I'll heal you."

"Firsht my fashe," he managed around broken teeth. "Den my hand."

"First your face," she said weeping. Still, the crowd's adulation flooded over them. Morgan looked to the man on whom it was poured: Lancelot.

He had just maimed her son, had just stolen top honors from him, and yet she knew he was the one. The one in one million.

Morgan watched for her chance with Lancelot. It came a month later, when he had ridden out questing, "to seek the king's justice." She intended quite a quest for him.

This wasn't revenge; Mordred was healed except for a withered left arm. Nor was it lust; Morgan had brought the three witches of Cumbria to make sure of it. Today's work was holy, the union between goddess and consort.

While Sir Lancelot and Sir Lionel rode the Winchester Road, above them, Morgan and the three witches rode the ley highway. They sat on snow-white mules, infertile creatures from Avalon. The beasts could not diminish the fertile energies in their mistresses, nor could the four eunuch guards who marched with them. One way to live with men was to unman them.

But not Lancelot. Morgan and the witches agreed about him.

"Lionel is the problem," Hilde said. She was no longer

queen—her lands lost and her husband slain—but still she rode regally. Like the other two witches, she had decked herself in a fine gown, suitable for ritual seduction. "He never leaves Lancelot's side. He never takes the fore in a fight. He never shuts up. . . ."

Cerewyn laughed. "There's one way to make him leave. A man like Lionel can't stand to talk without being listened to. A simple spell—"

"It's already begun," said Morgan.

She drew a rose from her hair and clenched her fist around the stem. A dozen thorns pierced her. She opened her hand and let the rose fall, blood drops raining all around. They tumbled beside the mule, slipped the ley road, and plummeted through the air above Lancelot. The droplets swarmed and buzzed, becoming scarlet bees. In lazy circles, they droned toward Lancelot. From flower to flower they flitted, beggar-ticks to yarrow, and set a soporific song in the air.

Bernicia watched avidly. "What's to keep Lionel from falling asleep?"

"He's not bored. He's too busy talking."

The mules huffed forward as Lancelot left the road. Red bees buzzed through the stalks around him. He came to a great old apple tree and slung himself from the saddle, which he unbuckled and pulled off to be a pillow. Lancelot lay down and folded his hands across his chest. His great white horse studied him a moment before wandered off to graze. Lionel talked awhile longer before he too gave up and edged away.

"A little farther now," Morgan urged quietly. "Be brave. Lancelot won't be up to listening for hours." Still, Lionel hesitated.

As if in answer to prayer, a vicious angel appeared. The man was huge and bestial atop a worse steed, and he led two more horses. On their backs lay two knights of the Round, hog-tied.

"Oh, what luck!" Bernicia said.

"Luck?" Morgan spat back. "And why do you think I've led them to this wood and put Lancelot to sleep? Watch. This ought to be fun."

Already, Lionel and the man shouted threats back and forth. In moments, they squared off and ran together, as ferocious and predictable as stag beetles. With one blow of his lance, the big man felled Lionel, who lay kicking in the dust. The victor returned, tied Lionel up, and slung him across his own horse. With a catch of three, he rode away to his hill fort.

"You *are* a schemer," Hilde said fondly.

Morgan replied only by saying, "Down we go." She leaned on the mule's neck, guiding him to press the ley line deeper. In mere strides, he came to ground, some half mile from where Lancelot lay. It was a drowsy stretch of meadow charged with blood bees.

"We cannot fight over him," warned Morgan, "any more than we would fight over a glass of fine wine or a select cut of steak. He is only that—made for consumption, for one of us. We cannot rip him into four parts."

Of course they argued. They thought he was the bull and they the cows to be inseminated, but Morgan was no cow.

"I knew of Lancelot du Lac before any of you. I watched him. I brought you to him. If he belongs to anyone, he belongs to me. But what does it matter? He is ours. I'll place on him an enchantment to keep him asleep until he lies within Castle Charyot. Then, let noble knight Lancelot choose among us which one he would serve." That shut them up. The fact was, they were witches, and she the avatar of a goddess, and she would win every argument.

Lancelot lay ahead, beautiful and young beneath the ancient tree. Morgan saw Tristan in him. Oh, if not for that horrible night, what a different life this would have been! She would have been like any other woman, who surrenders her maidenhead to a man, her godhead. Tristan was forever gone from her hand, first loved and first lost. Here, though, was one even more perfect and true.

As the other three rode up in a semicircle around the sleeping Lancelot, Morgan slid down from her beast's broad back. She knelt in the tall grasses beside him. Her hand still bled, the magma of her body like that of the earth. She reached to Lancelot, a drop of blood welling on her fingertip. She painted it along his jaw line, across his chin, and up onto his cheek.

"Sleep, child. Sleep, sweet son, and wake not until I call you." She continued to paint the blood mask on his face and murmured. "Sleep, dear Lancelot, and when you dream, dream of me, and believe." Her finger traced the last line across his eyes.

Breath rushed out of Lancelot, as if he had died, and Morgan stared in dread at him. A shallow breath entered him and departed again. His slumber was akin to death, but he lived.

Morgan swooned from the strain of the spell. To her eunuch guards, she said, "Bring my shield and cradle him in it. Bear him among you back to Castle Charyot." Even as the eunuchs came forward, Morgan grew faint. "Take us back, friends, to the castle. There, we will learn which of us he chooses." They lifted her toward the mule, and she knew no more.

29
Seduction

When they brought him before her in Castle Charyot, Morgan was drowsy, and so was Lancelot. They were waking from the same sleep, borne by the same strange hands to this place of safety.

Three eunuch guards led Lancelot in chains to stand in the center of the basilica.

Morgan rose from her throne. She couldn't bear to remain away from him. Descending the stairs, she came to a halt before Lancelot, but motioned for her cohorts to remain in place. Hilde dutifully kept her seat in the nave, Cerewyn in the south transept, and Bernicia in the north. They had done their part, bearing bride and bridegroom across the skies to be joined here together. They had even brought three pitchers of Avalon water to purify man and woman. The ritual was ready.

Morgan and Lancelot faced each other. Both were nubile, Lancelot grown too quickly and Morgan too slowly. Their flesh was smooth, their bodies were strong, their minds emerging together from oblivion. The only true difference between them was that Morgan was clean and well dressed, but Lancelot wore clothes seasoned with the road.

"Even through filth, your lines are clear," Morgan said quietly

He studied her lines as well. "I demand to know why you hold me."

Morgan spoke to the first eunuch. "Cleanse us."

The man lifted the pitcher and hurled the water so that it formed a great arch in the air. The glittering stuff fell heavily across them both. Brown water ran from Lancelot's armor, and it soaked into Morgan's clothes, pressing them against her body.

"You demand nothing here, Lancelot. You are no longer a swaggering knight, but something truer."

"What, a wet rag?"

"Cleanse us."

The second eunuch tossed his pitcher of water. In a liquid rainbow, it mantled them. The vital waters channeled between clothes and skin, bearing away sweat and perfume both and pouring them on the floor.

Morgan stepped nearer to him. "You are a consort, in the old sense of the term, a mortal partner to an immortal queen. It is why we desire you—we four and Guinevere and every woman. You are the one male in a thousand thousand who must sire. The first art learned by humanity was husbandry—the art of breeding animals through the careful control of the male member. One bull, one stallion, one cock, a host of partners, a nation of offspring." Her voice dropped. "But you are even more, Lancelot, not meant for the multitude but meant for the one. For me."

"I don't choose you—"

"Cleanse us."

The third gout was the coldest, and its waters trickled deepest.

Morgan spread her hands, the dress cleaving to her. "Choose."

"I want nothing to do with you—any of you, lewd witches that you are. On my life, I reject you all!"

Morgan swallowed hard. She folded her arms in around herself. "So be it! You are the one in a thousand thousand, Lancelot, but if you would squander it in the dungeon, so be it." She nodded to the eunuchs. The chains snapped tight around Lancelot, and they hauled him away.

Morgan sat up in bed and swung her legs down. She couldn't sleep, plagued with thoughts of Lancelot. He was the one, and she wanted him.

But everything she had done to gain him was wrong. This is rape, to take a creature against his will and force sexual acts on him. This is what has been done to you twice now, and it's changed you for the worse. Of course Lancelot rejected you. Any virtuous creature would have.

Shivering, Morgan went to the marble hearth and knelt by the embers. Tepid air brought out gooseflesh across her body. She laid a log in the glowing bed, but the wood sat inert. Ash formed a gray blanket between the heat and the fuel. Morgan blew away those cerements. Her breath struck coals that had turned black, and she coaxed the old fire to reawaken in them. Blowing again, she made the embers blaze, and flame leapt to virgin wood.

Morgan sat back on her heels. "I've turned to ash and coal. I need the breath of youth, the fire that will set Lancelot alight." She looked down at her body—voluptuous and mature—and it felt like bundled bags.

More deceptions, Morgan?

"Hush," she said, already beginning the enchantments. For this spell, she wouldn't even need to bring the blood out of her skin. It was there, in vessels and ventricles where it needed to be. Closing her eyes, Morgan drew in the breath of youth. It filled her lungs and woke embers in her blood. The heat rolled through her flesh and perfused it.

This is merely intoxication. You can't truly become young again, only have the appearance of it—strait and sallow, wide-eyed and pure.

"This is how I was on the night of Father's death, the night of terrors. Unspoiled. Virginal."

But you aren't.

"Hush." Rising, Morgan caught up the keys to the dungeon and walked from her chambers. Down the hall, she found a servant's closet and a maid's dress within. She donned it, smoothing it down over her narrow hips. In this simple garb and this pure body, she would undo the evils she had done to Lancelot. With a jackstraw, she lit a lantern and bore it with her toward the catacombs.

The basilica was cold, dark, and silent, and grew more so as she descended into it. Guards stepped from their posts to see who came. Some only nodded her on. Others called her to halt, but a simple smile and a word told them who this was. In fear, they backed again to their spots.

As she walked, Morgan worked out her plan. There had been a tournament a week before, and by it, North Galys had annexed the kingdom of Bagdemagus. The impoverished king would cherish a chance to win back what he had lost.

Yes, a tournament was the thing, and a king who needed a champion . . . and the beleaguered daughter of the king. . . .

The catacombs beneath the basilica were guarded by twelve gates, one for each apostle. They descended through tombs to Urien's oubliette at the bottom, where Lancelot lay. It was a great wrong for the highest man to sleep in that lowest place. One key at a time, gate after gate, Morgan made her way toward him. The lantern formed a cave of light and heat around her. At last, in the semblance of a servant, she stood above the metal grate, above the filth where Lancelot lay. He didn't move.

Through tears, Morgan stared down at the man. "I know you have refused them, though it is death to do so."

He was slow in answering, his voice full of despair. "It is a worse death to accept them."

"Yes, I know. I serve them because my father lost a wager with one of their husbands."

Lancelot shifted, craning to make her out. "Which husband?"

"The king of North Galys, and three knights of the Round, including the son of Queen Morgan. They defeated my father at tournament last Tuesday. Having already taken from him all else, they took me."

Lancelot stood and stared up through the grate. "What is your father's name?"

"King Bagdemagus."

The name brought a sigh. "A great king and a greater warrior. This is the sort of injustice I'm meant to right, but how can I while I languish in a cell?"

Morgan struggled not to smile. This was exactly what she had hoped for. She knelt beside the grate and set the lantern down so that it made her face glow. In a hushed whisper, she said, "Pledge yourself to me and my cause, and I will release you."

"Who are you, and what is your cause?"

"I'm a child who needs a champion. Fight for my father in the next tournament so he can win my freedom."

He reached up through the iron and grasped her hand. His flesh was feverish. "I pledge myself utterly to you."

She didn't want to let go. His touch made her heart ache.

Still, you awaken passion through trickery!

No. I will win him truly. In the joust, it will happen.

Prying her hand loose, Morgan withdrew across the floor and snatched up an iron pry bar. "Dawn is coming quickly. We must hurry. After I release you, you must ride to the monastery of the Broken Nard, three leagues from here, where you will meet my father." She returned to the oubliette, turned the key in the grate, and set the pry bar. With a heave, she lifted the grating. It clattered askew, opening a triangle of space through which he could climb.

Lancelot leapt up from the darkness. He dragged himself out like a lizard and knelt before her. "Forgive me. I'm filthy, outside and in."

You are filthy, too, Morgan. How you want him! This isn't just about a future brood, the fertility of the goddess and the necessity of the consort. This is about lust and love.

Morgan turned away, putting the key into the first gate.

"I will, of course, wash myself before I appear at the monastery."

"Outside and in," Morgan replied, striding through the first gate. "Wash your armor because it is grand, because it is meant to be clean and not filthy. Wash your soul for the same reason. A lofty purpose awaits your armor, but a loftier one your soul. Defend my father, free me, prove yourself, and transcend the sin of man."

You say too much. Surely he can sense your trembling desire. It's almost predatory. Why not make yourself a panther? Why not pounce on him and hold him under you?

She turned the next key in the next gate.

"I will, dear child, I will."

By dawn's light, Morgan sat at her window and watched Lancelot bathe in the river. He mounted his splendid steed and rode the swimming horse to the mainland. The stallion climbed the far banks and vanished among the trees.

Morgan whistled softly, a summons. From the battlements below, crows took flight. Three birds beat the air with their black wings and vaulted toward her window. Each landed, claws skittering on stone. They pranced, eager to hear what their mistress would say.

She paced, thinking. There were many messages—to Cerewyn and her husband, to Mordred on his questing, to Bagdemagus in sanctuary at the Broken Nard. It all had to be perfectly arranged. Let Lancelot avenge the child, let him win the day, let him face the Queen of Rheged from a position of strength. Then, he could not resist.

Morgan sat down at the window ledge, drew a small knife from her pocket, and brought blood on the end of her finger. She reached to the first crow, which held still in response, and painted a small red cap on its head. "You will fly to the Broken Nard and seek a broken man—Bagdemagus. . . ."

Every detail had gone to plan except one. Morgan hadn't thought Guinevere would be here. *That woman!* fumed the maiden within Morgan. *Priestess of the Celtic pantheons, chaste wife of King Arthur—and still she longs for Lancelot!* She had come in secret, of course, disguised and walking the ways of the fey, and now she watched Lancelot and wanted him. After so much work to shut out the three witches, Morgan now had to contend with a priestess-queen?

"Could you kill her, somehow, by accident?" Morgan whispered to Mordred. They stood in his pavilion atop a blustery hill. Mordred's squire had erected the tent and was even now busily preparing his armor for the day's jousts.

"Kill whom?" Mordred blurted. He winced and glanced surreptitiously at his squire. Cupping his hand to his mouth, Mordred whispered, "I'd have to be pretty bad with a lance to miss the rider and hit the queen."

"Or pretty good," Morgan spat. She wished the squire were gone so they could speak openly. "I don't want to kill her, not really. But if we could somehow . . . remove her from the competition . . ." Morgan cringed—the young maiden within her had gained control of her mouth. *Well, why not? This is about mating rights, after all!* "What about one of your substances? Something you could spread on your gauntlet and touch her, and she'd faint."

"I have just the thing, powerful. I use it on my lance tip. One touch, and she'll sleep for a day," Mordred replied. "But is that what you want? She'll swoon, and he'll rush to her and carry her to some bed somewhere and pine over her until she wakes up and they'll go at it."

The squire glanced dubiously at them.

"He doesn't love her," Morgan snapped.

A bluff laugh was Mordred's reply.

She lowered her head. "No, you're right. I'll devise something for her later. Today, he's my focus. Don't hurt him."

"Mother, this is revenge. I plan to kill him."

She sighed. As regarded Lancelot, what Mordred planned and what he accomplished were two different things. "Fine. Good luck today, Son."

"Good luck to you, too," he responded as she strode out of the tent.

In gown and veil, Morgan stood anonymously in the crowd on the plain. She might have been any noblewoman. Most certainly she did not look like Morgan le Fey.

Guinevere's disguise was less perfect. It leaked magic about the edges. And she put on a shameful display: gawking at Lancelot, cheering for him, cringing as he ran upon his foe, sighing when he rode away in victory. It was maddening, especially since Morgan caught herself doing exactly the same things.

There's a world of difference between an avatar and a priestess, but you and she act the same. That's because around Lancelot, you're both just wanting women.

The turmoil of Morgan's mind mirrored the tumult on the field. Knights and warriors rode and crashed. Men fell. Man by man they peeled away from the true duel—between dark and deadly Mordred and bright and beautiful Lancelot. At last, they faced each other as before, son and lover. Lancelot's weapon was clean of blood, but Mordred's dripped gore, and something else.

He means to kill your lover, Morgan. Your son has poisoned his lance.

The men kicked their steeds into a gallop. They converged across the field. Spears dropped level and roared toward hearts.

You can help one of them, but only one. It is the ancient decision: child or lover, motherhood or maidenhood?

Morgan bit her lip until she tasted salt and whispered words through the ring of blood.

Mordred's spear erred in his hand. The poisoned tip came nowhere near Lancelot's white flesh. Lancelot's weapon soared true and bashed Mordred's shield arm once again. It was a clean hit, bruising but not breaking. Even so, Mordred tumbled in the air, twisted around Lancelot's oaken shaft. He rolled in the grass and came to a halt. The angry way he kicked his legs showed that only his pride was wounded.

With all the other spectators, Morgan rushed down toward Lancelot. This was his moment, and it would be hers, as well. Instead of meeting him in weakness, she would meet him in strength. Morgan's blood rose, the fires stoking in every vessel. She was making herself a great spell. Unlike the last time, when she transformed outwardly for all to see, this time she transformed inwardly. None but Lancelot would see her, but to him, her immortal self would shine through. Already, her flesh felt numb, a husk that was cracking open to give flight to the down within. Her body jostled among other bodies, but her soul shone forth as no other.

Lancelot turned in confusion from King Bagdemagus and his daughter—the one Morgan had pretended to be. Beside them stood Prince Meleagaunce, angry at having been thrown down by Mordred. Lancelot stepped away from them, and Morgan pressed through a crowd of eager women, drawn to him like iron to a lodestone.

Suddenly—Guinevere. She clutched Lancelot's hands and nuzzled his cheek. She said something that made him smile with desire.

Morgan raged forward, and Guinevere melted away like wax before the flame. She was gone as suddenly as she had come, and Lancelot searched the wave of flesh. "Guinevere!"

Morgan flared. She could still save the moment. "I am not she. I am much more. Not only is she watching, but I am." Still, he looked past her. Desperate, Morgan caught his hands, dragged him to her, and kissed him full on the lips. He didn't return the kiss. Morgan pulled back. "Your greatest test is yet to come." It was all she could bear to say.

Morgan withdrew. She closed her magic around herself and was folded in among the shoving women. Lancelot seemed to be looking for her, but he called out: "Guinevere!"

That name was a fist to her gut. Morgan staggered. Twice she had bared herself to Lancelot and twice been spurned. She wished she could hit him back with that name.

She could.

While Lancelot struggled in the adoring throng, Morgan stepped up to Prince Meleagaunce. He was shaped like an iron oven and was just as hot. Biting her lip again, Morgan spoke through the blood. "Do you see the way the women want him? You have an admirer too—none other than Queen Guinevere. Your desire for her will grow to be an obsession. In the end, you'll have to have her, no matter the cost. . . ."

At first it seemed only a dream, torrid and passionate. Morgan and Lancelot twined like wrestlers, each vying to be on top. Everyone had such dreams. But as Morgan pinned him and straddled him, pressing herself down over him, she realized this was no dream. It was a spell. The succubus spell.

He was asleep, of course. He would remember the dream but not know it had been real. It was not rape, not really. He wanted her as much as she wanted him. It was merely theft, taking from him a tiny portion of his abundance.

How have you come to this? Of course it is rape.

"Hush." Morgan rode him until she had what she wanted. Then she vanished away into ether.

30

Desire Makes Fools

"S omething's . . . wrong!" Morgan panted between contractions. She gripped the handles of the birthing chair and shuddered. "Something's wrong. . . ."

A warm and leathery hand pressed her shoulder, and Daedra said, "No. Everything's fine. It's all progressing just fine."

"You're wrong. . . . This is my fourth . . . child. I know if something's wrong. Something's . . . wrong."

"And this is my, what—two hundred fiftieth child?" Daedra purred. At nearly fifty, she was well beyond the struggles of birthing, except for assisting others. "Trust me and stop worrying.

"Yes," Morgan gasped as the next contraction began. All through the pregnancy, she had worried. It was a new emotion for her: Worry was a luxury that only the secure and stationary could afford. By accident, Morgan had become both.

With Merlin's disappearance, she was now the most powerful sorcerer in Britannia. Her brood of goddess-believers grew daily, and soon they would be numerous enough to allow Avalon to be birthed on the world. The death of Camelot had become a certainty. Meleagaunce, Mordred, Owain, and even Lancelot worked toward it, whether they knew it or not. Morgan was not just the queen of Rheged and avatar of Gaea but also the puppet master of Camelot. She had nothing to worry about. . . .

Except this pregnancy. She regretted everything about it. It had begun without true consummation, for flesh had never touched flesh. A spell had gathered Lancelot's issue and borne it to Morgan's womb, a ménage à trois with magic. Morgan had wanted Lancelot and true union with him but instead had gotten only this child, so strangely conceived. . . .

"Something's . . . wrong!"

"The head is crowning!" Daedra said, kneeling before the seat. "One more big push, and it'll all be done."

Screaming, Morgan pushed, and she felt the head tear its way clear. The rest of the body slid, slick and smooth, from her. "It's dead! It's dead!"

Daedra caught the body, tissues and water and blood cascading down around it. "No! She's fine! She's pink and perfect."

Morgan's eyes dropped open in astonishment. "Breathing?"

"Yes. Breathing," Daedra said, lifting the child. Her skinny body was mottled in blood, but her chest rose and fell in easy breaths.

"How can she be?" Morgan asked. "The placenta's covering her face."

Astonished, the midwife only then saw the thick, clear membrane that covered the child's nose and mouth. She drew it off rapidly and put her ear to the babe's face. "No breath."

Flipping the girl over on her arm, Daedra patted her back, fetched a pig's bladder, and used it to suck out the mucous plug. She spanked the babe, but still she didn't cry. Daedra held her up. The little girl was pink, her lungs filled and emptied, but no breath came from her nose and mouth. "She's breathing somehow. . . ."

Morgan said, "What do you mean?"

"She's breathing, but not with her nose or mouth. It's as if she's breathing air from somewhere else."

Morgan clenched her fists. She turned her face away. Something was terribly wrong, and she was only beginning to glimpse it.

"Just give me a moment. She'll be clean. I'll cut her loose from you."

"Yes. Cut her loose," Morgan echoed emptily. "Cut her loose."

Daedra made cooing sounds as she worked over the child, but the noises were forced. She too sensed the strangeness of this baby. "What are you going to call her?"

Morgan shook her head, tears streaming into her hair. "Morfudd."

"Morfudd?" Daedra said, taken aback. "That's a . . . never mind. . . ." She finished swaddling the babe and handed her to Morgan. "Here, hold her on your chest. You'll feel she's breathing. You'll feel she belongs to you."

While Daedra bent to clean up, Morgan cradled her poor, silent girl. It was as if Morfudd had not even endured the traumas of birth, but lay the whole while in some safe crib, breathing some other air.

"What does this mean?" Morgan asked.

Daedra finished washing her and began to sew up the tears. "I don't know, Morgan."

"Two hundred fifty children, and you don't know?"

"I don't know."

Morgan lay awake and cradled her tragic child.

At three months, Morfudd breathed infrequently and nursed even less. She would lie on the breast and not take hold, but would later suckle by herself in her crib. Morgan had learned to listen for those sounds and bring her baby to feed then. Morfudd would coo to empty air but not to her mother. Her bright blue eyes would look right past Morgan and follow unseen things. She thrived, yes, but in a private world.

Just now, Morfudd began to laugh. In the middle of night, staring at the black ceiling, she laughed. The sound chilled Morgan.

"What've I done to you?" she wondered. Morfudd had been fathered by magic, and so she lived in magic places. She belonged to a spectral family, and her love was for them alone. "Where are you?"

Morgan sat up and lifted her daughter. The air beyond the blankets was crisp with fall. For a whole season, Morgan had tried to drag her little girl into the real world, but instead had been dragged out of it. There was another way.

"Lead me to you," Morgan prayed. There was divinity in this child. Her spirit called to Morgan, and she answered. Slipping a robe around her shoulders and soft leather shoes onto her feet, Morgan carried Morfudd to her chamber door. She unlocked it, pushed the handle, and opened it.

"Good evening, my queen," rumbled the eunuch Ananias, who guarded the door. He was a hulking shadow in the corridor. "Where are we headed?"

Morgan looked into his lightless eyes. "Somewhere." She strode past him.

Ananias fell into step with her. "You might want to stay inside. There's a good wind blowing."

Descending the stairs to the main basilica, Morgan said, "I didn't ask you to come."

"No, but you ordered me to guard you and your child."

Morfudd laughed, and Ananias beamed down at her.

Morgan studied the man. Here was another creature stranded between two worlds, neither male nor female. He was strong but gentle, quick but patient, watchful but kind— embodying the virtues of both genders without the vices. Where had it gotten him? He was a mere guard protecting a craven queen.

"What's it like, Ananias?" asked Morgan as they strode into the basilica and down the isle. "What's it like being . . . what you are?"

"I wouldn't want to be anything else, my queen."

"Aren't you lonely?"

"I was lonely before, when I wanted everyone but had no one. Now I don't want anyone. I can stand back and watch their follies and smile."

Morgan bristled a little. "Watch my follies, do you?"

"The queen has no follies," he said levelly.

Morgan nodded grimly. Who else spoke so candidly with her? "You don't think it folly to chase a man who's in love with another man's wife, to bear the man's child even though he doesn't know it, to carry the child away from bed and crib at midnight and walk the red way?"

"Ah, that's where we're headed," Ananias said evasively. Next moment, they stepped into the ley conjunction. Scintillating red walls surrounded them. Another step, and they were leaving the stony floor behind. Never once did Ananias hesitate or gasp.

"Well, is it folly?" Morgan pressed.

"To have follies, one must be a fool, and you are no fool, my queen."

She shook her head ruefully. "Desire makes fools of us all." Side by side, they stepped through the thick wall of the basilica and out into the brisk night. They walked across the sky, watching windows drop beneath them. "Men and women, women and men—fools all."

Ananias said nothing. He walked with one hand behind Morgan's back, his massive arm sheltering her.

"They stole my first child when he was three days old, and I never found him—not even his body or blood," Morgan said, her hand fidgeting with the swaddling clothes. "They stole my second child when he was three months old, and he nearly died before I could get him back. Arthur did it, you know, kidnapped a thousand babies to kill his single son."

Ananias only shook his head.

"No one tried to steal Owain—just a solid lad. I was so thankful. But now, Morfudd—abducted before she was born!" The baby stretched, straining against her mother's arms.

"Give her to me," Ananias said. "You look tired."

"I am." Morgan handed the baby to him.

Ananias wrapped one great arm around the swaddled girl. Another of his talents. They strode above the Tember, crossed the banks, and headed south. The forest below was black and endless. In the distance, the land was dotted with minuscule pools that shone back the stars.

"Lancelot is the one in a thousand thousand," Morgan said. "You can sense it in Morfudd. She has a divine spark.

But how can I rear a divine child? How can I nurture a girl I can't even reach?"

Ananias clutched the girl to his chest as if some force tried to drag her away. "She's like a dowsing rod. She's pulling me."

"She's pulling us toward the place where her spirit is." Forests flew by below. They opened on inky lakes amid folded hills. Westward, the Eire Sea shimmered with moonlight. Eastward, the land was black, and it met the sky with no clear distinction. Morgan stepped out above the Eire Sea, and then across the ragged coast of Gwynedd, and the Snowdonian Mountains. "Soon, it'll be Powys and Dyfed."

"You know where she dwells," Ananias said.

"There's only one place. All the leys converge there." Morgan strode above the Bristol Channel. "She is in Avalon, but I don't know why."

The red road dipped toward the Glastonbury Plains, converging with hundreds of other lines. They seemed the legs of a great spider, and Avalon its glimmering body. The power of the place tugged on Morfudd.

Ananias wrapped her more tightly in his arms to keep her from flying away. "I've never been to Avalon."

"It's enough to put desire into even you, Ananias."

Though the rest of the world lay cloaked in darkness, Avalon glowed. On the upper slopes, sacrifices in the great cauldron sent their light and heat into the night. Farther downhill, the heather itself gleamed. Sprites chased each other through the darkling air and naiads through sparkling streams. Foxfire danced among ancient trees and illumined faerie rings.

But no spot on that wide isle beamed as brightly as a single chimney of a single cottage. Its hearth fire sent sparks circling up in a smokeless spiral. The cabin's windows hurled trape-zoids of light onto the gardens around it. One old woman lived there, the infinite diminishment of Gaea. Once, her roof had been heaven and her garden Earth. Now, she dwelt under thatch, surrounded by furrows of carrot and leek.

Morfudd giggled.

"Of course," Morgan said solemnly. She climbed down out of the sky, drawing Ananias with her.

He struggled against the headlong pull of Morfudd, and when he touched ground, went to his knees in the grass. "She wants to go to that cottage. That's home."

Morgan took her daughter into her arms and approached the ragged wooden door. Light bled through its cracks, and the sweet scent of baking bread poured out. She knocked. "Brigid, come out. It's Morgan and Morfudd."

There came movement beyond the door, and the latch clicked. The wood drew back, and golden light spilled around the form of an old woman. "I've been expecting you," Brigid said. Her eyes shone with welcome in her sackcloth face. Silver hair haloed her head. Under a threadbare tunic, her shoulders were stooped, and she waved a gnarled hand toward her table and stools. "Come in! Come in!"

Clutching Morfudd, Morgan ducked under the lintel. "What about my bodyguard?"

"What bodyguard?"

Morgan turned, staring out across the dark hillside. Ananias was no longer there. "What happened to him?"

"He woke up."

"What?"

"Sit," the old woman said gently. "I'll explain all."

Morgan shuffled across the rush-strewn floor and settled onto one of the stools. Only then did she notice why Brigid looked so stooped. She held a baby on her hip, a baby that was the identical twin of Morfudd. She closed the door and walked slowly toward the table. "You shouldn't be so surprised that I'm helping you, and helping Lancelot. I helped rear you both. Morfudd is my great niece."

"But . . . but . . . ?" Morgan couldn't even form her question. She suddenly recognized Brigid's voice. She was the wise woman within. Dumbfounded, Morgan slowly shook her head. "All this while . . . you've been leading me. . . ."

Easing herself onto the other stool, Brigid changed the subject. "Nor should it surprise you that this is a dream."

"A dream!" Morgan said, standing. "So you aren't the wise woman? This is only a dream?"

"Not *only* a dream," Brigid replied. Her free hand grasped Morgan's and eased her back down, "but a dream, nonetheless. Many of the things you believe and know are dreams, Morgan. It has always been the case."

Morgan clenched her jaw. "I'm not mad. You can't convince me of that. You're no better than Morgause."

Nodding grimly, Brigid said, "You're right on both counts, but don't denigrate your sister . . . or your dreams. For most folk, dreams are unreal things. Your dreams, though, are the things that are coming into being."

Morgan blinked back tears. "You mean I see the future—?"

"I mean you *make* the future. A thought in your mind becomes a desire in your heart and then a reality in the world."

"And that's what this is," Morgan replied, "only the wish that Morfudd has another self somewhere—that her spirit dwells beyond her body. I'm fooling myself into believing that you are caring for her soul."

"You are wishing, my dear, yes, and your wishes have a way of coming true." She lifted the little girl in her arms—wide eyes in a heart-shaped face. She was the twin of Morfudd, but her eyes fixed on Morgan. "Let's trade for a few moments. You hold her soul, and I'll hold her body."

Now Morgan truly did weep. She received Morfudd's soul and handed over her body. "She's breathing. Really breathing. I can hear it." Beautiful blue eyes searched Morgan's face, as if seeing it for the first time. Fingers reached to touch her cheek and grab her hair. Morfudd's soul laughed in delight, and Morgan clutched the baby to her. "I only wish it were true."

Brigid rocked the other babe in her arms, its legs flailing loose. "It is true, Morgan, as true as it needs to be. Your daughter—my great niece—was conceived in dream, and her soul has been displaced in dream. Isn't it enough that I keep her soul here in dreams until she can be made whole?"

"She can be made whole?"

"Wish it, Morgan. Make it true."

Morgan held her child for the first time since she was born and rocked her. "If only I could take this part of her with me."

"Not out of dreams, you can't."

"How long can I stay, Brigid?"

"As long as you sleep. Whenever you sleep, you can return."

"I want to sleep forever."

"There's a name for that state, child. Don't wish for it."

The door bounded in its frame, and Ananias shouted, "Queen Morgan! Are you safe?"

"That's my bodyguard."

Brigid nodded grimly, handing Morfudd's body back to

her. "I know. As I told you, he woke up." She took the girl's soul in her arms.

Ananias pounded. "I nodded off. Forgive me! I had the strangest dream."

Morgan stood up, not from a stool but from her bed. The cottage was gone, and Brigid too—the light and the wonderful baby she had held all too briefly. Morgan crossed to the door and pulled the bolt. "Come in, Ananias."

He stepped across the threshold, eyes darting to the dark corners. "I dreamed you led me on a highway in the sky, and we went to Avalon. Then I woke up, and I heard you crying. Are you all right?"

"No," Morgan said bleakly.

"What can I do?"

"Sleep with me."

"My queen!" he gasped. "I'm—I'm—"

"I know. I don't need a lover, Ananias. I need a guard. I'll be walking that highway every night, and I'd rather not walk it alone."

Ananias seemed to consider. "Well . . . I have sacrificed greater things for you . . ." He turned and slid the bar in the door. "And I don't mind if people talk. It's like you said, desire makes fools of us all."

31

And with These Stripes

"Take her," Morgan said, pressing Morfudd into Daedra's arms. "I'll be back soon."

"I have no milk," Daedra said, fumbling to take the child—hastily wrapped and desperate to kick off those wrappings. "I'm not a nursemaid."

"Find one," Morgan snapped. She marched down the stairs toward the sanctuary of Castle Charyot. "Find whatever she needs—breast, clothes, bath, lullaby, warm arms—"

Daedra struggled to hold the kicking creature. "She doesn't need my arms, but yours. I don't know what she needs. You do."

Morgan nodded fiercely. "Yes, I *do* know! She needs you to care for her." Striding past black benches, Morgan reached into a pocket of her robe, pulled out a ring, and slipped it on her finger. This small circle would gather and channel her spells, increase their potency, and make them permanent. She flung off her robe and marched down the center aisle.

"Where are you going?" Daedra shouted.

"I'm going to heal her," Morgan snarled.

Even as she spoke, dark spots speckled her skin and then grew larger. The flesh between them became tawny, and a fine pelt rippled out across her. She dropped to her hands, now sleek paws with curved claws. The ring was bedded in her flesh, where its power transmuted her. Shoulders and hips narrowed into the joints of a predatory cat. Morgan snarled again, baring fangs, and leapt. With a flick of her spotted tail, she plunged into the leys.

The sanctuary seemed suddenly insubstantial beyond canyon walls of red. Morgan bounded up the fey road, slicing through the castle dome and out into sun-bright air. It was spring, and desire pulsed in trees and toads and men. It pulsed in Morgan, too.

This was her last chance with Lancelot, her last chance for Morfudd.

Morgan had spent six months dream-walking. Throughout the night, she cradled Morfudd's body and journeyed to the cabin where her soul lived, where both halves could be together. Still, Morfudd wouldn't be whole until the veil of magic was lifted between those halves. Only true consummation between her mother and father, true love between them, could heal her.

The gold and black cat ran across the skies of Britannia. Nominally, this was Arthur's nation, with knights riding the roads and pendragons on every pendant, but half the doorways bore the mark of the Sheila-na-gig. Morgan's army was massing in the very beds of her enemies. The war would begin soon, but first—Lancelot.

Even now, he rode toward the castle of Meleagaunce, where his beloved Guinevere was captive. Morgan's own spell had brought this about. It had taken Meleagaunce a year to succumb to his lust, but now he held Guinevere and fumbled around, trying to woo her. If Lancelot rescued her, they would consummate, and Morfudd would be doomed.

Morgan had foreseen all these things in a bowl of blood, and this was her only chance to stop them from happening.

There he was. His white stallion tore along the Westminster Road, a pinion of dust rising behind him. Lancelot crouched low on the creature's rippling back. The mane of the beast and the hair of the man seemed apiece, shaped by wind and colored by sunlight. The ley highway passed above the road, and Morgan's faint but gigantic shadow swooped across Lancelot.

She couldn't catch him here. The ley line didn't touch down until it reached a wood beyond the river. The road cut through the forest, and Lancelot would have to ride right beneath her. Morgan tore on above the Westminster Bridge, seeing only then the malicious men that waited by the pilings.

"No," she growled.

The first wicked shafts jagged out toward horse and rider and swarmed them. Most of the arrows ate air, but one struck the horse's chest, and another Lancelot's shoulder.

"No!" Morgan roared, spitting blood.

The droplets plummeted and formed a fiery veil. It fell from the sky atop the bridge and the ambushers. The spell flashed. Arrows dissolved, and bows blazed. Lancelot rode amid the stunned archers, his sword laying the men down as a scythe cuts wheat. The stallion's hooves glinted red in the trampling. Then beast and rider thundered on across the bridge. A few smoldering shafts were flung desperately after them, only to tumble and extinguish themselves in the river.

Morgan yowled. Look at how well we are matched, Lancelot! The heavenly queen and the earthly warrior! Spells and swords! You complete me and I complete you. Together, we will complete our daughter.

Morgan dashed ahead of him, down the throat of the sky. The ley way slanted above a farm field where an ass switched its knobby tail. I need you, Morgan thought, and she roared. The feral sound billowed over the beast.

It raised tufted ears, and the roar morphed them into feline form. The sound changed the beast's brain, too. In waves, the animal transformed. Its shaggy jowls grew a leonine mane. Shoulders broadened and turned golden. Ribs widened, and tail lengthened. The sturdy legs of the beast became stealthy limbs covered in velvety fur, and its hooves split into claws. Most important of all, the stubborn set of its eyes changed to a hungry glint.

The lion lifted its head and sniffed the wind. It heard hooves rumbling up the road and saw the unmistakable dust cloud of a frightened beast. Twitching in anticipation, the lion stalked toward the hedgerow, ready to pounce.

Morgan le Fey leapt from the ley highway to the lofty boughs of an ash tree. Her claws sank into the gray bark, and she clung on, panting. The heat of the day enveloped her.

You'll pursue from below and take down that great stallion, she sent to the lion familiar. *I'll pursue from above and take down his master.*

Lancelot came into view. His horse cantered unsteadily, an arrow wedged in its chest and a line of blood reaching down its foreleg. Lancelot languished in the saddle. He had driven the arrow through his own shoulder and out his back, and a blood-soaked rag jutted from either side of the wound. They cantered toward the forest.

Morgan's savage heart labored. Yes, they would be easy

prey, too easy. She'd not come here to slay him or seduce him, but to win him truly.

Do not hurt the man, she sent to her lion comrade. *Not even his horse. We must stop them, yes, but we cannot hurt them.*

The lion snarled in reply.

Lancelot glanced fearfully over his shoulder. He set heels to his steed, and the wounded creature went from a canter to a three-legged gallop. They plunged into the forest, rushing just beneath Morgan. Behind them, the lion bounded over the wall and trotted afterward. He sniffed the air, not yet committed to an all-out charge.

Morgan leapt to a nearby branch and onward to two others. She ran along the tangled boughs as she had along the sky. Claws sank into bark and hurled her through the canopy. She soon bounded just above Lancelot and his limping steed. They couldn't run and wouldn't even reach Meleagaunce's castle.

The lion charged. Its claws lashed out and bashed the stallion. The poor beast shrieked and fell. Lancelot raked his sword out even as he went down. His injured shoulder struck the ground first, and he shouted as he rolled. The blade fell from his hand and was pinned beneath the fallen horse. The lion gathered to spring atop them both.

Enough.

The lion snarled sullenly, and then sat beside the horse.

Morgan stalked down from the treetops, as regal as a lady down a stair. Tail twitching, she leapt to the ground and padded to the place where Lancelot lay.

He froze, watching her with wide eyes.

Morgan casually draped herself across him, a great cat claiming her prey, and pinned him to the ground. Only then did she transform. The spotted pelt melted to smooth, young skin; the face grew human and beautiful though no less ferocious. Her claws, resting on his chest, became slender hands. She straddled him, and he couldn't move.

"Morgan le Fey," Lancelot breathed. His face reflected her beauty.

"I'm more than that," she said. She extended her arms to either side and was transfigured. Her very flesh grew candent, and fire lit her eyes. The air sung around her. "I am the avatar of Gaea, the goddess of old. For millennia of millennia, I have sought the perfect consort, and you are he."

Lancelot shook his head, lifting a bloodied hand to shield his eyes. "No. You're a witch."

"Once I was, perhaps, and then a priestess, and now an avatar. I've transcended all I have been, and now I would bring you up with me."

"Why?" he bleated. "Why?"

"Love, Lancelot. For love. Once I thought it would be enough to have your child, but for lack of love, she and I both have been destroyed. No. I want a mate. I want you."

Tears filled his squinting eyes. "I — I must save Guinevere."

"She belongs to Arthur, not to you. Don't you see? Guinevere can never be yours, but I can be yours forever. I'm offering you eternity, Lancelot." She reached to him, and even her fingertips sent rays of light out through the woods. "Take my hand. Transcend the sin of man and become my true consort. We'll live together in the Garden. We'll bring bounty to the world. Take my hand."

At last, all the writhing uncertainty was gone from his face. He could see past his own petty fears. This was a goddess, and she offered him the glories every man dreamed of. He reached for her hand, his fingers trembling with hope.

"Yes, Lancelot," she said. "Yes."

He fumbled, and Morgan felt something come loose in her grip. It was the ring. He had yanked it from her finger, and with it went her focused powers. Glory fell in layers from her like the skin from an onion. She was left small and mortal. Her eyes no longer shone, the air no longer sang, and the lion had become once again an ass.

Lancelot wore a look of desperate triumph as he rammed the stolen ring on his own finger. It would empower him for the moment, yes, be enough to salve his wound, but in time it would sap his heart.

Morgan was unmoved. Naked and mortal, she sat atop him. "It changes nothing. I still love you and want you, Lancelot."

He shoved her brutally aside and staggered to his feet. Madness filled his eyes, perhaps from Meleagaunce's poison, perhaps from the intoxication of the ring. "You're no goddess, Morgan. You're hardly even human. Something broke in you early on, and instead of healing it, you aggravated it, made that broken part swell and take over your whole being. Now it's all you are—delusion!" His hand clenched and released around the ring, and he looked like he would strike her.

Morgan shied back miserably, naked of magic.

"I don't want you, Morgan. I never wanted you, and no amount of witchery will change that." As the stallion struggled to its feet, Lancelot reached down and snatched up his sword.

Morgan fled. She ran up the road, past the donkey. With a humorless bray, it trotted after her.

She wept in agony. It wouldn't matter if Lancelot leapt on his horse and rode her down. He had rejected her, now and forever. His words had been brutal and true, touching on the very wound he had named: Delusion.

The ass bolted past her, kicking at imagined pursuers.

Was that all this was? Delusion? Had she merely imagined this world where a goddess waited in the fecund and immemorial earth? Even Brigid had said that her mind made wishes real. . . .

No, Brigid hadn't said it. Her *delusion* of Brigid had said it.

What is real? Is anything?

The red road lay just ahead, as slender as a rope out of danger. If she grasped that rope and it carried her out of the world, she would return to delusion. If she didn't grasp it, she would die here, naked and alone in the chaos wood. She leapt, and her hands clasped the slender cord, and she plunged into the red way.

Magic closed around her, magic or delusion. The result was the same. She left the horrible world and was safe again, folded in fey. She lay down on the road, only inches from its beginning, and gathered her mind.

Her first impulse was to slay Lancelot outright. How dare he torment her this way? How dare he toss her aside to embrace Guinevere? Lancelot would see how real her magic was when her spells tore him apart. . . .

No, she was not like Meleagaunce.

Morgan glanced back. Lancelot and his stallion pressed on toward the distant castle. He would surely die, destroyed by Meleagaunce and his men. Her heart snagged on that thought. She couldn't allow it. She loved Lancelot and couldn't bear the thought of his death. Better that he be wrapped in another woman's arms than that he be gone.

Morgan stood and walked up the red way toward the castle. She had calmed herself, breath and thought coming easily now.

How could this be delusion when she had such power, such compassion? She passed through trees and out above their tossing heads. Her bare feet walked on the sky. The wood fell away beneath her, and then the rolling plains of Westminster. Lancelot was but a small white dot moving along the road toward a large black fortress, but he wore her ring.

Morgan bit her lip and tasted blood. "Shield him. Shroud him. Surround him," she said. Her arms reached out to hold the emptiness, and leagues away, her magic held Lancelot.

None too soon. An arrow from the castle wall struck her spell and burned to nothing. Morgan felt the shaft pierce her magic and sensed its heat as it burned away. A second arrow blazed, a third, and five more. Morgan bore them all, and Lancelot felt none of them.

Beneath the fiery storm, he cried up to the battlements. A figure appeared there, racing before the guards, and flung herself from a crenellation. She plunged whitely through the air and into the castle moat.

Lancelot dismounted and ran forward to drag her from the black waters.

"Shield them. Shroud them. Surround them."

He climbed from the moat, carrying her. Arrows hailed down upon them, but none found their mark. Wrapped in arms of magic, Morgan's beloved bore his own beloved out of torment and death. Lancelot climbed the bank, lifted Guinevere to his stallion's back, and swung his legs up behind her. They rode, lovers shielded by the goddess.

They stand together in the Otherworld, Queen Guinevere and King Lancelot. They are wed, joined, skyclad on the verdant moss. This moment had been promised decades before, when these two children of fey were betrothed. Today, the promise is realized.

Morgan watched Lancelot and Guinevere become one. The vision tore her in two. Morfudd would never be healed.

It would tear apart Arthur too.

In her agony, Morgan at last saw the end of Camelot. She had given up her lover, but she had gained this one great boon.

Plagued with arrows outside and in, Morgan bore Lancelot and Guinevere safely away.

Daedra startled awake. Someone was in the sanctuary. She stared out through the darkness and clutched Morfudd tightly to her.

In the central aisle, a figure moved. It was Morgan, covered in burns and small wounds. She held her arms out and seemed to be dancing with an invisible partner.

"Queen!" Daedra said. She levered herself out of the creaking chair where she had slept and carried the babe forward. "What happened? Did you find a way to heal Morfudd?"

Dancing, Morgan said, "No."

"What happened, then? *You* need to be healed."

"And with these stripes, I am healed," the queen replied. Her arms opened out, and she spilled onto the ground.

Daedra ran to her and knelt. She wrapped one arm around Morgan and the other around Morfudd and said, "It'll be all right. I'm here. . . . I'm here. . . ."

32

Circle of Goddesses

*A*mid a company of soldiers and priestesses, Morgan rode beneath the antlered archway of Camelot castle. The horned gate was mounded with snow, and beneath it the flagstones were slick. White clods clung to the fetlocks of the horses, and steam rose from their backs. They clomped toward the great hall. Morgan pulled her deerskin cloak more tightly around herself and her six-year-old girl.

Morfudd hadn't thrived. She was small and lost in her own world. She spoke a nonlanguage to nonbeings and played with empty air. The real world and all its inhabitants were phantasmal to Morfudd, and her own phantom world was true. Still, Morgan loved her. The poor lost child had redoubled her mother's visionary powers. At last, it was time to make visions real.

Morgan's horse tossed its head, clomping to a halt before the great hall. Lifting her daughter, Morgan stepped down from the saddle. The soldiers and priestesses did so too. Stable boys ran across the snow and snatched up the reins, leading the great beasts away. Morgan's horse shook his hooves, eager to be rid of the clods.

Ahead, the double doors opened, spilling heat into the silver sky. Out stepped King Arthur. He wore furs atop his samite finery, opulent despite these hard times. His beard had grown bushy and gray, and his eyes had lost their brightness. They gleamed like glass. Here was a king abandoned by his queen and his greatest knight, left with a scheming court. Morgan's own sons quietly worked to destroy him, and Arthur had the look of a man whose gut was full of worms.

Spreading his arms in welcome, Arthur said, "Sister." That single word held such emotion—hope and dread, friendship and fear, but loneliness most of all. "I'm glad you've finally arrived."

"The roads were near impassible east of Shrewsbury," Morgan said simply, approaching him. She didn't hold out her hands, clutched still around Morfudd.

Arthur wrapped them both in a genuine embrace. "It's good to have you here, Sister."

Morgan drew back and looked him levelly in the eye. "Sister, am I now? Not half-sister?"

"Let's be done with half measures between us," Arthur said, clinging to her shoulders. "Winter is lying on Camelot—not just this white stuff, but a real chill that's freezing our souls."

"That's why we're here," Morgan replied. She didn't add that her sons and other agents had brought this winter to the land.

Arthur's troubled eyes searched her face. Eventually, his expression eased, as if he had decided to trust her. Good boy. He had no other choice. "Then, come inside, Sister. It's been a long trail. Chambers are ready and baths are drawn. The stable boys will bring your bags around, and we will feast tonight."

"Yes, Brother. We will feast."

The great hall fireplace was large enough for a horse to stand in, and it burned logs as large as men. The fire filled the room with heat and a little smoke, but it stole away the light. The hall was cave-dark. Even tallow chandeliers couldn't dispel the gloom.

Arthur had tried. He had thrown a feast of boar and eel, baked carrots and turnips, braided bread and mulled wine. Each steaming dish only added mist to the already murky rafters. While they ate, Arthur told tales of his knights, roaming Britannia and administering justice. Each story grew more colorful, more emphatic, and Arthur began to pace, his face lit with desperate joy. Beneath it all, the fire droned of doom. At last, he spent himself, slumping in his chair and staring at the ravenous flames.

He was ready, and Morgan began. "Brother, this is indeed the winter of Camelot." He only nodded, ruminating the flesh of the boar. "It has lasted more than a season, and may never end."

"She'll come back," Arthur said. He glanced up as if wishing he could gather those words back in.

"Five years, Arthur," Morgan said. "Your wife has been gone for five years, and Lancelot, too."

His nostrils flared, and he said, "They're not dead."

"It might be easier if they were," Morgan said. "They're alive and together."

"Where?" Arthur asked.

"In the Otherworld—not Avalon, but their ancestral realms."

Bedeviled, Arthur shook his head. "What are you talking about?"

"Lancelot du Lac is an orphaned prince of a fallen kingdom of fey. Guinevere is a faerie changeling princess. They were betrothed at birth."

He silently echoed the last sentence. Some part of him must have sensed the truth of it, for he took in this revelation as dry skin takes in oil. "Have they . . . ?"

"Not yet," Morgan replied. "But it is inevitable. You'll lose your queen. Already, her love of you wanes, and the love of the people does as well. Winter has drawn its cold blanket over your kingdom, Arthur, and there may never be another spring."

Arthur picked at a bread loaf, tearing off hunks and letting them tumble onto the tabletop. "Why are you telling me all this?"

"Without Guinevere, you rule nothing. She is the power of the land. But your power may be greater." Morgan slowly stood. "You will soon lose Guinevere, but you may yet ally with the goddess."

"You?" Arthur barked, incredulously.

"My powers are tenfold those of Guinevere, the equal of Merlin's. We would not be husband and wife, but king and goddess. It would not be a marriage but a dynasty. Subject yourself to me, Brother. Give up war. Follow me, and I will bring a glory to Britannia like it has never known."

His amazement teetered on the brink of derision. "How? How will you bring glory to Britannia?"

She strode to him and stood by his seat. At last, there was true light in that black place, for Morgan's flesh shone. "I will burst the gates of Avalon and birth it across the land. I will bring the Otherworld up from the earth and make it true once more. I will end the Age of War and bring back the Age of the Goddess."

Arthur buried his face in his hands and shook his head. He seemed to be sobbing. When he lifted his eyes, though, his features were twisted with laughter. "The apple doesn't fall far from the tree," he said. "Especially the Avalonian apple."

"What?"

"You! You and Morfudd. What a pair you are! I've seen Avalon, yes, but it's dying, Morgan. You would revive my kingdom by resurrecting a dead world?"

Morgan's gaze grew hard. "Know, half-brother, that you are deciding your fate. Right now, you are deciding it."

Arthur waved her words away. "Go talk to Morfudd about it."

She turned, storming away.

He shouted after her. "Stay as long as you wish, Sister. You shouldn't be traveling . . . in your condition."

Morgan stalked from the room, driven out by laughter.

Morgan flung back the door of her chambers. They were half lit with candles and a dying fire. In one corner stood Morfudd, singing in a high and eerie voice. Her caretaker, a young priestess, sat before her, back straight and hands knotted in white dread. She bolted up when Morgan arrived.

"Sh-she's been singing, Mistress. I couldn't stop her."

"Thank you, Celia," Morgan said summarily. "You may go."

Celia gave a huff of relief and, head ducked, walked

quickly toward the door. She nodded and hurried out, drawing the door closed behind her.

Morgan stared at the white marble floor and listened to her daughter's plaintive song. She shivered. Arthur's response was what she had expected, but its finality had come as a blow. He had little choice, after all—ally with Morgan or decline unto death. She had engineered his downfall and given him a final chance to escape with his life, but Arthur had refused, preferring damnation.

Morgan walked to the fireplace and leaned on the mantle. Candles illumined her hair and face. "Damnation." Had he agreed to bow, she would have had a kingdom, an army, a knightly class, and countless nobles at her disposal. She could have done her work openly. Now, it would all remain secret and shadowy, and she would have to do it alone.

Not alone. There were hundreds like Celia, priestesses of Gaea, and tens of thousands of believers. The Goddess of the Open Door marked countless lintels across Britannia. Her people rose like floodwaters behind a dam. A simple cloudburst would overtop the barrier and send them gushing out across the land.

Morfudd's strange song hitched and grew softer. She nodded in irregular time and reached out as if to take the unseen hands of others. She began to turn and twirl. All the while, her wailing song went on.

"Then, she'll be whole," Morgan told herself.

Snatching a cold hunk of coal from the fireplace, Morgan strode to Morfudd and gathered the girl in her arms. She stepped to the center of the white marble floor. While her child sung, Morgan knelt and scribed a black circle around them, and then tossed the chunk of coal back on the embers. It tumbled in the heat and began to burn. It was a good sign.

Sitting down in the center of the circle, Morgan positioned Morfudd on her lap. She listened to the girl's wailing song, so pure and haunting, and shut her eyes to everything else. Nothing existed beyond the circle where they sat. Even the heat of the fire dissipated across her back. Only the song remained, and the rhythm of her heart. With slow breaths, Morgan tuned her pulse to the ley, joining blood to note. At last, mother and daughter were in the same place, entwined in song.

Other noises intruded now—hooves on baked ground, the clang of pans, voices dickering. Morgan opened her eyes.

They sat on a street corner in a city of tan stone. The sky overhead was cloudless and bright blue, and the street was paved with brick. A peddler led his donkey past, and it towed a cart covered with brass pots. The man's skin was dark, his head wrapped in cloth. As he went, he wailed rhythmically, hawking his wares. The singsong lilt of his voice and the strange tongue he spoke matched perfectly the song Morfudd had been singing.

"Where are we?" Morgan wondered aloud.

Morfudd sat on her lap and sang, but her eyes met her mother's. That was astonishing enough. Then she pointed down the crowded street, toward a stepped pyramid in the distance. It was huge, and the scaffolds and slave teams told that it would be bigger still.

"The ziggurat," Morgan said breathlessly. "The Tower of Babyl." Morfudd had not simply carried her to another place, but also to another time.

The girl turned and pointed the other direction up the road. In the distance stood a great palace, wide and massive in stone. It seemed to float above the ground. Square pillars held up its outer walls, and enormous stone drums supported its gates. Whole plazas jutted out over empty air and spilled greenery in rampant locks. It was a miracle anything would grow in this desert heat, but the place was verdant.

"The Hanging Gardens," Morgan said, amazed.

Morfudd took her hand and stepped across the air, and they were there.

A cool garden spread all around them. Fronds jutted into the sky and leaves as large as Morgan riffled like flags in the wind. Lush lawns filled level upon level of the place. Meandering streams followed stony beds to lips of rock, where they poured into chattering cascades. Vines chased their way up ancient boles, flowers hung in brilliant curtains, and fruit dangled pendulously above the paths.

Morgan went to her knees. She sensed the presence of Gaea.

Welcome, Morgan and Morfudd, came a voice, ancient and mellifluous.

Morgan buried her face in her hands, but Morfudd stood beside her, singing still. The words formed themselves out of the nonsense song.

You stand in my dwindling garden. Once all the land between the Tigris and Euphrates was lush this way. It was the birthplace of the races of the world. I guided your race up out of Africa, across the shallows of the Red Sea, and along the ocean to this verdant land. For hundreds of thousands of years, you dwelt here in my garden, gathering its bounty and hunting its beasts. From here you spread throughout the world.

But some who had left the garden returned to conquer it. The great age of warriors had begun. Under their boots, the garden dwindled. Now, this is all that is left, a man-made paradise ruled by the greatest and most vicious of the warriors: Sargon. To him, the garden is no temple, but a prize. He builds the ziggurat there to glorify himself above the goddess, to make himself a god.

Morgan still lay there, fearful to look. She murmured a prayer, "Great Gaea, I am unworthy to be here with you."

No, Morgan, I sent for you. You have come. To do in Britannia what you wish to do, you must see this garden, and other things.

The song of Morfudd took hold of them again, and the Hanging Garden of Babylon vanished. Only darkness remained. Morgan reached out desperately to grasp her daughter's ankle. Their roles had reversed. Morfudd now was the guide and protector, and Morgan the clinging child.

A modal scale ascended to a single sustained tone. It rang clear and pure, as if Morfudd were a bell that pealed. Other voices joined the tone, human voices speaking some barbaric tongue, and around all of the sounds came a rumble like sustained thunder. Metal rattled—not loose metal but bolted panels pummeled as if by fists. Sound enveloped them, and gray light.

Morgan lifted her face to see a strange sight. She was inside a mine, its walls made of metal and braced with steel. At the peak of the mine were two oblong windows out to a cloudy sky. Three strange thrones faced the windows, and three strange kings sat in those thrones. The high-pitched sound seemed to come from the metal wall beneath the windows, where tiny stars flashed and implements jutted. The kings spoke to each other. Other men moved through the metal mine around Morgan and Morfudd, oblivious to their presence.

"What is this place, Mother Gaea?"

This is the place where the Age of War will end.

Morfudd tapped her mother's shoulder and pointed back behind them.

Not twenty feet away was a great fat barrel made of metal and lying on its side. It had weird flanges in back, and runes written on it. Underneath the barrel, the floor of the mine shifted. Metal panels separated and dropped. Beams cradled the barrel so that it didn't fall through, but the roar of the wind grew terrible. Morgan peered down through the opening hatch and saw what could only be a coastline far below. It was as if this mine flew in the sky.

The kings up front spoke, and they worked the implements before them. With a clang, the barrel's cradle gave way, and the barrel dropped through the opening.

"This is the end of the Age of War?" Morgan asked.

Yes.

"When does this metal mine fly?"

Fourteen hundred years from your time. Men will make war for fourteen hundred years.

"What is this great barrel?"

It is a weapon so horrible that all-out war becomes unthinkable. After this weapon falls, no nation will gather armies to stand from horizon to horizon. No longer will it profit kings to march into other lands and kill and dominate. In the aftermath of this weapon, there will be a fifty-year war of silence and secrecy, and the world will turn from its warrior gods back to me.

"I will change this future. I will end the Age of War now."

Before Gaea could respond, there came a blinding flash through the gaping hatch, and a great silver monster roared up out of its abyssal home. Its head was a rolling chaos, wider than a storm cloud, and its killing arms reached out to lash the land all around.

The kings were standing and peering down. One shouted in despair before slumping into his throne.

Then the roar of the monster reached them, a sound like

the plate of the world splitting and oceans and nations pouring through the crack and into the void. The noise solidified the air, and they all were gripped in its terrible fist.

Morgan clutched hands to her ears and hunkered down. In time, the sound eased and thinned, becoming the soft and slender voice of her daughter, singing. Morgan lashed out, clinging to her again. The song bore them through leagues and ages. It rose and lilted on tumbling winds and bloomed into other tones. Birds sang, and winds spoke amid shushing heather.

Morgan opened her eyes.

She knelt in grass, and apple blossoms fell in a fragrant storm around her. Morfudd still stood at her side, but there was another person here, too, an old woman in tattered robes of brown.

"Brigid!" Morgan said.

The woman nodded gently and reached out a gnarled hand. "Yes, but you must stand, Morgan."

Taking her hand, Morgan rose to her feet. Even as she stood, the ruler of Avalon, the once-great Sky Goddess of Eire, went to her knees.

"Why do you kneel to me?" Morgan asked.

The old woman's face was sweet in its wrinkles. "Because, you are the Second Eve, the Second Gaea. You will bring us all back to the world."

33

In the Secret House

Morgan stood numbly between her daughter and the kneeling goddess of Avalon. A frisson of delight and desire swept over her, and she breathed the air of the Otherworld. She had worked toward this moment all her life, but now she didn't know what to do.

Brigid gazed in wonder at Morgan and seemed to read her mind. "We've been on opposite courses, you and I. I began in the skies of Eire, worshiped by every soul on that isle. A simple monk named Patrick changed all that, and I fell and became a servant to the Christ. Devotion to me waned until I was but a forgotten old woman in a hovel on the outer edge of Avalon. This whole place would have faded from memory too if not for you, Morgan."

Morgan drew a ragged breath.

"And what have you done? You began as a mere mortal, a girl who lived more in vision than in truth. You made them true. You've dreamed a new world, a very old world, and made yourself the goddess who can realize it. You're at the moment of ascension, Morgan, from avatar to goddess, and

I—oh, in hopeful desperation I cling to you, that I might ascend as well."

Morgan could stand no longer. She knelt beside Brigid and her daughter and laid her arms across their shoulders. "I don't know where to begin."

"You've begun, Mother," said Morfudd.

Morgan gaped at the six-year-old. "What did you say?"

"You've begun," Morfudd replied. She reached out and laid her little-girl hand along her mother's cheek. "I'm here now."

The lost girl wavered behind a curtain of tears, but Morgan dashed them away. "You're talking! You're talking!"

Brigid wore a bittersweet smile. "She has always been talking. Now, she is talking to you."

"But always before it was . . . some angel tongue."

"It still is," said Brigid, "but your ears are changed. You hear thoughts, not languages. You hear what she means, not what she says. You will understand every person, every creature who lives and once lived or will live."

Morgan stared beyond Brigid to her cottage, its ragged wooden door standing just slightly ajar. "This is she? The girl you've raised all this while?"

"Yes," Brigid replied, "and the girl you have raised. The twin Morfudds, body and soul, have been united now in this one child." Every wheal that the ages had struck on Brigid's face curved upward in a manifold grin. "She's the firstborn of your new brood, Morgan. You've united the body and soul of your daughter, and soon you'll unite the body and soul of every woman in the world."

Morgan fiercely wrapped her daughter in her arms, and she let the tears pour from her. "My sweet girl. . . . My sweet, sweet girl . . ."

"For five thousand years—since Bahomet slew Tiamat and all the other warrior-gods fashioned swords to slay their goddesses, to make them wives or whores or nothing at all— our beings have been in schism. Our souls have been forced from our bodies and driven underground to hide in other worlds. While our flesh was traded and stamped and used, our spirits waited and pined for you."

Morgan still clung to Morfudd, though the girl herself pulled back.

"Come, Mother. We want you to see Avalon."

Sniffing, Morgan shook her head and stroked Morfudd's cheek. "All I want to see is you. Besides, I've been here many times, drunk from the immortal stream, climbed the world tree. . . ."

Morfudd laughed gently. "Those things are just on the outside." She took her mother's hand and lifted her from her knees. "There's lots more downstairs."

Wonderingly, Morgan stood. She helped the old woman do so as well. Brigid's hand was withered but strong, and her sparrow-light body had a spry gait as she led toward the root cellar beside her cottage. "I keep lots of things down here."

"Brigid, you could be any age," Morgan said. "Why do you choose to be old?"

"Because I am old. I feel old. When I feel young—and that will be soon—I will be young. No longer must we live in the world as it is, but as it should be." She grasped the cellar doors and yanked them open. Moldered stairs delved into the dark earth. "It's a good, deep place for storing up preserves— apple, of course." Down she went, the dank scent of worms billowing up around her.

Morgan clutched her daughter's hand and took a hesitant step. "You've been down here?"

"All the time. It's my secret house." She led her mother down the stairs.

Wet air enveloped Morgan. She stooped beneath a low beam and entered a small chamber with dim shelves leaning against walls of earth. Jars filled them, jingling like bells as Brigid brushed past. She descended another set of stairs, deeper into the hillside. Without pause, Morfudd followed, and drew Morgan afterward. Even the gray light of that place died in the lower chamber. Walls pressed close for a time, ragged wood grazing their knuckles, and then they came to a dead end—a wall of rock with water trickling down. It chattered into a small channel that bore it through the cellar.

"A dead end."

"No," Brigid replied, "though in a way it is. Below lie the dead generations of Avalon. Only I and a few others remain above, willing to converse with the world. In the deep reaches are the old powers—half dead and growing more so with each day. They live fragments of lives, perseverating on the matters they left undone."

"Below?" Morgan wondered, lifting her hands toward the cascade. "Do we have to swim?"

Brigid laughed lightly. "No, this was just to keep Lancelot from finding the door."

"Lancelot?" His name still made her heart leap.

"Before I took care of his daughter, your daughter, I took care of him. He lived nearly twenty years here—all within a few months. If I hadn't put a waterfall here. . . ." Brigid set her hands on the streaming wall and pushed.

It swung backward, pivoting soundlessly. Bright light spilled past the swinging stone. Brigid grasped the hands of mother and child and guided them over the wet path. They crossed onto gold-veined marble, and the door swung closed behind them. It boomed, fusing seamlessly with a curved wall in limestone.

The waterfall was gone. Brigid, Morgan, and Morfudd stood in a small domed room. Onion-shaped windows gave views of a pale sky, and an arched double door opened onto a balcony.

"Where are we?" Morgan asked.

"Go see," Brigid said, gesturing toward the doors.

Morgan walked to the threshold and stepped across it, out onto a stone balcony. Its white balustrade hung above a dizzy drop. Hundreds of feet below lay a great and strange city.

"Avalon," said Brigid, at her side.

Roofs of tile and slate, shake and living grass covered buildings of stone and wood, wattle and daub. Some were mean little hovels befitting wild folk, and others were great palaces befitting royalty. They made a conglomerate city, the hearts of a thousand sacred settlements pressed together. Amid these mortal structures rose immortal ones, spires impossibly tall. They soared like columns, burying their heads in the rocky heavens. Other palaces floated, their foundations set in dreams. Fantastical fountains gave watery music to the air. Flocks of doves and murders of crows soared in lazy motion among the buildings.

"It's beautiful," Morgan breathed.

Brigid nodded. "Graves often are." She pointed out across the staggering spaces to a garden. A grove of silver trees stood at its center, their boles so long and slender they seemed made of crystal. Their mirrorlike leaves trembled. "That spot, for instance." Brigid wrapped one arm around Morgan's waist and the other around Morfudd's, and with a strength that belied her age, lifted them and stepped over the rail.

Morgan gasped and lunged backward, but already her feet were stranded in air. Kicking, she clung to Brigid.

Morfudd laughed into her hand, "Hold still, girlie!"

"That's what I used to say to her," Brigid said.

Below their dangling dresses, pinnacles of stone jutted skyward. They passed beyond a henge and above a long-house, its roof like the overturned hull of a dragon ship. Next came a cluster of ivy-strewn barrows. The shadow of the women crossed a wide avenue crowded with Tuatha dé Danann, Seelie hounds, bogeys, and drifting spirits, their paths interlacing. A few lifted their heads and watched the three women drift across the sky.

"They know you," Morgan said.

"Yes," replied Brigid quietly, "but they are looking at you." Many of the folk below shifted to follow them. "You'll have to work quickly." The silvery circle of trees loomed ahead. Descending, Brigid reached out with one foot and came down on a berm of clover. Even as she released Morgan and Morfudd, Brigid was running up the slope toward the grove.

Morgan followed quickly, her heart pounding. The trees shimmered, and their leaves chimed overhead. She passed among crystalline boles and into the sacred circle.

Brigid already stood there, gazing at a pile of jagged white stones. The cairn lay in the precise center of the circle, on the highest ground. At the peak of the pile lay a marble cross. Brigid read the inscription: "Here lies Saint Brigid of Eire, servant of Christ."

Morgan blinked. "Your grave."

"Yes," the old woman said, "though no body lies here. My godhood does. The priests piled up stones and inscribed a monument. They pointed to it and told the people the great

saint of God had died. They pretended to honor me, but
with these stones they dragged me down from the heavens
and made me a mortal servant. And I allowed them. I
would've rather lived a saint than died a god," she paused
before adding, "until today."

At last, Morgan knew what to do. She climbed up the
cairn, grasped the stone cross, and heaved, lifting it. The
monument was cold, its edges sloughing earth down onto
the white stones. Setting her teeth, Morgan hoisted the cross
above her head. "This is . . . what's buried you." She flung
the cross down.

It struck the cairn and, with a great crack, split into four
pieces. The body, arms, and head of the cross tumbled opposite ways down the pile, but the heart had shattered utterly. Its
inscription was gone forever. Shards pattered across the white
stones of the cairn, transferring their motion. Rocks began to
shake and bounce. They clambered over each other, gathering.

Morgan stepped down the shifting slope and felt old
magic prickling her feet. It had lain here for a century, imprisoned by the ward of the cross, but now it was loose. As she
left the pile, it rumbled violently.

Stones boiled up from the center of the heap or bounded
in from its edges. They met in midair and joined. What had
been ragged shards of rock connected into smoothly chiseled
forms. At each fissure, divots showed the hammer blows that
had smashed this great statue. Even they filled in with gravel
and grit. The pieces vaulted together into a large and beautiful figure in white marble.

Her face was young and strong, beautiful and vigilant. A
holly wreath crowned her braided hair, and elegant robes
draped from shoulders to sandaled feet. On the pediment
beneath her was inscribed BRIDA.

"It's you," Morgan said, turning toward Brigid.

The old woman was gone. In her place stood a woman who was, flesh and blood, the image of this goddess. "I had always liked this statue," she said. "It was carved five hundred years ago by a Roman artisan. He set it in this sacred grove, and he and I believed it would be here forever. That very year, though, three thousand miles away, a boy was born who would be the end of us all." Brigid turned toward her. "But you have brought me out. And you will bring out thousands of others."

A mounting roar came nearby. The folk of Avalon City rushed across the street and up the berm of clover. They cried out in the ancient tongue of the Tuatha. "Deliverer! Deliverer!"

Morgan knew the word and knew those who spoke it: Blodeuwedd the May Queen, the weaver Ariadne, Cailleach the hag, Macha of war, the ever-drunken Maeve. . . . These were the voices she had always heard in her head. They had come not from within but from without, goddesses praying to a mortal girl. All her life, these ancient powers had trained and advised her, patiently guiding her to this spot and this day. More of them came: Epona the mare and Cerridwen the sow and Irusan the cat. . . . In a mob, they rushed among the trees of the sacred grove intent on Morgan.

"And you!" Morgan said, turning toward Brigid. "You are the wise woman!"

Brigid only nodded.

"Deliverer! Deliverer!" The throng converged, their hands reaching for Morgan. In their voracious hope, they might have torn her apart.

"Back!" Brigid cried, stepping defiantly before Morgan. The command rolled out from her in a great wave, lifting the throng and hurling it back. The creatures tumbled to the ground and stared up, dazed. "This is my grove, my sanctuary. You'll not defile it!"

"They come for the same reason you came. . . ."

"Yes. They want you to awaken them from death."

"I will, Wise Woman," Morgan said. "I will awaken them all."

Brigid nodded again. "But one at a time, and you choose which."

With a deep breath, Morgan approached the fallen goddesses. Her gaze moved from one to the next, and at last settled on the wan, strangely smiling face of a small woman. Morgan reached to her and said, "Sheila-na-gig, Goddess of the Open Door, rise."

The woman took her hand and stood, adoration in her eyes.

"Your sign has freed a hundred thousand households throughout Britannia, but you yourself are bound still."

She nodded.

"Take me to the place where your divinity died."

Sheila-na-gig smiled, crooked her finger, and led Morgan away from the sacred grove. Brigid and Morfudd followed, and the rest of the crowd fell in line, too.

Morgan and the multitude went from the great cauldron at the center of the city to the sacred pools at its verge. At each site, a goddess was reborn, and all along the way, more folk joined the throng. Soon, they didn't need their feet to bear them, for a tide of divine power swept them along.

Ancient songs began among them, melodies unheard for centuries. Once, mortals sang these hymns, but now the goddesses had become their own believers. The deliverer had come, and she was returning them to life, one by one. Soon, the false sun in the stony sky was outshone by Morgan and her pantheon.

"With each goddess you raise," Brigid said to her, "you have recovered another piece of the great Goddess. She was shattered by the warrior-gods, reduced to rubble, but you are reassembling her. When we all are joined, Gaea will be reborn!"

Morgan nodded. She felt feverish—hungry and thirsty, weary beyond all measure.

"Once the Tuatha goddesses are raised, we'll descend to the Fir Bholgs in the world beneath."

"Fir Bholgs?" echoed Morgan.

"They ruled before the Tuatha, and the Formorians before them." Brigid set a gentle hand on Morgan's weary shoulder. "The sidh is deep, with layer upon layer of slain deities, back to our Mother. But don't fear. We immortals will lend strength to your mortal body."

Huffing, Morgan crouched and caught her knees. "I need strength, Brigid." She crumpled to the street, grasping ancient stones in her trembling fingers.

Brigid and Morfudd knelt beside her and held her up. Sudden fear filled Brigid's face. "I've been a fool, Morfudd. This day has been a week in the world outside. I forgot how fragile she is. . . ."

"I never knew how fragile she was," Arthur said. His face was pale within his graying beard as he stared at the woman, collapsed on the floor. She lay within a black circle, drawn with a piece of coal. "I assumed her people were tending her."

The chirurgeon shook his head. "We must get some water in her." He rose and grabbed the pitcher and basin.

As Arthur lifted his half-sister's head, he said, "Where's Morfudd?"

The chirurgeon trickled water into her open mouth. At first, it welled up there like blood, but then she swallowed. "I don't know."

"We had to break down the door—bolted within," Arthur said. "What happened to the little girl?"

34

Transformations

She was breathing. That was the first thought that came after the long silence. It felt good, the steady flow of air into her. For a long while, breathing was enough. She shifted to her side, and a tingling chill crept from her shoulders down her spine, the parts that had pressed so long into the bed. Her limbs lay on each other, and breath sieved into her chest. For a time, it was enough.

But beds belong to someone, and this bed was not hers. She was . . . she was a queen . . . in the north . . . Queen Morgan of Rheged. . . . And this was—She sat up, gasping.

A man in black garb gripped her arms. One hand was strong and whole, but the other was twisted and somehow ever stronger. He pushed her back down.

"No!" she said, though she couldn't resist him. "No!"

"Now, Mother," the man said. His voice was both familiar and unsettling. "They told me you were coming around, at last."

Morgan lay in the well of heat and stared at this man— tall and curved, his smile crowded with teeth. This was her son, Mordred, the one that Arthur had tried to kill. "Where am I?"

He spread his hands to his sides and said grandly, "Camelot, of course."

"Why am I here?"

"You were visiting King Arthur, trying to get him to throw over his wife for you." There was glee in Mordred's face. He used words like daggers, delighting in the way they gleamed. "He said no, and you fainted. That was almost a year ago."

"A year!"

Before she could sit up, Mordred firmly pressed her shoulder. "It's all right. I've been watching over Rheged for you, practice for the day that Camelot will be mine."

Morgan looked warily at her son. "You've been busy. . . ."

Mordred nodded. "Already, I'm halfway there. Your brother—"

"Half-brother—"

"Half-brother, half-lover, whatever—Arthur's beside himself. Guinevere and Lancelot have been gone six years. Everyone knows what they're up to, but Arthur won't admit it. Of course, I've been very supportive of my old pa. He's withdrawn into himself, and I've been taking more responsibility. The knights need a leader."

Blearily, Morgan was trying to put it all together. "I thought you said the knights hated you."

"Lancelot and his cronies, yes, but they're out of favor, or out altogether. I lead the others." His fingertips rubbed across each other. "I've found it takes only a little nudge to change hearts—a pinch of this in one man's ale, a pinch of that in another's. . . . I can make them love me and hate anyone I wish. . . ."

"You seem to relish this task I've set you."

"He kidnapped me and tried to kill me," Mordred said with sudden heat. "I'm just returning the favor—kidnapping his kingdom and killing him." He shrugged away his defensiveness. "I'm your good son, Mother, saving your kingdom and winning another, all while you slept."

"It wasn't sleep," she blurted, and then wondered at that. "I—I was doing something."

"Resting your eyes, I suppose."

Morgan shook her head, picking among pieces of dream and assembling them. "No. I was . . . in Avalon . . . awakening goddesses. . . ."

"Mother, you were in a coma. You couldn't even wake yourself."

"I drew a summonation circle . . . and sat in it with Morfudd . . . and she took me away. . . ."

"Mother," his tone softened, "Morfudd is gone. No one has seen her since this coma began."

A small smile formed on her lips. "No, she's not gone. She's in Avalon, with the goddesses. She can talk now, Mordred. She's whole. I united her body and soul, and Brigid's too, and dozens of others. I'm their deliverer."

Mordred shook his head slowly. "Mother, you need to rest."

"No, I'm fine, and you've done well, too, better than I could have hoped." A tearful smile filled her face. "You're tearing down Camelot while I'm building up Avalon. We're bringing Gaea to the world."

"No, no, Mother," Mordred said. "I'm not destroying Camelot. I'm destroying Arthur and those loyal to him. Camelot will be stronger than ever when I ascend the throne."

Morgan shook her head slowly. "No, Mordred. There can't be a Camelot, and certainly not a *king* of Camelot. The Age of War is drawing to a close."

"You're . . . Mother . . ." He lifted her hand and patted it. "You're sick. You don't understand."

"I *do* understand. The reason you're here is to bring down Arthur and Camelot—"

"Listen to you! 'I woke up Eve! Morfudd is talking with faeries! I'm the new queen of the world!' You're delusional, Mother! These things aren't visions. They're *lies* you're telling yourself and everyone else—not just telling us, but shouting at us, demanding we believe. Nobody believes except you!"

She stared at him.

"You need to sleep, Mother. You're not well."

"You're doing this, aren't you?" Morgan said. "Not the original coma—I should have gone physically to Avalon—but when they found me, you took charge of me and you started using your poisons."

Mordred's face was a mask of incredulity. "You're mad! No, I've not used my poisons on you."

"You've taken control of me and Rheged. If I were dead, you wouldn't have the power to rule, but as I lie here, month after month, year after year, you gain the power. . . ."

He loomed over her, his jaw knotted with indignation. "I've never used any alchemy on you, but I will now, Mother." His healthy hand grabbed her jaw, fingers squeezing brutally to force it open. His twisted hand dumped a small vial of powder onto her tongue, and he rammed her jaw closed.

Morgan swung at his arms, trying to knock them away, but she was too weak. The bitter powder dissolved on her tongue, making it numb. It formed a thick syrup that ran toward her throat. Morgan tried to blow it out past clenched teeth, but Mordred clamped his hand over her lips.

"It's for your own good, Mother. You need to rest. You're delusional. If I let you go, you'll end up strangling Arthur," Mordred said, spittle flecking his lips. "Now, lie still!"

She hadn't any choice. Her mouth and throat were insensate, and the enervating stuff spread through her. Arms dropped and went limp. Eyes lost their focus. She was drifting away. . . .

"There," Mordred said, taking his hand away. "Good. You rest, Mother. You'll be better soon. Let your mind catch up to your body." The same hand that had forced her jaw closed now gently patted her shoulder. "I love you, Mother."

She wanted to say that she loved him too, but her mouth wouldn't work. Then it didn't matter at all. She was gone.

Morgan awoke in the company of goddesses. They sat all around her, perhaps fifty of them, arrayed across the inside of a giant stone bowl. Morgan lay at its center.

She sat up. Balmy air rolled into her. "Where am I? What's happening?"

One goddess stood up, young and strong in robes the color of the zenith. A crown of holly was plaited through her beautiful hair. She wended her way among the others, reached Morgan, and knelt. It was Brigid in her sky-goddess aspect. Gentle hands took hold of hers. "We brought you here, to the great cauldron atop Avalon. We're an offering to Gaea. Our power, her power, has poured down into you to save you."

Morgan panted. "Mordred . . . He's kept me in a coma for a year. . . ."

"A year," Brigid echoed gravely. "Time has piled up at the door. Only a day has passed here."

"He's taking my nation, and Arthur's too. He'll not destroy Camelot, but take it over. He'll be a warrior-king even worse than Arthur—a war-tyrant."

Brigid wrung her hands. "Are you in danger? Will he poison you?"

"Not until he's ready to seize power," Morgan said. She straightened her back. "I must be ready by then." She stood, holding her hands out to that crowd of goddesses. "Come with me. I need your strength. There are more of you to waken—among the Tuatha and the Fir Bholgs and the Formorians, and the elder goddesses, back to Gaea herself."

As one, the deities came to their feet and then above their feet. They lifted into the air, with Morgan floating in their midst. The stone cauldron dropped away, and the green mountainside around it. The women soared out across the sky and then plunged suddenly through heather and soil, rock and water, to the world below.

She descended through the great sidh of Avalon, world upon dead world, and brought the goddesses up to live. She shattered the chains that had kept Arianrhod from her home in the stars; slew the horse that dragged Godifu naked through the streets; melted the sword that impaled the wyrm of the Geats; unearthed the braid of Niamh in the land of the dead. . . . For each of Hercules's twelve labors, Morgan performed twelve times twelve—and did so as a mortal. She dug through the immemorial hill and gathered the shards of Gaea and rebuilt her. Each new feat drained her even as the risen goddesses empowered her. When at last she had reached the deepest, darkest places in Avalon, there were many thousands of goddesses.

"It is enough," Brigid said. She stood beside Morgan. Around them, the divine company filled an antediluvian cavern, vast and lit with their magic. "We're not every part of Gaea; there are other splinters of her—Tiamat and Isis and Mary and thousands more—but we are enough to bring her back."

"Yes," Morgan said, slumping in the woman's arms. The great depth and the endless labors weighed on her. She trembled.

"Our time is done. Lancelot and Guinevere have returned to Camelot, and Mordred uses them against Arthur. Soon, there will be war with Benwick, and then civil war in Camelot. You must ascend now."

"Yes." Morgan's breaths were labored. "I can do no more."

"I know," Brigid said quietly. As Morgan fainted away, Brigid lifted her as if she were a sleeping child.

Morfudd tugged on her sleeve. "Is she all right?"

Brigid nodded uncertainly. "For the moment, but not much longer. We'll take her where she must go and do what must be done." Tilting her head back, she stared toward the ceiling of the cave, the womb of the goddess. Brigid flew slowly upward, cradling Morgan in her arms. All around her, the great company followed in a vast and shimmering veil of divinity.

"Forgive me, Mother," Mordred said, stroking her sweaty forehead.

All the while that he had reworked the politics of

Camelot, he had tended Morgan. For seven years, she had lived on milk, a babe who would never grow. Mordred administered the feedings himself, nursing her as she once nursed him. Of course, others changed her and bathed her, but his devotion had won him many admirers.

At last, her time was done. All of Mordred's plans had come to fruition, and he no longer needed his invalid mother.

He carefully poured the powder into the ewer of milk and mixed it, making sure not to spill. Then, leaning over her, he gently pried her mouth open, set the spout on her lip, and poured.

"Forgive me."

Brigid laid Morgan in the center of the great stone cauldron. She was pallid, her heart trembling in a thready rhythm. She hadn't awakened, and might not ever. The poisons of Mordred were turning her blood blue. Brigid kissed her forehead "Not long now." She lifted her eyes to the heavens. A host of divinities floated there. "Hurry, now, all of you!"

They rushed down. As joyous as they had been in their resurrections, they now were solemn, almost sad. Ten thousand fragments of Gaea packed themselves in concentric rings around Morgan and Brigid. Shoulder to shoulder and back to front, the goddesses pressed together. Power shot galvanically through them, magic seeking its polarities. Already, they were becoming one.

It would not be enough. They were bound together, but their power would have to be channeled into the one mortal in their midst, and that would require mortal blood. Brigid knelt above Morgan, her fingers tracing out the blue network of her veins. It should have been Morgan's blood—but not this poisoned stuff.

Morgan stopped breathing. She lay there as still as stone.

"No," Brigid murmured. "Not yet." She turned to the circle of divinities around her, packed in brutally. Not one of them had mortal blood, except. . . . the girl that waited just beyond the cauldron. "Morfudd!"

Brigid leapt into the air and soared above the heads of the goddesses. She stooped like a falcon, snatching up Morfudd in her arms. They shot above the green hills of Avalon, turning back toward the cauldron. "You must be brave now, Morfudd."

"I am brave."

"We must help your mother."

"I will do whatever I must."

"Good girl."

Brigid soared above the cauldron. It seemed a giant eye staring up toward heaven. Energy arced across the living iris of that eye, and in its dark pupil lay a single tragic figure. Brigid hovered directly above her.

"Open your hand," she said to Morfudd. The girl did, and Brigid drew a ceremonial knife from her belt. She placed its handle in the child's grip. "Good. Now hold your other hand out above your mother, palm down." As she complied, Brigid said, "She needs your blood—just a few drops, enough to join her to the cauldron and focus its power." Brigid shook her head. "Forgive me, child, for asking this—"

Clear-eyed, Morfudd rammed the dagger into the palm of her hand. "Anything." She drew the blade out. Blood cascaded in a crimson stream, two rivulets that interlaced as they fell. The sanguine line reached down into the eye of the cauldron, to the creature at its focus, and joined daughter to mother.

Brigid wept. "Just a moment more. . . ."

Morgan's side was painted in red, and where it struck her blue-white skin, the contrast was stark. She looked dead already. Power coruscated throughout the great circle of divinity, but none of it was channeled into Morgan.

"What's wrong?" Morfudd asked.

Brigid reached to the child's bleeding hand and drew it back. "I'm sorry. It's too late."

"No!" cried Morfudd, "it can't be!" She hurled her hand out over her mother. The red rain resumed, but Morgan did not stir.

Mordred sat at his mother's bedside, watching her breath grow slower, shallower. Finally it ceased. He waited, listening. She was not breathing. He set his hand on her mouth, with one finger beneath her nose so that he could feel if she breathed. He counted to fifty, and then one hundred, and one hundred fifty.

Mordred stood, wiping his hand on his waistcoat. "It is finished. Britannia says good-bye to her daughter." He bent, kissed her forehead, and then straightened. He took a single step toward the door but stopped. "No. I'd best make sure." He sat back down beside her and lifted her hand, already growing cold, and began to count again.

At five hundred, he left her. Morgan's chapter was done, and his was only begun.

Magic crackled in a vortex above the goddesses. Power leapt being to being and gained strength with each jump. No longer were these separate entities, but parts of a whole. Lines of force pulled at the goddesses, attenuating them and braiding them together. Their power converged. It arced into the stream of blood, pouring down into Morgan—but also fountaining up toward Morfudd.

"Back!" Brigid yelled, grabbing Morfudd's hand and hurtling away from the cauldron.

Beneath them, the great stone bowl boomed deafeningly. Ten thousand divine beings dissolved. Their souls flooded into the one in their midst.

Morgan lurched into the air, her arms and legs flung outward. Power roared from her. Her hands shot beams that split the sky. Her feet poured rays that laved the cauldron. Her eyes, though, were fixed on the two creatures that fled away from her, and power like fire roared out after them.

Tightly clutching Morfudd, Brigid flew away. They were the last goddess and last mortal in Avalon, the only witnesses to the birth of Gaea.

35

The Eye of Gaea

J shine above Avalon. Soon I will shine above the world.

O Brigid, O Morfudd—I see how you flee from me, and I am grieved! I am your daughter, your mother . . . but the wondering terror in your eyes gives me another name. Goddess. Gaea.

I am Gaea. I am.

Myriad, plethoric, summative—I hold within me the once-dead goddesses of Britannia. Melusine twines her serpent scales through my thoughts and Eostre dances her spring dance through my wants. Sul bathes my flesh in sunlight, the triple goddess laves my mind in the moon, and Sirona pours starlight on my soul. I've always had them with me—Meg the midwife and Morrigan the phantom queen, birthing and devouring—but now we are one.

I withdraw my light from Avalon. It has probed the deeps of the lake and known each blade of grass on her shores. It has drunk from the eternal spring and eaten from the world tree. No mysteries remain for me in Avalon or Britannia. When Arthur is gone and Camelot is dismantled, I will merge world and Otherworld, and all the isles will be mine. Then, I will take into me every goddess on the continent and throughout the earth.

I am but the eye of Gaea now—her vision to the future. In time I will be her all.

But first: Arthur.

I am within his bedchamber. [Thoughts are footsteps to me: I think of a place, and I am there.] The plastered walls and gilded ceilings, the canopied bed and rugs from Old Babylon all reek of his torments. He lies even now upon the sheets and tosses in sleeplessness. For decades he has rolled on that bed, wishing for his wife, whom he has never touched. He is suspended between a woman and a kingdom, and the tug of war has drawn him thin. I will make him thinner still.

I kneel down beside his bed. [He cannot see me except as a phantasm of dream.] I whisper in his ear, *She loves Lancelot, and he loves her.* Even now I see them, across the hall, their faces inches apart as they struggle together toward climax. *They are making a cuckold of you.*

"Cuckold," he groans, rhyming it with a Saxon vulgarity. Arthur rolls onto his side, his face turned toward me.

He's still handsome under his mask of sorrows. Beneath his bushy beard and mustache, his face is that of a boy. I feel deep sadness for this man. In better times, we might have been brother and sister, not halves that do not mesh. To bring better times, though, I must be rid of Arthur.

You're losing the Power of the Land, and the power of Christ has evaded you. The Grail sundered your knights. [I see the quest sketched in full, the Round Table circling in mad scribbles, and I am appalled.] *Galahad is gone to heaven with the cup of Christ, and lesser men to the monastery or the grave. Oh, that*

Lancelot had been undone, but he remains to undo you. Your castle and city and nation are tumbling down around you, and you've no will to save them. [It is true: Camelot is in decay; but I want it destroyed utterly, and that will not happen unless Arthur acts.] *Lie there, Arthur, yes. Let your dreams become your mausoleum.*

He sits up. *Good boy.* He reaches for Excalibur and Rhiannon, hanging above his headboard. *That's it, Arthur. Strap on the scabbard and draw the sword. Cross the hall and kill them both—your unvirgin wife and her unloyal champion. The people will understand. You will be king again.*

Arthur stands, barefoot in his nightshirt. His fingers tremble in rage as he buckles the scabbard around his shoulder. He grips the sword and yanks it forth. The blade leaps into the dark air and shines. It wants to be wielded, to separate bone from marrow and get at the truth. Arthur swings it once through the air, and then steps toward the door.

A knock comes. I see through the wood to the silhouette of Mordred, leaning narrowly against the post. "Father," he says in a tremulous voice, though a smile is tucked in the corners of his mouth. "It's me, Mordred! Terrible news!"

Arthur hesitates. He sheaths Excalibur but does not unstrap the scabbard. Striding to the door, he flings it open and stands defiant. "What is it?"

Mordred blinks, amused by the king in nightshirt and sword, but a moment later, his face is awash in grief. "It's Mother—your sister. . . . She's dead. . . ."

"Morgan. . . ." Arthur steadies himself against the doorpost. I'm impressed with his acting, but a simple peek into his heart tells that this is *true* grief. "It's been . . . how many years—?"

"Twelve."

"And I still regret my last words to her." He heaves a sigh. "Poor Morgan. Alone all her life. . . ."

"And alone in death," Mordred says. "I went in to kiss her goodnight and found her dead." *Oh, Son, such a deceiver you are. You've deceived even yourself. You think you've murdered me, but you'll see.*

"Take me to her," Arthur says. He undoes the scabbard and leans it and the sword beside the door.

Mordred's eyes avariciously watch the jeweled scabbard, but he says, "Shall I wake the queen to come with us?"

Yes! Wake her! Kick the door in before she can roll off of Lancelot.

"No. Let her sleep. Morgan was nothing to her."

Not even the other woman.

Arthur slings an arm over Mordred's shoulder, and the two of them walk down the corridor. *I will join them soon, but first I step into Guinevere's chambers.*

Naked, they stand and cling to each other just within the door. They have listened even as they make love, and guilty smiles fill their faces.

"Poor Arthur," Guinevere sighs, and Lancelot kisses her neck. "He's torn in every way."

"He shouldn't mourn that witch."

Guinevere holds her head back, as if listening. "I would've expected to sense her death. She was supremely powerful. I knew the first moment I saw her."

"Enough," he says, lifting her and carrying her to the bed. "I have other interests."

Guinevere lies beneath him, his kisses raining on her neck. "She's not gone, Lancelot. She's more powerful than ever. I can sense her presence."

Only that stops him. "You mean *here?*"

She nods.

A slow smile reveals his teeth. "You know, I dreamed I made love to her once—more a wrestling match. She pinned me."

A flush of jealousy crosses Guinevere's face, and she rolls Lancelot onto his back, straddling him. "Like this?"

My touch inflames them. They'll wear each other out tonight and for a fortnight. This is chess. I've positioned the knight and queen in the conjunction where they will be most deadly together. Now, back to the king.

"—I don't think so," Mordred is saying. "Of course I didn't lock the door. Why would I think to lock the door?"

Arthur stands above my bed, the blankets still arched in my shape, but my body is gone. "For this very reason!"

"Who would've stolen her body?"

The king's teeth clench in anger. "Her damned followers, of course. They've taken her body, and they'll claim she's risen. She always talked about being the female Christ, and now her followers will make sure she is."

No. *I* will make sure of it. I will appear to them and tell them to prepare for the fall of Camelot.

Mordred stares at the spot, stoops, and picks at the blankets. They crumple. "I'll begin an investigation."

"No," Arthur says, gripping his arm. "It would only draw attention. Let's wait. Whoever proclaims Morgan's resurrection will be the culprit. Anyone who breathes a word of it must be brought in and questioned."

Nodding, Mordred says, "We'll need a coffin. We'll fill it with stones and bear it, son and brother, with a candle at her head. We'll bury the box in the castle garden and post a guard to keep witches from digging it up. She'll be as good as dead."

Arthur's eyes flare. "She *is* dead."

"Of course."

The king says, "I'm glad I can count on you in this, Son."

Mordred smiles. "This, and many other things." I nudge him. *Mordred, mention Lancelot and Guinevere. Plant the seed of his demise.* "I can help you restore the glory of Camelot, weed out the . . . unfaithful. There's lots of talk among the knights, damaging talk—"

"Your mother just died, and someone's stolen her body, Mordred. There will be time later—"

"Of course."

They are so bound by time. I am not, and this matter of Lancelot and Guinevere burns in me. They will bring Arthur down. Before I leave these two—son and husband-brother— I tap Mordred's mind and say *You'll need an accomplice in this.* He thinks of Owain. *Someone brighter and less loyal.* He thinks of Agravain, and I know he has found the right one. *Tell him that you must catch Lancelot and Guinevere in the act, and must charge them both with treason.* Mordred cannot tell my thoughts from his own. He smiles, thinking he is brilliant, though indeed he is very dark.

That should be enough to begin the plot between the sons of Morgan and Morgause. They are sparks to ignite a fire. I step a week ahead of them, to the time when they will talk to Arthur.

The king sits in his room, impatient and suspicious. "You've just accused my wife—your queen—of infidelity, and you have the audacity to offer me cakes?"

Mordred gestures to the tray between them. "The tea is quite fine too—honeyed." I see the substance that curls through Arthur's tea, a potion that first brings credulity, and then paranoia and rage. Mordred lifts the cup and hands it to his father. He then lifts two others and gives one to the other knight with him—Agravain.

He had been my own age, but now he is old. His face looks like weathered wood. Still, his wit remains. He casts sidelong glances toward Mordred as if they share a secret joke.

Arthur sips his tea, and the lines of irritability soften. "What were you saying? Something about Guin?"

You know what they will say, Arthur. You know it will be true.

"Well, it's widely known at court that the queen spends many of her nights with Lancelot. Either in his chambers or hers."

Arthur sighs. "There have always been suspicions. I've had my own. But what of proof?"

"There's none, as yet. But we could gather some. It really is your decision—you know what's best for Camelot."

"What's best for Camelot is that we turn a blind eye. Why destroy what we have for sake of pride?"

Mordred's alchemy has failed him. Arthur could not have endured a dozen years of suspicion only to crumple because of a little syrup. All may be lost in this moment. As Mordred fumbles for words, I whisper the key one—*cuckold.*

"—you'll not be much diminished by this, even as a cuckold. You are the greatest ruler this land has seen since Caesar."

"A cuckold . . ." Arthur echoes.

I touch his head, speckled with sweat. I show him Lancelot and Guinevere clenched together. Their bodies beat like the two halves of a heart. He remembers the night he had drawn Excalibur to cut them apart: He stood, trembling and alone, and through door and wall they lay together and laughed at him.

"The ones who are truly diminished are Guinevere and

Lancelot," Agravain adds, with a sly glance toward Mordred. "Pretending to love you, but all the while mocking you this way."

"Mocking me. . . ."

Lancelot laughed even as he rode her, and he boasted, "I slept with his sister once. . . . She pinned me," and Guinevere avidly rolled him and straddled him and said, "Like this?"

Arthur can't breathe, and he spills the poisoned tea in his hands. "What should I do? Suddenly, I can't seem to decide anything."

"Don't worry, Father. You said you needed proof. That's what we'll do next—get proof."

You will arrange with Arthur himself to abduct Guinevere from her room. Use your poisons to enrage him. Then post Agravain in her place. When Lancelot arrives, Agravain will attack and subdue him. He must not slay Lancelot. There must be a trial and imprisonment, time and woes to rip up the belly of Camelot.

Mordred believes these thoughts. He is ready to act.

The white queen and white knight are in position, and the black knights close in. I control all the pieces. I step back, now, to the night of my death, to comfort my people.

Daedra weeps. Her old hands are knotted on her bed-clothes, and she kneels on the floor. Word could not have reached her, here in Castle Charyot—moments after my passing. She has sensed my death. The circle drawn before her and the guttering candles at its lodestone points tell that she had sought the will of the goddesses—and none had replied.

Her door flies inward, and Rachel, now middle-aged herself, rushes to the bedside. "Do you feel it?"

Tears speak for Daedra. "What's happening? My spells've failed, and I feel like my insides've gushed out."

Rachel's smile is beatific as she lifts her mother and wraps her in her arms. "Don't weep. This isn't the end but the beginning. She's been gathering the goddesses, and now they are one in her."

Daedra pulls back from the embrace and stares. "All these twelve years, you've believed, but I could only wish. Now, it's all gone."

"No," Rachel said, shaking her head. "Your spells are gone because they were rooted in goddesses that are gone." She points at the summonation circle. "Who have you beseeched?"

"Arianrhod, my guardian."

"She's gone. Kneel and call to Morgan herself." Oh, Rachel, so faithful you are! She helps her mother down to her knees and then sits beside her, and Rachel says, "Great goddess Morgan, our friend, who was the Avatar of Gaea and is now and forevermore her embodiment, come to us."

I do. I step into the circle, and the ritual candles illumine my invisible form. *It is I.*

Daedra faints dead away.

Rachel catches her and weeps for joy. "I knew you would ascend, Morgan. I sensed all your work in the Otherworld. I have diligently taught your people to watch for this day."

I step from the circle and wrap her in my arms. *Rachel, greatest of my priestesses. You are faithful. You will boast on the day when the Otherworld is birthed across the land, but not yet. Arthur will slay anyone who says I live, so speak in secret and only to our faithful. Call to me, and I will answer. Draw your power from me. We will bring down Arthur and Camelot, and then Avalon will burst forth—the holy mountain.*

Rachel nods, tears streaming.

Be faithful and true. Prepare your sisters for the fall of

Camelot. I pit our foes against each other, and soon the world will be remade!

She tries to cling to me, but I pull back. There are many more I will visit this night—Bernicia in her island home and Cerewyn in North Galys and Hilde in the hot east; Lydia and Clare in Gododdin; and believers great and small throughout Britannia.

But first a little mischief.

They stand at midday around the coffin, draped in purple samite as if it were my color. Arthur is at the head and Mordred at the feet, and the Knights of the Round have gathered as witnesses. Not one of them weeps for me. They think that after this day, no one will be able to say that Morgan yet lives.

A priest stands above the grave, a great golden cross bobbing in his hands as he speaks the Latin prayers. I know the words. He asks that God should have mercy and Christ should have mercy, and the Holy Ghost should have mercy on this fallen one. He asks that my sins be forgiven and that I be covered in the extravagant blood of Christ. These are all fine wishes if I were subject to him.

He lays his cross upon the coffin, as if it might purify my sin. I will purify it. The gold melts easily and sets fire to samite and wood. Arthur falls back a step as the lid burns through. The knights are just beginning to gasp when the top of the coffin falls to ash and its sides blow away, revealing the rocks piled where my body should've been. Molten gold covers them in an odd figure.

The knights crane forward to see, but they will not recognize it—the Sheila-na-gig, Goddess of the Open Door.

No, but my faithful will. They will see and hear and know that I live.

Tonight it all begins. Arthur crouches with Guinevere in his arms and rage in his veins. He keeps her still and silent and wishes he could do more than simply hold her. My brother has sworn chastity, though, and he abides his vows, unlike Guinevere.

In her bed lies Agravain, smirking in the dark. He wears armor instead of bedclothes, and his sword is ready. *You'll not kill him. Only subdue him. Make him kneel and be kneeling when the others come through the door.*

Mordred and his friends among the knighthood wait in a nearby room, listening for Agravain's shout.

Put away your sword, Agravain. Lancelot will only gain it and use it against you. Flatten him with blows and kicks.

Agravain clings to the sword. Behind his smile, he is fearful.

I drag my finger across the sword so that it will be as dull as a club on Lancelot's skin.

Lancelot lies in his chambers below, and I lie upon him. I breathe desire into his ears. He sweats under me. I swim over him until he can stand no more. He rises, wearing only a breechcloth, and goes to his balcony. He climbs to Guinevere's room and steals in.

"Guinevere, it's me. Don't be afraid."

It will be a delight if he actually tries to kiss Agravain. The warrior thinks so as well, struggling to keep his breaths smooth and even as he lies there.

"Sweetheart, don't be afraid. It's your Lancelot. Wake gently." He crosses the sheepskin carpet and sits at the bedside. He reaches a caressing hand toward Agravain's shoulder.

Only beat him. Do not kill him.

Agravain lunges, grasping Lancelot's hand and ramming

it up behind the man's bare back. He could have caught Lancelot in a headlock and flung him to the floor, but his sword is in his other hand. It comes clumsily up, missing the man but catching its crosspiece on his shoulder.

Lancelot grasps the metal to yank the sword away.

Growling, Agravain holds tight.

Instead of stealing the blade, Lancelot flips the man over his rounded back. Agravain wails as he tumbles in the air, but his head comes down on the floor and his neck bends in a way that it shouldn't. He is a broken mess. I can see he is dead, but Lancelot cannot.

Staggering away, he turns and readies for another attack. "Who are you?" he asks the corpse. "What are you doing in the queen's quarters?"

I could step back and do this differently, save Agravain from this terrible death, but they all must go, one way or another. No. I will not drive myself mad by revisiting every moment of every day in every place and nudge things different. The plan proceeds apace.

"Who are you? In the name of the queen's champion, answer me!" He lights a jackstraw from the embers of the fire and transfers the flame to a taper on the mantle. Flickering light paints his comrade's death and his own horror.

"Collgrevaunce," he murmurs, but he is wrong. Both men had dark mustaches, and that bashed face could have been either of them. It didn't matter. Collgrevaunce is among the men rushing down the hall, and he will likely die tonight too.

Lancelot hears them and sets the candlestick beside the kill. He leaps to the door and bolts and braces it. Next moment, it bounces in its frame. Mordred and a score of other knights pound on the other side.

Stand guard here, Mordred, and send the rest downstairs to break through Lancelot's door. He complies. As Mordred shouts to Lancelot, most of the company rattles down the stairs and rams his door in. They rush through the shattered wood and out onto his balcony and begin to climb.

He's trapped now, where I want him. He lifts Agravain's sword from the floor and yanks free as much of the man's armor as he can. With deft hands, Lancelot arrays himself for battle. It comes.

I let them fight. Why not? This is what warriors do. Collgrevaunce is the first to die, and Gyngalyn next. Lancelot shoves their bleeding bodies to one side so that he does not slip, but the deaths anguish him. They will anguish all the Table Round. The more he kills tonight, the more this company will be unable to recover. An impaled eye, a severed neck, an eviscerated belly—the work of the warrior gods is gruesome.

And then Mordred makes the climb. His good hand clutches his sword, dipped in poison, and that leaves only his claw to drag him up. Clumsy and slow, he scuttles over the railing. Lancelot could have killed him ten times over except that I whisper of honor in his ear. I also warn him of the poisoned sword.

Panting, Mordred says, "Where is Guinevere? I thought you fought only for her. You certainly seem willing to fight for yourself."

Lancelot does not take the bait. "You know where she is."

I touch my son and speak through him. "Yes, I do. Arthur's got her. He's teaching her what it feels like to have a real man inside."

Lancelot jags like lightning and would kill my boy except that I bat his sword from his hand. Mordred thinks he's done it, but when has Mordred ever bested Lancelot? Unarmed and staring down a poisoned blade, Lancelot knows he must submit.

Mordred knows it too. "So easy. I should have reached you first. It would've saved a few sides of meat. Now, the question is, do I take you captive, or do I kill you here?"

You take him captive. But Mordred isn't listening. Murder rises in his heart.

"Either way, I might as well have you kneel. I'd like to see the great Lancelot on his knees before Sir Mordred. Kneel." He plans to take the man's head. He'll take it with one sword stroke and pike it on the Lance of Longinus and ride it around the walls of Camelot. Even now Mordred imagines the gory prize raining down on his hand as he rides. "I said, *kneel!*"

Lancelot dips his knee. Mordred raises his sword overhead and brings it whistling down. It sliced through skin and muscle and bone—not Lancelot's, but Melyon's, for I have made his corpse lunge up as a shield. Mordred's blade passes halfway through but hangs up, poisoned tip stopping short of the man.

In reflex, Lancelot lunges, shoving Melyon into Mordred and hurling both over the balcony rail.

My son falls, crying as he goes. I could return in time, but Mordred has made his choice. I'll keep him from dying, but also from following Lancelot. Yes. He must get free. It will do the most damage to Camelot and Arthur. Even as my son hits the ground and thrashes, Lancelot is climbing down and making his escape.

The chessboard is in disarray. The white king and queen are cornered by the black knights. They will take her first, and Arthur will be left in checkmate.

36

The Still, Small Voice

There she stands, tied to the great stake. Its rough thews drive deep into the earth. Wood mounds around its base, and ropes wrap its shaft. There stands Guinevere, caught as all women are caught on the claims of father and brother and husband. Of course Arthur sentenced her to death. She stole his most prized possession, her own body, and gave it to another man. It is an old, old crime. There are a hundred names for women who commit it, but only one sentence: Death.

Flame leaps from the brands of Gaheris and Gareth, laid gently on the wood mound. Fire rises in a curtain around Guinevere. It climbs the hill, converging on stake and woman.

Of course I must save her.

I ride with you, Lancelot, my arms hard around your waist and my hands clinging to your breastplate. You don't feel me sitting here, with my face pressed up against your golden curls, but you will survive today because of me. Your sword flashes, driving back the crowd. They shrink from us, parting in a canyon. Your horse, Rasa, charges through their midst. The knights stand and reach for their swords, but their hands are stayed by your friends among them. You will plow past them all and reach her.

Gaheris and Gareth turn. They have no weapons, not even the burning brands, which they have left on the pyre. They have no time either. Rasa barrels into them. Knees drive them onto the burning logs and hooves strike their big, noble hearts.

I am sad for my sister—three sons killed by Lancelot. Gawain only survives, and his grief and fury will make him a monster. He will tear the heart out of Arthur.

We burst into a wall of fire. It ignites the horse's pelt and your hair, Lancelot. Even your fingernails are limned in flame. I draw a cowl of magic about us, and it descends to suffocate the blaze and keep us inviolate within. You ride on, Lancelot, and beneath your cloak you harbor a dozen roses. You plucked them from an Otherworld bush, each bloom filled with the dew of that place. You hope to fling the dew out across you and Guinevere and Rasa, riding its potencies to the Otherworld. Such romance, but you know nothing of magic.

I could let you burn, all three, a heartrending end to your tragic love, but you will do more for me by living.

This cloak of mine is woven of Otherworld power, and it sweeps out around Guinevere too. You draw out that bundle of flowers, Lancelot, and swing it like an aspergillum to bless your love, and I draw my cloak tight about you all and whisk you away. It is the second time I have saved you from a jealous lover.

It is a heavy burden to bear horse and rider and lady in my arms this way—especially this rider and this lady. You might have been mine, and the world would have been different. I would never have raised the goddesses or combined them in me. I would not have ascended to become what I am. Thank you, Lancelot, for rejecting me. . . .

You are dying, all three. Even my magic is not enough.

I lay you in a chattering creek on Avalon, tributary to the immortal stream. Let these waters lave away your pain. You'll not live forever, but your burns will ease, and you won't die today. I leave you here with a kiss, not of longing, but of care.

Go, sweet Lancelot. Wage your Otherworld war and regain your lost kingdom. Take Guinevere to Benwick and rule there happily.

I step away from them and back to Camelot—to you, Arthur, where you stand and gape at the empty stake. Fire piles on fire, rending wood and rope to nothing, but your wife is gone and your greatest knight too. You tremble, not from outrage but from relief. Dear brother, how alike we are now! You punished her for not loving you, and I punished Lancelot for not loving me, but in the end we wish them to be together and safe. We who are born of Tintagel have never found true love, not even with each other.

You sit, breathing in shock. "It's over."

I sit beside you and wrap you in my arms. *It isn't over, you know. If they had died, the insurrection would have ended. Now you must pursue them wherever they go. Instead of punishing a single woman and a single man, you must punish a whole nation.*

A tear stands in your eye. You are so weary, Brother, the inevitable end of all warrior-kings. You tire of war, your domination wanes, and younger bullies take what you once took. "I will endure this. I will diminish but not die."

No, Arthur. You will fight. The old lion has one last great rampage in his blood. You'll go after your bride and her thief wherever they lair, and tear them down, and take their lands for your own. Then all will know that Arthur ruled, not some Tuatha queen. You will be augmented by this.

Your shoulders square beneath your silken tabard. Yes, there is strength left in you, and I will spend every ounce of it.

Leave your kingdom in the hands of your son, Mordred—the son you once kidnapped and tried to kill. He almost gave his life again in capturing this traitor. You owe him this much, and your trust will bring him back to you. Your Round Table has lost so many to the Grail, and now more to Lancelot. The ones that remain need you at the head of your armies, marching and fighting as you did to gain this land.

You nod in slow decision. "I'll lead my armies."

I am glad. Arthur will spend himself and his men. All the stags of Camelot will run together and crack their skulls on each other until not one remains.

Just now, one such stag bellows below—Gawain, who drags his brothers' bodies from the fire. He uses his own tabard to smother the flames that burn their faces, and kicks dust onto their torsos. All the while, Gawain mourns.

I step to you, bereaved nephew. I grieve with you. *They had been good boys, the philanderer and the true believer. They had been unarmed, ridden down like dogs and cast like refuse on the burning pile. Such villainy! He steals the wife of his king and slays his own friends—three of the sons of Lot!*

Beneath your breath, you say, "He will wish he had slain the fourth."

Yes, he will. *Already, Arthur's heart burns for war, Gawain, and you will lead it. You could not defend your brothers in life, so at least you might avenge them in death.* Your eye rises from these smoldering corpses—oh, how destroyed they are!—to your king, the one man more wronged than you. *Yes, go to him now. Stand above him, lest Lancelot's allies in treason strike at Arthur himself.*

Even as he goes, I turn aside to speak with Mordred. He lies infirm in Camelot Castle, bones broken in his fall from Guinevere's window. Both his good arm and his twisted one are splinted, and one leg. Poor boy. He is my child, and I love him, though he had tried to murder me. Indeed, he thinks he did, but he has another think coming.

I sit down on your cot, Mordred, and take your hand in mine. Your eyelids flutter slowly apart, and you stare through the musty shaft of sunlight to see my figure. I am not whole, but neither am I ghostly. I am here, and I know you see me because your eyes are dull with guilt. "Mother, I'm sorry—"

I've given this matter into your hands, Son. Camelot will be yours, just as you had hoped. You begin to sit up, but I press you back down and motion for you to be silent. *Rest. Let your limbs mend. You'll need your strength. In time, Arthur will come to you, and you must play the wounded child, seeking his long-overdue and much-deserved love. Win his heart, Mordred, and without your poisons. Gain his truest heart, and he will give Camelot into your hands when he leaves to pursue Lancelot and Guinevere. . . .*

"Are you a dream?" you whisper incredulously.

I am a divinity.

"If only you were real."

Sit up. Call the healer. Tell her you need her to see some-thing.

You struggle against your splints, and the cot squeaks as you lever yourself upright. You lean your back against the cold stone of the infirmary wall and call out, "Magdalena, come here."

She is one of my own, and bears the sign of the Sheila-na-gig within her blouse. It is well, for I am soon to teach them all the truth about me. Magdalena walks to the foot of your cot and stands there. "What is it?"

Tell her she is about to see proof that your mother still lives. Point to the chandelier. I reach up to the contraption. It is a wide wheel of wood fitted with metal implements that hold eight candles. None are lit now, at midday. As you tell Magdalena about the sign, I tighten my grip.

No sooner has the healer looked toward that light than I yank on it. The chain snaps halfway to the ceiling and pulls free. The wheel plunges to strike ground broadly, throwing hunks of metal out around it. Two flagstones chip, and all the patients bolt up in their cots.

You smile toothily, my son, and Magdalena searches the air for me. I open my cloak of magic to her for but a moment, and say into her mind, *Tend these wounded and tell them what you have seen and heard. When you are done here, go tell your sisters in faith.*

She falls to her knees and reaches for me, but already I am gone.

I step a year ahead, when Mordred sits the throne of Camelot. You sense me, don't you, son? You know my anger.

If only you had listened. You shift uneasily on that ill-gotten throne, floating on a tide of poison. *You didn't trust my power but yours. You used your potions to gain Arthur's love and that of his nobles. They'll not love you long, and when they turn, they'll spit that poison back.* You stand from the throne. Your gaze darts among rafters, as if I would lurk there. I tap your shoulder, and you spin, drawing a poisoned dagger. *You*

*poisoned me once, or don't you remember, son? You can't do it
again.*

"I am king of Camelot," you hiss, "and of my own doing,
not yours."

*Foolish child. You knew I would kill whoever sat the throne of
Camelot, and now you've made yourself that man.*

"I am king! You can't take the throne from me!" you
shout, uncaring that your servants stand and stare.

Why reply to that? I let your hollow echo answer you.

I leap the channel and find more foolery in Benwick.

Arthur, Gawain, and their army hunker down outside the
city walls and wait to starve the people out. Meanwhile
Lancelot, Guinevere, and their nation wait within—well-
stocked and well-sexed.

I grow impatient. This siege must turn to storm.

I lie upon you at midnight, Gawain, and whisper into
your ear: *Your brothers haunt Camelot. They cannot join the
Resurrection until you avenge them.*

You groan on your back, great bear that you are, and weep.

*Call out the coward. Challenge him. Slay him and end this
siege. Your strength waxes with the rising sun and wanes with its
setting, so challenge Lancelot at dawn and do him dead.*

Next morning, he does. He challenges Lancelot to a duel
to decide the siege. Lancelot accepts, and the two ride
together and throw each other down. They duel with swords.
I watch avidly, glad at whomever might win. Should it be
Gawain, he will take Benwick and march back to battle Mordred. Should it be Lancelot, he will do the same. To me, this
battle is a spinning coin.

Then, a stroke. Lancelot's sword comes down with the
weight of a cudgel. It lays back Gawain's breastplate, the
cloth and skin beneath it, the muscle and bone under that,

and bares the great man's thundering heart. Lancelot pulls up short, not slaying him, and backs away as blood hides the organ of courage.

Gawain goes to his knees and weeps. He pleads to be slain, but Lancelot will not do it. More's the pity. They drag Gawain back to the half-timber house that had been his head-quarters. It becomes his sick house for three months, and now his mausoleum.

Arthur, Brother, I stand beside you, above this grave of your last true friend. The earth is deep and black here before your feet, and the setting sun casts the shadow of the cross down atop Gawain. His face seems almost living, taking on the hue of the bloody sky. In the distance, trees shiver in the face of autumn's first breezes. There are hundreds of warriors behind us, Arthur, and yet we stand alone.

Here lies the last son of Lot. Who defends Camelot now, Arthur? Only you yourself? And now autumn, and soon winter, and it will be another season of suffering for your men.

You stare bleakly at that noble face, the mended breast-plate and the wound beneath it that would never mend. You lift your hand to your heart, and many men weep to see how affected you are. I know the love you had for this man and for all those you have lost. I know what else grieves you—the message that came this morning. Mordred has concocted reports of your death, has won the nobles to his side, and has usurped your throne. You stare at the death of this one man but are seeing the death of many things.

Go to him, Arthur, the only friend you have left. Go to Lancelot, though it slays you to do it. Break the siege and seek alliance against Mordred. Let your armies fight side by side to regain your throne.

You want nothing more than to do it. You love

Lancelot, and your heart aches to heal this rift. And yet you know also that if you turn from vengeance, you have given up Guinevere.

Your kingly hand descends to the black earth, mounded before you, and you cup a fistful. Reluctant, reverent, you pour the rich ground down upon his face, and the priest says, "And at the end of your days, you will return to dust, for dust you are."

No. That is a perversion of the goddess blessing: "At the end of your days, you will return to the earth, for the earth's you are." Gawain is not a corpse but a seed, a dry husk laid down in the ever-fecund body of his mother, and from him new life will spring.

You sigh deeply. "Lancelot."

I know you have chosen, and it makes me glad.

I step forward in time and cross the channel. The whelmed armies of Benwick and Camelot fill a vast armada beneath me. They battle Mordred's ships and make landfall. The armies sweep north and west. Against Lancelot and Arthur, the knights of Mordred cannot stand.

"Mother, my poisons have poisoned me. I repent of trusting my own strength over yours. I had thought to make Arthur's death true, to stop the armies of Lancelot on the channel, to bring the faerie queen in chains to my throne. All that I had accomplished is now undone. I beg you, Mother, if ever I was your son, your anti-Arthur born to end his kingdom, come to me now and help me end it."

I have waited so long to hear just these words from just these lips. He is praying to me. At last Mordred realizes my divinity. That is reason enough to go to him. I love him also, and I go for last words between a mother and son.

He is kneeling at a windowsill—oh, precious boy!—and I form myself out of his shadow. Mordred senses my presence and turns. He is middle-aged and gaunt, twisted and terrified. I stand before him as a young woman with smooth white skin and eyes untouched by terror. *Thank you for calling me, Child.*

"Mother," he breathes, remaining on his knees, "will you do it?"

I already have been doing it, in a thousand ways. I've embraced each actor in this great tragedy and whispered the lines he will speak. All are playing their parts, and it is time for you to play yours.

"Can you convince Arthur and Lancelot to encamp for the winter and wait for warmer weather . . . ?"

Of course not. You must surrender.

"What?"

If you surrender, you can dictate terms—retain your knighthood and title as Prince Mordred, receive a large see in Powys, and be named Arthur's legitimate heir upon his death.

"I have to wait until he's dead?"

You're a poisoner, Mordred. You decide when he's dead! Do this, or you yourself will be dead within the fortnight.

He is sullen and sad. He had hoped I would grant him a miracle, but his will is not mine. Now he knows it is not a question of whether he will fail, but how.

Draft the surrender today. Couch these terms in more outrageous requests so you will have room to whittle them down. Be willing to give up all provisions but these, and you will have a treaty.

"It will be easily done," Mordred says.

I fade in the way of shadows. *Not as easily as you think. Good-bye, Son.*

If he says good-bye, I do not hear it. I race ahead to the day when the treaty will be signed, when Camelot will be destroyed. I watch from the treetops, boughs mantled in snow.

It is a frosty morning. On the western banks of the Somerset Cam stands the army of Mordred. Its main forces wait within the wood, lest they be caught in the open by the greater forces of Arthur and Lancelot. On the eastern banks mass those very troops. At their head rides an honor guard of knights, surrounding the two kings. Their horses clomp across the shallow ford, and then chuff as they plod up the bank. Icicles form on their legs, and their breath flees away like ghosts.

Mordred waits with his own honor guard at the brow of the hill. Both sides wear ceremonial armor but bear true blades. No man in either army may draw steel, though, or the treaty will be shattered and peace will turn to war.

Such a knife's edge you walk, Brother. My best to you this day, that it might all be done quickly.

Arthur and his retinue dismount. Mordred and his retinue kneel. He produces the treaty that they all will sign, and sign in blood. Without drawing his sword, Mordred nicks himself. He signs the paper first, and the characters of his name steam in the cold air. He hands the treaty to Arthur, who takes it and reads it. All the while, Mordred stands with his finger dripping on the hoarfrosted ground.

It is so easy to turn that line of red into a viper. It swells up and snaps at Arthur's legs.

Lancelot cries treachery and draws his blade and chops the snake repeatedly until its sections lay dead. By then it is too late. There is an omnipresent roar, from west and east, from forest and plains. The men have seen naked steel and blood upon it, and both armies converge to destroy each other.

Good-bye, my son, my brother.

37

Morrigan le Fey

They are dying by the thousands, these best and brightest of Camelot.

I fly above them in three bodies, the three crows of the Morrigan. They are part of me now. I am the black witches of death. My wings are as broad as men, my beaks as sharp as swords. I shriek, and they groan; they fall, and I rise. We meet in the air, the goddess of death and the newly dead men. They dance with me, macabre in their twisting. They sing a song like the scream of pigs. It is a horrible harvest. White souls pour from severed necks, and heads fall like acorns.

Owain, my son! How well you fought, how horribly well! Always your flesh was stalwart and true. You're done with flesh now—it lies there gutted and trammeled—but I draw you up to new life. This is your second birth, and I bring you up into it. . . .

Of course they are shrieking: They are fresh from life as from the womb. There is blood and pain in plenty, and terror at what is to come, but they have entered a larger world.

Tristan, my love! How did I lose track of you? We have sieved down separately through the years, and you have grown old. Rest now in the arms of your maiden lover. The flesh that once divided us is gone, and now we consummate our souls. . . .

I am not just the Morrigan, the hoary harvesters, but also Niamh of the Golden Hair. I am the smiling maiden who stands in the midst of this whirling dance. My golden locks spread like sunshine, warm and bright. The warriors cease their lament and turn toward me. They smell the clean scent of my hair and think of their lovers or mothers or sisters. *There, there. Don't cry. I'm here for you.* I wipe the terrors from their eyes, and they reach for me. I gather them into my arms, sweet smelling and gentle. *There, there. I'm here. I'll take you from this place of torments to a place of delights—Tir-na-nOg.* I whisper to them of the Otherworld they have hoped for but never seen.

Come with me, sweet souls.

I breathe them in as if breathing mountain air. The spirits of Camelot whirl into my bosom. I rise into the wintry sky and curve toward Glastonbury Tor.

The rumpled island rises from an ice-choked swamp. Its abbey crouches on one hillside, smoke dragging from its chimneys. The whole land huddles beneath the winds of winter.

I dive through its bedrock. The souls within me wait in silence like a held breath. Then we burst out upon the city of Avalon. It is wide and bright, fantastic beneath a beaming sun. Over rooftops of grass and slate I fly. In my wake, rainbowed windows shudder in their frames. Dead gods look up to see me, the apotheosis of every departed goddess. They weep for joy that I have returned, and they run and fly to follow.

We soar among spires and minarets, out beyond the lofty battlements of the city wall. A cliff face drops away below us.

Nine great cataracts pour over its edge and plunge whitely a thousand feet to the sea below. Beneath its sapphire waves move great things—leviathans and serpents, naiads and selkies and sea sprites. . . . My shadow passes over them, and they lift their heads to see me. I am life to them and to all creatures, and the beasts of the sea sport and play in my shadow.

On I fly, the breath I hold growing anxious within me.

At the far edge of the sea is a green land, wide and verdant. I am there in a moment. Grasses and wildflowers cloak rolling hills. Groves of fruit trees stand along singing streams. Here is Eden, the primeval garden.

I pour the souls from my lungs across that glorious place. They soar out of me and come to ground running. Their spirits take form, naked and unashamed. No longer are they men of Camelot, but new creatures in a new world.

Welcome, my children, to the Garden prepared for you from the foundations of the world. Eat of every tree and drink of every stream. Taste of all knowledge and receive eternity. I will bring more like you, men and women, both. I will bring all of you here to live together forever, to tend the garden and walk with me in the cool of the day.

Anguish has become ecstasy. I am grieved no longer. I rise and return to the Battle of Camlaun, to my black-winged aspect, and shriek and gather.

"Mother! Mother, what have you done to me?" Mordred cries. He crouches within a rocky cleft and summons me.

I do not go to him, too busy gathering souls, but I will speak from the shadows. *Did you think you were the only one who wanted to win this war?*

"I thought you were on my side. I thought if I won, you won."

No. I want no man to rule this land. I have arranged all of this not so that you or Arthur will win, but so that no man will. . . .

"So, you intend that this day will be the death of Camelot. The death of us all?"

At last he understands, as much as he is able. He does not realize that every death is a birth, that soon he will be born again.

I fly. I call the souls of the dead to dance with me in the sky. They rise and don black feathers, their feet stomping on air. In the turn of the dance, the plumes become golden, and I gather them in and whisper them comforts. We soar to Avalon, to that green land where there is no more misery or dread.

Brigid stands there. She is old again, her hands fretful. She kneels on the grass and bows to me, as she should, and I whirl in a wreath about her.

"It is your great day, Gaea."

It is.

"Must they all die?"

They must. And more than this—you must reclaim Excalibur. I'll not have it floating about, making a new warrior-king.

"If I will take back Excalibur," she said quietly, lifting her silvered head, "I would take back Arthur too. Grant him to me."

Yes. It will be best that he rest on Avalon.

I leave her. She has gotten more than she deserved, and the souls are calling me.

O Mordred, my son! Already? I had not known it would be so soon, while I was elsewhere. Come into my arms. I carry you here next to my heart, but I must see your body. Where do you lie?

The thought bears me to a rocky valley, where shelves of

stone jut above a small stream. The rocks are painted in blood—a handprint here and a trail there. I see the cleft where you had hid, and the red line that showed where you lurched into the open. You lie there on your side, a spear in your heart. That same weapon, the Lance of Longinus, stabbed the heart of Christ and slew him too. That lance had belonged to your father.

Mordred, forgive me. He killed you at last, and this time I did not save you.

The wound still pours, blood going down into the earth and spirit going up with me in the air. I take you in my arms and rock you, my son—so tragically conceived and born and stolen and reared and slain.

There is the man who did it. King Arthur. He sits near you, his hand on your ankle. I had not seen him before, for he still lives, but not much longer. Your sword bashed in his helmet and a good part of his brain. The edges of the staved helm crimp in around the wound, and no doubt your poisons even now kill him.

I stand above you, Arthur—husband-brother. Do you hear me?

"Morgan," you say blearily. Blood has painted your nose red, and it runs down your lip.

You've killed our son, Arthur, but we've killed you. Blame Lancelot if you wish, but he was only a tool of mine as you were a tool of Merlin's. The old sorcerer built up your kingdom, and the old witch tears it down. Jove created a new nation to dominate, but I have destroyed it and return it to the patient and forgetful earth.

You shake your head wearily. "Sister. . . ."

Yes, Brother. I am waiting. I will comfort you and carry you away to a land of endless beauty. Bid the world begone.

Your fists clench like iron beside you, and you set your teeth.

They come, as I knew they must—Lancelot first. In a rage, he rides Rasa over the hill and yanks the stallion to a halt. Leaping from the saddle, Lancelot runs to you, pries your hand from Mordred's ankle, and cradles you as I will do soon enough. He weeps. He knows now that this is the end of his king and of Camelot, and he knows he was the cause.

In Lancelot's cries, he shouts for his beloved Guinevere. She is Tuatha, a priestess, and she has been mustering the numena of the wood to aid in the battle. Now she comes down out of battering boughs and takes solid form. She rushes to the side of her lover and bends over the form of her husband.

We four have torn apart Camelot—these three with their passions and I with my visions. Whatever hatred I may once have felt is now gone. I love these souls. They are my comrades, my adversaries, my peers.

I touch the trickling spring where it forms an ice-crusted pool. Now, the water is sacred, and the well goes to other water very near. I whisper to Guinevere what they must do.

Lancelot hears it from her lips and lifts Arthur in his arms. Guinevere yanks the Lance of Longinus from Mordred's heart—he looks so small, so broken!—and uses the spear to break the ice that encrusts the pool. Lancelot reaches it, steps in, and plunges, swallowed by the chill waters. He and Arthur are gone. Guinevere follows. I go with them all.

It is black and cold in the watery ways. I have always walked the ley lines instead of swimming these dark passages, but I go now the way of Guinevere. We tumble together, the four killers of Camelot, and arrive at the shores of Avalon Lake. I bring them out not on the isle, but on the mainland, for there is one last matter they must attend.

Excalibur.

"Excalibur . . . ," Arthur murmurs. "Merlin first hid the sword here . . . hid it from the gods. Rhiannon formed around it and hid Excalibur. Now Rhiannon is destroyed. Now Excalibur must return to the waters . . . hidden from the gods. . . ."

And from men.

Arthur demands that Lancelot draw the fabled blade and throw it again into the waters. He demands it thrice, and at last, Lancelot pulls the peerless sword.

I circle around it. This is the great other, beautiful and deadly. Jehovah himself fashioned this blade to slay all the other gods, that he alone might rule the heavens. I am drawn to Excalibur, for I know it is a power utterly opposed to mine. For one rebel moment, I wish that I might know the mind of the God who folded such a sword, leaf by steel leaf, until it was perfect.

No, there is to be no god. There is only the goddess, Gaea. Her consorts are only mortal creatures. In all the world, she alone is divine. Gaea is alone.

Throw it.

Lancelot's arm draws back the blade. With a great heave, he hurls it. Excalibur flashes end over end through the cerulean sky. It sings as it goes, slicing air as once it sliced bodies.

I circle the blade. My dark wings bear it toward its death. I am Badb and Macha and Nemain—the Morrigan. White steel and black plume whirl together to the heights and plunge together toward the depths.

Brigid waits, mistress of these waters. Her hand had brought that god-killing thing up from the depths, and her hand will bear it back down. She reaches from the lake, and her fingers open. I carry the sword down to her and gently place its hilt in her hand. I would not have her slain by this thing. With slow reverence, she withdraws the blade from the world. The waters of Avalon close over it, and it is gone.

Join me, Brigid. We will bear Arthur to Avalon.

We stand on a raft in the midst of the lake. Brigid, beside me, wears her sky-goddess radiance. How she shines! I do not begrudge it of her. Soon, she too will rejoin me, and her radiance will be mine. I wear a youthful semblance in black samite. We seem sisters, she the shine and me the shadow, but we will be one. Behind us stands the ferryman, who is Charon and Bron of the floods and who poles between the lands of the living and the dead. His shaft reaches down to murky depths and pushes us to the shore.

"Bring him," Brigid says simply, holding her arms out to Lancelot, Guinevere, and Arthur.

Lancelot lifts his king, steps onto the raft, and kneels to rest Arthur across his legs. Guinevere follows and drops down to sit beside them. The ferryman shoves away from the shore.

Lancelot looks at me accusingly. "Why are you here?"

I am his sister.

Brigid says, "She is the land's true power. She has grown up to be my spirit and the spirit of every goddess. This is her day."

Guinevere shivers. "You can heal him, Brigid. Mordred's poisons can be nothing to you."

She looks to me, and then says, "This wound was struck

long before Mordred, and its poisons are manifold and potent. Some wounds are mortal wounds."

"Then you," Guinevere says to me. "Surely you can heal him."

I shake my head slowly. *He is the sacrificial king. Unless he dies, the world cannot be reborn.*

We arrive on Avalon. Lancelot lifts Arthur and climbs the green hillsides. Apple blossoms make the air into mead, and he and Guinevere are drunk with it. They cannot abide the specter of death on this sun-dappled hill. They rush toward Brigid's cottage, and they laugh with hopeless hope.

But I follow. They will not escape me this day, none of them.

Flinging back the cottage door, Lancelot bends down and carries his king within. Guinevere crowds after him, and they are surprised to find Brigid and me standing within already. Brigid now is a crone in homespun brown robes, but I remain as I was, the death-garbed maiden.

Lancelot crosses the floor and goes to the simple straw mat where he himself slept as a boy. There, he lays the king of Britannia.

Guinevere kneels down beside him and caresses Arthur's bloodied beard. She is weeping as she kisses him. "What will I do without him?"

"What will any of us do without him?" Brigid asks. She stares at the poor, sobbing woman and quietly says, "Lancelot."

He looks up, and sees the shovel she holds. "Good-bye, good king," says Lancelot. He rises and stalks toward her, takes the spade, and strides from the hovel. His feet crackle on the stones outside the door, and he is gone.

How much more deeply Guinevere breathes now. There

are things she could not say in front of Lancelot. "Arthur," she says, lifting his hand between hers. "I'm so sorry. . . ."

His hair is matted in blood and grime, but his eyes are stunningly blue. "Whatever . . . for . . . ?"

She weeps, her shoulders shaking. "You deserved better. . . . You deserved everything."

"I've had . . . everything."

Guinevere kisses his hand. "Everything but me." She stares into his eyes, waiting for a response, but there is nothing left. His gaze is glass. "Oh, no. . . . No!" She screams and embraces his dead body.

Arthur's spirit flows from the wound in his head. He coils up through the air and across the cottage, into my arms. I gather him in.

Guinevere rises from her knees and lunges toward me. "Let me go with him! I know you have the power, Morgan. I know we can be together!"

It is as I had thought. She who had Lancelot would give him up for Arthur. He is her Tristan. Their flesh was the barrier between them, and while they lived in it, Lancelot was her choice. Now, though, nothing needs to separate her from Arthur.

Come into my arms.

Guinevere's eyes are clear as she enters my embrace. Arthur's spirit trembles, pressing against her flesh. As soon as my hands close around her, a little sigh escapes her lips, and she slumps against me. The spirit that had buoyed her flees now between dead lips. She and Arthur twine together in death as they never had in life. I will bear them to the Garden, the new primeval couple.

I carry her body across the rushes and lay her down beside her man. It is right that they are together.

I turn to you, Brigid, and see that you are weeping. *We will dig three graves today.*

"Three?" Your eyes flash.

Lancelot cannot survive this grief. It will kill him to learn of Guinevere—kill him or drive him mad.

Your old face blanches. "You know this?"

I nod.

You begin to pant, staring at me as if I were death. I am. Death and life both, brilliance and madness. "May I choose for him?"

What woman would ask to make that choice?

"A mother would. I am that to Lancelot."

Yes, then. You may choose. You nod solemnly. On stiff legs, you head through the door and toward the cellar. Another shovel waits there. Your fingers fasten on its handle, smooth with work and the oils of human skin. For a long while you lean on that implement, the wet darkness swathing you. At last, you walk back up the steps and carry the shovel. You've made up your mind. It will be madness, not because that will be kinder for Lancelot, but because you can't imagine going on without him.

Poor woman. You, too, will be surrendering your identity to me soon enough. Now, though, with arms full of souls, I walk from the hovel. I descend into the cellar, past the deep waterfall, and to the heights of Avalon City. The souls I hold are glad to see it—Arthur and Guinevere and Mordred.

I am glad to bring them here.

38

Glory

King Arthur and Queen Guinevere are dead. The only true heir to the throne, Prince Mordred, is gone as well. Sir Lancelot is insane. The Knights of the Round Table are decimated. The great armies of the land lie broken on the Camlaun. Camelot is a corpse, and the folk that scramble all over her are but flies begetting maggots.

I appear above them: Sky goddess, earth mother, Morgan le Fey and Gaea la femme. I hang above a benighted land and am their only light. My radiance pours over rooftops and pierces shutters. They have been closed against lawlessness as against a storm, but I am the dawning sun. Doors swing open, and faces peer up at me. Folk caught in the street are swept to their knees by my refulgence. What guards remain in any garrison or on any wall stand with swords half drawn and mouths full open.

Believe, people of Camelot! It is I, Gaea. I am returning to you. Trust no more in king or God, but in me. The old things are being swept away, and all is made new. The Goddess rises from her long sleep and casts the dominators down. Receive me, enter into the feminine mysteries, take the sign of my coming, and you will inherit the earth. Those who cling to war will inherit nothing at all.

They hear me not in their ears but in their minds and hearts. Many believe. They cry to me and receive me, and I place my mark on them. Others quail, caught between God and Goddess, wrathful father and embracing mother. Some few decry me:

A priest stands on the height of the basilica and shouts, "Hear the words of the Revelator: 'I saw a woman sit upon a scarlet colored beast, full of names of blasphemy, having seven heads and ten horns. And the woman was arrayed in purple and scarlet color, and decked with gold and precious stones and pearls, having a golden cup in her hand full of abominations and filthiness of her fornication: And upon her forehead was a name written, Mystery, Babylon the great, the Mother of Harlots and Abominations of the Earth. And I saw the woman drunken with the blood of the saints, and with the blood of the martyrs of Jesus.'"

He calls me the Antichrist. I am, and also the Antiwotan, the Antijove. I will be rid of all warrior-gods. Though Jesus was the meek and lowly Son of Man, men have made the Christ a warrior god, and I will be rid of him.

Still the priest harangues, speaking of seven hills and a fallen king, the ten rulers of the north, and the beast out of the abyss. All the while, my lichens grow across that great basilica. Stone seems hard to human hands, but its yields to tendrils of plant. They sink small white fingers into the crevices and break them apart. Dressed blocks become rubble and rubble becomes gravel and gravel becomes sand. It coheres a moment more, an enormous sandcastle, but then disintegrates beneath the railing priest.

He falls in a whuffing cloud of grit, which buries him to his waist. Whoever waited within the basilica is buried deeper—they who had not emerged to see my coming. They lie among their crosses and stained glass, and I let them lie.

Behold, people of Camelot, what awaits those who cling to war. On the day of my return, every structure that does not bear the sign of my mysteries will fall, and every person within will be buried. Christ does not draw these folk forth, but today I will. I reach my hand to that sand pile, and power rakes through it, unearthing a dozen gasping folk. They are the color of dust, and they cough and sputter blood. *I save them today, but will not on the day of my coming. Behold and believe. Receive the mysteries, and receive the whole earth.*

I leave the poor folk of Camelot. Such terrors they have known, and they think I am just another, but I will bring them into paradise. On I go, to Bath and Worcester, Stratford and Leicester, Cambridge and London and Canterbury. I go first to the cities, for they will be most decimated by the coming Garden. The people will decide what remains and what falls, whether they will inherit the new world or be outcast from it. I warn the priests to prepare their boats and take their faithful to Brittany or Saxony. My great and terrible day is coming.

But enough for those who do not believe. I have spent the winter among them. The spring belongs to my people.

From door to door, I go, wherever the Sheila-na-gigs wait on post or lintel. The women within know me, and I know them, each by name. Lydia, Clare, Rachel, Daedra, Morfudd, Cerewyn, Hilde, Bernicia, and a hundred thousand more. We speak every night. They have waited and wanted, and I bring good news.

My day is at hand. Tomorrow, with the dawn, the Garden will break out across the world.

Dawn arrives. I stand on the peak of Avalon, in both worlds at once. One eye peers down the slopes of Glastonbury Tor, where a skin of grass stretches across the bony earth. The other eye gazes on the glories of Avalon—the immortal stream and world tree, the great cauldron where I was born, the apple groves and the deeping lake. They are overlaid, these worlds. Mortals are fated to wander one or the other. Not I. In me, the worlds are one. They pour their sights into my eyes, and the light awakens thoughts in my mind, and the thoughts combine into a single thing.

You make the future, Brigid had said. A thought in your mind becomes a desire in your heart and a reality in the world. Your visions, Morgan, become the truth.

In me, vision and truth are one.

The rock beneath my feet grows soft and verdant. From the fecund ground jut shoots that unfold into blades and become a carpet of grass. It rolls down the rocky hills before me, welcoming me to Glastonbury Tor. The hill is growing into a true mountain. It rumbles up from the earth and lifts me to the clouds. It drags warm air into cold heights, and snow begins to fall.

I descend from that glorious height, not on feet but spirit wings. I soar just above the advancing wave of green. Where it strikes a sapling, the tree grows with sudden urgency. It spreads its boughs as if to welcome me, and well it should. I am returning the world to its primordial abundance, before sword and ax, before war and ruin. The tree grows massive in a moment, ten tight rings followed by one great ring wider than a man.

Every tree will be the world tree, every woman my daughter, every man my son.

I fly above the abbey, a cloister among hermits' huts. The

wave of grass sweeps past the chapel, and vitality enlivens the mosses that cling to it. They tear apart mortar and rock, and the church collapses. Dust rolls into the air as, beneath it, grass grows from the pulverized stone. The nuns and priests lie in fresh-made tombs. They had known this day was coming, had prayed in earnest against me, but their champions are gone. Their decision is made.

A different tomb awaits the hermits in their huts. The green wave envelops them. Crude planks swell to new life, fuse to each other, and grow. Their doors cleave to their frames and take root in the earth. Huts become trees, with monks trapped in their heartwood hollows. The trees rush skyward. Perhaps the monks can climb down the boughs that spread from them. Perhaps they will simply join their God in heaven.

I fly on from land to lake. Beneath me, rushes transform into lilies and brackish pools become deep water. Spirits dance along the surface. I would join them, but I have all of Britannia to awaken today. There, on the far side of the lake, the River Brue is ennobled. It churns with rapids over ancient stones. The transformation runs upstream, toward the distant headwaters. It bears this change eastward, and I follow its path, heading for Camelot.

There are her towers, the dream of Merlin made real. Now my dream will overtake his.

Beneath me, flowers bloom in every tree, on every stalk. Their bright panoply garbs the world. This first blush of color deepens as each blossom matures to fruit according to its kind. Britannia is becoming the Garden of old, a paradise meant for all people.

An old farmer walks the Cadbury Road, leading his mule and hay cart.

Believe!

He hears me, sees me. The breath of Eden rolls over him. He goes to his knees and believes. I sweep by. The hay piled in his cart redoubles, and the cart itself roots into the ground. The old man is young again, a new creature in my new world.

Camelot is silhouetted black against the bright morning. All atop her walls, folk stare toward me. In every window, in every tower, they reach out, hoping.

Believe!

The growth wave crashes against the walls, and they tumble into mounds of sand. Many men fall with the dust, but others dangle in air, held up by sudden belief. Beyond them, bricks crumble and houses cave. Half timbers transform into tangled woodlands and thatch grows into knolls of grass. Towers topple like felled trees, stranding some folk in the air and smashing others to the ground.

Believe!

Inhabitants run out into the street in terror. They see me. Some are slain by fear. Others are saved by hope.

The Fount of the Bountiful Weirds turns to verdigris and dissolves in a green puddle. King Arthur's palace shatters like glass. Hunks cascade atop each other. They will dissolve to dust. There will be none of it left, not even foundations. The jousting grounds overgrow. Quintains become trees in a glade. The lists where so many men had died bloom with red orchids. The sanctuaries of war become paths in a sacred garden.

Among plunging towers and dissolving streets are some few houses that stand resolute. The Sheila-na-gig marks their lintels. Sudden forests bristle around them, and dawn's light deepens to a green murk. These will be cottages in the forest—a shop here, a pub there, the glad believers living in a sylvan wonderland.

They will need no ruler, for I am the friend of all. They will need no coin, for I call them to share all they have. They will make no war, fear no evil, and live not by their sweating brows but by my bounty. And when they die, I will gather them all to the Otherworld garden.

This is how humanity lived when there were no gods, but only me.

Believe!

Camelot is done and will never be again. Its buildings are rolling meadows and woods. Its walls are mounds that ring the hills. Few will remember Camelot, and those who do will find nothing when they dig. I am glad.

On, I fly, on across Britannia. Other cities will fare better than this one, where many buildings will remain. One city will fare best of all—my Gailhom in Rheged. It is my holy city, and it will remain. While this great green tide sweeps away the evils of Arthur, I fly north toward my home.

"She's coming," Rachel said. She lay on the floor of Castle Charyot, fingers feeling along the foot-worn crevices between stones. Her cheek was white, pressed against the floor, but she smiled. "I can feel her. Can't you feel her, Mother?"

Daedra knelt nearby. Her hands lay in a dead tangle on her thighs, and wrinkles form a nest around desolate eyes. "Yes, Daughter. I can feel it."

Rachel sat up. Her eyes were too bright to see her mother's darkness. "Now is the hour! All we've hoped for comes true. Gaea is restored. The Garden sweeps from sea to sea. War is no more."

"Many things are no more," Daedra said.

At last, Rachel's smile flattened and slid away. "What's wrong? Everything is born anew."

"No, Rachel. Not everything. Some things die. Many people do."

Rachel moved to kneel in front of her mother, pried up her hands, and held them tightly. "Arthur and his knights chose what they chose. They broke themselves on each other. Morgan only turned their warfare inward rather than out. You can't grieve for those horsemen and their cavalier ways."

"I can grieve for the great cities."

Mouth gaping, Rachel said, "What great cities? Do you remember what the cities did to us before Morgan found us? Do you remember what Arthur and his soldiers did to Gailhom and her baby boys? No, Mother, this is the only great city, and Gaea will enliven even it. It will be a beacon to the world."

"You know what I will miss?" Daedra said, her eyes suddenly aflame. "Men. Real men. I don't mean rapists and killers. They aren't men but monsters. I mean strong, kind, decent men—"

"There are many such men who believe in Gaea—"

"No, I mean ones that think differently than we do, and act differently. Men that aren't women. See, that's what's happening today. Two thousand years of history are being wiped out, along with the men who made it."

"For two thousand years, they've kept us in chains!"

Daedra nodded. Her eyes were black in her pallid face like fist holes in mud. "We aren't even giving them chains, but graves."

A shudder ran though Rachel. She shook her head as if her hair could erase the words from the air. "Today is her day, the day of Gaea. I will not be grieved today." She stood, pulling the old woman up from the stones. "And what are we doing kneeling here?"

Soft tears rolled from Daedra's eyes, and she lifted her hands to the gray vault of stone. "This is her sanctuary."

"Not today," replied Rachel with a broad smile. "Today her sanctuary is Britannia."

Clinging to the old woman's hands, Rachel walked down the aisle toward the great double doors. At a touch, they swung back, their black bulk replaced by a sky radiant with noon.

Sunlight splashed across the stone porch and played in sharp angles on the roofs of Gailhom. Light limned the city wall and swarmed the waves of the river. It cast the south-lands in shadow, though something massive moved there.

Across the land surged a tidal wave of magic. Before its breaking edge, the ground was fertile but fallow. Behind it, tree and grass and flower burgeoned.

"She's coming," shouted a woman in a nearby window.

"Morgan!" cried another.

"Gaea!"

Women began to sing a strange and lilting song, the sort used to lure lovers.

"Do you hear them, Mother?" Rachel asked.

"Yes, of course."

She pointed toward the distant line, sweeping toward her. "Do you see?"

"Of course."

At the head of that tide flew a figure they all knew. She had freed them when they hadn't even known they were pris-oners. Morgan had dreamed for them all and made her dreams come true.

The shutters of Gailhom were thrown open, and faces

filled the windows, gazing in awe. Paeans poured from a thousand mouths and made the air shimmer with desire.

Rachel fell to her knees and pulled her mother down beside her.

The green wave rushed down the far bank. Morgan flew above the river, and her shadow shot through its depths. She crossed the battlements of Gailhom, each gate bearing the sign of the Open Door. Every plot of land grew in abundance, and every tree sprouted and thickened. Some buildings fell with a sad noise, but their roofs grew new gardens before their Queen. Most of the buildings stood, though, enlivened by ivy and moss.

Morgan soared toward Castle Charyot. Beneath her flying form, thistles and wildflowers proliferated. She descended and touched down before Rachel and Daedra. A wave of transformation swept out around her and continued north across the city.

Hands at her hips and young face beaming, Morgan stared at her old friends, her worshipers. *Rachel, Daedra! Rejoice with me. It is my day!*

"Today and every day," Rachel said, falling to her face. "We will rejoice with you today and to the end of time."

Daedra didn't bow but slowly stood. Tears streamed down her face. "It's your day, Morgan, but it isn't my day."

What?

Shaking her head, Daedra said, "I'm too old for a new world, Morgan. I wanted all this—beauty, truth, freedom, life—but the cost is too high."

While Rachel stared in amazement, Morgan stepped forward. *Your own daughter said it. There is only one day now, my day. And only one way out of it.*

Daedra nodded and walked into the arms of the goddess. They closed around her, and she slumped.

"Mother!"

Her body, old and finished, slid down the figure of the goddess and lay at her feet as if in worship. Rachel clambered to her and grasped her hands, stilled now. "What's happening?"

It's a new world for new creatures, Rachel. Your mother goes to another garden beneath the world. Don't fear. You'll see her there. Everyone will be there. As if cradling an invisible child, Morgan rose into the air. Her cloak of vitality whirled around her. Britannia would never be the same.

"Glory to you, O Goddess," Rachel muttered in her tears. "Glory."

39

Consummation

From the Outer Isles to the channel, from Eire to Essex, the Garden is all. My lands spread wider than Arthur's ever did, and within their borders, all is bounty and beauty. Primeval forests stand above pristine lakes. Rushing rivers spread into primordial fens. Fruit hangs on every tree, and grain crowds every field.

I am glad, and my people are glad.

They live in the depths of a new, rough paradise. The great Bedgrayne Forest extends from the Thames to the Trent, engulfing Oxford and Ely and Peterborough. Each is but a cluster of cottages on a river. London, York, and Edinburgh have escaped the woodlands, but they brim with flowers. Camelot has escaped nothing. It is a verdant forest with but a few homes, surrounded by wild wheat. A woman walking the Cadbury Way can gather enough sheaves for a week. A man wading the River Brue can reach down and grasp a salmon in each hand. A child can wander the woods and feed on berries as large as grapes, and grapes as large as apples.

Britannia is gone, and Albion has returned out of the

ages. It is a paradise for my people, daughters and sons and beasts. Game roam in huge herds. Harts and wild goats, prairie hens and creatures dead for an age of ages. The great stag has returned, the mammoth, the dire wolf. Their bones have been hidden in my body, but time is full, and I give them new birth. Many more of their brethren lie at the bottom of the channel, where they had roamed when last I was queen. I will raise them too on my way to the mainland.

I will go to gather the continental pieces of me. Goddesses long dead must be found, raised, and subsumed, and the champions of the gods thrown down. Then I will take Europe, and soar on to the Levant, to Egypt and Æthiopia. I'll turn east into Persia and cross the Tigris and Euphrates, where Eden once was, sweep north to the Rus and south to the Hindoos and east to the Celestial Empire. All will be remade in my image.

But now, it is enough that I am Gaea over Albion. It is more than enough.

I need not call for a celebration of my triumph. Life is celebration. There is no need to shuck woes and embrace joy, for there is only joy. Laughter fills my garden. Every glad word is a prayer to me. I hear my people marveling in their new world, feasting on fat meat and drinking new wine. Their joy could not be more complete, except . . .

Huge and myriad, I appear in their skies. Above the sacred peaks of Snowdonia, the steepled heights of Gailhom, the seaside splendor of Canterbury, the strange fastness of Caerleon—my arms open in welcome to my people.

I called you to believe, and you believed! The world is yours. I, Gaea, am yours, and you are mine. The Goddess and her mortals . . .

Hearts leap at my voice, and faces turn toward me as leaves toward the sun.

Rejoice with me, my people. Eat and drink your fill; sing and tell tales; gather around your hearths and gather in your beds as it pleases you. Be glad.

They are glad, and I am too. They want for nothing, and I . . .

I am alone.

No, I am surrounded by my people—flowers yearning toward me. I need only seek the most beautiful one, pluck him, and be alone no more. Through a thousand eyes, I gaze at my folk. They peer back at me lovingly. So many fair-haired men, their skin so smooth, with eyes like sapphires and teeth like pearls. Were it merely a matter of comeliness, I would have thousands to gather, but I seek the right one.

All my life, I have wished for a true consort. Tristan was too pure, Arthur too fierce, Urien too weak, Lancelot too fey . . . I have had every type of wrong man, but never the right one. Now, I will have him. I am Gaea, and I will find the perfect consort.

There he is, sandy-haired and aster-eyed. This young man wants me as much as I want him. His mind and spirit are attuned to me like no other's. He wears the mud-stained tunic of a farmer and clutches a hoe in his hand, but nobility lurks under the crude clothes. I draw him up. Tunic and breeches flutter down, empty beside the hoe. Mud and dirt fall too. Only the man, perfect and clean, comes to me.

I gather my countless selves into a single body and wrap the man in my arms. We lie upon the heights of Avalon, within the great cauldron. At first, it is enough simply to cling together and feel the warm contours of flesh on flesh. Our hearts beat in separate rhythms, the sound caught by that great stone bowl and sent out into the heavens. Slowly, though, his pulse aligns with mine.

I roll him onto his back and cover him with kisses. He trembles with each one. He caresses my face, my neck, and gathers me in his arms. The young man is tender with me as if I were a virgin. I am reverent with him as if he were a god.

At last, consummation. For all the miracles I have wrought, this is my truest. Before this moment, men were pests and their warrior-gods foes. I had only ever fought them, whether with blades or words or beds. I had never come into true commun-ion with these irreconcilable opposites. Now, on the heights of Avalon and in the depths of the cauldron, we are one.

The sun flashes through the heavens. Night blinks its starry lid closed. Another dawn and another dusk, and a third . . . The world can tend itself while I lie here in his arms. Bliss. I have felt such overwhelming peace and joy but once in my life, when I held my first child, Mabon.

Suddenly, I realize who this is—this young man whose soul is tuned to mine. Lost these four decades, stolen by Morgause and spirited to an abbey, growing strong among the people of God and yet able to embrace the Goddess—he cannot know who he is, but I know. A space opens between us, cold and hard like steel. It is impassible.

This is the ancient rite, of course, that the consort of the goddess is her very son. It cannot be otherwise, for all men are born of her and all return to her, but it sickens me. I still feel the taboo deep in my flesh.

Before Mabon, I had thought I was utterly alone. Now I *know* I am, forever.

I leave him and run across the sky. He stares after me, and we both are weeping. This ache will kill me. I can't bear it alone, but alone I am. I've made this solipsism, and it is my prison. I've transcended myself and my world, and I am alone. Who can be a confidante to the Goddess?

There is one.

I step down into her cottage. Its migration to the world has left it unchanged: sturdy walls in stone and stick, pole rafters hung with drying spices, a small table and two stools, two pallets, a hearth. The woman at the hearth hasn't changed either. She's old and bent, her silver hair gathered loosely at her neck. She looks up at me when I arrive, and then glances away.

"I know why you've come."

Do you?

She nods, lifting two warm ciders in wooden cups. "You've come for me."

Yes.

Slow breaths saw into and out of her. "Well, I suppose I'm ready, but I'd hoped to live out whatever days remained to me."

I take a cup from her and sit at the hearth, hunching to warm myself. *What are you talking about?*

She stares at me, and I know what she thinks. "I'm human now, or nearly. The power is all yours. There's a whit or two left in me, but no more. I'm just an old woman living on the mountain of the Goddess and I—well, I wondered if I had to be subsumed."

So gentle are her words, though I see fear boiling in her belly. I reach to her, a young hand on her old, old jaw. *O Brigid, that's not why I came. I came because you're the only one left like me.*

"But I'm not like you," she objected, panicky. "Not anymore."

No. No one is like me anymore. I've made sure of that. What a fool I've been. *It's just that . . . I needed some cider,* I say to her, lifting the cup.

Her fear falls away like a veil, and she sees me for the first time. "Goddess. What is it? Has something happened?"

I'm sad, Brigid.

"How can you be sad? You did everything you set out to do. You began life as a little girl, a little human being who saw things no one else did. You brought your visions into being. You made yourself a goddess—*the* Goddess—and made your private world into the world for everyone. You defeated every foe and won every prize. You've gotten everything you wanted."

What she says is true. The pledge I made as a frightened child, that I would be the Second Eve, is fulfilled.

"You weren't born to fate, Morgan. No god or goddess shaped you toward this. You mothered yourself, tutored and advised yourself, and tore down a kingdom to build your theacracy."

But I'm alone.

She takes my hands in hers, old trembling twigs, and peers fervidly into my eyes. "Of course you're alone, Morgan. You've always been alone. You're without peer."

I'm not Morgan, but Gaea.

Her face falls, and she is penitent. "Forgive me, Great Mother."

But you are right. I have always been alone. I'm much older than the priests say—not five thousand years, but five thousand million. From the beginning, I've been alone, this great spinning sphere hanging in cold, dark emptiness. Just me. At first I was fiery and furious, and I still hold that rage inside me. Then I became fertile and began to bear the basest of creatures. Slowly, they grew, and slowly I changed them. I sought another mind and found none. For thousands of millions of years, I found not another thinking thing. At last, for a hundred thousand years, I had someone—small and vicious, but someone.

Brigid nods.

I set them to dreaming and made them dream of me. They made images of me and carved them in stone. Throughout the world, they took round rocks and carved into them my great breasts and thighs and worshiped the power of my fertility. These were my children, and I was their all. I had no peers, and my lovers were my sons. For ninety-five thousand years, it was enough.

"And it is enough again," Brigid says hopefully.

No, I changed them again, as I had changed all the beasts in time. I gave them a new occupation: War. It made the males do new things and dream new dreams. In their dreams lurked heroes, which they made into gods. Do you see what I was doing?

The old woman can only shake her head.

As I had given birth to every creature, I now was giving birth to gods. I wanted them to grow, change, develop, perfect themselves. I set them against each other, so that one god would subsume another god until they would be One, until at last I had a divine consort. That's what has been happening these five thousand years of history. Heroes became anima became gods became God. Even now, this great Other is featal, not ready to be born. And do you see what I've done?

"You're killing Him. You're killing the One you have waited five thousand million years to meet."

I cradle the wood in my hands and sip the cider in it. It is still hot, and it goes down bitingly.

Brigid can only stare at the fireplace. "When will He be ready to be born? When will you have a God who is your peer?"

I knelt with Morfudd in a metal mine and watched a great barrel fall through the floor and saw a blinding flash. *Not for fourteen hundred more years.* I weep. *I thought Gaea wished me to end the Age of War, but now I am Gaea, and I see that she was warning me that war must go on for fourteen hundred more years. She was telling me that these were the birth pangs of her Beloved.*

Humans cannot conceive a God who would be my equal until they have learned the secrets of the worlds and stars, until they can kill me as surely as I can kill them. Then, their God will be real and true, and we will be consummated. But not until then.

Brigid shakes her head in misery. "Can it truly be?"

To me, the future is real already. I know it as a certainty.

"What are you going to do, Gaea? You can't turn back the sun. Britannia is changed now and forever. The paradise you have brought to this isle will draw all humans here to worship you. Your God will never be fully formed.

There is something I can do, Sweet Brigid, though it grieves me to do it. I lift the cup and its bitter cider and study it. The firelight makes a warm glow against its edges. *There is a cup of death, Brigid. Thrice as a woman I thought of drinking it to kill the thing that grew in me, but each time I put it aside. As the Goddess, though, I've drunk of that cup five times.*

"Five!"

Five times I have killed the creatures growing in me. Not all of them, but enough to bring a new start. If the world is to give birth to my God, I will need to poison my paradise.

Her eyes are bright as if candles are lit within them. "Well, my friend, it would be both of our wishes come true. You would have your bridegroom back, and I would have been a mortal again for my final days."

I set down the cider and lean to her and wrap her in my arms. *I'll be here with you, sweet daughter. You'll not be alone. And I will carry you to my paradise beneath the world.*

She clings to me, too. Oh, if only someone had held me this way!

Even as my hands of flesh hold that frail old woman, my hands of spirit reach to the skies.

There is a white murderer tumbling out there in the

blackness. It is only ice, but it is larger than Camelot. It will do what needs to be done. I tap it. The killer shifts from its oblivious path, which would have borne it past me and into the eye of the sun. Instead, it tilts toward my heart, this fragile chain of islands where I have made my vision true.

The icy mountain plunges. Its edges melt and whirl off in a white tail. It diminishes, but not enough to save us.

I'm here, sweet daughter. I'm here.

The killer is peeling away as it strikes the air. Ice burns. A roaring wound opens across the sky, and this white thing is the sword that slices it open. It will do worse to the ground—burn everything and cover it in a pall that will kill crops for five years. It will create a Dark Age, when all that I have done and all that Merlin did, and Arthur, will be forgotten. Even Rome will not awaken from this sleep, not for a thousand years.

Tumbling in its corona of fire, the icy mountain splits the sky and plummets toward us atop Avalon. The mountain will be gone, a scoured finger of stone amid cratered hills. We will be gone too—Brigid beneath the world and I within it.

I'm here.

Before it even hits, the white killer erupts. I recognize the flash—just like the one from that steel barrel fourteen hundred years from now. Silver energy roars down across the mountain and strikes us. It is so quick that there is no sound.

EPILOGUE
I'm Here

Jt's been a good morning for a picket. The sidewalks are clear, and the weather fine. The Lord knows we're saving His babies, and His sunlight is like a warm pat on the back.

There's just one woman in the clinic. We did everything we could to show her the love of Jesus and let her know there are other ways. She heard what we said, I know she did, but she was so distraught. I prayed with her, but she went in anyway. Poor girl. She's probably ten years younger than I'd been when I had Jeremy.

Well, we keep walking and nobody else comes except a meter maid. Nancy laughs and points at the meter. It says, "Expired." The girl'd forgotten to put a coin in. Nancy nudges me and says, "I guess this little visit'll cost her extra."

"It's costing her enough," I say and put a quarter in.

Nancy's face goes white as bone. "What're you doing?"

"I'm putting a quarter in."

She flings her arm out toward the doors. "She's in there killing her baby, and you're saving her from a fifty-dollar parking ticket?"

I shrug. "It's what Jesus would've done."

"Next you'll be driving the getaway car," Nancy says.

Linda pats her shoulder to cool her off. "It'll take more than half an hour. The meter maid'll be by again."

So I put another quarter in.

All the time, Trent and Jake are like, "Let us see. Seriously," and I'm like, "No, way," and they're like, "What's the big deal? Do they show everything?" and I'm like, "It's just a disc for girls. Since when're you guys girls?" and they're all, "I bet they show the boobs and the snatch and everything," and so I'm like, "Mr. Dylan wouldn't let you near that disc," and they're like, "he always goes for a smoke third period and you're in here for an easy half hour. You said nobody ever signs out the little TV-DVD, so just let us sit in the back room and see it," so I'm like, "Sure, on one condition, that you gotta watch the whole thing," and at first it's just ha ha and fox whistles and stuff, but when they are showing the scope up the tubes and showing the egg coming out of the ovary and the blood and everything, it gets real quiet in there. And then in comes Mr. Dylan and he goes, "Who's in there?" and I tell him and he goes, "What're they watching?" and I tell him, and he gets all red and I go, "Are you mad or embarrassed or what?" and he goes, "I don't know" and heads out like he's gonna have another smoke, so I shout at him, "It's nothing to be ashamed of. The female reproductive system's a beautiful thing!"

I sit on the edge of Tony's desk, and he says, "So, let me get this straight. When Bill hits on you and you say no and he keeps hitting on you, that's a crime?"

"He's my boss," I reply. I stare out into the nighttime skyline.

"And when Roger hits on you, it's not a crime?"

"Well," I say, crossing my arms and liking the way the silk sleeves feel. "Not legally. But Roger hitting on *anybody* would be a crime."

We both laugh.

Then Tony coughs and says, "And you coming in here after hours and sitting down on my desk and looking at me the way you are, that's not a crime?"

"I'm not your boss. We're both acquisitions editors—equals."

"Not a crime in the legal sense, sure," Tony says, "but what about in the Roger-sense?"

I smile because I know I've got him. "I've only asked you out for a drink, and already you're talking about rogering?"

He blushes. I love when men do that. "You're avoiding the question."

"Is it a crime for me to hit on you?" I ask. "Well, that's up to you, isn't it?"

Tony nods down at his hands. "The thing is, I'm kind of used to making the first move."

"It's a new world, Tony," I say, standing back up. "So what's your answer?"

He shrugs—a shrug that starts at his fingertips and rolls all the way up to his earlobes, as if I've just taken something huge out of his hands. "What else am I gonna say? Sure."

King, J. Robert (John
Robert)
Le morte d'Avalon

K527mor